MANHATTAN

MICHAEL GRANT

ACKNOWLEDGEMENT

Special thanks to Elizabeth Grant and Diana Salesky for proofreading the manuscript. Nevertheless, any errors that remain are mine alone

Books by Michael Grant

In the Time of Famine
When I Come Home
A Letter to Ballyturan
Line of Duty
Officer Down
Retribution
The Cove
Stalker
Appropriate Sanctions
Back to Venice
Krystal
Dear Son, Hey Ma
Precinct
Who Moved my Friggin' Provolone?
The Ghost and the Author

CHAPTER ONE

Manhattan
September 1850

Michael Ranahan couldn't sleep on this, the last night of his and Emily's long, grueling voyage. In utter darkness, he lay awake in their cramped berth listening to the now familiar creaking of the ship's timbers, the sloshing of the water in the bilge, the snap of canvas sails catching the wind, and the snores and pitiful groans of his fellow passengers. After forty-three harrowing days at sea, he could scarcely believe it was almost over. At first light, they had been told, they would be sailing into New York harbor and disembarking at a quay on the southern tip of an island the Indians called *Manna-hata* and the English call *Manhattan*.

Their ship, the *Catherine Dee*, wasn't one of the dreaded coffin ships in which so many had perished under appalling conditions, but, still, the accommodations were dreadful. Steerage passengers, over two hundred men, women, and children, had been crammed below decks into an open cabin measuring seventy-five feet long by twenty-five feet wide and with headroom of less than six feet. Running along the starboard and port sides of the ship were rows of berths made of rough planks. Each berth—ten feet wide and five feet long—was designed to accommodate six adults. The narrow aisle between the berths, barely five feet wide, was jammed with passengers' baggage, cooking utensils, and sacks of food that passengers had brought with them as a safeguard.

Food was supposed to be included in the price of the ticket, but disreputable captains routinely cheated the passengers by allocating less than the agreed upon provisions. In some cases, ships ran out of food before reaching their destination. What food was available was far from appetizing. Beef, pork, and fish were pickled in brine. Biscuits or "hardtack" were made of wheat flour and dried pea flour cooked into saucer-shaped discs. Passengers were forbidden the use of the galley, which the ship's cook used exclusively to feed the first-class passengers and crew. Up on deck there was, however, a hearth-box—an open topped sand box atop bricks—which steerage passengers were permitted to use on a rotating basis during fair weather. Over the course of weeks, the food became more and more inedible. The hardtack—true to its name—had to be pounded with a hammer into small pieces. Meat and fish became moldy and infested with maggots, weevils, and rodent droppings.

The only exit from the dank, musty hold was up a hatchway to the deck above. The lattice hatch cover, the only source of air and light, was locked down at night and at all times during rough weather. Michael and Emily and their fellow steerage passengers were allowed up on deck in small groups for no more than one hour a day. The captain had said it was for safety reasons, but Michael knew better. He'd seen the look of utter revulsion on the faces of the first-class passengers who promenaded on the upper deck. To protect their delicate sensibilities, the captain determined it best to keep steerage passengers out of sight as much as possible.

By the third day out, the poorly ventilated hold already reeked of vomit, sweat, and human waste that sloshed in buckets until it could be tossed overboard in the morning. As days at sea ticked off, conditions grew worse. The fetid witches' brew of mold, mildew, stagnant bilge water mixed with human waste, as well as the proximity of the passengers, proved an ideal Petri dish for the spread of disease. Typhus raged through the cabin. Within a week people began to die. Mostly babies, but, as time went on, old men and women who were already weakened by years of famine. Michael always knew when someone had died because the nerve-wracking keening of the women would reverberate throughout the cabin. Anyone who died during the night had to be kept below decks until morning when the crew unlocked the hatch. Barely a prayer was said before the crew unceremoniously tossed the canvased wrapped body overboard. Michael didn't know how many had died during the voyage. He stopped counting after fifteen.

The three terrifying storms they'd encountered in the mid-Atlantic made life below decks even more frightening and miserable. As the seas picked up and the wind howled through the rigging, the hatch was battened down. Immediately, the air became suffocatingly foul; the gloom, claustrophobic. With each pitch and roll of the ship passengers were violently thrown from their berths and onto a deck awash with bilge water and vomit. The air was filled with the terrified screams of passengers and the high-pitched shrieks of babies.

The *Catherine Dee* was what sailors called a "wet" ship. High winds and pounding seas exerted a great strain on the masts, causing the ship's planks to separate. Sea-water poured down into the hold, soaking passengers—and bedding, which could take days to dry, if at all. During these storms, candle lanterns could not be lighted, nor could the stoves topside be used. For days, while the storm blew itself out, passengers existed on only hardtack and brackish water.

Emily stirred beside him. "Is it time to get up?" she whispered, throwing her arm across his chest.

He looked toward the hatch and could see a faint light. "Soon," he said, smoothing her unruly auburn hair. "Soon, it'll be over, Emily."

"Thank God for that," she said, a weariness in her voice.

Now that they were almost at their destination, he was becoming increasingly more worried about her. How would she fare in this new world? It was true that she'd gone through her fair share of trial and tribulation in the last few years in Ireland. Her father, Lord Somerville was murdered, and the estates, her inheritance, was lost to debt. But before the famine she'd led a privileged life, attending private schools in Switzerland and France.

The voyage had been particularly hard on her. She'd been seasick almost the entire time. She'd lost a great deal of weight and the dark circles under her eyes attested to the many sleepless nights she'd endured. To take her mind off her constant nausea, she'd busied herself teaching Michael how to read. And to her delight, she found he was a quick learner. They plodded through *Pride and Prejudice* and *Sense and Sensibility.* Neither book held much interest for Michael, but he did enjoy reading *Frankenstein*, which he'd laboriously worked his way through several more times during the voyage. She'd even been able to teach him some simple arithmetic. Now he could add and subtract reasonably well, but he was still mystified by multiplication and division.

"So, we're finally here," she said, turning carefully so as not to wake the woman sleeping inches from her. Next to the woman was her husband, and next to him were their two children. All six occupants represented the complement of their ten-foot wide berth.

He kissed her forehead. "Yes. America. The beginning of our grand adventure." He tried to ignore the knot of tension in his gut, but truth be told, he was terrified of what lay ahead. Leaving famine Ireland for America had seemed like the right thing to do at the time, but now that they were almost here, he realized he didn't know what to expect. His mind was awhirl with questions. Where would they live? How much would lodgings cost? Could he get a job? Doing what? And it didn't help his nagging uncertainty that some passengers, who already had relatives living in New York, related conflicting descriptions of the city. Some said it offered unlimited opportunity, while others said it was the most dreadful and soulless city in the world. The latter were the ones who were usually bound for distant cities in the Midwest. Still, despite the naysayers, he told himself that they were young and in good health. He was only thirty and she was just twenty-five. *They would make it in America,* he told himself firmly. *They would make it in America.*

Michael heard the locks being undone and the hatch swung open. "Ahoy, down below," a crew member shouted, "everyone look smart now. The master says we'll be dockin' in a couple of hours. Pack your belongings and be on deck ready to disembark."

Michael had anticipated the crush and confusion of almost two hundred people trying to organize themselves in the cramped cabin. The night before he'd packed what little belongings they possessed into their two battered cloth bags and they'd slept in their clothes. "Come on," he said, helping Emily out of the berth. "Let's go."

They made their way through the sleep-deprived and befuddled throng of weary passengers and were the first to come up on deck. Gratefully, they breathed in the glorious, fresh sea air, a welcome respite from the fetid air below decks. The sun was rising on what promised to be a fine day. A stiffening breeze coming from the southwest gently drove the ship over the rolling waves. Michael and Emily made their way forward, being careful not to get in the way of the crew scurrying about the deck preparing to shorten sail in preparation for entering the harbor.

At first, as they stood in the bow looking forward, they saw nothing but open sea. But slowly, as the ship plowed forward, they began to see low-lying specks of land. Off to the left was a hilly mass that looked like an island. Michael thought that might be Manhattan, but the ship veered toward a low-lying mass of land to the right. As they closed on the land, everything slowly came into focus and they were stupefied by the sight before them. As far as the eye could see was an impenetrable forest of ships' masts. Most were anchored, but countless sloops, lighters, schooners, yachts, barges, and ferries maneuvered in and around the anchored vessels. To the unpracticed eye, it seemed that at any moment there must be a terrible collision, but miraculously there was none.

Michael gripped the rail and his eyes widened. "*Jesus*!" It appeared that they were heading directly toward a line of anchored ships. Just when he was certain they would plow headlong into one of them, the ship hardened up into the wind. Amidst shouted instruction from the captain and mates, the sails were smartly furled while an anchor gang let go the anchor chain.

"Why are we stopping out here?" Emily asked. "We must be a good mile from shore."

Michael shook his head. "I have no idea."

Now that the ship had come to a stop, a wind blew offshore toward them bringing a stench that made their eyes water.

"What in God's name is that?" Emily said, quickly covering her nose with a handkerchief.

"I don't know ..." Michael said, stifling a gag reflex. "I thought the stench below decks was bad, but this is much worse. Could this be what Manhattan smells like?"

What they were smelling was a noxious combination of more than six-hundred thousand pounds of manure and twenty thousand gallons of urine deposited every day by the city's twelve thousand horses. And then there were the pigs. For years, pigs—some domestic, some feral—had been allowed to roam the streets of Manhattan. But the stench and destructiveness of the animals had finally roused the city's reformers. Policemen rounded up over five thousand pigs out of cellars and garrets and drove the herd to the upper wards of Manhattan. All to no avail. Eventually, the pigs returned. To add to the stench, lower Manhattan was also home to over two hundred abattoirs that butchered three hundred seventy-five thousand animals a year. Then there were the more than five hundred butcher shops, the tanners with their piles of stinking hides, and the stench of assorted animals—over five thousand a year—who simply dropped dead in the streets.

By now most of the passengers, looking frightened and disoriented, were on deck. The captain, a rail-thin man with an enormous red nose, came out of his cabin and called for attention. "There is no berth for us at the piers," he said, "so we will be going ashore using lighters. First class passengers will disembark first, followed by steerage. Make sure you have all your belongings as there will be no coming back on board once you leave this ship."

It took almost three hours before it was Michael and Emily's turn to board the lighter. The small boat weaved its way through and around hundreds of anchored ships and finally tied up at the Canal Street pier. The huge quay was swarming with confused passengers disembarking from a half dozen docked ships. Horse and wagons carrying luggage and provisions to the ships barreled through the crowds as though they weren't there, dodging stacks of barrels, sacks, boxes, hampers, and bales.

As soon as Emily and Michael set foot on solid ground, they both began to stumble, as though they were drunk. So, too, they noticed did every other passenger, all to the amusement of the lighter crew.

"What's so funny?" a confused and irritated Michael asked.

"It took you days to get your sea legs, didn't it?" a leathery-faced sailor explained with a toothless grin. "Well, after forty-three days at sea, it'll take you awhile to get your landlubber legs back. Don't you know—"

He was interrupted by great shout. Michael and Emily turned to see a spectacle the likes of which they had never seen before. Twenty companies of uniformed fireman in bright red shirts, complete with their colorful fire wagons pulled by teams of men, came marching through thousands of spectators crowded on the quay. They stopped at the foot of the gangway of a steamer ship named the *Atlantic*.

A plain, middle-aged woman wearing a lovely silver-gray silk dress and a pale-blue silk hat appeared at the top of the gangway and another roar went up from the crowd. Led by a couple of top-hatted men, she quickly descended the gangway and climbed into a waiting carriage. As it made its way through the mass of spectators, she was showered with flowers thrown by the cheering throng.

Emily had seen crowds in London and Paris, so for her this was not unusual. But Michael was speechless. He'd never seen that many people in one place in all his life. "Who was that woman?" he asked no one in particular.

The old sailor puffed on his pipe. "That, my young friend, would be Jenny Lind."

"Who?"

The old man shook his head in disbelief. "Paddy, do you mean to tell me you never heared of the Swedish Nightingale?"

Michael was more confused than ever. "No. I never have."

"She sings that opera music and they say she has a beautiful voice. That old rascal P.T. Barnum has brought her here to make millions for the both of 'em. I hear tell that some seats are being sold for more than six hundred dollars each."

"That's an awful lot of money," a shocked Emily said.

"Aye, a king's fortune. But I reckon that sly old Barnum knows what he's doin'."

As soon as the carriage left the quay, the crowd quickly dispersed.

Michael and Emily made their way off the wharf and stepped onto Canal Street, an insane cacophony of street noise and chaos. Hundreds of horse-drawn wagons carrying everything from ice, coal, and lumber to beer barrels zigzagged up and down the street in every direction. One oddity they saw among the lumbering wagons were "bulletin" wagons that carried signs advertising everything from local theaters to medicine to Barnum's Museum.

The sounds of hundreds of iron horseshoes and iron wheels clattering over the cobblestone streets raised a fearful din. To add to the pandemonium, carters loudly cursed their horses and one another with equal vehemence. What Michael and Emily were experiencing was a typical day in lower Manhattan and on a typical day, fifteen thousand wagons rumbled along a maze of narrow cobblestone streets.

Lining both sides of the street cheek to jowl was a profusion of commercial sail-lofts, counting houses, warehouses of every description, and cheap eating houses.

As the couple stood there taking it all in, a young man wearing a bright green tie and a bowler hat tilted at a jaunty angle, approached them with a wide grin.

"And welcome to New York the two of youse. And where might you be from?"

"Ireland," Michael said.

"And didn't I know it," he said with a thick Irish brogue. "Sure, you have the very map of Ireland all over your face. May I inquire—do you and the missus have accommodations?"

"No," Emily said. "We've just come off the boat and—"

"Ah, then you're in luck." He elbowed Michael and winked. "The luck of the Irish as you might say. My Uncle Tommy owns a boardinghouse on Greenwich Street that caters to Irish immigrants such as yourselves. It's a modest hotel I will admit, but you'll find the prices very reasonable."

Emily looked at Michael. "Well, I don't know ..."

"I'll wager you have a lot of questions about New York."

Emily nodded. "As a matter of fact, we do."

"Well then, the hotel is just the place. You'll meet other Irishmen such as yourselves. They'll be able to answer your questions such as you might have."

Michael and Emily looked at each other, unsure of what to do next.

"You don't have to stay there," the young man said in a reasonable tone. "But at least take a look. Here, let me carry those bags. You must be exhausted after such an arduous journey." Before Michael could protest, he snatched the bags. "Come on, follow me. It's not far."

And with those words he darted into the bustling street with reckless abandon. They thought he would surely be run down and trampled, but to their amazement he dodged in and around the chaotic traffic with the grace of a dancer and made it to the other side of the street unscathed.

An apprehensive Michael surveyed the busy street and took Emily's hand. "Well, if he did it, I guess we can. Come on."

As soon as they stepped into the street they were met with a barrage of rude curses and shouts from carters and wagoneers.

"Mind where you're goin ..."

"Step out of the way you damn fools ..."

"Are you gormless eejits all together ..."

Frightened and confused, they scurried back on to the sidewalk. As Emily caught her breath, she looked up and went pale. "Michael, he's gone."

Michael looked across the street and muttered a curse. "Wait here."

Before she could stop him, he rushed into the street. Anger drove all fear from him. Disregarding the shouts and imprecations of drivers, he dodged in and around the wagons and miraculously made it to the other side without being trampled. He looked around frantically, but the man was nowhere in sight. He ran to the next corner, still no sign of him. On the next corner, he saw a man wearing a blue tunic with a line of brass buttons running down the front and a large eight-point star on his chest. He assumed he must be a policeman and ran up to him.

"Excuse me, sir ..."

The big policeman took a step back and wrinkled his nose in disgust. At first Michael was puzzled by the man's behavior, but then it suddenly occurred to him that he must smell something awful. In the forty-three-day voyage, because of the shortage of water, they had only been able to take a handful of sponge baths. The clothes he was wearing he'd been wearing for at least three weeks. He took a step back, feeling ashamed.

"Well," the policeman said, twirling his baton, "what is it?"

"We've just come off the boat, sir. This man came up to us and offered to take us to his uncle's boardinghouse and—"

The officer grinned knowingly. "Was he wearing a bright green tie?"

"Yes. Exactly. Do you know him? He—"

"Paddy, you've been swindled by a trickster."

"I… I don't understand."

"It happens all the time. They're called 'runners' and there are hundreds just like him. They prey on youse paddies coming off the boat promising to help their fellow countrymen and all that Irish malarkey. Did he get anything from you?"

"My two bags."

"Consider yourself lucky. If he'd taken you to his 'uncle's' boardinghouse I guarantee you the place would be a filthy hell-hole. Instead of comfortable rooms, you would be shoved into vermin-infested hovels with eight or ten other unfortunate souls at prices three or four times higher than what was proper. Consider yourself lucky he only got your bags. Was there anything of valuable in them?"

"No, just some old clothes, a handful of books, and ..." His heart suddenly pounded in his chest. *Sweet Jesus. There was something else. The money. The money Emily had made from selling her ring to the gombeen man. It was all they had in the world.*

Without another word, he spun on his heels and raced back to Emily. He was so distracted as he crossed the street that he was almost run down by a huge wagon loaded with beer barrels.

Emily saw the look of fright on his face as he ran up to her. "Michael, what's the matter?"

He grabbed her by the shoulders. "I spoke to a policeman," he said, gasping to catch his breath. "He told me we've been robbed. The bags are gone."

"Well, the devil take him and the bags. There was nothing of value in them anyhow."

"The money," he said, hoarsely. "Emily, your money from the ring was in there."

She took his face in her hands and kissed him. "No, it wasn't, Michael. I sewed the money into this very dress," she said, twirling in a circle.

A relieved Michael scooped her up and spun her around. "Oh, Emily, thank God one of us has some common sense."

"Put me down," she said, feigning anger. "We're making a spectacle of ourselves."

But of course, they weren't. They would soon learn that New

Yorkers paid absolutely no attention to the antics of other New Yorkers.

"What'll we do now?" she said, smoothing her dress.

"We're both exhausted. Let's find lodgings, get a good sleep and a hot bath."

"That sounds wonderful."

They walked east on Canal Street dodging a relentless army of newsboys, peddlers, apple sellers, and hot-corn girls who all sang the same refrain: "*Here's your nice hot corn, smoking hot, smoking hot, just from the pot!*"

At the corner of Canal and Mulberry Street they spotted a small hotel.

"That looks decent enough," Michael said. "Do you think we should we go in?"

"Please. I don't think I can walk another step."

Behind the desk an elderly man with bushy gray sideburns looked up and smiled. "Yes, may I help you?"

"We'd like a room for the night," Michael said.

"I'm sure I can accommodate you."

As they stepped up to the desk, the man recoiled, as did the policeman earlier.

Michael reddened, knowing the cause. "I apologize for our… appearance, but we just came off a boat and—"

"Quite so," the man said with a kindly smile. "I understand." He opened the register. "That will be fifteen dollars a night."

Emily and Michael looked at each other indecisively. They both were thinking the same thing. *That was an awful lot of money for just one night's lodging.*

Emily made the decision for them. "Very well. We only have a handful of American dollars. Will you take English pounds?"

The man shook his head. "I'm sorry, miss, that isn't possible."

"Is there someplace where we can convert our money?"

The man looked at the wall clock behind him and shook his head. "I'm afraid not. It's past five and all the currency establishments are closed. There's one at the entrance to the quay, you must have missed it."

"Look, we need a place to stay," Michael said with a note of desperation creeping into his voice. He was bleary eyed with exhaustion and he knew Emily was too. "Can you offer us any advice?"

The man scratched his chin. "How much American money do you have?"

On the ship Emily had taught Michael how to count American currency, but he still didn't trust himself. He gave the handful of bills to her.

She quickly counted it. "Almost six dollars," she said.

"I'm afraid you will not get decent lodgings for that amount."

"Sir, we're desperate," Michael said. "We'll convert our money tomorrow, but we need a place to stay tonight."

"I understand, but I'm not allowed to extend credit. There is, however, one place in the city that can accommodate you, but I hesitate to suggest it."

"Where?"

"Have you ever heard of the Five Points?"

Michael shook his head.

"When tourists come to the city they always ask to see two things: the mansions of Washington Square Park and the hovels of the Five Points. It's a very nasty part of town, but you will be able to find lodgings there. The Old Brewery charges between two and ten dollars a month. Bad houses can be had for five to ten cents a night."

Michael looked at Emily and shrugged. "What choice do we have? It'll just be for a night."

CHAPTER TWO

It was called the Five Points because it was at the intersection of five streets—Mulberry, Worth, Park, Baxter, and Little Waterford. In the time of George Washington, the site of the Five Points was a pond surrounded by swamp-land. As the city began to expand, the swamp was drained and buildings were constructed on landfill.

By the 1840s the Five Points had become a sinkhole of vice, degradation, and wretchedness populated by thieves, loafers, and vagabonds. It was a notorious breeding ground for disease, crime, poverty, wretched drunken misery, and every other vice imaginable. It was also a source of obscene profits for disreputable landowners who converted single family frame houses, boardinghouses—even stables and sheds—into a bewildering maze of rabbit warrens.

Twenty-nine thousand people, most of them Irish, crammed into these hovels with two or three families sharing a single filthy space. The Old Brewery alone, which had once been an active brewery, housed over a thousand tenants. It had close to a hundred rooms with only a few having windows.

When Charles Dickens visited the Five Points in 1842, he described the Five Points as "hideous tenements which take their name from robbery and murder: all that is loathsome, drooping, and decayed is here."

A survey in 1850 showed that in just one block there were thirty-three underground lodgings and twenty grog shops. The *Police Gazette* said the Old Brewery was "the wickedest house on the wickedest street that ever existed in New York."

Five Points was also the home of dozens of gangs who preyed on the poor and warred against each other. Among the more notorious of the colorfully named gangs were the Dead Rabbits, the Plug Uglies, the Roach Guards, and the Bowery Boys.

It was into these miserable and frightening surroundings that Michael and Emily stepped. In their short time in the city, they'd almost gotten used to the pervasive stench of horse manure and urine. But here, the reek, even more powerful, was a combination of horse manure, urine, dead animals, stale beer, and rotting garbage through which pigs rooted for food scraps. The thick, malodorous air seemed to absorb the very light.

The foul streets were lined with ancient tenements and low clapboard houses. Cellars ten feet below the street were lodging houses with little ventilation and no windows. At every corner were grog shops and pawnbrokers.

People with unfocused eyes stumbled along sidewalks slippery with garbage and filth. Pale-faced, emaciated men slumped in doorways or lay stretched out on the filthy pavement. Dirty and slovenly women moved in and of darkened narrow alleyways carrying babies bundled in rags. Children, barefoot and dressed in grimy scraps of clothing, played in the garbage-strewn gutter. To her horror, Emily saw one child slumped in a doorway draining what was left in a bottle of whiskey.

They stopped in front of a massive and unusual looking building. "What do you think that is?" Michael asked.

"I don't know. But it looks vaguely like an Egyptian tomb."

They kept walking and finally came to the hulking, dilapidated Old Brewery. To the side of the building was an alley three feet wide, which led to a room called the Den of Thieves. Seventy-five men, women and children, Negroes and white, made their homes there without furniture or other amenities. Many women were prostitutes and conducted their business there. The far end of the dark alley was known as Murderers Alley and was all that the name implied.

Michael gripped Emily's arm. "We can't stay here."

"I don't like the place either, but what other choice do we

have?"

Michael stared up at a looming, vaguely threatening, building and took a deep breath. "All right, let's go in."

The gloomy hallway smelled of stale urine and sour beer. Cautiously, they climbed a broken, almost impassable, staircase. Most of the room doors were open and they saw that one room, barely twelve by fifteen feet, was inhabited by at least fifteen people.

Emily was appalled when it occurred to her that here, in this claustrophobic place, was where these people ate, drank, and slept. Another room about the same size contained five Negro men and women.

Suddenly, there was the scraping of boots on the stairs and a gruff voice shouted out of the gloom, "*You, there. What are you doin' here*?"

The owner of the voice was a middle-aged, red-faced man with a bulbous nose. He squinted at them suspiciously. "Well? What's your business here?"

Michael recoiled from the strong smell of whisky on the man's breath. "We've come about a room."

"Oh. I thought you was one of them damn missionary do-gooders. They're always coming in here and riling up my tenants." He wiped his sweaty forehead with a dirty handkerchief. "I imagine I can accommodate you on that score. It'll cost you four dollars a month. In advance."

"We only want to stay one night," he said.

"Well, that'll cost you fifty cents."

He led them to the room with a closed door. He pushed it open without knocking. The tiny windowless room, barely eight by eight, was dimly lit by a single flickering candle. Its only occupant, a frail woman wrapped in a black shawl, sat huddled in the corner. The room was devoid of furniture, save for a pile of rags on which, presumably, the woman slept.

"These two will be staying the night with you," he said gruffly.

In a shaky voice the frightened woman said, "But ... I paid for the entire room for meself."

The man's laugh was harsh. "You expect the entire room to yourself, do you? Then I suggest you go over to Broadway and check into the Astor House. I'm sure they'll honor your lady's request."

He slammed the door, leaving the three occupants to stare at each other self-consciously. Finally, Emily broke the strained silence.

"Hello," she said, tentatively, "my name is Emily and this is Michael."

The woman pulled her shawl around herself defensively and nodded. "I'm Maureen. I'm supposed to have this room to meself, you know," she said, accusingly.

"Well, we know nothing about that. But we're only staying the night." Emily felt sorry for the pale, rail-thin woman who seemed terribly frightened about something.

Cutting off all further conversation, the woman crouched down in the corner and blankly stared at the walls.

Michael looked around the room in growing frustration. With their bags stolen, they had only the clothes on their backs. "Emily, how can we stay here? We've no bedding nor blankets, nor ..."

"It's only for the night, Michael."

"All right, but at least we can open the door. It's stifling in here."

As soon as he touched the doorknob, the woman screamed, "*No, no, don't open the door!*"

Startled by her outburst, he jumped back. "Why not? It's terrible hot in here. There's not a breath of air."

"*Don't open the door,*" she shouted again, now almost hysterical. "*For God's sake, don't open the door!*"

Emily knelt beside the woman. "What's the matter, Maureen?" she said, soothingly. "Why can't we open the door? It is awfully hot in here."

Maureen looked around, her eyes barely focusing. "There's a man looking for me. I mustn't let him find me. He'll take me back to that terrible place. I won't do that anymore."

"Maureen, how old are you?"

"Twenty-two."

Emily was stunned. She judged the woman to be in her mid-forties. "Have you no family?"

"They're all back in Ireland. I came out here alone. When I got off the boat I was frightened and afraid. Then this man approached me. He was so kind. He said he would find me safe lodgings. He said he would find me a decent job. I went with him. But then he ..." Here she broke in to tears.

Emily patted the woman's hand. "Well, you're safe with us. He won't find you here."

She shook her head vehemently. "He's a terrible man. Everyone in the Five Points is afraid of him."

Emily smoothed out the pile of rags. "Why don't you get some sleep. Tomorrow, we'll take you to the authorities. They'll help you."

"He'll find me. I know he will ..." Almost before her head touched the rags, the exhausted woman was asleep.

Emily stood up. "The poor thing."

Michael stared at the sleeping woman and shook his head in dismay. "Emily, what kind of madhouse have I brought you to? This is not at all what I thought America was."

"I'm sure it's not all like this. Tomorrow, we'll convert our money to American dollars and then we'll find decent accommodations. Let's get some rest. I can't keep my eyes open."

He blew out the candle and lay down on the floor next to her. Both exhausted, they quickly fell into a deep sleep.

Sometime during the night, they were awakened by sounds in the hallway of doors being banged open, followed by shouts of angry voices and scuffling feet. Just as Michael got to his feet to investigate, their door was violently flung open and a heavyset, brutish-looking man with beady eyes and a broad bent nose burst in. He held the lantern up, peered into the room, and spotted Maureen curled up in a ball pitifully trying to hide under her rags.

"*There you are, you little bitch*," he bellowed. He grabbed her by the hair. "You'll come with me."

"Take your hands off her," Michael said.

The man looked at him with contempt. "And who might you be? Her pimp? Sorry, she's my girl."

As Michael stepped forward to pull Maureen away from him, the man backhanded him sending him crashing into a wall. Michael came off the floor and charged the man, driving him into the opposite wall. The force of the impact made the man drop the lantern. Emily quickly righted it before it could start a fire.

Michael drove his fist into the man's gut and he went down with a loud exhalation of air. Michael pounced on him and drove his fist into the man's face. The man rolled away and suddenly there was a knife in his hand. Michael jumped back as the man swung the knife in a wide arc toward his stomach.

"So," the man said, stumbling to his feet, "you think she's worth your life, so be it."

He charged at Michael, but he was big and clumsy and drunk and Michael was able to sidestep him and yank his arm backwards. He heard a loud snap and the man screamed in pain as his arm broke. The knife clattered to the floor and Michael snatched it up. He pointed it menacingly at the man. "Get out of here. *Now.*"

The man looked at Maureen then pointed a finger at Michael. "I'll get you for this." Then, holding his useless arm, he stomped out the room.

Maureen was hysterical. "*I told you he'd find me,*" she wailed. "*Oh, Jasus, what am I to do?*"

Emily put her arms around the distraught woman. "It's all right, he's gone. You're safe now." But the frightened look on Emily's face belied her soothing words.

Michael closed the door. "You two go back to sleep. I'll stay awake in case he does come back."

Michael sat with his back against the door and the knife in his hand. He didn't know how long he stayed in that position, but at some point, he heard the soft murmuring of voices and the lazy shuffling of feet in the hallway. Evidently, it was morning.

The three of them went downstairs and out into the gloom of an early morning rain. As bad as the air smelled, it was a welcome break from the foul air of their claustrophobic room. Michael looked up and down the street for signs of the man, but all he saw were drunken men staggering on the sidewalks so drunk they could hardly see, women sleeping in doorways, and pigs rooting in piles of rubbish.

"Come on, Maureen. Let's find a policeman and we'll tell him what happened."

"*No*. I can't do that."

"Why not?" Emily asked. "The police will help you."

"They'll do no such thing. Don't you know all the policemen

are paid off by the likes of him?"

Emily and Michael were stunned. They wouldn't have been surprised if they'd heard that back in Ireland. It was common knowledge that the police and the army were under the thumb of the landlords. But they thought it would be different here in America.

Before they could stop her, Maureen darted into Murderers Alley and disappeared into a darkened building.

"Should we follow her?" Emily asked.

Michael took one look at the rough men loitering in the alleyway and decided it would be a mistake to pursue her. "No. We have to attend to our own business."

"But what's to become of that poor woman?"

"I don't know." He surveyed the derelicts all around them. "It would seem that this city is full of people like Maureen and we can't help all of them."

As the hotel clerk had said, they found the currency establishment at the foot of the quay. Before they'd left their room, Emily had removed the money from the lining of her dress. Now she put it on the counter in front of a young, bespectacled man. "I'd like to exchange this for American dollars."

"Certainly, madam." He quickly counted out the money and gave her the equivalent in dollars. He looked them over carefully. "May I presume you are just off the boat?"

Once again, Michael was painfully aware of their disheveled appearance, not to mention their odor. "We are. But now that we have money we're off to find decent lodgings, a hot bath, and some new clothes."

The clerk looked at Emily's thread-worn dress and nodded sympathetically. "Well, there's Lord and Taylor's on Catherine Street. But for ladies clothing, I would highly recommend A.T. Stewart's Marble Palace located on Broadway and Chambers Street. You can't miss it. It's not called a marble palace for nothing. The store is so well-known there's no sign on the front. My wife tells me the store advertises regular and uniform prices. She appreciates not having to haggle over prices. As for the gentleman, I would recommend Devlin and Company at the corner of Broadway and Grand."

"Perhaps you could recommend a place where we might find decent lodgings at an affordable price?" Emily asked.

"I know of none personally, but there are any number of boardinghouses along Greenwich Avenue. You might try there."

"Thank you very much for the information."

"Not at all. My uncle came out from Ireland a couple of years ago and he had a hard time of it in the beginning. It takes a while to get your bearings."

"I imagine it does," Michael said, thinking of the scoundrel in the green tie.

"Oh, and one more thing. That's quite a bit of money you have. I would advise you not to carry all of it on your person. The streets are full of amusers and their ilk. A word to the wise."

"*Amusers*?" Michael asked.

"It's the latest trick of the criminal trade. They throw snuff or pepper in your face and while you're temporarily blind, they rob you." He chuckled. "Perhaps that's the origin of the term getting robbed blind."

When they came out of the currency house, Emily said, "First thing is we must find a place to stay and take baths. Then, we go clothes shopping."

"That's fine with me. It's getting so I can't stand my own stink."

Asking directions and getting lost a couple of times, they finally found Greenwich Avenue. True to the clerk's word, there were any number of boardinghouses lining both sides of the street.

"This looks grand," Michael said staring up at handsome three-story brownstone building.

They climbed the stoop stairs and knocked on the door. A plump woman with rosy red cheeks and her gray hair pulled back in a severe bun opened the door.

"Yes? She gave them a critical once over with her eyes. Judging by the frown on her face she wasn't impressed with what she saw.

"We're looking for lodgings," Emily said.

"Quite impossible. You can't afford my rent."

"We have money," Michael said, irritated by the woman's haughty tone.

She fixed him with a steely gaze. "It's forty dollars a week."

"Forty dollars *a week*? They both said in unison.

"Try the boardinghouse at 515," she said and slammed the door.

Back on the street, they reconsidered their options. "We could afford that rent for a while," Emily said. "But until we're both gainfully employed, we'd better settle for something less expensive."

The house at 515 Greenwich Avenue was a great comedown from the first house they'd visited. It was in need of painting, the stoop's bricks were crumbling, and two shutters were hanging at odd angles.

A small, elderly man with a push broom mustache over a weak chin opened the door. "Yes, what is it?"

"We're looking for lodgings," Michael said.

"Come in then, come in. I'm Coyle, the landlord. The rent for the two of youse is ten dollars a week, payable in advance. The price includes meals. Come with me, I'll show you what I have available."

He led them up a staircase covered by threadbare carpeting. A strong, musty smell permeated the air. He led them down a dark hallway to a small room containing a bed, a dresser and a chair.

"This is what I have available. It's quite suitable."

Michael took one look at the worn-out bedspread, the rickety chair, and the peeling wallpaper and wanted to say it wasn't suitable, but he held his tongue.

Emily was underwhelmed by the room. "This will do. We need a hot bath. Is that available?"

"It is, but it'll cost extra."

After much-needed baths, they set out to look for A.T. Stewart's Marble Palace department store. After a few wrong turns, they found their way to Broadway and stopped in amazement at the utter confusion. Traffic was almost at a standstill as dozens of horse carts and cursing, red-faced cart men dodged and maneuvered their way around piles of timber, mounds of bricks, mountains of packing-cases, pyramids of stones and stacks of goods blocking the street.

A.T. Stewart's Marble Palace was as the exchange clerk had said. Michael stood in amazement at the sight. He'd never seen so large a building. It was indeed a marble palacc sheathed in dazzling white Tuckahoe marble. Standing five stories high, it spanned the entire length of the block between Chambers and Reade Streets. Its street-level facade boasted fifteen plate-glass windows, behind which were displayed beautiful fabrics for dresses, muslin, as well as a wide range of cloaks and bonnets. Adding to the traffic chaos on the street, dozens of carriages were lined up outside the store awaiting their shopping mistresses.

The magnificent interior of the store was organized around a large circular court covered by a domed skylight that soared five stories above the main floor. Beautifully displayed on polished mahogany counters and marble shelves were all manner of clothing and goods, including silks from Lyon, gloves and dresses from Paris, carpets made in Brussels, Irish linens, French laces, English woolens, paisley and cashmere shawls, some of which—to Michael's amazement—cost two thousand dollars. Emily had shopped in London and Paris, but she had never seen anything quite this opulent.

A handsome young man, one of the store's two hundred clerks, approached them. "May I be of service to madam?"

"Yes. I'm looking for dresses and shoes."

"Very good. Right this way, madam."

He led her to the dress department. "May I ask, are you employed in the domestic service?"

"No, why do you ask?"

He looked around and dropped his voice. "Lately, we've been getting complaints from some of our wealthier customers."

"About what?"

He grinned. "It seems that these mistresses are quite vexed because their servants buy our dresses and become virtually indistinguishable from them. That's why most of them insist that their employees wear costumes suitable to their station in life."

"How silly."

"True. But I just wanted to warn you. Some domestics have been forced to return their dresses because their employers thought them above their station."

"Well, I'm not in domestic service and I don't intend to be."

"Very good, madam." He held up a yellow dress. "Would madam like to try this on?"

Emily ran her hand across the soft fabric. "Yes, I would."

While Emily went to try on dresses, Michael wandered about

the store, marveling at the sheer volume of clothing on display. On the second and third floors, he saw carpets, ladies' suits and a bewildering assortment of shawls.

When he returned to the dress department, he caught sight of Emily and couldn't believe his eyes. After weeks aboard the ship with scarcely a change of clothes or a decent bath, he'd almost forgotten how beautiful she was. She was wearing a bright blue hoop skirted dress and a flowered bonnet that highlighted her soft auburn hair.

She spun around. "Well, what do you think?"

"It's beautiful," he stammered. "And so are you."

"Thank you, kind sir. Now, let's get you some suitable clothing."

On their way back to the boardinghouse, weighted down with their clothing purchases from Stewart's and Devlin's, they witnessed an extraordinary sight. Just three blocks from their boardinghouse, a building was on fire. Suddenly, there was the sound of bells and a fire wagon, pulled by a dozen men, came rushing up the street. Then, from the opposite direction, came another fire wagon with bells ringing came. Both groups reached the building at the same time. Then to Michael's amazement, the two groups ran at each other and started clubbing each other as the fire continued to consume the building.

They arrived back at the boardinghouse just in time for supper. Seated around the table in the small dining room was a young girl in her early twenties, an older woman in her fifties, and a middle-aged man with enormous whiskers and a strong, pleasant aroma of tobacco about him.

The whiskered man stuck out his hand. "Greetings. I'm Gaylord Temple."

"I'm Michael Ranahan and this is my wife Emily."

The young girl nodded shyly. "Hi. I'm Sarah Kavanagh."

"And I am Mrs. Winslow," the older woman said with an air of authority.

As they sat down, Gaylord whispered to Michael, "The food's not much, but old man Coyle's always good for seconds."

"Unfortunately, the subpar quality of the food does not entice one to seek seconds," Mrs. Winslow intoned with an arched eyebrow.

Just then, Coyle came into the dining room carrying a tureen. "I heard that, Mrs. Winslow. If the food is not to your liking, you might wish to dine at Delmonico's over on Beaver Street with all the other swells."

Ignoring his comment, she said, "And what is on the menu tonight, dear Mr. Coyle?"

"It's a stew if you must know, Mrs. Winslow."

"Stew again. How enchanting."

"Well, I can't feed the likes of you steak with the paltry rent you pay me."

"Perhaps if you refurbished your establishment, you could charge more."

"Refurbished?" Gaylord chuckled. "He'd have to pull the entire building down and start over."

Coyle gave him a dirty look and Mrs. Winslow said, "Mr. Temple, I do believe you have just forfeited your chance at seconds tonight."

"Not at all. Mr. Coyle knows I was kidding. Right Mr. Coyle?"

Coyle slammed the tureen down on the dining room table. "You can all serve yerselves," he said, and stomped out of the room.

As Michael ladled stew into Emily's bowl, he said, "We saw something very strange today. A building was on fire and two fire wagons showed up at the same time and they started fighting with each other."

Gaylord chuckled. "It happens all the time. There are dozens of volunteer fire companies in the city and only the company that puts out the fire gets paid by the insurance company. The competition is fierce. Men have been killed over it. For added muscle, some of these fire companies employ the Dead Rabbits, the Plug Uglies, and the like."

"Dead Rabbits?" a puzzled Emily asked.

"Gangs, madam. The city is full of gangs. Just last year, over at the Five Points a couple of them battled in the streets for two days."

"My goodness. Why?"

"The Dead Rabbits are made up mostly of Irish immigrants. The Bowery Boys are nativists and anti-immigration. They went at it for two days with brick-bats, stones, clubs, and guns. Over a thousand gang members were involved. When the police came to break it up, the two gangs joined forces against the police. Overwhelmed, the police had to call out the militia to stop the riot. Over a hundred men were injured and eight died. At least that we know of."

Seeing the look of astonishment on Michael's face, Mrs. Winslow said, "You will find, Mr. Ranahan, that New York City is a very violent place."

"It is that," Gaylord agreed. "If you ever have the occasion to walk by a firehouse you'll see a bunch of loafers hanging about. When there's a fire, they follow the firemen to the scene and take advantage of the chaos to pick pockets and conduct all sorts of mischief. Some even dress like firemen complete with red shirts, fire hats, and badges and they go into the burning buildings to loot whatever they can."

"How do you know so much about it, Gaylord?" Michael asked.

"I'm a reporter with the *New York Tribune*. It's my job to know everything that goes on in this city."

"So, you cover crime and such?"

"Lord, no. My editor, Mr. Horace Greeley, will have none of that in his newspaper. We gather news with good taste, high moral standards, and intellectual appeal. Police reports, scandals, dubious medical advertisements, and flippant personalities are barred from its pages. Still," he said with a wink, "I keep my eye on the ne'er-do-wells and blackguards in the city."

"Perhaps you could explain another unusual building we saw the other day," Emily said. "It looked like some kind of Egyptian tomb."

"Ah, that would be our city prison affectionately known as the 'Tombs' and it's where our rapscallions and rogues of the Five Points are frequently housed. When Charles Dickens saw it, he had only one question: "'What is this dismal fronted pile of bastard Egyptian, like an enchanter's palace in a melodrama?'"

"I would agree," Emily said. "It seems like a very fancy building just to house criminals."

"No doubt graft and the passing of huge sums of money had something to do with it," Mrs. Winslow sniffed.

"It's true. There was plenty of graft to go around," Gaylord said. "The building was badly built on the site of the old Collect Pond and started sinking the very day it opened. There are calls to tear the damn thing down." He turned to Emily. "So, what are your plans now that you have arrived in our fair city?"

"We're both going to be looking for work tomorrow. Does anyone have any suggestions where we might start?"

"I work at Stewart's," Sarah said. "I believe they're hiring."

"We were just there today. It's a lovely store. Are you a sales clerk?"

"Goodness, no. Mr. Stewart hires only handsome young men to be sales clerks."

"Whatever for?"

"Well, it is a store for ladies, and he believes that ladies would rather deal with an attractive young man than a woman."

"You've got to hand it to old Alexander T. Stewart," Gaylord interjected. "He's a crafty old Irishman who came here from Belfast. He opened a small dry-goods shop over on Broadway and parlayed that into the magnificent edifice you shopped in today. The man's a genius. Until he came along, the time-honored custom in clothing stores was for a clerk to engage a customer as soon as he came through the door. Prices were purposely not fixed and after a time of tedious negotiating an agreed price was struck. Old Stewart realized that if he was to move his merchandize faster, he would have to change the whole system."

"What did he do?" Emily asked.

"He instituted regular and uniformed prices. Absolutely revolutionary."

"That's what the man at the currency exchange told us."

"Furthermore, he outsmarted all the other merchants in the city."

"How so?"

"He created a store that would fill a woman's every need. Before he came along, merchants expected women to purchase fabrics, bonnets, furniture and the like at small specialty shops scattered along Broadway. His idea was quite radical, but it worked. A.E. Stewart's is one of the most successful department stores in the city. Everything you need is under one roof."

"Obviously, a man of vision." Emily turned to Sarah. "So, what do you do there, Sarah?"

"I'm a seamstress."

"What kind of wages does the store pay?"

"For women, somewhere between fifty cents and two dollars a week."

"Are those good or bad wages?" Michael asked, still unfamiliar with American currency.

"They're terrible," Gaylord said, ladling more stew into his bowl, "and that's because it's assumed a woman is not supporting herself and is merely supplementing her husband's wages."

"An unwarranted assumption, I might add," Mrs. Winslow huffed.

"What do men earn?" Michael asked.

"An unskilled laborer can earn around seven dollars a week."

"That doesn't seem fair," Emily said.

"My dear," Mrs. Winslow said, "in New York City fairness has nothing to do with anything. Sarah is fortunate to have a position with Stewart's. Some factory seamstresses are forced to work fifteen-to-eighteen-hour workdays for appalling wages."

"Working at Stewart's is better than most stores," Sarah agreed. "I have a friend who works in a millinery shop on Pearl. She makes only two dollars a week, but just last week she was fined sixty cents for sitting down."

"Isn't there a law requiring seats for saleswomen?" Mrs. Winslow asked.

"There is," Gaylord said, "but it's generally ignored. Sarah, why don't you get a position in domestic service? I understand they make twice as much as store workers."

"I prefer what I'm doing. It's freedom that I want when my work is done. I know some girls who make more money and dress better and everything for being in service, but they're never sure of one minute that's their own when they're in the house. My day is ten hours long, but when it's done, it's done, and I can do what I like with my evenings. And besides, one day I hope to become a dressmaker working for myself."

"Is that possible?" Emily asked.

"Oh, yes. My friend, Molly Kelly, has done it. Of course, now she calls herself Madame Odette."

"Did she change her name because she's Irish?" Michael asked.

"Oh, no, nothing like that. French dress-makers are all the rage in the city. She subscribes to French fashion magazines and keeps up with all French designers. She even has a woman in France who sends her dolls dressed in the latest styles. Molly, I mean Madame Odette, copies them and sells ever so many caps, bonnets, mantles, and lovely dresses to wealthy women."

"How much money do you need to start up your own business?" Gaylord asked.

"A lot more than I have now. But I'll do it."

Emily saw the steely determination in the young girl's face and patted her hand. "I know you will, Sarah. I know you will."

Still not fully recovered from the anxiety of their voyage and their frightening night in the Five Points, a weary Michael and Emily undressed and threw themselves into bed. The creaky bed was lumpy and sagged, but it was a bed worthy of an emperor compared to the rough planks of the ship.

Emily flapped her arms. "My God, Michael, all this room. I don't know if I can sleep with so much room."

"Aye, and you don't have to worry about waking up your bunk-mate, poor Mrs. Callahan." Michael slipped his arm across her body and whispered, "And we can make love without waking the whole damn ship."

Emily settled into Michael's arms. "Indeed, we can," she said, slipping out of her nightshirt.

CHAPTER THREE

Early the next morning, Michael set out to find a job, thinking it shouldn't be too difficult. While they'd wandered the streets looking for a hotel on their first day in the city, he'd noticed lots of "Help Wanted" signs. As he walked the streets, he was puzzled by the abundance of oyster stands, seemingly on every corner, that advertised one-cent oysters and oyster stew for six cents. One stand had a sign that stated: "All you can eat – 6 cents."

Never having had an oyster, he was about to buy one, but then he saw the man shucking them and decided oysters were not for him.

On the corner of Canal Street and Mercer he saw a "Help Wanted" sign in the window of a butcher shop. The sickening smell of blood and animal guts was overpowering, but he went inside anyway.

A burly man wearing a striped apron caked in dried blood was supervising the loading of sides of beef onto a wagon. He turned toward Michael. "Yeah, what is it?"

"I've come about the sign in the window. I'm looking for work."

The man shook his head. "Jesus Christ. All you goddamn paddies are the same. Isn't there a one of youse who knows how to read?"

Michael reddened in embarrassment. He knew he was still shaky reading words, but he thought he'd read the sign correctly. "I'm sorry. I don't understand."

The man brought him outside and pointed to the sign. "What does the sign say?"

Michael stared at the sign. It was simple enough. What could the man be talking about? "It says help wanted."

"And under that?"

"N-I-N-A. Is that a woman's name?"

"No, you goddamned mackerel snapper. It means *no Irish need apply*. Now be off with you before I call a cop."

A dumbfounded Michael stood on the sidewalk staring at the sign, unsure what to do next. Then, he heard the man say something to the others loading the wagon and they all laughed. Humiliated, he hurried away.

Now that he knew what to look for, he was astonished to see those letters—*NINA*—on almost every help wanted sign. Some signs even spelled it out: *No Irish Need Apply*. Wherever he walked—along Canal Street, Grand, Delancey—he saw the same signs again and again.

He found himself aimlessly walking up the Bowery, which soon turned into Third Avenue. He noticed that north of Houston Street the pattern of the streets changed. Instead of the confusing jumble of crisscrossing streets, the streets began to form a rectangular grid. And the cross streets had numbers instead of names—something that as a newcomer he found easier to negotiate.

The farther north he walked the more the buildings began to thin out and there were less people on the street and wagons in the road. He was suddenly aware of an unaccustomed silence and realized something was peculiar about the roadbed. The center of the street was paved with a surface of compacted small stones—something he had never seen before—making the sound of iron carriage wheels on this surface much quieter. And yet, each side of the street closest to the curb was left as soft dirt.

Distracted by his lack of success in finding a job and wondering what to do next, he started to cross Third Avenue when he heard a shout. He looked up and saw two carriages, side by side, racing toward him. One was a sulky pulled by a single horse, the other was a phaeton pulled by two horses. He jumped back just in time as the two carriages roared by him, missing him by inches. Scared out of his wits, he scurried back to the sidewalk.

The man who had shouted the warning was leaning up against

the gaslight lamppost smoking a pipe. He grinned and nodded toward the galloping carriages receding into the distance.

"You're a lucky fellow, mister. You came within a cat's whisker of being run down by Cornelius Vanderbilt himself."

"Who's Cornelius Vanderbilt?"

The man took the pipe out of his mouth and knocked the ashes out against the lamppost. "You're just off the boat, aren't you?"

"Aye."

"Mr. Vanderbilt happens to be one of the richest men in the world. Makes his money in steamboats and railroads. And his racing companion is Robert Bonner, the owner of the *New York Ledger*. I came all the way out from Brooklyn just to see his horse, Dexter."

"Why?"

"Mr. Bonner paid thirty-three thousand dollars for that magnificent trotter."

"*Good God*!" Michael wasn't sure how much that amount was but it sounded like a king's ransom. He was beginning to believe that New York was a very strange place indeed. Firemen fighting with each other while a building burns, people living in virtual pigpens in the Five Points, and now a man spending a fortune on a horse. And on top of that, the all-consuming, frustrating question that was now nagging him: would there be no man in this city who would hire an Irishman?

It was getting late and he started back down Third Avenue. After a while the two carriages that had almost run him down came trotting down the avenue side by side, the two drivers laughing about something. He stopped to look at the horse that cost a fortune. It was indeed a magnificent animal. Back in Ireland, before the famine, Emily's father had had a stable of splendid animals, but nothing to compare to this horse. He looked at the other driver, Cornelius Vanderbilt, who was supposed to be so rich. He was balding with pointed features and bristling side whiskers. Actually, quite ordinary, Michael thought. But one look at the custom-made phaeton and the sleek pair of Chestnuts and even to Michael's unpracticed eye it was evident the man was wealthy.

At the corner of Third Avenue and Tenth Street, he saw a horse tack shop with a help wanted sign in the window. Now that was something he could do. He understood horses and horse tack. Hadn't he worked in Lord Somerville's stables since he was a young boy? As he grew nearer to the store, his heart sank. At the bottom of the sign were the now dreaded letters NINA. He was about to keep walking, but he stopped and ran his fingers through his thick curly black hair in frustration. Maybe that ignorant butcher didn't like the Irish, but that didn't mean it had to be true for everyone else in the city.

He went into the shop. A man in a leather apron, polishing a saddle, looked up. "Yeah?"

"I've come about the sign in the window. I know all about horses," he added, hurriedly. "And I—"

"Didn't you read the sign?" the man snapped. "I don't hire Irish. Be on your way."

"But why not? I'm only thirty years old, I'm healthy, and strong. I'm a good worker."

The man squinted at him. "That's what you all say. But I'm on to your type. You'll say anything to get the job, but the next thing is you don't come to work because you're too drunk or you were thrown into jail for beating your wife. You're all shiftless, lazy drunks. Now get the hell out of my shop before I call a policeman."

After that shameful encounter at the tack shop, a furious Michael continued down Third Avenue. After a while it occurred to him that he was purposely wandering the unfamiliar streets of Manhattan because he was too ashamed to go back to the boardinghouse and face Emily.

Third Avenue led back to the Bowery and the next thing he knew he looked up and saw the Old Brewery where he and Emily had spent their first night. He was back in the Five Points. He realized he hadn't eaten anything since breakfast and he stepped into a grog shop. The low-ceiling gave the gloomy shop a cave-like feel. In one corner stood a broken stove with a crooked pipe from which the smoke leaked at every joint. The bar consisted of rough boards propped up on boxes. There were a few men standing at the bar. A few more slept at tables made of planks across old barrels.

The man behind the bar was a huge barrel-chested man with a

long scar running down the side of his right cheek. "What'll you have?"

"You serve Irish here?" Michael snapped, surprised that those words had come out of his mouth. All the pent-up anger, frustration, and humiliation had come tumbling out of him with those words.

Taking no offense from Michael's tone, the bartender wiped the top of the bar with a dirty rag. "I'll serve the devil himself if he can pay for his drink."

"I'll have a beer. Have you any food?"

The bartender laughed, revealing three missing teeth. "It's a grog shop, not a fine eating establishment. That'll be three cents."

Michael took his beer and sat down at one of the barrel tables. He wasn't there long before two men came in. One of them looked familiar, then, alarmed, he saw that the man's arm was in a sling. *He was the one he'd fought in the Old Brewery.*

The man spotted Michael. "So, it's you again, is it? I told you I'd get you." Suddenly, there was a revolver in his hand. Instinctively, Michael threw his beer in the man's face and rushed him. With only one arm to defend himself, he fell back and Michael easily yanked the firearm out of his hand. As the man's friend made a menacing move toward him, Michael pointed the gun at him. "Just… just take your friend and… and get out of here, the pair of you."

Giving Michael a murderous look, the man helped his friend up and they stumbled out the door.

The bartender stuck his hand out. "The name's Big Bill. What's yours?"

"Michael Ranahan."

"You handle yourself well, Ranahan."

A befuddled Michael threw the gun on the bar and shook the man's hand. "I'm only in this county a couple of days. I'm just trying to find honest work. Is it always this crazy here?"

Big Bill shrugged. "More or less. So where are you living?"

"Coyle's boardinghouse."

"The one on Greenwich?"

"Aye."

He studied Michael as though trying to make up his mind about something. "Are you the one who broke Feeny's flipper?"

"Feeny?"

"The man you just took the gun away from."

"Oh, I guess I did. I was only trying to defend a young woman—"

"Maureen? Well, you were wasting your time. He found her, slit her throat, and tossed her into the East River."

"Oh, my God ..."

Big Bill slid the revolver back to Michael. "I'd advise you to hang onto that."

"Why?"

"Feeny is one mean sonofabitch. You bested him twice. He won't forget that."

Michael stared at the revolver on the bar for a long moment. "Aren't they illegal here?"

Bill shrugged. "Sort of. If you get caught you can always buy your way out of an arrest."

Now in a complete state of confusion, but wanting nothing to do with a firearm, Michael pushed the weapon away from him and hurried back to the boardinghouse.

Emily was sitting in their room reading a newspaper when he came in. "How did it go?" she asked.

"Not good. Not good at all," he said, slumping into the rickety chair.

She saw the troubled expression on his face and put the paper down. "What happened?"

He told her everything that had transpired during the day, leaving out only the news that the young woman had been murdered. "Emily, what am I to do?"

"I think you should talk to Mr. Temple. Perhaps he can offer some advice. Meanwhile, I've been reading the employment advertisements and I see what you mean. Listen to this one. *Wanted, a girl of neat and industrious habits and amiable disposition to take the entire charge of two small children. No Irish need apply*. Here's another one. *Wanted, an American or German girl, about fourteen or fifteen, to assist a small family. No Irish need apply.*"

"My God, Emily, what are we to do?"

"I know what I'm going to do. I won't tell anyone I'm Irish."

"And well you can. You don't have the brogue."

She smiled. "All those years of schooling in England and France may pay off yet."

"Well, that's all well and good for you, but what about me?"

Emily frowned. "Talk to Mr. Temple. Let's see what he says." When she saw the dejected look on his face, she opened the paper. "Listen to this one."

Michael waved his hand in dismissal. "Please Emily, I don't want to hear anymore Irish Need Not Apply advertisements."

"No, this one is funny, in a strange sort of way." She read: "*Ho! For the execution. The beautiful and commodious steamboat Chicopee will leave this city on Friday morning for the purpose of affording all on board an opportunity of witnessing the execution of John Hicks, the pirate. The boat will lay near the island until the ceremonies are over. This will be a fine chance for sea captains and seafaring men generally to view the exit of one of the most atrocious of these scourges of their profession. The Chicopee will afterwards run up the North River as far as West Point, taking in a view of the countryside. One dollar.*"

She looked up at him and grinned. "Do you want to go?"

Michael shook his head in amazement. "This country is daft all together."

That night after supper, Michael pulled Gaylord into the parlor and told him everything that had happened. The newspaperman listened attentively and when Michael was done, he said, "First, I would advise you to stay away from the Five Points."

"Why? Do you know this Feeny person?"

"No, but there are hundreds just like him. Pimps and scoundrels are as common in the Five Points as fleas on a dog."

"But what if he comes looking for me?"

"Highly unlikely. The denizens of the Five Points rarely stray outside the confines of the Five Points. Having said that, you should have kept that firearm. Just in case."

"But it's illegal, isn't it?"

"Your friend Big Bill was right. You can always bribe your way out of an arrest in the unlikely occasion that you would be searched by a policeman."

Michael ran his hands through his hair. "All I want is to find work, but no one will hire me because I'm Irish."

"I understand. Unfortunately, this city is full of nativists."

"Nativists?"

"Back in 1835, the New York Protestant Association sponsored a meeting at Broadway Hall to discuss the question: Is popery compatible with civil liberty? Well, a bunch of Catholics forced their way into the meeting and generally tore the place up. In response, a couple of months later, the Native American Democratic Association was formed to—how did they phrase it? —'protect American industry from foreigners'—read Irish—who they described as destructive as locusts and lice were to the Egyptian fields. Almost poetic, don't you think?"

"So, are these the ones who won't hire an Irishman?"

"They're not the only ones. There's the Order of the Star-Spangled Banner, a secret society with clandestine meetings, rituals, secret signs, and handshakes. They're commonly called the 'Know-Nothings' because that's the response they always give when asked about the nature of their organization."

"What do they have against the Irish?"

"Well you may ask. It is a puzzlement. After all, unless these lads are native born Indians, they're immigrants as well. But the thing is, now that they're here they want the door shut to other immigrants."

"But why?"

"Jobs. They're afraid that the newly arrived immigrants will undercut their own jobs by working for less money."

Michael shook his head. "So, there's no hope for me, is there?"

Just then there was a knock at the door and Coyle answered it. Michael stiffened when he heard a man's voice mention his name. A flurry of thoughts flooded his brain. Could it be Feeny or one of his henchmen come to get him? No, it couldn't. No one knew where he lived—but then he remembered. He'd told the bartender where he lived. He stood in the parlor, tensed, preparing to fight, and regretting that he hadn't kept that firearm after all.

Coyle came into the parlor and handed Michael a note. "He told me to give this to you."

With trembling hands and a shaky voice, Michael read the note aloud. *Michael Ranahan, come to my office in Tammany Hall tomorrow morning. Tommy Walsh.*"

"What does this mean?" Emily asked. "Who is Tommy Walsh?"

"He's the local ward boss," Gaylord explained.

"What's a ward boss?"

"A Tammany Hall ward boss is the local vote gatherer and provider of patronage. Tammany Hall has been very helpful to the Irish community."

Michael stared at the note. "What do you think he wants of me?"

"Perhaps he can get you a job."

"Oh, that would be grand." The smile on Michael's face faded. "And what would I have to do for this service?"

"Just promise to vote for their candidate in the next election."

"But, I'm not a citizen."

Gaylord grinned. "A minor detail. Don't be surprised if you are asked to vote more than once."

Michael shook his head again. "Gaylord, I feel like I'm living in some kind of mad dream." Gaylord slapped him on the back. "Welcome to the new world, Michael."

CHAPTER FOUR

The next morning, in a soaking downpour, Michael made his way to Tammany Hall, an imposing five-story building at the intersection of Nassau and Frankfort Streets.

Tammany, named after an old Delaware Indian chief called Tammend, was an organization founded in 1789. The leader was called the Grand Sachem and the workers, Braves. Every year the members elected thirteen Sachems. Then those thirteen elected one of their own to be the Grand Sachem. In recent years, Tammany had been taken over by Irish politicians and it was now the place for Irish immigrants to go to get help finding work or a place to stay.

He went into the building and approached an elderly man seated behind a desk who was engrossed in a newspaper. “Excuse me, could you tell me where I might find a Mr. Tommy Walsh?”

“Second floor, room 212,” he answered without looking up.

On the door of room 212 was a name in gold lettering—*Thomas J. Walsh.*

Inside he found a jowly man, in his early thirties with flaming red hair smoking an enormous cigar. He looked up from his newspaper.

“And what can I do for you, sir?” he asked with a wide grin.

“Are you Tommy Walsh?”

“That I am. And who might you be?”

“My name is Michael Ranahan and—”

The broad smile vanished from the man’s face and tears welled up in his eyes. “God bless you, Ranahan,” he said coming around the desk and vigorously shaking a puzzled Michael’s hand. He motioned to a chair. “Sit down. Sit down.”

Michael, bewildered by the man’s strange behavior, sat down. The ward boss continued to stare at him, saying nothing. Growing more and more uncomfortable by the minute, Michael pulled the note from his pocket. “I believe you sent this to me?”

“I did. I did. I want to thank you for helping my sister.”

Michael shook his head. “Sister? I don’t think I know your sister. There may be a misunderstanding …”

“You stayed at the Old Brewery a couple of nights ago, did you not?”

“I did. My wife and I had just arrived and we had no American money for decent lodgings, so we had to stay there for one night.”

“And that night you saved my sister from Feeny.”

“You mean the young girl, Maureen?”

“Her real name is Bridget.”

“I don’t understand. She said she had no family here.”

“She was lying.”

“Why would she do that?”

“My sister has never been right in the head. She’d been in and out of Blackwell’s Lunatic Asylum for years. We’d bring her home and she’d run away the first chance she got. I’ve been looking for her for these past few weeks, but ...” he shrugged. “It’s easy to disappear in this city, especially into the Five Points.”

“How did you know I helped your sister?”

“Big Bill told me.”

“Big … Oh, the bartender?”

“The same.”

Michael looked away from the man’s intense gaze. “Then you know ...”

“Yes, my sister is dead. Feeny murdered her.”

Michael was surprised by the lack of emotion in his voice. “Will he be arrested?”

“No need. As of last night, Mr. Feeny is no longer among the living.”

Michael nodded solemnly. He knew better than to ask what had happened to him.

Walsh slapped his knees, breaking the somber tone. “So then,

Michael Ranahan, if there is anything I can do for you, just ask."

"Well, the thing is, Mr. Walsh, I'm having no luck finding a job. They all say—"

"No Irish need apply. I know, I know," he said, returning to his desk. He picked up his cigar and waved it in the air. "Those damn bigoted Know-Nothings control this city, but that will soon change. We Irish have discovered that the only way to gain power in this city is through the ballet box. Eighteen-forty-seven was the first big year of famine emigration. Fifty-two thousand Irish Catholics arrived. And it's been steady ever since. Do you realize the Irish now make up a quarter of the population of this city? That's almost a hundred and thirty thousand souls. Every day more than forty passenger ships arrive here in Manhattan. Do you know there are more Irish in this city than in any other city in the world save Dublin?"

"No, I didn't know that."

"Well, it's true. And that, my lad, is a huge and powerful voting bloc."

All the while he'd been talking, he'd been looking out the window as though he could see all those thousands of Irish immigrants marching outside his window. He turned back to Michael. "We've got to become the biggest voting bloc in the city. It's a matter of self-preservation, pure and simple. Did you know that the Know-Nothing Party up in Massachusetts has actually been *deporting* Irish?"

"No."

"Well, they are. They've manipulated the colonial poor law to develop laws for deporting foreign paupers—meaning the Irish. Thousands have been sent back to Ireland already."

They very thought of being sent back to Ireland made Michael's heart pound. "Could they do that to me?"

"If the Know-Nothings here in this city have their way, that's a distinct possibility."

"Then they must be stopped."

"That's what we in Tammany are trying to do with the help of the Irish in this city. So, Mr. Ranahan, how long have you been living here?"

"I've just arrived. It was a desperate voyage I can tell you."

"I know, I know. The North Atlantic can be very unforgiving."

"Our ship had over two hundred souls aboard."

"Well that's a pretty small boat. Some of the larger ships carry up to a thousand men, women, and children. And most of those passengers are Irish."

Walsh put his feet up on the desk. "So, Michael Ranahan, what did you do in the old country?"

Michael told him about his life as a tenant farmer, how he'd lost all his family, how Emily had lost her father and his estates, and why they'd decided to come to America to escape the famine.

Walsh crushed the stub of his cigar in an overflowing ashtray. "It's a familiar story, Michael. I've heard it a thousand times."

Just then the door opened and a tall, handsome, dark-haired man with an immense black mustache and wearing a black frock coat came in. He had a prominent nose and black slicked-down hair. Walsh jumped up. "Mr. Wood, may I be of service, sir?" he asked in a deferential tone.

The man looked at Michael. "I wanted to talk to you about something. When you're done with your business here, please come to my office."

"Yes, sir. Oh, by the way, I'd like you to meet our newest voter, Michael Ranahan. Ranahan, this is Mr. Fernando Wood, former congressman and currently our Grand Sachem here at Tammany Hall. And, if we have anything to say about it, he'll be our next mayor, God willing."

Wood bowed slightly and shook hands with Michael. "Are you new to New York, sir?"

"I am. I just arrived from Ireland."

"And he's looking for a job," Walsh interjected.

"Do you have anything for him, Tommy?"

"I do. I'm going to send him to see Cully."

Wood nodded. "Good choice. Cullinane owes us a few favors. When you're done here, Tommy, I'd like to see you in my office." Wood bowed toward Michael. "Good luck, Mr. Ranahan," he said and left.

Walsh wrote a name and address on a piece of paper and handed it to Michael. "Tomorrow morning, you'll go see this man. I think he'll be able to find work for you."

Michael gratefully pumped Walsh's hand, feeling for the first time since setting foot on Manhattan Island an absence of dread and fear. Maybe things were going to work out after all. "Mr. Walsh, how can I ever thank you?"

Walsh slapped Michael on the back and grinned. "I'm sure we'll find a way, Ranahan. I'm sure we will."

CHAPTER FIVE

Emily had carefully thought out her plan to find a suitable position. She had gone back to Stewart's department store and, swallowing hard, spent an obscene portion of the money they had left on new dresses, shoes, and blouses. But it was all for a good cause she told herself. She had to make herself look presentable.

The night before she'd read a promising advertisement in the newspaper: *Wanted: An experienced young woman (preferably French or English) of good repute. Purpose: To tutor a twelve-year-old girl in the French language. No Irish Need Apply. Inquire at 15 Gramercy Park N between 2 and 4 pm.*

Earlier that morning, Emily had met Mrs. Winslow in the hallway.

"Mrs. Winslow, do you know where 15 Gramercy Park is?"

Mrs. Winslow arched her eyebrows. "Yes, of course. It's one of the more fashionable neighborhoods in the city. The homes surrounding Gramercy Park, I am happy to say, are mercifully free of the epidemic of humbug and sham finery and gin-palace decorations seen in far too many homes of the nouveau riche. Why do you ask?"

"I'm going there to answer this advertisement." She handed the paper to Mrs. Winslow.

"Well, it's a very exclusive neighborhood," the older woman said, discretely eying Emily's rather plain dress.

Emily reddened. "I intend to wear something more suitable than this."

"Quite so. Gramercy Park is inhabited by some of the city's most illustrious luminaries. It's home to, among others, Peter Cooper, Cyrus Field, James Harper, and George Templeton Strong."

"And these are rich and influential men?" Emily asked, with growing trepidation. Until this moment, she had every confidence that she could obtain the position by passing herself off as English. But now she wasn't so sure she could pull it off.

"Yes, they are *all* rich and influential men."

Nestled between Twentieth and Twenty-First Streets off Third Avenue, the land where Gramercy Park now stands was once a swamp. In 1831, Samuel B. Ruggles, a real estate man and advocate of open space, proposed the idea for the park due to the northward growth of Manhattan. The swamp was drained and the park built. In time, the wealthy residents of the city flocked to the area for its tranquility and relief from the cacophonous noise of the city's streets.

Thirty-nine red-bricked houses were arranged in a broad rectangle around the pleasant, fenced in central garden. The park was private but, as a concession to the city, it was open to the public for one day a year.

Hurrying down a bucolic tree-lined street, Emily stopped in front of 15 Gramercy Park. Taking a deep breath, she climbed the steps and struck the gleaming brass knocker on an impressive solid oak door. A young maid with a heart-shaped face and wearing a black and white uniform opened the door.

"Yes?"

"I'm here about the position of tutor."

"Please come in." She led Emily into a parlor. "If you will remain here, I'll get the mistress of the house."

The focal point of the spacious, high-ceiling room was a piano draped in velvet. The walls were covered with bright red flock wallpaper. Thick dark green curtains blocked most of the delightful view of the park across the street making the room almost claustrophobic. The rest of the room was cluttered with an unfortunate excess of Chinese vases, porcelain statuary, and oil paintings. Scattered over the oak floor were oriental rugs of various sizes. A massive mahogany bureau set against the far wall was crammed with a confusing jumble of bric-a-brac. On one side table rested a silver tea set replete with a dozen delicate porcelain cups and saucers. On another side table Emily noticed four books and immediately knew what they represented. *How to Observe Morals and Manners, Wealth and Pedigree of the Wealthy Citizens of New York City, The Art of Good Behavior,* and *A Calendar of Wealth, Fashion and Gentility* were all of a genre of "courtesy books" that dealt with etiquette, behavior, and morals. These books were designed to instruct the uninitiated in how to comport themselves in polite society.

Emily pushed aside the heavy window curtain and watched several maids wheeling their charges in large ornate parabolas while older children ran with their hoops.

"So, you're here about the tutor position."

Emily turned to face a woman in her early thirties with her blond hair pulled back in a severe bun. She was wearing a dark green printed wool challis day dress. She would have been more attractive if she didn't have such a stern look on her face.

"I am."

"You're not Irish, are you?"

Momentarily stunned by the question, Emily muttered, "What… Oh, no. I'm English."

"Good. My husband has given me strict instructions. I am not to hire anyone Irish." She motioned toward a Chesterfield sofa near the fireplace. "I'm Mrs. Vera Ingersoll. Please be seated."

Emily watched the fussy woman smooth out her dress and began to wonder if she'd made a mistake coming here.

"*Comment t'appelles tu?*" she asked, suddenly.

"Emily Somerville."

"*Parlez-vous français?*" she asked.

"*Oui, bien sûr.*"

"*Où avez-vous étudier le français*?"

"I studied at the Sorbonne and at a Swiss finishing school," Emily answered, switching to English, mostly because the woman's French was so atrocious.

"C'est bien." Giving up on the French, she, too, lapsed into English. "My husband, I, and my daughter are going abroad next year and he wants Lucy to be able to converse in French."

"An excellent idea. How often would you want me to come?"

"I think three days a week. Shall we say two hours a day?"
"That would be fine."
They quickly agreed on salary and work requirements. Then Mrs. Ingersoll rang a small bell on the table and the maid came into the room. "Letta, would you bring Lucy in here?"
A minute later, Letta brought a gawky, shy young girl into the room. With her dark hair, brown eyes, and dark complexion, she looked nothing like her mother.
"Lucy, this is Miss Somerville. She is going to be your French tutor. Say hello to Miss Somerville."
Barely looking up, the girl said, "Hello," in a soft voice.
"Hello, Lucy. Are you excited about learning French?"
"I guess so."
Mrs. Ingersoll gave her daughter a sharp look. "Very well. You can go now."
Emily stood up. "Shall I start tomorrow?"
"Yes, that would be satisfactory. Subject, of course, to my husband's approval."

At supper that night, besides Emily and Michael, there was just Mrs. Winslow and Gaylord seated at the table. Sarah was still at work.
Mrs. Winslow queried Emily. "So, how did your interview go?"
"It went very well. I have been retained by the Ingersoll family to tutor their daughter."
Mrs. Winslow's eyebrows went up. "The Ingersolls are quite wealthy."
"You bet he is," Gaylord said. "He's in shipping I believe. He has a counting house on Water Street. As I recall, he has an interest in three ships that ply the Atlantic trade. But, still, he's not up there with the Astors or the Belmonts." He lowered his voice. "He's what they call *nouveau riche,*" he said in a confidential tone.
"What does that mean?" Michael asked.
"It means he has the money, but not the pedigree," Mrs. Winslow explained. "Rest assured, he'll never be invited to an Astor ball or to the finer homes in New York City. He's one of the "Shoddy" element and always will be."
"What do you mean by shoddy?" Emily asked.
"I'm afraid it's what many of the *nouveau riche* are, my dear. If

you know what to look out for they are pathetically obvious. For one, they overdress. They compensate for their lack of taste with an ostentatious display of expensive, but vulgar, clothing and jewelry. But all to no avail. Their coarseness betrays their common beginnings. They lack what the French call *comme il faut* – proper social usage"

"Aren't you being a little harsh?" Gaylord asked.

"I think not. I find it humorous that they have the audacity to look down their noses at those with lesser fortunes while at the same time idolizing those who are richer."

Emily studied the older woman, wondering if she might be talking about herself as one of those with "lesser fortunes."

After a moment of uncomfortable silence, Gaylord turned to Michael. "How about you? What news have you?"

"I went to see Mr. Walsh and he's given me the name of someone to see tomorrow morning."

"What kind of business is it?"

"I don't know. I'm just to see a Mr. Cullinane."

Gaylord tapped his spoon on his bowl. "Cullinane. The name is familiar. Where are you to meet him?"

Michael took the piece of paper and read it. "Twenty-Five Pearl Street."

"Ah, that's it. There's a Cullinane Construction Company on Pearl Street. I hope you have a strong back, Michael. Construction in this city can be brutal."

"I don't mind. I'll just be glad to have a job."

"Do you know how Pearl Street got its name?"

"He doesn't," Henrietta said. "But I'm sure you'll tell him."

Ignoring Henrietta's dig, he said, "When the Dutch first came ashore on Manhattan Island they noticed huge mounds of oyster shells deposited by the Indians. They called them oyster middens. There were dozens of middens along the path of the road they were building and so they called the path Pearl Street."

"You are an absolute font of wisdom," Mrs. Winslow said with a raised eyebrow.

Gaylord nodded. "It's true. I am a great repository of information. Alas, none of it is very useful."

Back in their room, Michael picked Emily up and whirled her

around the tiny room. "Isn't it grand? Here we are only a few days in New York City and we both have jobs."

Emily kissed him. "I never doubted it for a minute."

He put her down and frowned. "Well, you were more optimistic than me. There's a lot of hostility toward the Irish in this city."

"That is no concern of mine," she said with a sly smile.

"And why not?"

"Because I'm English."

"So you are," he said with a grin. "So, you are."

CHAPTER SIX

The next morning with great trepidation Michael set out early for Pearl Street. He'd lost track of how many times he'd already gotten lost in the confusing jumble of intersecting and crisscrossing streets that was Manhattan and he didn't want to be late getting to the Cullinane Construction Company.

Following Gaylord's handwritten map, he made his way east on Barkley Street, to Fulton, and finally to Pearl. He found himself standing before a large warehouse-like structure and read the sign over the door: *Cullinane Construction Company*. He stepped inside and was met with a fearful din of hammers and saws. The air was filled with a not unpleasant smell—a combination of brick dust and wood chippings. Even at this early hour the warehouse was bustling with activity. A handful of men were loading several wagons with brick, stone, sand, and wooden beams, while others were busy sawing lengths of planks.

Above the noise, he shouted to a man loading a wagon. "I'm looking for Mr. Cullinane. Could you tell me where I might find him?"

The man pointed to a small office in the corner.

Sitting behind an old desk piled high with floor plans and architectural drawings sat a heavy-set, roughhewn man in his early sixties. He was bald, but his cheeks bristled with bushy gray muttonchops.

He looked up at Michael over his round steel-framed spectacles that perched at the tip of his nose. From his expression, it was clear that he didn't appreciate being disturbed. "Yeah, what is it?"

From the man's brusque and dour demeanor, Michael was afraid he was going to tell him that no Irish need apply. "Mr. Thomas Walsh sent me," he said, nervously.

Cullinane threw his glassed on the desk in disgust and shook his head. That damn Walsh. Why does he send me every damn Paddy that comes off the boat? I suppose you're looking for a job?"

"I am."

"The last five Paddies he sent me didn't last a day. Construction is hard work."

"I can do it, sir."

Cullinane squinted at him. "What makes you think so?"

"I need a job," he said, trying to keep the desperation out of his voice. "Mr. Cullinane. I'll do whatever it takes."

The old man grunted. "We'll see. What's your name?"

"Michael Ranahan."

"Come with me, Ranahan."

Out on the warehouse floor, he called out to a small, wiry man preparing to drive a loaded wagon out the door. "Flynn, hold up."

"What is it, Cully?"

"Take this man—what was your name again?"

"Michael Ranahan."

"Take Ranahan with you."

"What's he to do?"

"Anything you damn well tell him to do. Mind, if he slacks off, give him the boot."

"I will." Flynn grinned, revealing several missing teeth. He motioned to Michael. "Climb aboard, Ranahan. Can you drive a horse?"

"Aye."

Flynn handed him the reins. "All right, then. Let's go."

Glad to have something to do, Michael snapped the reins and clucked to the horse. "Come on, boy. Let's go." For a moment, he wondered if the horse would understand his brogue. But the horse responded immediately. He began to relax. Finally, he had a job. But his newfound sense of serenity evaporated as soon as they cleared the warehouse doors. Outside the street was crawling with horse drawn wagons and men pushing wheelbarrows and fruit carts. Everyone seemed to be shouting at each other at the same time.

"Take a left at the corner," Flynn said, lighting up a cigar and seemingly unperturbed by the chaos around him.

At the corner of Pearl and John Streets, Michael took the turn too close and the rear wheel of the wagon bounced over the curb.

Flynn grabbed the bench with both hands. "Jasus, man. Are you trying to kill us all together?"

"I'm sorry. That other wagon cut me off and—"

"Sure they *always* cut you off, Ranahan. You're not on some quiet country road in Ireland now. Give no quarter and ask no quarter. That's how things are done in this city, me boyo."

Keeping his hands tightly on the reins, Michael followed Flynn's directions. Soon they were skirting a lovely park with trees and an open field that looked very much out of place in such bustling surroundings. "What's this?" Michael asked.

"This is Washington Square Park."

"It's lovely."

"If you think this is lovely, you should see Gramercy Park."

"That's where my wife is going to be working."

"She get a position as a maid?"

"No. She's going to teach French to a young girl."

Flynn looked at Michael askance. "French, is it? What Irish peasant learns French?"

"Oh, she's not like me. She's the daughter of my late landlord."

"Then how did the likes of you end up with an aristocrat?"

Michael told him the story of their experiences in the famine.

When he was done, Flynn said, "That's pretty much everyone's story. Turn right here onto Fifth Avenue."

Michael turned onto a wide road that ran straight as an arrow north. It was a welcome relief from the narrow and twisting streets from which they had just come. But the air was suddenly filled with a choking dust thrown up by passing wagons and carriages. "My God, is the air always this bad?"

"Aye. In the summer, the streets and sidewalks are covered in dust. And then, come the fall, these same streets will be ankle deep in mud. And in the winter the mud turns to rock-hard ruts that will jar the teeth right out of your head. It's a grand city you've come to, Michael Ranahan."

As they moved north, Michael stared in astonishment at the

piles and piles of cow manure covering the street as far as the eye could see. "What's this about?"

"There must have been a cattle drive come through here last night."

"Do you mean to say they drive cattle through these streets?"

"Aye. They used to do it during the day, but the city council has forbidden it. Now they can only drive the cattle at night."

Michael was beginning to suspect that nothing that went on in this city made any sense. "Have you been here long, Mr. Flynn?" he asked, changing the subject.

"You can cut out the *mister* for Jasus sake. I go by Flynn. That's all anyone ever calls me. We came from Cork twenty years ago. I was just a young gossoon. I'm the only one left now. My father abandoned us within weeks of us coming to America. Then, two years later, my mother died of the cholera. I took care of my young sister and brother as best I could. But within a year, they were both dead as well. My sister of the fever. My brother ... I have no idea. Probably something in the stinking, foul water we drink."

"This is a rough city, isn't it?" Michael asked. It was more a statement than a question.

"It is that. There's no one going to give you anything. You must fight for what you want or you'll never have nothin'."

As they continued up the broad avenue, Michael observed the same phenomenon that he'd seen on Third Avenue. The road traffic had thinned out and houses became sparser and gave way to open fields.

'Have you been with Mr. Cullinane long?"

"Goin' on ten years."

"What kind of man is he?"

"He's not a bad lot." Flynn lit up another cigar. "Demanding, but fair. Give him a good day's work and you'll have no trouble from him. The old man's tough as nails. Comes from upstate Albany. Ran away from home when he was thirteen. Lived in the streets and slept under bridges until he got a job as a hod carrier."

"Married?"

"The wife died in the cholera epidemic of forty-nine. That was a bad time. More than fifteen thousand died that year. Anyhow, Cully worked his way up to foreman and finally saved enough money to buy out the owner."

Flynn stared off into the middle distance. "That's what I'd like to do someday. Of course, I'm only a foreman now, but someday…"

After a long silence, Michael said, "So where is it we're going?"

"Fortieth Street," Flynn said, snapping out of his reverie.

Michael looked at the cross-street sign. "My God, we're only at Twelfth Street. Does anyone even live that far north?"

"Precious few. Mostly just some scattered hog pens, orphanages, farms, inns, cattle markets, and shanties inhabited by the Negroes and the Irish. Although, we'll be passing the great mansion of Mr. Waddell. Truth be told, I don't know how anybody in his right mind would move all the way up there into that wild country. There are plenty of fine homes on Union Square and Madison Square and even here on Fifth Avenue up to Twenty-Third Street. Mr. John Harrington might not be crazy, but he certainly is odd."

"Harrington?"

"He's the man whose mansion we're building, a millionaire who made his fortune in fur and now real estate. He's good friends with John Jacob Astor."

"Astor?"

"Jasus, don't you know about anyone in this city?"

"I'm only here a few days," Michael said defensively.

"True enough. Astor made his fortune in real estate. The Astors are known as the landlords of New York."

"There's an awful lot of rich people in the city, isn't there?"

"Aye, but even more poor. And those rich people don't even notice them. They spend their money on big houses and private clubs and such and the devil take the poor."

"Apparently, they like expensive horses as well. The other day I was almost run down by man I was told was Mr. Vanderbilt. He was racing some other fellow on Third Avenue."

"They come almost every day with their fast trotters and pacers. Vanderbilt, Belmont, even the Reverend Henry Ward Beecher. Although I don't know that horse racing is the proper sport for a preacher."

"Does Mr. Harrington race?"

Flynn laughed. "Lord, no. For all his money, he's tight as a tick he is. Certainly too cheap to spend money on a fine horse. Do you know he had old Cully draw up the plans for the house?"

"So?"

"So, Cullinane is only a contractor. He's no architect."

"Why didn't he hire an architect?"

"To save money on the architect's fees. These rich people are a strange lot. I'll tell you that."

As they approached Thirty-Seventh Street, Michael saw a huge house with towers and chimneys sprouting from the roof. "And what in God's name is that?"

"Ah, that would be the fine mansion of Mr. Coventry Waddell. We had a hand in building that back in '45." Flynn chuckled. "Mr. Waddell's brother said it looked like a collection of condiment bottles." He stared up at the profusion of towers and chimneys and said, "By God, I think he's right." After he finished lighting his cigar, he said, "Do you know his lot extends all the way to Sixth Avenue? He has a field of wheat growing there for the use of the household. The rich are a strange lot, I'll tell you."

As they approached the building site on Fortieth Street, Michael's eyes widened in amazement at a massive Egyptian-like structure two blocks north of them. "What in God's name is that? It looks like some kind of Egyptian tomb."

"Ah, that would be the Croton Distributing Reservoir. Now that's a lovely piece of work and I'm proud to say I had a hand in building that back in '42. We worked on that job for three years. The land down toward Sixth Avenue was the city's potter's field and it had to be cleared before building the reservoir."

"Potter's field?"

"That's what they call the graveyard where the poor and destitute are buried. They took thousands of bodies out of the ground and buried them again on Ward's Island."

"What does this reservoir do?"

"It supplies drinking water to the whole city. The water comes down from a great dam up in Westchester County and ends up here. The reservoir opened on July 4th and what a celebration it was. There were parades and such and it went on for days. Along the tops of those fifty-foot walls are public walkways, offering a lovely view of the countryside. One day you should bring the missus up here to see it."

"I will." It occurred to Michael that since they'd arrived in America, they'd done nothing but work, sleep and eat. It would do them both good to get away from the boardinghouse for the day.

Michael pulled the wagon up to the building site. "Here it is. The Harrington mansion."

Michael was taken aback by the strange, cube-like three-story, red brick brownstone. It seemed stunted and squat, as though rooted in the ground. It looked nothing like the grand Waddell mansion he'd just seen. In fact, most of the buildings he'd seen in his wanderings were much more stylish and impressive.

"Would you believe it?" Flynn said, shaking his head. "A great huge house like that just for a husband and wife and three children."

When Michael pulled the wagon up to the mansion workmen were swarming all over the building. Some were on the roof installing slate trimmed with copper, others were cutting and measuring beautiful lengths of mahogany, while still others were carrying building material inside.

"Let's have a few men here," Flynn shouted.

Immediately, six men rushed up to the wagon.

Flynn jumped down. "All right. Let's get this wagon unloaded. Everything is going to the third floor." One man groaned and Flynn gave him a sharp look. "And what's the matter with you?"

"Why does everything have to go the top floor?"

"Because the lower floors are finished, you eejit. Now, get to it." He looked up at Michael. "Do you think you're going to sit on this wagon all day like some grand pooh-bah? Get down here and help them carry the bricks upstairs."

One of the men loaded bricks onto Michael's hod and he followed the others into the house. He nearly dropped his load of bricks when he saw the interior. In the style of the times, these brownstone houses were rather simple on the outside, but the interiors, decorated with Italian statuary, rich tapestries, and expensive porcelain, were where the wealthy spent their money. The ceilings in the enormous foyer had to be thirty feet high. A beautiful curving staircase of gleaming mahogany led to the second floor. Everywhere was marble and gleaming wood.

For the rest of the day he and the others carried wood and bricks to the long three flights of stairs. Finally, just when Michael thought they would never stop working, Flynn called out. "All right, that's it for the day."

As the workers piled into the wagon for the ride back to Cullinane's warehouse, Michael asked a man next to him for the time.

The man looked at his pocket watch. "Just seven."

No wonder he was tired. They'd been at it for almost twelve hours. Michael slumped on the floor, grateful that Flynn had picked another man to drive the wagon. After such a long and tiring day, he had no desire to drive back into the chaos of lower Manhattan.

That night only Gaylord, Mrs. Winslow, and Emily came to dinner. When they'd finished, Gaylord patted his stomach and in a mocking tone said, "After another one of Mr. Coyle's fine stews, I feel the need to recuperate. Ladies, why don't we adjourn to the parlor?"

Mrs. Winslow stood up. "You'll have to excuse me, Mr. Temple. I believe I'll retire for the night."

"Very well." As Mrs. Winslow left the dining room, Gaylord turned to Emily. "How about you, young lady?"

"Yes, I think I will. To tell you the truth I prefer to spend as little time as possible in that dreadfully small room. But are we allowed? Will Mr. Coyle mind?"

"No, not at all. He's a strange old duck. As far as I can tell, he spends all his time in the kitchen. Doing what, I have no idea."

"Is there a missus Coyle?"

"He and his wife ran this boardinghouse for fifteen years, but she died a couple of years ago. As you can see he's let the place go. Still, it's cheap lodgings and it's reasonably clean."

"Well in that case, let's go. Michael should be coming home from his work soon."

"So, he got a job?"

"I hope so," she said, sitting down on a lumpy settee. "He's been gone all day."

Shoveling a scoop of coal onto the dying fire, Gaylord said, "It's a shame Mrs. Winslow didn't join us. She spends entirely too much time alone."

"She does seem rather distant. Why is that?"

"She's had a tragic life, the poor woman. Do you know anything about the financial panic of '37?"

"No, I don't."

"There were many and complicated reasons for it, but the upshot was that hundreds of banks collapsed, businesses failed, prices declined, and thousands of workers lost their jobs. One of those banks was owned by Mr. Winslow. Three days later, he committed suicide."

"Oh, my goodness ..."

"Mrs. Winslow was left almost penniless. She lost her mansion on Union Square and almost everything else she owned. She's been living here ever since."

"What a tragic story."

"It is, but from what Michael has told me, you suffered a similar fate."

"True. We lost our estates in the famine, but my father didn't commit suicide, he was murdered."

"I'm so sorry."

"It was a difficult time in famine Ireland." Changing the subject, she said, "Were you born in Manhattan?"

Gaylord flopped down on an old chair badly in need of reupholstering. "No. I was born and bred in Boston."

"That's in Massachusetts, is it not?"

"Correct. My father is a preacher. He wanted me to go into the church so I could follow in his footsteps, but that would have been quite impossible."

"Why?"

"Because I'm an atheist." He gave her a sly smile. "Does that shock you, Emily?"

"No, it does not. It's funny, I haven't given it much thought, but I suppose I'm an atheist as well."

"Because of the things you saw in the famine?"

"Exactly." She looked into the fire and watched the glowing red coals. "I can't believe in a God who could allow that kind of death and misery for so many people." She turned her gaze away from the fire. "So, what brought you to Manhattan?"

"When I was in college, I got the grandiose idea that I would become a writer of novels. And New York seemed the obvious place to begin my illustrious career."

"But you work for a newspaper."

He grinned. "Much to my chagrin I soon discovered that a writer of novels without any monetary support will starve to death very quickly."

"So, you went to work for the ..."

"The *New York Tribune*. Although the paper is a daily, it's highly influential nationally through its weekly edition, which is circulated in rural areas and small towns. Mr. Horace Greeley, the editor and chief of the newspaper, is probably most famous for his admonition that all young men should go west."

"Are you keeping company with anyone?"

"Lord, no. I am forty-five years old and a confirmed bachelor, if for no other reason than I can barely support myself."

"I am sorry for all the questions. You must think me a meddlesome person."

"Not at all. How else do you get to know someone? Besides, I spend my day asking questions."

Just then, the front door opened and Michael came in.

Emily jumped up when he came into the parlor. "You look exhausted."

"I am that. It's been a long day, but at least I'm gainfully employed."

"I'm glad to hear that. Let's get you upstairs. You have a good evening, Gaylord."

"You, too. I'm about ready to turn in myself."

As soon as they got to their room, Michael fell onto the lumpy bed and groaned. "Every bone in my body is sore. I thought working on the road gangs back in Ireland was tough. This is much worse. At least in Ireland there were no stairs to climb."

"Have you eaten today?"

"No."

"I'll go downstairs and see if Mr. Coyle has something for you to eat."

"Don't bother. I'm too tired to eat."

She wrapped her shawl around her shoulders. "Nonsense. I'll just be a minute. You must ..." She stopped talking when she saw that Michael was sound asleep.

CHAPTER SEVEN

When Emily awoke the next morning, she was surprised to see that Michael had already gone. He'd looked so tired yesterday, she wasn't sure he would make it to work today. When she went down to the dining room for breakfast, Mrs. Winslow was already there.

"Good morning, Mrs. Winslow."

"Good morning, Emily. Are you off to your tutoring job?"

"I am."

"And how is that going?"

"Very well. Of course, I've only just met my student. She seems quite shy, but, if I'm not mistaken, I think she will be a quick learner. I'm confident she'll be able to converse in French by the time the Ingersolls go on their holiday to France. And you, Mrs. Winslow, have you been to France?

"I have. Several times. When Mr. Winslow was alive we went to France every year."

"France is a beautiful country, is it not?

"Indeed, it is. Certainly better than this odoriferous excuse for a city."

"If you feel that way, why do you stay here?"

"I have my reasons," she said.

"I see." The way she said it, Emily thought it prudent not to pursue the matter further. She looked at the clock. "Well, I must be on my way."

She walked to the corner of Broadway and Grand to wait for an omnibus, which was Manhattan's main form of public transportation. Essentially an oversized stagecoach, it carried twelve to twenty people. The driver had no fixed stops. If one wanted a ride, one simply waved at the driver to stop. In winter, the carriage wheels were removed and replaced with runners.

She waved one down and climbed aboard. Most of the omnibuses heading north were not crowded this time of the day. But the ones heading south were often so full that people climbed up on the roof or clung to the sides of the vehicle.

When she saw that the omnibus was nearing Twenty-First Street, she pulled on a leather strap that was connected to the driver's ankle to let him know she wanted to get off.

When Letta opened the door, she whispered to Emily in a low, fearful voice, "Mr. Ingersoll is home and he wishes to see you."

Emily waited in the parlor for almost fifteen minutes and gpt more nervous by the minute. It had been relatively easy to fool Mrs. Ingersoll into thinking that she was English, but it might be another matter entirely when it came to an experienced businessman like Mr. Ingersoll.

Finally, Thaddeus Ingersoll came into the room. He was an imposing man with a full white beard and muttonchops. He was wearing a loosely cut waistcoat that did not hide his rather large stomach. His high and pointed shirt collar seemed to be strangling him. Emily judged him to be in his early sixties, which surprised her. She expected him to be nearer the age of Mrs. Ingersoll.

He fixed her with piercing gray eyes. "Miss Somerville?" he asked with a dour expression.

"Yes."

"Be seated." He pointed to a chair near the fireplace. "Mrs. Ingersoll tells me you're English."

"That's correct."

"I've been to England many times myself and know it well. Where did you live in England?

"Actually, my family lived in Ireland."

His busy eyebrows shot up in disdain. "Ireland? Whatever for?"

Emily suddenly realized that this snobbish man was just like so many wealthy American men of common birth she'd met in England. They were so much in awe of England and titles that it was laughable. It was ironic that these American men, so extremely wealthy, should revere penniless dukes and earls. And it wasn't just the men. She'd met more than a few rich American women who went abroad with the express purpose of marrying a title. It was often a marriage of convenience for both. She got a title, and the title got the money.

Now she understood the reason for those courtesy books. The Ingersoll's were not to the manor born. Despite their money, they were, as Gaylord had said, *nouveau riche,* and as such they were unsure of their social status. Now that she had taken the measure of the man, she decided to lay it on thick.

"My father, Lord Somerville, was the eighth Earl of Devonshire, Mr. Ingersoll. My family has had estates in Ireland since the time of the Norman Invasion."

His eyes widened. "Oh... I see. Yes, of course." Immediately, his whole demeanor changed. He slapped his hands on his knees. "Well, then." He stood up. "It was a pleasure talking to you, Miss Somerville." His façade of intimidation in ruins, he practically slinked out of the parlor.

A minute later, Mrs. Ingersoll came with a look of surprise on her face. Mr. Ingersoll was very impressed with you, Miss Somerville."

"And I with him," Emily said.

"Oh... yes, of course." Momentarily befuddled by Emily's unexpected self-assurance, she shouted, "*Letta—",* but stopped, suddenly remembering what the little bell on the table was for. When Letta appeared, Mrs. Ingersoll said, "Please bring Lucy in here. It's time for her lesson."

As Emily surmised from her earlier introduction, Lucy was a painfully shy child. Emily had no doubt she would be able to teach her French, but first she would have to find a way to penetrate the child's wall of isolation. When they were alone, Emily said, "Lucy, where would you like to begin?"

The child shrugged. "I don't know," she mumbled."

Emily picked up a book. "Lucy, *ceci est un livre.*"

Lucy shook her head in confusion.

"It's a book. *Livre*. Can you say *livre*?"

" *...Livre...*"

"Very good. *Très bon.* That means very good."

Emily studied the child. She appeared to be a quick learner, but she seemed to be afraid of something, even going so far as to flinch when she heard a noise in the house or out in the street. If she was going to successfully teach Lucy French, she was going to have to get to the bottom of that puzzling issue.

Emily began to roam about the room picking up objects and naming them in French and asking Lucy to repeat the names in French. Then she began to put those words into sentences. Despite her shyness, Lucy was a quick learner and the two hours went by quickly.

CHAPTER EIGHT

Michael had been working for Cullinane for almost three months and in that time, he had fallen into a familiar, if boring, routine; get to the warehouse by seven and work till six—if nothing unforeseen came up. Go home to the boardinghouse eat and fall into bed exhausted. And in that time, he'd also mastered the art of weaving a heavy-laden wagon through the insane traffic of downtown Manhattan.

It was early November and the weather had gone from the hot, humid days of September to the biting cold of oncoming winter. If there was anything good about the cold, it was that the pervasive putrid odors of the city were not quite as bad.

He and Flynn were heading north on the Bowery to deliver a load of bricks and lumber to a building site on Fifth Avenue and Twentieth Street. A cold wind sweeping off the East River made both men pull the collars up around their necks.

"They call it *Kleindeutschland*—Little Germany," Flynn said.

On these long, tedious trips Flynn had fallen into the habit of taking this time to enlighten Michael on his newly adopted city. With a sweep of his arm, Flynn said, "Kleindeutschland starts on Division Street all the way up to Fourteenth Street. And it goes from the Bowery all the way to the East River."

"Are there many Germans there?"

"Thousands, but not as many as us. They're a different breed of animal altogether. They didn't come here fleeing a famine. Many of them are farmers, shopkeepers, and bakers. And they do love their beer." Flynn poked Michael. "Truth be told I like it well enough meself. There are dozens of breweries in Kleindeutschland and they all make good beer."

After they unloaded the wagon-load of bricks and lumber, Flynn said, "I'm feeling a powerful thirst. I think we need to stop off at the Volksgarten for a beer."

When they got below Fourteenth Street, he directed Michael to turn east to Avenue B, or as he called it, "German Broadway." The avenue, running from Houston Street to Fourteenth Street, was lined with beer halls, oyster saloons, and assorted grocery stores.

At Seventh Street, he told Michael to pull up in front of a building with the name *Volksgarten* printed in large Gothic German script over the door. Across the street was a park surrounded by a high wrought iron fence. It was similar to Washington Square Park, but not as well maintained. "What's that?" Michael asked Flynn.

"That would be Tompkins Square Park."

"It looks a little shabby."

"Aye, that it is. When it opened in '37, the city had great plans for it, but then the panic hit and all work stopped. Maybe someday they'll get back to it. Now it's used mostly as an assembly spot for assorted protest rallies. Come on," Flynn said, climbing down from the wagon, "I'm dying of the thirst."

Inside the Volksgarten, Michael was surprised at how large the interior was. He'd only been in that one dingy grog shop in the Five Points, but he'd passed by numerous other saloons and grog shops and they all looked pretty much the same. But unlike those grog shops, this spacious interior had room for rows and rows of rough wooden tables and benches. And the walls were covered with brightly painted frescoes of young women and men dancing in fields.

"It's quiet this time of day," Flynn explained, "but you should see this place on Sunday. Men and women of all ages drinking and dancing. In the summer, they open the back yards and turn the space into a beer garden. I come here quite often meself."

"So, the Irish come here as well?"

"No, not a'tall. I wager I'm the only Irishman who does. But I like it. The Germans are a good lot. Hard workers and hard drinkers."

He stepped up to the bar and slammed his hand down. "Can I get some service here?"

Michael was taken aback by the rude tone in Flynn's voice, but the bartender, a portly man with an enormous handlebar mustache grinned. "Flynn, my old friend," he said with a heavy German accent, "ver have you been?"

"Working. What else? Say hello to Michael Ranahan."

The bartender wiped his hands on a white apron that was almost up to his chest and shook Michael's hand. "A friend of Flynn is a friend of mine. What will you boys have?"

"How about two glasses of your fine beer?"

As Otto poured the beer, Flynn said, "So, Otto, have you saved enough to buy your own beer garden yet?"

The bartender made a face and shook his head. "I save what I can, but the wages are poor and"—he looked around furtively and lowered his voice— "old man Beyersdorf is a skinflint, I can tell you that."

"Ah, you'll get there, me bucko. Chin up."

"Will I get there before you own your own construction business?" Otto asked with an impish grin.

It was Flynn's turn to frown. "My wages are worse than yours, my friend. But I'm not discouraged. I'll manage it somehow."

Just then an obese man came out of the back. "Otto," he bellowed, "did you get that barrel from the cellar yet?

Otto jumped. "Not yet, Mr. Beyersdorf. I was just on my way."

Flynn took a slug of his beer. "Well, what do you think of it?"

Michael sniffed at his glass warily. "I don't know. I'm used to the poteen at home."

"Well, you won't find poteen here. Go on. Give it a go."

Michael took a sip and made a face. It was better than the beer he'd had in the Five Points grog shop, but that wasn't saying much. "It's very bitter."

"That's what good German beer tastes like."

"Is Otto really saving to open his own beer garden?"

"Aye. It's the only thing to do. A workingman in this city doesn't stand a chance. They work you to death for starvation wages and when you're worn out they toss you aside like the carcass of a dead dog."

"Is that why you want your own construction business?"

"It is. I want to be my own man. Control my own life. I've learned a lot about the construction business from my time working for Cully. I could do this on my own. I see more and more building going on in this city. There's great opportunity here, but…" His voice trailed off.

"You need money to start a business."

"Aye." He shook his head to clear away the daydreams. "And what about you?"

Michael was taken aback by the question. When he'd left Ireland, he'd had only a vague idea of what he would do once he got to America. And now that he was here, he realized that the prospects were not good for a barely literate Irishman. He was grateful for the job that Cullinane had given him, but he didn't see himself hauling bricks and lumber for the rest of his life. "I don't know, Flynn. I don't know what I'll do."

Flynn drained his glass. "Come on, we'd best be getting back or Cully will have a conniption."

When they pulled into the warehouse, Michael was surprised at how eerily silent it was. There was none of the usual shouting, sawing, or hammering. And then Michael realized why; it was late and all the workers had gone home for the day. All except for Cully, who was standing at his office door with an irritated look on his face. Michael's stomach turned. They were in trouble. They shouldn't have stopped for that beer. He was certain he was going to lose his job.

"Flynn, Ranahan," Cully called out. "In my office, right now."

Cully slid behind his paper-strewn desk and motioned for the two men to sit down. "Tomorrow's an election day," he said, dryly.

Flynn slapped his knee. "Ah, Jasus, I completely forgot."

"Does Ranahan know the drill?"

"No, I haven't told him yet."

"Is this your first election, Ranahan?" Cully asked.

"Yes."

"Tomorrow morning you and all my other employees will report to Tammany Hall at five."

"Do we have a job there?"

"You could say that." Cully sat back and laced his fingers

behind his head. "Flynn, explain it to him."

Flynn lit up a cigar. "There's a big, important election tomorrow. The Whigs against the Democrats."

"Who are they?"

"It doesn't matter. Just know that you're a Democrat. We're *all* Democrats."

"And what does that mean?"

"It means that tomorrow you and all us good Democrats are going to vote for, among others, one Fernando Wood and one William Magear Tweed."

Michael's head was spinning, barely able to follow what Flynn was talking about. "I met Mr. Wood at Tammany Hall. But I'm an immigrant. I don't think I'm allowed to vote."

"Don't worry, it'll all be arranged."

Michael didn't like the sound of that. He suspected there was something illegal and underhanded about this whole business. "What happens if I don't go to Tammany Hall tomorrow?"

"Then you lose your job, Cully said flatly. "It's as simple as that."

"But ... but that's not fair."

Cully chuckled. "*Fair*? Do you hear him, Flynn? It's *fair* he's talking about."

"I hear him," Flynn said, grinning.

Michael felt his anger rising. "I don't understand what's so funny."

Cully stopped chuckling. "Fairness had nothing to do with it, Ranahan." There was a hard edge in his voice now. "How do you think you got this job?"

"Mr. Walsh sent me and—"

"And Mr. Walsh works for Tammany Hall. I'll give it to you that for these past few months you've been a good worker, Ranahan, but I would never have hired you if you hadn't been sent by Tammany."

"But, why not?"

"Because," Flynn interjected, "all the jobs that Tammany controls go only to the men who support the Democrats and Tammany. If it wasn't for Tammany, you'd still be walking the streets looking for work."

"You're either with us or you're agin us," Cully said. "There are only two ways to control this city. Either you've got money or you've got power. The Irish don't have the money, at least not yet. So that leaves power. And we get power through the ballot box. When we put more and more Irishmen into political positions, we gain that power."

"So, what do you say?" Flynn asked, flicking an ash onto the floor. "Will I see you at Tammany Hall tomorrow morning?"

Michael's mind was a confusion of emotions. He was angry, he was frustrated—and, he had to admit, he was afraid. If he got in trouble, could he be deported? Why was he being asked to do this? All he wanted was to do his work and earn a decent wage. He wanted nothing to do with the politics of Tammany Hall. He was about to tell them that he wouldn't do it, but then he thought of Emily. How could he go back to the boardinghouse and tell her that he was out of work after so short a period of time? He also suspected that Flynn was right. Remembering all those NINA signs he'd encountered, if he went looking for work without the support of Tammany, he probably wouldn't find a job. "All right," he heard himself say, "I'll be there."

"But … but, that preposterous," Emily sputtered indignantly.

They were sitting in the parlor alone and Michael had just told her about his conversation with Flynn and Cully.

"It is that, but there's nothing I can do. I—*we*—can't afford for me to lose my job."

"That's true. We can't survive on my part-time tutoring position."

Just then, Gaylord came into the parlor. He took one look at their solemn faces and said, "Is it a wake I'm interrupting?"

"I've been told I have to vote tomorrow," Michael blurted out. "But I'm only an immigrant and—"

Gaylord shook his head grimly. "That's the way it is in this city, Michael. Politics is a dirty business and both sides engage in outrageous chicanery and often criminal behavior."

"They told me I must vote for Fernando Wood and someone named Tweed."

Gaylord nodded. "Wood is a very ambitious man who wants to be mayor. Have you heard of the gold rush in California?"

"No."

"Last year, Wood made a great deal of money shipping goods out to San Francisco to supply all those prospectors. As for Bill Tweed, he, too, is an up-and-coming figure in the Democratic Party. He grew up not far from here on Cherry Street. And quite a rogue. A big fellow with clear blue eyes and an amiable disposition. But don't let that appearance fool you. Tweed is a rough sort. Last year he and a couple of friends organized their own fire company with the highfalutin' name of the Americus Engine Company, Number Six. As you saw the other day, these fire companies often battle with the competition. On one of his outings, Tweed led his men in an ax-wielding assault on his competitors and a couple of them were badly hurt. Tweed was expelled from the company."

"And this man is running for political office?" Emily asked incredulously.

"He is. The Democratic politicians in the Seventh Ward in their infinite wisdom have decided that a man like Bill Tweed could be of use to the party. He's running for assistant alderman for the Seventh Ward."

"And I must vote for him," Michael said, glumly.

"I'm afraid you do," Gaylord conceded.

Emily was perplexed. "Gaylord, how can the good people of New York tolerate such blatant fraud?"

"A good question, Emily. It seems the good people of New York have adopted a peculiar belief that respectable and educated classes of New York should abstain from voting. I've heard some boast that they are utterly indifferent to politics."

"So, they don't care who gets elected?"

"Precisely. Those of refined taste are not keen to mingle with the coarse rabble that surround voting places. The unfortunate result is that the good people of New York leave the control of politics in the hands of the worst and most vicious classes."

Michael shook his head. "If I live to be a thousand, I'll never understand this city."

"It is a puzzlement," Gaylord agreed. He leaned into Michael. "A word of warning, my friend. Be careful tomorrow. Sometimes these elections get out of hand and heads get broken."

And with those uneasy words, Emily and Michael retired to their room for a restless night's sleep.

CHAPTER NINE

A steady, early morning rain made the gray, drab streets of Manhattan even more dreary than usual. It was just before five when Michael arrived at Tammany Hall and found Flynn huddled in the doorway smoking a cigar. "So, you showed up."

Michael, still irritated and apprehensive about what was going to happen today, snapped, "I'm here, am I not? So, what's next?"

Flynn took his arm. "Let's go inside and find out. The meeting's about to start."

They took a seat at the back of a large hall where there were at least a couple of hundred men.

Fernando Wood stepped up to the podium. "Good morning, gentlemen. As you all know, this is a big day for Tammany and the Democratic Party. Today our job will be to make sure we get the votes for me and our other candidates. The Whigs are a wily bunch and we'll have to keep a sharp eye on them." He turned to a man seated behind him. "Bill, do you have anything to say?"

"That's Bill Tweed," Flynn whispered.

Michael was surprised at how young he appeared. He'd been expecting an older man, but Tweed appeared to be in his mid-twenties. And he certainly was big. Well over six feet tall with a big barrel-chest and a full beard.

Tweed stepped up to the podium. "I'm running for assistant alderman in the Seventh Ward. I would appreciate anything you can do to get me elected." He waved a big fist in the air and shouted, "Let's get out there and defeat them goddamn Whigs."

The crowd roared its approval.

Wood came back to the podium. "On your way out see the men at the desk in the back of the hall. They'll tell you the saloon you are to report to."

Michael leaned into Flynn. "Saloon?"

"That's where most of the voting is held. Most of the saloons in this city are owned by politicians. It's said that if you want to clear a council meeting just shout, *your saloon is on fire* and there won't be a soul left in the room."

Wood continued. "Your most important job after you vote is to make sure the vote goes Tammany's way. And you know what that means. All right, on your way. Don't forget to come back here tonight. Drinks are on Tammany."

At the back of the hall, Flynn stepped up to the desk. "All right, Casey," he said to the curly black-headed man seated at the desk, "which fine establishment am I to vote in today?"

The man consulted the list. "That would be Halloran's over on Division."

"And what about my young friend here, Michael Ranahan?"

Casey ran his finger down the list. "Ranahan. You'll go with Flynn to Halloran's. I see you're not a citizen."

"No, I'm not," Michael answered, hoping he would be told he couldn't vote.

Casey grabbed a slip of paper out of a pile and handed it Michael. The name Donald Maclean was written on it. "You'll vote using that name."

As they were leaving, Michael saw Tommy Walsh talking to a group of six men with beards and muttonchops. He overheard Walsh tell them, "After you vote, go the barbershop, get that facial hair scraped off you and go back out and vote again."

When Michael and Flynn got to Halloran's there were dozens of men milling about outside. They squeezed past the men and stepped into a spacious saloon with high ceilings and a wooden floor covered with sawdust. It was barely six o'clock, but men were already lined up three-deep at the bar.

"Do you want a beer?" Flynn asked.

"No, it's too early for me."

"Suit yourself," Flynn said, elbowing his way through the

crowd.

A half hour later, four officious men came in carrying a black box with a lock on it.

"Ah, the ballot box is here." Flynn drained his beer and wiped his mouth with his sleeve. "Let the games begin."

The box was set up at the far end of the bar. "All right, gentlemen," a self-important, bald-headed man said, "the election may commence."

Michael studied the slip of paper Casey had given him. "I'm supposed to be Donald Maclean. Who is he?"

Flynn shrugged. "Some dead guy, I suppose."

When it became Michael's turn, the man asked him, "Name?"

He almost blurted out his real name, but he caught himself just in time. "Um… Donald Maclean," he muttered.

After consulting a list, the man handed Michael a ballot. Holding his breath, Michael put an X next to Wood and Tweed's names and dropped it in the box. At any moment, he expected a policeman to grab him by the scuff of the neck and arrest him. But all the man said was, "All right, move on. Next."

Feeling relieved, Michael went outside where Flynn was waiting for him. "Well, that wasn't so bad now, was it?"

"It's done. Can we go now?"

"Not a'tall. Our work is just beginning. We're to stay here till the balloting is closed."

"When will that be?"

"Usually eleven."

"*Eleven at night?* What are we supposed to do in that time?"

"Keep an eye out for Whig shenanigans."

As the day went on, Michael's uneasiness left him. Remembering what Gaylord had said about busted heads, he was worried there might be a disturbance. But everything seemed to be going smoothly. All day long a steady stream of men came to vote, drank a beer or two, and then went on their way.

It was almost ten when Flynn slipped up behind Michael. "There's trouble afoot," he whispered.

Michael looked around. "Where? I don't see anything wrong."

"Do you not see those three great big brutes at the bar?"

In fact, Michael had seen them come in. They were the only

ones who hadn't voted and he thought that odd.

"They're what we call 'shoulder-hitters.' If something starts up, they'll be in the middle of it. You can be sure of that."

"Are they Tammany men?" Michael asked, beginning to feel uneasy again.

"They are not. They're part of the Whig contingent."

Michael could feel his heart pounding in his chest. "What are we supposed to do?"

"Keep an eye on them. They might go for the box."

Michael spun around to face Flynn. "What do you mean they might *go* for the box?"

"Steal it."

"Why would they steal the ballot box?" Once again, Michael felt as though he was in some mad dream.

Flynn shrugged. "If they think we have more votes in the box than they do, they'll go for the box."

"But what about the police?"

"Look around you, Ranahan. Do you see any policemen here?"

He didn't, and he found that strange. Even in Ireland there were always constables at the polling locations. But he hadn't see a policeman all day.

Casey, the man who'd sent them here, suddenly appeared in the doorway. When he saw Flynn, he nodded and went back outside.

"Come on," Flynn said. "We're wanted."

They followed Casey around the corner to where a group of men were crowded around Tommy Walsh.

"Here's the deal," Walsh said. "Our watchers have determined that the Whigs have more votes in the box than we do."

"I thought it was the other way around," Flynn said. "They've got three shoulder-hitters in there."

"I know. But they're not there to go for the box. They're there to protect it from us."

Standing with the group were four very large men whom Michael assumed were Tammany's shoulder-hitters. "What do we do, Tommy?" one of them asked.

"We go in there and when I give the signal, you grab the box."

"What do the rest of us do?" Michael asked in a voice constricted with apprehension.

"Do whatever you have to do to see that the box goes out the door with us."

Michael and Flynn went back to the saloon first. The rest of the men wandered in two and three at a time. Walsh was the last man to come into the saloon. When he saw that everyone was in place, he shouted, "*Now*!"

And all hell broke loose.

Tammany's four shoulder-hitters rushed toward the ballot box. But the three Whig men jumped them, clubbing them with iron pipes they'd concealed under their coats. As Michael stepped forward to help them, somebody hit him over the head with a stool and he went down. Then a boot came out of nowhere and he felt a sharp pain as he was kicked in the side. Bleeding from the head wound and grimacing from the kick, he rolled on the sawdust-covered floor among shuffling feet. He managed to stagger to his feet just in time to see another man take a swing at him. He blocked the man's punch and drove his fist into the man's face.

After that, amidst the shouted curses, kicks, and screams of pain, Michael, fighting for his life, swung at anyone within range, not knowing, nor caring, if the man was Tammany or Whig. After what seemed a lifetime, he saw one of the Tammany shoulder-hitters racing for the door with the ballot box tucked under his arm. The other three shoulder-hitters ran interference, clubbing anyone who tried to stop them.

He felt a tug on his collar and turned to confront his attacker. But it was Flynn. Wiping the blood streaming from his nose with his sleeve, he said, "Come on, Ranahan, our work is done here."

When they got outside, Michael saw the man carrying the ballot box jump into a waiting carriage, which then raced up Division Street, scattering pedestrians and other carriages.

"Ah, that was a good night's work," Flynn said, with a gap-toothed grin. "Let's go back to Tammany and have a few beers."

Michael's head wound was still trickling blood and, when he moved a certain way, he felt a sharp pain in his side. The last thing he wanted to do was go back to Tammany Hall for a beer. "No, I think I'll go home."

"Suit yourself. See you tomorrow."

It was almost midnight by the time Michael got back to the boardinghouse. An alarmed Emily jumped out of bed when she saw him. Dried blood had caked in his hair and there was blood—

some of it his, some of it not—on the front of his shirt.

"Good God, Michael, what happened to you?"

"I … I voted today ..." he mumbled and collapsed onto the bed.

CHAPTER TEN

The next morning Emily awoke and was surprised to see that Michael had already left for work. Judging by the way he'd looked last night, she didn't think he'd be able to get out of bed this morning. All night, whenever he turned, he groaned and clutched his side.

Down in the dining room, Emily sat down to have coffee with Gaylord, who was reading a newspaper. "How did the elections go?" she asked.

"Not well for Tammany. The Whigs took the election."

"So that Mr. Tweed didn't get elected?"

"He did not, nor did Fernando Wood, who lost to Ambrose Kingsland."

"Michael will be disappointed. Apparently, he had a rough night."

"He wasn't alone. There were donnybrooks at almost all the polling locations. Bottom line, the Whigs stuffed more ballot boxes than Tammany."

"It all seems so illegal."

"It is, but that's the way things are done in this city."

She looked at the timepiece over the mantel. "Well, I'm off to tutor little Lucy."

Gaylord put the paper down. "And I'm off to interview Mr. Wood."

As usual, Lucy was jumpy in the house, startling at every

sound. As Emily listened to the child recite her French words, she peered out the window and watched a parade of governesses and maids pushing perambulators around the park. It looked so peaceful and quiet. Suddenly, Emily had an idea.

"Lucy, what do you say we continue our lesson in the park. Even though it's November, it's really quite mild outside."

Lucy's face lit up. "Oh, yes, could we…" Then her smile vanished as quickly as it had come. "Oh, I forgot. I'm not allowed in the park."

"Why not?"

She shrugged. "Because father doesn't want me to."

Just then, Mrs. Ingersoll came into the parlor. "How is the lesson proceeding?"

"Fine, Mrs. Ingersoll. I was just saying to Lucy, it's such a lovely day, why don't we finish our lesson in the park?"

"Oh, I'm afraid that's not possible. Mr. Ingersoll doesn't want Lucy to go there."

"I don't understand," Emily said with a tight smile. She was growing irritated with the woman's unwarranted intransigence. She stepped to the window and pulled the curtain aside. "Look, it's perfectly safe. The gate is locked. And there are children playing there."

Mrs. Ingersoll became flustered. "What if you should lose the key? You would have to pay for a replacement key, you know."

Emily, struggling to keep her mounting anger in check, smiled sweetly. "I'm only going across the street. But if I lose it, I'll be happy to pay for another."

Not knowing what else to say, the flummoxed woman fetched the key.

Once they were in the park, Lucy seemed to visibly relax. There was something about the house that made her uncomfortable and Emily hoped that one day Lucy would tell her what it was.

As they continued their lesson, three girls about Lucy's age ran by chasing their hoops. "Do you know those girls?" Emily asked.

"No."

Emily found that puzzling. According to Letta, the Ingersolls had been living here for over two years. It was hard to believe that in all that time she had not become friendly with the neighborhood children. She also noticed something else strange. As the governesses passed, they gave Lucy a curious look, as though they'd never seen her before. It was all quite perplexing.

Wincing, as he gingerly touched the scab wound on his scalp, Michael said, "Do you mean to tell me I almost got beaten to death for an election we lost?"

Flynn calmly lit up a cigar. "Aye. Both Wood and Tweed got whipped good, but they'll be another election for alderman next year and I'm sure Tweed will win. He's not the kind of man to lose twice in a row."

"Is being an alderman an important job?"

"It is that. It's the aldermen who hand out building contracts, and they make the contractor pad the bill for their graft. They award contracts to firms run by relatives. Sometimes they own outright the business they give the contracts to. And then there's the policemen. The mayor appoints all policemen, but he must choose them from a list provided by aldermen. And here's the kicker. These appointments are for one year only." He winked at Michael.

"I don't understand."

"Don't you see, man? If a copper wants to be reappointed, he'd better tend to the needs of the aldermen. They're a powerful bunch these aldermen."

"Copper?"

"It's a term applied to policemen because their badges are made of copper."

"So, what happened? If they and Tammany Hall are so powerful, how did they lose the election?"

"Truth be told, not everyone in Tammany likes Wood. But, it's like they say, you can't win 'em all. Mr. Wood may be down, but he's not out. There'll be an election for mayor in four years and Wood and Tammany are determined to win that race."

They were traveling up Fifth Avenue on their way to deliver a wagon load of bricks to a job site at Fifth and Fortieth Street. As they passed the Harrington mansion, now completed, Flynn stared at the building with a look of disgust. "Have you ever seen such an ugly building in all your born days? I'm ashamed to say I had anything to do with the damn thing."

"I've seen better." Indeed, Michael had had the opportunity to see plenty of buildings as he traveled throughout the city delivering bricks and lumber, and the Harrington Mansion was by far the most ungainly building he'd seen.

"That's what you get when you're too cheap to hire a real architect," Flynn said, spitting toward the building.

At the end of the work-day, they started back down Fifth Avenue. "Do you see all this empty space?" Flynn asked.

"I do." As far as the eye could see there were only a smattering of homes and farmhouses.

"This is why I want to become my own building contractor. There's great opportunity here. No one wants to live way up here now, but mark my words, one day there will be houses on every corner."

"How can you be so sure?"

"Everything is slowly moving north. I've been watching the movement for years now. Back in '35 the rich folk lived in houses on Greenwich Street, Broadway, and Bowling Green. Then there was a great fire and it destroyed hundreds of houses. Those fine old houses were replaced by stores, warehouses, and offices, and the rich moved north to Union Square and Gramercy Park. We helped build a beautiful mansion right on Union Square. It cost nearly a hundred thousand dollars, it did." He shook his head at the extravagance of it all. "When I was a lad, there was practically nothing north of Canal Street, now the northern border is Fourteenth Street. Pretty soon it'll be Twenty-Third Street." Flynn's eyes had a faraway look. "I'll tell you, Ranahan, there's great opportunity for a man who's not afraid of hard work."

"Well, I'm not afraid of hard work, but I imagine it takes an awful lot of money to start a business."

Flynn laughed. "Aye, that it does. You should have let Mr. Vanderbilt run you down when you had the chance. He might have given you some money for your troubles."

CHAPTER ELEVEN

1851

After a reasonably mild December, the New Year started out bitterly cold, which, Michael found, made working on outdoor construction sites all the more challenging. The cement men complained about cement freezing before they could use it. The horses tended to come up lame more often from trying to negotiate the frozen, rutted roads. And the men, like Michael and Flynn, who had to work outdoors were continually fighting off hypothermia and frostbite.

For the past few weeks, Michael and Emily had made it a habit of strolling over to Broadway after dinner. Despite the bitter cold, the fresh air was a welcome relief from the stuffy and claustrophobic boardinghouse. By day, Broadway was a bustling, cacophonous scene with wagons of all shapes and sizes rattling up and down the street and sidewalks crowded with shoppers. But at night, when business ceased, Broadway turned into a much quieter scene. Emily and Michael found it amusing to watch the dandies with their stovepipe hats, monocles, and gold-tipped canes strutting like peacocks up and down the street. But this evening they were nowhere to be found on Broadway. Instead of the usual parade of dandies, the street was packed with hundreds of angry, shouting men.

Michael stopped one of them, a short, red-faced man. "What's going on?"

"We're on our way to Longstreet and Company to protest unfair wages. We're tailors and we deserve a decent wage and those penny-pinchers at Longstreet refuse to meet out demands." The man glanced down Broadway and shouted to the others, "They're coming, men. Stand your ground."

Michael turned to see a dozen or more policemen running up Broadway toward them. With their breath creating clouds of steam in front of their faces, the policemen reminded Michael of a stampeding herd of cattle.

The picketers started shouting in unison, "*Union, union, union* ..."

As soon as the police reached the men they waded into the crowd swinging their nightsticks. Some men tried to fight back, but they were no match for the better armed policemen. Soon, men were falling in the streets, blood streaming from their heads. A large police wagon drawn by two horses raced up Broadway. The protesters who hadn't been clubbed senseless scattered into the side streets. Those who were wounded or unconscious were unceremoniously tossed into the wagon.

Michael put his arm around Emily. "Come on, let's get away from this."

Back in the boardinghouse parlor, a breathless Michael recounted what they'd seen to their fellow boarders.

Gaylord shook his head. "This unionizing business has been going on for some time now. For once it has nothing to do with ethnic differences. The men you saw are Irish, German, and American tailors. Longstreet and Company, one of the largest clothing manufacturers in the city, is notorious for low wages and anti-unionism. Lately, there's been talk of forming a tailor's union and the wealthy men who own these factories don't like that kind of talk."

"How can they stop them?"

"You saw it tonight. The owners employ the use of the police to do their bidding. They don't want unions. For them, unions mean better wages and working conditions for the men and less profit for them.

"Unions have no future in this city," Mrs. Winslow said with firm finality.

"Why not?" Michael asked.

"Because, it's as Gaylord said, the owners will never permit workers to control their businesses."

After a momentary silence, Sarah said softly, "I have some

news. I'm leaving my position at Stewart's."

Mrs. Winslow's eyebrows went up. "Really? What will you do, my child?"

"I'm going into business with my friend, Molly Kelly… I mean Madame Odette."

"That's wonderful news," Emily said. "I knew you would do it, but I thought it would take you a little longer."

"Well, the truth is it won't be a true partnership as I haven't enough money right now. But Molly said as I put more into the enterprise, I will eventually become a full partner."

"Will you be staying on here?" Gaylord asked.

"No. To save money, I'll be moving in with Molly."

"Well, we'll miss you."

Sarah blushed. "Thank you, Mr. Temple."

Later, back in their room, Michael blurted out, "I want to open my own business."

Emily stopped brushing her hair. "Where did that come from?"

"It's the only thing to do. This afternoon when Flynn and I were coming down Fifth Avenue he said that someday there are going to be houses filling all that empty space above Fourteenth Street."

"Really? From what I hear no one wants to live way up there. It's not a very desirable area."

"True, but Flynn says he's been watching the city slowly moving north. If he's right, they'll be plenty of work for construction companies."

"But it must cost a fortune to start your own company."

"It does. But a wage-worker is treated like dirt in this city. I see that now. There's no future in working for someone else. You saw what the police did to those protesters tonight. I don't want to spend the rest of my life working for someone who can fire me on a whim or reduce my wages for no good reason. You heard young Sarah. Even she is going to work for herself. So is Flynn, when he gets enough money together. A while back, he introduced me to a German fellow named Otto. He's only a bartender now, but someday he wants to open his own bar as well. I'm going to do it. Somehow, I'll get the money."

Emily put her arms around him. "I have every confidence you will, Michael. But something has come up and you may have to rethink your plan."

"What's that?"

"I'm with child."

It took a moment for Michael to digest what she'd just said. Then he lifted her off the ground. "Oh, my God, Emily, that's wonderful news."

"Are you sure? I'm not certain we can afford to have a baby just now, nevertheless, there it is."

"We'll manage. Don't you worry about that. When is it due?"

"July."

"My God, that's only six months away." Michael sat down on the bed with a faraway look in his eyes. "I'm going to be a father ... and you're going to be a mother ... Imagine that."

"So, you're happy?"

"I couldn't be happier. I just wish my mum and da had lived to see this."

"I know. As soon as I found out I was with child, I thought about my father."

"What'll we name it?"

Emily laughed. "It's still an *it*. Let's wait to see if it's a boy or girl before coming up with a name."

"Oh, right. Of course."

When Emily arrived at the Ingersoll home for Lucy's French lesson, Letta opened the door and shrugged in embarrassment.

"Don't tell me," Emily said with a frustrated smile. "They're not home."

"Mrs. Ingersoll and Lucy are at the doctor's."

Emily shook her head in exasperation.

"Letta nodded sympathetically. "I know. But please come in. The coffee pot is on the stove."

In the beginning, Emily had been irritated by Mrs. Ingersoll's rather rude habit of not being home when it was time for Lucy's lesson, but it did give her the opportunity to get to know Letta better. The young German girl was pleasant and much more relaxed when the Ingersolls weren't around.

In the kitchen, Letta poured a cup of coffee for Emily and smiled shyly. "I know it must be a great inconvenience for you, but I'm glad when Mrs. Ingersoll isn't home. I enjoy talking to you."

"And I enjoy talking to you, too, Letta. Thanks to you, I'm learning more and more about the city. You never told me how long you've been living here?"

"My family came to America from Germany when I was just a little girl. My parents own a bakery in Kleindeutschland."

"And yet you prefer to be in service rather than work at the bakery?"

"Ya. My father is very strict. Working here I have much more independence. I can stay out late with my friends without having to answer to him."

"How long have you been working for the Ingersolls?"

"I came here two years ago, right after they got married."

"So, Lucy is not Mr. Ingersoll's child?"

"No. Mrs. Ingersoll's first husband died three years ago. He was an engineer and he was killed in an accident while working on the Croton Aqueduct."

"How sad. Do you think that's why Lucy seems so quiet?"

"I don't know. She's been that way since I came to work here."

"What happened to Mr. Ingersoll's wife?"

"I understand she died in a cholera epidemic about ten years ago."

"Do you like it here, Letta?"

"Um, yes ..."

Emily noticed she hesitated before answering. There was something strange going on in the Ingersoll house. Why was Lucy so skittish? Why was Mrs. Ingersoll so high-strung? And why was Letta hesitant about saying if she liked it here?

Just then they heard the front door open. Letta jumped up and straightened her apron. "They're home."

Emily took advantage of the unseasonably mild weather to take their lesson in the park. She was just finishing up when a well-dressed woman approached.

"Excuse me," she said, offering her hand, "my name is Delia Hainsworth." She pointed to a brownstone house on the north side of the park. "I live just over there."

Emily shook her hand. "And I am Emily Somerville."

"When you're finished here, I wonder if you would mind stopping by. I have a proposition for you."

"Certainly," Emily answered, wondering what the proposition could be.

Fifteen minutes later, she was sitting in Delia's parlor. It was much like Mrs. Ingersoll's, but much more tastefully done without the clutter and piles of tacky bric-a-brac. When she was seated, Emily said, "Mrs. Hainsworth, you said you had a proposition for me?"

"Please, call me Delia."

"And please, call me Emily."

Emily was pleasantly surprised—and slightly shocked—by Delia's informality. Judging by the expensive, yet tasteful way her home was furnished, plus the understated elegant dress she was wearing, it was obvious that Delia was a refined woman of good breeding. Nevertheless, it was a refreshing experience to meet someone so open and relaxed after dealing with the stiff Mrs. Ingersoll.

"My maid tells me you're teaching French to the little Ingersoll girl."

"I am."

"I was wondering if you would have the time in your schedule to take on our Abigail. My husband and I have wanted her to learn French, but we haven't been able to find a suitable teacher. She's only fourteen, but she does so want to learn French. I'm sorry she's not here to meet you."

She *wants* to learn French? Emily was happy to hear that. Lucy was a bright child, but she seemed… distracted, if that was the right word. Perhaps she didn't really want to learn French. In any event, it would be a joy teaching a willing student, not to mention the welcome extra money.

"I would be delighted to teach your daughter. I come to Mrs. Ingersoll's three days a week. I could come to you after Lucy's lesson."

"That would be fine."

Back at the boardinghouse an excited Emily told Michael about her second student.

"Well, that's great news," he said. "With a baby coming, we can certainly use the extra money."

"The only thing is, I don't know how I'll be able to teach these girls when the baby comes."

"We'll cross that bridge when we come to it," Michael said with more confidence than he felt. Now that he was going to be a father, he felt the pressure to earn more money.

The next morning, Michael got to work extra early because he knew Cullinane was always the first one to arrive. The old man was in his office working his way through piles of invoices and architectural drawings when Michael knocked on the door. "Cully, can I have a word with you?"

The old man looked up. "Yeah, Ranahan. What is it?"

"Might I sit down?"

Cullinane tossed his glasses on his cluttered desk. "Go ahead," he said without much enthusiasm. "What's up?"

Michael wiped his sweating palms on his trousers. "I … I just wanted to let you know that my wife is pregnant."

"Congratulations," he said, reaching for his glasses. "Was there anything else?"

The old man was not making it easier for Michael. "Well, with the baby coming and all, it's going to be an added expense."

"Babies usually are. If you're looking for a raise, forget it."

Michael's heart sank, but he continued, determined to make his pitch. "Cully, I've been here for over four months. Haven't I been doing a good job?"

"You have."

"So why would a raise be out of the question?

Cullinane put his glasses back on. "Because I'm going to make you a foreman."

"A … foreman …?"

"We're getting busier and busier. Flynn's just not up to the task so I'm giving you a crack at it. Don't screw it up."

Michael was elated that Cully was promoting him to foreman, but he was uncomfortable with the fact that he would be replacing Flynn, a man who had become his friend. "Cully, I don't know if I can take the job …"

"If you're thinking of Flynn, forget about it. I already spoke to him and he's fine with my decision." He waved a hand in dismissal. "Now get out of here; we both have work to do."

An apprehensive Michael waited outside for Flynn. He didn't

want to talk to him about the switch in front of the other workers. Finally, he saw him coming down the street with his hands stuck in his pockets and the ever-present cigar in his mouth.

Flynn grinned and stuck his hand out. "Congratulation, Michael. The headaches are all yours."

"Are you sure you're okay with this? If not, I'll go in there and tell Cully I don't want the job."

"Don't be daft. To tell you the truth, I'm relieved. I can see now that I'm not one for responsibility or bossing men around. I'm not cut out to own my own business, so I've gotten that notion out of my head once and for all."

"Okay, if you're sure."

"I'm sure." He tossed his cigar into the street. "Now come on, we've got a wagon load of bricks to deliver to that site on Delancey Street. Oh, I forgot," he said, slapping Michael on the back. "That's not my problem anymore. It's yours."

While the other workers drifted in one by one, Michael went to inspect the wagon. He'd helped load it yesterday and he didn't like the way it had been done. It was just another example of the wasteful inefficiencies he'd been noticing. He'd said nothing because it was none of his business. But now that he was the foreman, things would change.

As soon as all the men were in the warehouse, Michael said, "Men we'll have to unload this wagon and reload it."

Brian Larkin, a chronic complainer and loudmouth said, "So who died and made you boss?"

"Cully. As of today, I'm the new foreman."

Larkin looked at Flynn. "Is this true?"

"It is, and I'm very happy to become just one of you lot again."

Larkin glared at Michael. "It took us hours to load the bloody wagon yesterday. Why do we have to unload it?"

"Because it was done all wrong. Look, we piled all this lumber on top of the bricks, but we'll need the bricks first. That means we'll have to unload the lumber and leave it in the street while we unload the bricks. It's double the work."

Larkin shook his head. "Well, what's done is done. I'm not going to undo yesterday's work."

As the newest man here, Michael assumed there would be some who resented him becoming foreman. And he knew that his authority would be challenged at some point. But he didn't expect it to happen so soon. "Larkin, you'll do as I say."

"And what if I don't?"

Out of the corner of his eye, Michael saw Cully standing in the doorway to his office with his arms folded and an inscrutable look on his face. Michael stepped up to Larkin. They were about the same height, but the beefy man had him by a good twenty pounds.

Looking him right in the eye, Michael said, "You'll do what I tell you or you're fired."

Larkin's face turned red and, without warning, he tried to sucker punch Michael. But Michael was expecting it and he easily blocked it. He drove his fist into the man's fat stomach and Larkin sunk to the floor groaning in pain. Michael stood over him. "What'll it be, Larkin, will you unload the wagon or will you get out?"

A sullen Larkin stumbled to his feet and shuffled toward the wagon. "Well, let's get the damn thing done."

Michael looked back to see Cully's reaction, but he was no longer standing there.

Now that Emily was sitting in the Hainsworth's parlor, she was having second thoughts about agreeing to take on the Hainsworth child. Despite what Delia had said, maybe Abigail didn't want to take French lessons. She dreaded the thought of dealing with two recalcitrant students.

Just then, Delia and Abigail came into the room.

"And here's my Abigail," Delia beamed. It was apparent to Emily that Delia was very proud of her daughter.

Abigail, with an oval-shaped face was tall for her age and, like many fourteen-year-old girls, at that gawky, awkward stage. Her red hair was in a long braid that ran down her back, and her green eyes flickered with a charming mischievousness. Emily could see that in a few years she would grow into a beautiful young lady.

"Abigail, this is Miss Somerville."

Abigail bowed slightly and held her hand out. "I'm pleased to meet you, Miss Somerville."

Emily took her firm hand. "And I'm pleased to meet you, too."

Emily was immediately impressed with Abigail's confident manner and openness; so unlike unhappy little Lucy.

"Well, shall we get started?"

"I'll leave you two to your work," Delia said, closing the door behind her.

"Abigail, do you know any French words at all?"

"Last Christmas we had many visitors to our home, which is our custom on Christmas Day. One of the gentlemen was French, but I didn't understand a word he said. We had over a hundred gentlemen callers you know. I wrote all their names down in my diary. Some of the gentlemen didn't stay long, but some stayed for oysters and cake. The gentlemen kept dropping in all day and until long after I had gone to bed. The horses looked so tired, but the livery men made lots of money."

"That sounds very exciting," Emily said, trying not to laugh at Abigail's unexpected loquaciousness. "What games do you like to play?"

"I ever so much enjoy rolling hoops and jumping rope."

"In French, jump rope is pronounced, *corde à sauter.* Can you say that?"

Abigail wrinkled her freckled nose. "C*orde à sauter*?"

"Very good. And roll hoops is pronounced, *arceaux*."

"Arceaux."

"Excellent." Emily was relieved to see that Abigail was a bright child and a quick learner. As she had done with Lucy, they spent the rest of the lesson picking up objects in the parlor and pronouncing them in French.

At dinner that evening, Emily delighted Mrs. Winslow and Gaylord as she described her remarkably bright and funny new student. "My, the child does like to talk. Among other things, I found out her favorite bakery is Mr. Walduck's."

"I know it," Gaylord said. "It's on Sixth and Eighth. And indeed, it is my favorite bakery as well."

"Abigail also tells me her favorite cream puffs cost three cents each. And she informed me that Dean's candy store has molasses candy that is the best in the city."

Gaylord clapped his hands. "She's spot on. I, too, frequent Dean's for their molasses candy."

Abruptly changing the subject, Mrs. Winslow said, "With a baby coming, I presume you'll be leaving here soon. Do you have any plans?"

Michael frowned. "No. But between my move up to foreman and the income from Emily's two students, I'm hoping we'll find something suitable."

Mrs. Winslow took a newspaper out of her handbag. "I happened to be reading the paper today and I saw an advertisement that might be of interest to you." She handed the paper to Emily, who read the circled advertisement aloud.

"*To let: Eight entirely new, two-story cottages, piazzas, and veranda fronts, courtyards, thirty-five feet deep, filled with elegant forest trees. Each house contains four bedrooms, two parlors, and kitchen, and hard-finished walls with cornice and center-piece. Possession given immediately; terms very moderate …*"

Emily put the paper down. "My goodness, that sounds … wonderful."

"That sounds too good to be true, if you ask me," Michael said. "And if it is true, it must be terribly expensive."

Emily glanced back at the advertisement. "It says here the rent is four hundred dollars per annum."

"What are you paying here?" Gaylord asked Emily.

"Ten dollars a week."

"That's five hundred and twenty dollars a year."

"My, it's expensive when you look at the annual cost."

"Residing in a boardinghouse has its conveniences, but it can be quite expensive."

She turned to Michael. "It's costing us more to stay here than to rent a house."

Still doubting the possibility of renting such a fine home, Michael interjected, "But our food is included here. If we rent a house, we'll be responsible for buying our own food. Then there's the heating and… God knows what else."

"That will be the case wherever you go," Mrs. Winslow pointed out.

Michael was not swayed. In his short time in this city he'd learned that people made lots of promises, but just as often went back on their word. "Where is this house anyway?"

Gaylord picked up the newspaper. "West Fortieth between Sixth and Broadway."

"That's way up," Michael said.

Gaylord tossed the newspaper on the table. "Michael, the farther south you go, the more real estate costs. As neighborhoods go, West Fortieth isn't bad."

Despite his doubts, Michael had to agree. He'd seen with his own eyes that the most desirable—and expensive—neighborhoods were all south of Delancey Street. Looking at the expression on Emily's face, he could see she was very excited at the prospect of moving into a new home. "We'll have to think about it," he said noncommittally.

Back in their room, Emily could barely contain her excitement. "Michael, it has *two* parlors. We can turn one of them into a classroom."

"A classroom for what?"

"To teach French. With a young baby, I won't be able to travel up to Gramercy Park three days a week. Besides, Delia Hainsworth hinted that she might know of a few women who would like to have their daughters learn French."

"But what if they won't come to you? Then all we'll have is my foreman's pay."

"If it comes to that, won't that be enough?"

"I suppose. But if—" He was interrupted by a knock at the door.

Emily opened the door and Mrs. Winslow was standing there. "May I have a word with you?"

Emily nodded. "Certainly, please, come in."

Mrs. Winslow sat down on the rickety chair, Emily sat on the bed, and Michael remained standing.

The older woman turned to Michael. "I know you're concerned about being able to afford the rent for that house."

"I am. That's what we've just been talking about."

"I have a proposal for you that I think will be advantageous to the three of us."

"And what is that?"

"If you decide to rent that house, why don't I move in with you? I will of course pay you the five dollars I now pay Mr. Coyle each week. That's an additional two hundred and sixty dollars a year for you, which will more than pay your rental expenses."

When she saw them staring at her with their mouths open, she added, "And, Emily, I would be most happy to be a nanny to your baby while you're teaching your students." Mrs. Winslow looked down at her lap. "Mr. Winslow and I were never able to have children and I've always regretted being childless. I think I can be an asset to your young family and you would do me a great honor if you would accept my proposition."

Mrs. Winslow's proposal had literally taken Emily's breath away. It was, to say the least, a great surprise. Gaylord had told her about Mrs. Winslow's tragic past and she'd assumed the woman just wanted to live out the rest of her life alone.

"Mrs. Winslow, I … don't know what to say."

The older woman smiled. "Yes, would be a good response."

Emily looked at Michael for help. She knew he was just as surprised as she was but his expression was neutral. She wasn't sure if he'd want someone else living in the house with them.

"Mrs. Winslow, I think we need some time to consider your very generous offer."

"No, we don't," Michael said abruptly. "It's up to you, Emily. I'll go along with whatever you want."

Emily was surprised—and pleased—with his response. She had a feeling that he didn't really like the woman, who, admittedly, could be at times be caustic and abrasive. Emily stood up and straightened her dress. "Well, in that case, we accept your generous offer, Mrs. Winslow."

Mrs. Winslow stood up and the two women hugged. "Please, Emily, call me Henrietta."

After Mrs. Winslow left, a stunned Michael and Emily stood staring at each other in silence, hardly able to comprehend what had just happened. Any doubt that they could afford their own home had been suddenly, and finally, put to rest by Mrs. Winslow.

Emily sat back down on the bed. "Can you believe our good fortune, Michael? Thanks to Mrs. Winslow ... I mean Henrietta, our rent will be only one hundred and forty dollars, and she's willing to help with the baby as well."

"I'll admit it sounds good, but, still, I have my doubts about her. She can be a bit highfalutin'."

"That's only because she's been alone for so long. She's a lonely and frightened woman. I think she realizes she needs to be with people, to be wanted, to count for something. We can help her as much as she can help us."

The next night at dinner, they broke the news to Gaylord.

"Well, that's wonderful news for the three of you. But what'll I do now? God help me, it'll just be me and Mr. Coyle."

Mrs. Winslow patted his hand. "Gaylord, there will be new tenants with whom you'll be able to regale with your tales of this wicked city."

"Perhaps. But to tell you the truth, I'm a little jealous. I wish I were going with you."

"We won't be far away," Emily said. "As soon as we get settled in, we'll have you over to dinner."

Michael tapped the tureen with his fork and grinned. "And you can be sure it won't be stew she'll serve up."

CHAPTER TWELVE

On Sunday morning, an anxious Emily and Michael took the Sixth Avenue omnibus up to Fortieth Street. The advertisement had painted a pretty picture of the house, but given the exaggerations and outright lies of unscrupulous landowners, they weren't sure what to expect.

Fortieth Street was mostly vacant lots with a few squatter's shanties scattered here and there. It didn't look very promising. Then they saw the eight houses as described in the advertisement.

Tears welled up in Emily's eyes. "Oh, Michael, look." The row of eight, shiny new houses were even more beautiful than she'd dared imagine. Each house had a patch of grass in front surrounded by a picket fence. "Isn't it beautiful?"

Michael grunted. He was expecting to find a hidden catch in all this business. Still, Emily was right. They were beautiful homes.

Arthur Schaefer, the property manager was waiting for them in front of building 407. "Ah, you must be the Ranahans."

"I'm Michael and this is my wife, Emily."

The short, rotund man shook both their hands. "Well, let's see the property, shall we?"

Off to the left and right of the modest vestibule were the two parlors. They stepped into the one on the right. Emily squeezed Michael's hand. "This could be my classroom," she whispered.

"Come on, let me show you the upstairs," Schaefer said.

The second floor consisted of four bedrooms and a small bathroom. Emily was especially taken with the bathroom as she imagined never having to share a bathroom with other boarders.

"What do you think, Michael?"

"I have to admit, it's better than I thought." He turned to Schaefer. "The paper said the rent is four hundred dollars a year. Is that correct?"

"It is, and I advise you to make up your minds as quickly as possible. Six of the houses have been rented already."

Emily looked at Michael. "Well?"

All along, he'd been expecting some unpleasant surprise—shabby construction for example, or a pig farm next door, but everything appeared to be in order. "I guess we should take it," he said with a shrug.

The property manager clapped his hands. "Excellent. Now if you'll come to my office on Worth Street tomorrow and sign the papers, you can move in the first of the month."

To celebrate the renting of the house Emily suggested they stop at a small restaurant off Broadway.

Looking in the window, Michael said, "This looks very expensive."

"We'll just have tea and crumpets."

"Tea and—?"

"Never mind." She firmly took his arm and led him through the front door.

Ill at ease in such a fine establishment, he squinted at his teacup. "Look how small these things are. And so delicate. How's a man supposed to pick the damn thing up without breaking it?"

She picked her cup in demonstration. "Gently. See? Just use your thumb and forefinger."

"I'd rather have a mug. And what are these things?"

"Jam and clotted cream. You spread them on your crumpet."

"Clotted cream? It sounds like something's gone bad."

"No, it's good. Try it."

Despite his complaining, he ate his—and some of Emily's crumpets. He especially enjoyed the clotted cream.

The bill was exorbitant, but to Emily it was well worth it. It was the first time since they'd arrived in New York that she felt civilized. The last time she'd seen linen tablecloths and decent tableware was back in Ireland before the famine. Thinking of it made her sad to remember how things used to be.

Shaking that unhappy thought from her mind, she said in a brighter tone, "Isn't this a refreshing change from Mr. Coyle's endless tureens of bad stew?"

"Aye, I'll give you that. But we can't be eating crumpets every day."

"No, but with my own kitchen, I'll be able to feed us something besides boardinghouse fare."

She took Michael's hand. "I sense a new beginning for us, don't you?"

He grinned. "Aye. Our own new home. A baby coming. And with the money coming in from Mrs. Winslow, I'll be able to save more money for my business. It's all good, Emily."

Rushing to get everything in order before the first of the month, Michael found the last week in January a blur of activity. Over the course of several days, he borrowed one of Cully's wagons to pick up furniture from various junk dealers throughout the city. Flynn and several of the men he worked with helped him move into their new home. Without any great mishap, Emily and Michael were finally in their new home.

Michael looked around at the sparsely furnished parlor. "It's not much, is it?"

"It's a start," Emily said, trying, but failing, to sound as upbeat as she'd hoped.

"It's a damn site better than Mr. Coyle's boardinghouse," Henrietta added, making them all laugh. "Don't worry, Emily, it'll look a lot better when you get some curtains up."

"I'm sure it will. Meanwhile, I'm off to see my students and find out if I'll still have them by next week."

After Lucy's lesson, Emily asked to see Mrs. Ingersoll. The woman came into the parlor frowning. "Is there something wrong?"

"No, not at all. It's just that I wanted to tell you that I'm pregnant."

Mrs. Ingersoll gave her a tight smile. "Congratulations."

"Thank you. As you can imagine, having a young baby will complicate my life somewhat."

"In what way?"

"Well, I won't be able to travel."

"Oh, does this mean you will no longer be able to teach Lucy?"

"No, not at all. My husband and I have rented a house on Fortieth Street where I plan to set up a classroom to teach French.

Would it be possible for Lucy to come to me?"

Lucy clapped her hands. "Oh, yes, I would like that."

Clearly, she was delighted at the prospect of going uptown for her lesson, mainly, Emily suspected, so she could get out of the house.

Mrs. Ingersoll gave Lucy a sharp look. "I will have to discuss this with Mr. Ingersoll."

"Of course. I understand."

At the door, Letta gave Emily a hug. "I am so happy to hear about the baby and your new home, but I'm sorry that we will no longer have our coffee and chats."

"I will miss that, too, Letta. But when we get settled in you must come for a visit."

"I will," she said with tears in her eyes. "I will."

Breaking the news to Delia Hainsworth was a lot easier.

"I understand perfectly," she said. "You can't very well travel about the city with a brand-new infant. By the way, I talked to my three friends and they want their daughters to study with you. They live in various parts of the city, so it will be easier if they agree to send their daughters to you. I'm sure they'll agree."

CHAPTER THIRTEEN

Over the next several months, they settled into a comfortable routine. As Michael got used to being a foreman, he experienced less and less resistance from the troublemakers among the men, especially when they realized that his efficient ideas saved them extra work.

As he traveled about the city he was ever on the lookout for discarded furniture to add to their meagerly furnished home. Of course, there was never a scrap of wood to be found in the poorer neighborhoods; it was all used for firewood. But it was different in the upscale parts of the city. On Fifth Avenue, he found a beautiful mahogany dining room table and eight matching chairs. A week later he found a fine oak bed outside a mansion in Union Square. He was amazed at what these rich people left at the curbside. As far as he could tell, there was absolutely nothing wrong with the furniture he picked up. Flynn said he'd seen that sort of thing all the time. Rich people routinely threw away perfectly good furniture in favor of the current fashion. Michael thought they were daft. But it was their loss and his gain.

Emily, too, was settling in. As her pregnancy progressed, she found it much easier not having to travel to Gramercy Park three days a week. She had turned her parlor into a classroom of sorts with a mix of desks and chairs. She was delighted when Michael brought home six school desks that had been salvaged from a school building fire. A little cleaning up and they would be suitable for her students. In addition to Lucy and Abigail, she now had three other students. Mary, Beatrice, and Nora were all from wealthy families, but they, too, were attentive and quick learners. With all five students in one place it became easier to work out a curriculum geared to the level of each student.

It was a bright Monday morning in early June when Emily's students began to arrive. As usual, Lucy was accompanied by Letta. Mr. Ingersoll had reluctantly given his permission for Lucy to travel, but only if Letta came with her. Emily was delighted with that arrangement. It gave her an opportunity to resume their coffee and chats after class.

When all the girls were seated and settled down, Emily said, "All right, girls our new term for today is *faire des courses.* Does anyone know what that means?"

They all shook their head no.

"*Faire des courses* means to go shopping."

Abigail's hand shot up. "Miss Emily, yesterday my mother and I went shopping at A.T. Stewart's store on Chambers Street. Then we went to Constable's on Canal Street where they keep elegant silks and satins and velvets. My mother always goes there to get her best things."

Emily smiled. "That's very interesting." Abigail could always be counted on to interrupt the class with some tidbit of information. But she was so exuberant about it that Emily couldn't be angry with her.

As Emily walked between the desks leading her students in reciting today's list of words, she was startled to see an angry bruise on Lucy's neck just at the collar line. Lucy had been acting unusually timid—perhaps frightened was a better word—since she'd arrived for her lesson. She stumbled over her words and seemed more distracted than usual.

At the end of the class, as all the other girls hurried into the kitchen to sample Henrietta's cookies, Emily said, "Lucy, could you stay behind a minute?"

"Yes, Miss Emily." Lucy remained in her seat.

Emily sat down next to her. "Lucy, is everything all right?"

"Yes." Her answer came too quickly.

"I couldn't help but notice you have a nasty bruise on your neck. What happened?"

"Nothing."

Emily could see she didn't want to talk about it, and she knew it wouldn't be wise to push her. "All right, why don't you join the other girls in the kitchen."

The idea of making cookies for an after-class snack was Henrietta's idea. It was a great way for the young girls to socialize while they awaited their chaperons to pick them up. The other girls seemed to enjoy their time together, except Lucy, who always hung back from the group.

Emily took a tray of tea and cookies into the parlor where Letta was waiting for her. As Emily poured the tea, she said casually, "How are things at home for Lucy?"

"Well enough, I imagine."

Emily sat down on a chair close to Letta. "I think there's something wrong with Lucy."

"Whatever do you mean?

"Did you see the bruise on Lucy's neck?"

Letta nodded as she stirred her tea.

"Letta, I know it isn't a servant's place to gossip about their employers, but—"

"No, it is not." Letta said firmly.

"But I have to ask you these questions because I believe Lucy may be the victim of some kind of abuse."

A visibly upset Letta abruptly put her cup on the table, sloshing tea into the saucer. "Emily, please don't ask me these questions. I can be terminated for talking about anything that goes on in the Ingersoll household. And if I'm dismissed, I'll not get a good reference from them."

"I understand," Emily said, reluctantly. "We won't speak of this again."

At dinner that night, Henrietta noticed that Emily seemed preoccupied. "Emily, is there anything wrong?"

Emily put her fork down. "As a matter of fact, there is."

"My dear, what is it?"

"I'm worried about my student, Lucy Ingersoll."

"Is she not grasping her lessons?" Michael asked.

"I wish it were as simple as that."

"Well, then, what is it?

"I think Lucy's being abused," Emily blurted out.

Henrietta dropped her fork. "Oh, my God!"

"Why do you say that?" Michael asked sharply.

"It goes back to the first time I met her. She seemed

extraordinarily timid and withdrawn."

"Aren't most twelve-year-olds? Henrietta asked.

"Not like that. I also noticed that she flinched at every little sound in the house. She's afraid of something."

"Afraid of what?" Michael asked.

"I'm not sure. When I first started teaching her I suggested that we do our lesson in the park. She was delighted at the prospect, but her mother said Mr. Ingersoll didn't want her in the park."

Henrietta's eyebrows went up. "Gramercy Park? My goodness, whyever not?"

"I don't know. I finally convinced Mrs. Ingersoll to let us go. I can tell you Lucy was visibly relieved to get out of that house."

"Are you sure you're not imagining all this?" Michael asked.

"I am not imagining it," Emily said sharply. "While we were in the park, three girls her age came by rolling their hoops. She didn't know who they were. Michael, they're neighbors for God's sake."

"Is there anything else?" Michael asked, not convinced there was anything amiss.

"Today, I saw a large bruise on Lucy's neck."

"Oh, my heavens …" Henrietta muttered.

"And I can't tell you how many times I would come for my lesson and Lucy and her mother were at the doctor's."

"I understand your concern," Henrietta said. "But I think you'll have to admit, it is all quite circumstantial."

"I know. I just feel there is something I should do."

Michael shook his head. "Mr. Ingersoll is a wealthy and influential man in this city. I can't imagine the likes of him abusing his own daughter."

"Who says it must be Mr. Ingersoll," Henrietta asked.

Michael had no answer for that.

Emily put her napkin down. "Gaylord is coming to dinner on Sunday. I'll ask his advice."

In the short time Henrietta had been living with them, she continuously surprised Emily. The cookies were one example. The cookies, which were absolutely delicious, were her grandmother's recipe, Henrietta explained. And then there was the cooking. Emily had no illusions about her cooking skills, still, she thought she must be a better cook than someone who has lived a life of leisure for many years. Wrong again. It turned out that Henrietta was something of a gourmet cook. Unfortunately, there was no money for gourmet fare, but Henrietta could turn the toughest piece of beef into something wonderful. After Emily turned out a meal of mutton with dubious results, it was tacitly agreed upon that Henrietta would have dominion over the kitchen.

At precisely five o'clock that Sunday, Gaylord arrived for dinner armed with a bottle of claret.

As Gaylord entertained them with descriptions of the new quirky, weird, and strange boarders who had taken their place at Coyle's boardinghouse, Emily's mind was only on Lucy. As dinner was winding down, she couldn't hold her questions in any longer. "Gaylord, I would like to ask your advice about something."

He poured more wine in their glasses. "Of course."

She told him everything she'd told Michael and Henrietta. When she'd finished, the usually buoyant reporter looked grim. "Emily, you may have tapped into the ugly, under-side of the upper class in this city. There are dozens of religions and charitable organizations that tend to the needs of the poor and destitute who are victims of child abuse. But it must never be suggested that such despicable activity could ever happen in our better households."

"Just because they have money doesn't mean they're not immune to such bad behavior," Michael said indignantly.

"True enough. It's just that you'll never find our affluent brethren discussing such a distasteful topic. And it's not just child abuse. You'll never hear anyone in that circle talk about wife beating, alcoholism, or rampant gambling."

"So, they are immune," Emily said in exasperation.

"I'm afraid so. Let's assume your hunch about the little girl is true. And let's assume the culprit is Mr. Ingersoll. To whom would you go to for relief?"

"The police I suppose."

Gaylord shook his head. "Out of the question. The police in this city are under the thumb of the mayor. Did you know that they are all appointed annually at the discretion of the mayor?"

"I didn't."

"Under those circumstances, they will do nothing to jeopardize their positions by taking on some one of the stature of Mr. Thaddeus Ingersoll."

"So, what's to be done?" Henrietta asked.

"I'm afraid there's nothing to be done."

Michael slammed his hand down on the table. "I can't accept that, Gaylord. We have a baby coming soon. I don't know if it's to be a boy or girl, but I can't accept a world that would allow my daughter to be abused without some sort of justice and reckoning."

Gaylord drained his glass. "Well, I'm sorry to say, there it is. Now mind, it's only my opinion, but I do believe I'm right about this."

Despite what Gaylord had said, Emily vowed to keep an eye on Lucy and if she saw any more signs of abuse, she would go to someone. Who that someone might be, she had no idea.

CHAPTER FOURTEEN

It was the beginning of the workday and Michael was supervising the loading of the wagons for the day's work. There wasn't much for him to do. Having convinced the men that loading a wagon properly would save them time and effort, they automatically loaded the materials in proper sequence. But how many men should go on what job was another problem he'd been watching. Today, he would address that.

As the men were getting ready to climb onto the wagons, Michael tapped Larkin on the shoulder. "I want you on the Fifth Avenue job wagon today."

"What for? I'm always with this crew."

"That job is going to finish up today, I don't need six men there. You'll go with the Union Square gang. They need all the help they can get."

"Why me? You're always picking on me, Ranahan."

"It's not just you." He pointed at three men. "Foley, Dunn, Clark, all of you will go with the Broadway crew." When he heard the muttering, he said, "Listen up, men. We're here to make money for Cullinane Construction. If Cully makes money, we get work. If he doesn't make money, we're out of work. Any questions?"

There were none.

It had been raining since six that morning and Fifth Avenue was a sea of mud. The gloomy, overcast day matched Michael's sour disposition. He couldn't get the conversation they'd had last night with Gaylord out of his mind. He kept hearing the reporter's words, *I'm afraid there's nothing to be done.* He shook his head in bewilderment. What kind of city was this where a young girl could be abused and nothing would be done?

At the end of the work day Michael was riding up front next to Flynn, while the other men sat in the back of the wagon. As they neared Fourteenth Street, Michael saw another wagon coming towards them. It was the only time he smiled all day. The overloaded wagon was being pulled by a large white horse that reminded him of Shannon, Emily's spirited stallion back in Ireland. Of course, unlike Shannon, this horse's head hung in defeat and he had difficulty keeping his footing in the slippery mud. Whatever pride and dignity he may have had in his youth, had long since been beaten out of him.

Suddenly, the horse stumbled and went down on his knees. As Michael watched in horror, the carter, cursing furiously, jumped down from the wagon and began beating the poor horse unmercifully. Passersby hardly gave him a second look. Other carters, annoyed at the delay, maneuvered around the fallen horse and continued on their way without a glance.

Without thinking, Michael jumped off the wagon and reached the man just as he was raising his whip to deliver another blow. He ripped the whip out of the surprised man's hand and brought it across his face. As the stunned man fell to the ground, Michael roared, "Leave him alone, you bloody beast. Can't you see he's worn down?"

"Who the hell are you?" the man shouted, wiping blood from his cheek. "It's my goddamned horse and I'll damn well beat him to death if I so wish. The useless creature isn't worth the feed I give him."

The carter's callous attitude infuriated Michael even more. "And maybe you're not worth living either," Michael hissed, bringing the whip down on the man's head again and again. Suddenly, he was in a bear hug and the whip was yanked out of his hand. Flynn and some of the other men pulled him away.

"Come away, Michael," his friend said, eyes wide with fright. "Surely, you don't want to kill the man, do you?"

Michael stopped struggling. "No… no…. It's just that I can't stand people being cruel to dumb animal—or … *young girls*."

Flynn was puzzled by his reference to "young girls." He took Michael's arm and led him back to their wagon. "Come on, old Cully will be wanting to know why we're late."

They continued down Fifth Avenue in silence. Even the men in the back, who usually carried on a constant line of chatter, were quiet. As they were passing Washington Square Park, Michael gazed at it wistfully. The lush green grass, the trees and shrubs, even the steady downpour, reminded him of Ireland and it made him homesick. He missed the fields and the peacefully grazing animals. He missed his friends and the little cottages that dotted the hillsides. Then he shook his head in dismissal and castigated himself. *What are you thinking, you damn fool?* That was not the Ireland he'd left. Most of the cottages had been tumbled and most of his friends were dead. There was nothing left for him in Ireland. Still, he wondered if he'd made a mistake taking Emily to this godforsaken city.

With tears in his eyes, he said, "It's a damn cruel city, isn't it, Flynn?

Flynn took a long puff on his cigar and squinted. "Aye, it is that."

CHAPTER FIFTEEN

For the next two weeks, every time Lucy came for a lesson, Emily examined her closely, looking for any physical signs of abuse. But, thankfully, she saw nothing. After each lesson was over, she tried to engage Letta in conversation about Lucy's life at home, but the servant girl was maddeningly vague in her responses. Emily understood her young friend's predicament, but she didn't like it. If there was abuse, she was certain that Letta, living under the same roof with the Ingersolls, would have to know about it. But by mid-June, Emily began to believe her suspicions were unfounded.

Then, Lucy came to class with a bruised eye.

"Lucy, what happened to you?"

Looking embarrassed, she gingerly touched her cheek. "Mother says I'm so clumsy. I walked into a door."

Later, while the girls were having cookies with Henrietta, Emily pulled Letta into the parlor and closed the door.

"Letta, you must tell me how Lucy got that bruise."

"I was told she walked into a door."

"Who told you that?"

"Mrs. Ingersoll."

"Did you see it happen?"

"No."

Emily took Letta by the shoulders. "Letta, for God's sake, tell me the truth. Do you believe that's what happened?"

Letta began to weep. "No … I… don't ..."

"What's going on in that house?"

Through convulsive sobs, she said, "It's Mr. Ingersoll. He's a brute to Lucy and to Mrs. Ingersoll. He's never done anything in my presence, but I've heard things …"

"Like what?"

She fell into Emily's arms. "I've heard the sounds of someone being slapped … punched … Oh, God it's terrible. I put the pillow over my head, but I can still hear the sounds."

"Letta, I'm going to ask you a question and I want you to answer me truthfully. To your knowledge, has Mr. Ingersoll ever sexually abused Lucy?"

Letta bit her lip. "I hear things …"

"What sort of things do you hear?"

"Sometimes, in the middle of the night … I hear doors opening and closing."

An ashen-faced Emily sat down hard. "Oh, my God. Oh, my God …"

Letta dropped to her knees and took Emily's two hands in hers. "Emily, you must never tell anyone I said such things."

Emily squeezed the distraught girl's hands. "Don't worry. I would never get you in trouble with the Ingersolls."

"What are you going to do?"

"I don't know."

A despondent Letta stood up and wiped the tears from her eyes. "I'd better take Lucy home."

Tears welled up in Emily's eyes. "I can't bear the thought of that poor girl spending another night in that horror house."

"Neither can I, but what choice do I have?"

"None," Emily said dully.

After the last of the students had left, Emily sat at the kitchen staring into the fireplace.

Henrietta sat down next to her. "Emily, what is it? You look so worried. Is it the baby?"

Emily automatically patted her stomach. With an expected due date less than a month away, she was growing bigger and bigger by the day. "No, it's not the baby." She started to cry. "Henrietta, Ingersoll is molesting his daughter."

The older woman dropped a plate of cookies. "Oh, no … no ..."

"What am I going to do, Henrietta?"

"You heard what Gaylord said. Who could you go to?"

"I think I've found a place." She opened the newspaper on the table and flipped through it until she found the classified section.

"Here's a place I might go—The Society for the Relief of

Orphan and Destitute Children. It's located on Greenwich Avenue."

She stood up and pulled her shawl around her.

"Where are you going?" Henrietta asked in alarm.

"I'm going to tell them what's going on."

"Emily," Henrietta pleaded, "at least wait until Michael gets home."

"There's no time to waste. I've got to get that child out of that house as soon as I can."

Before Henrietta could say anything more, Emily was out the door.

The building in which The Society for the Relief of Orphan and Destitute Children was housed was impressive. In a previous incarnation, it might have been a proud merchant bank.

An elderly woman was seated at a desk in the foyer. "May I help you?" she asked with a kindly smile.

"Yes, I want to report a case of child abuse."

The woman nodded knowingly. "I understand. We get these referrals every day. What's going on in those terrible neighborhoods like the Five Points is a disgrace to this city. But, that's what we're here for—to do our part in saving the children from abuse and neglect."

She opened a notebook. "What is the address where the child abuse has taken place?"

"Gramercy Park."

The woman dropped her pencil. "Did you say … Gramercy Park?"

"I did."

The woman looked puzzled. "Does this involve a servant or a tradesman?"

"No. It involves the master of the house."

The woman pursed her lips. "Wait right here." She jumped up and hurried down the hallway.

A minute later she came back accompanied by an anxious middle-aged clergyman who directed her into a small office.

"Please be seated, Mrs. …?"

"Ranahan. Emily Ranahan."

"I am the Reverend James Fowler, the director here. What is the nature of your complaint?"

"As I told the woman at the desk, I want to report and incident of child abuse."

"And you claim this so-called 'child abuse' occurred in a residence in Gramercy Park?"

"That's correct." She didn't like his use of the word "claim" or his characterizing her complaint as "so-called." She realized Gaylord was right about these people. They would not—or could not—accept that one of their own could be a monster.

The reverend, bald except for tufts of white hair sprouting above his ears, studied her with an undisguised look of incredulity. "Do you know the name of the alleged miscreant?"

She realized his whole tone and demeanor was designed to discourage and intimidate her, but she'd come this far and there would be no turning back. "His name is Thaddeus Ingersoll."

The clergyman started. "That's… that's… preposterous," he sputtered. "Mr. Ingersoll is an upstanding member of my church. Why, he's the chair of our Congregational Council. You must be mistaken."

"I don't believe I am."

His eyes narrowed. "What sort of proof do you have?" he snapped.

"What kind of proof would you expect me to have? If I'd come here to complain about some poor drunken father in the Five Points, would you ask me for proof? No. You would investigate the claim as I expect you to do now."

The reverent stood up. "There will be no investigation," he said coldly. "I know Mr. Ingersoll personally. It is not possible that he could ever do what you claim. And I will not be party to a scheme to destroy the reputation of an upstanding member of this city and of my congregation. Good day, madam."

Emily stood up. "And what about his daughter? Don't you care about what happens to her?"

"I am not worried about his daughter because I will stake my reputation that nothing is amiss in the Ingersoll household."

Emily pulled her shawl around her shoulders. "Reverend, I hope to God you're right."

An angry Michael was waiting for her when she got home.

"Emily, what could you be thinking? You're eight months pregnant. You've no business gallivanting all over the city on a fool's errand."

"It was not a fool's errand."

"Of course it was. You heard what Gaylord said."

"I had to do it, Michael. Someone must stand up for Lucy."

"And what was the outcome of your meeting?"

Tears welled up in her eyes. "It was a fool's errand. They won't do anything. My God, what's going to become of her?"

Michael put his arms around her. "Emily, you tried. That's all you can do."

The repercussions of Emily's visit to The Society for the Relief of Orphan and Destitute Children was swift. Within days, a nervous Letta appeared at the door.

"Come in" Henrietta said.

"I can't. I'm here to deliver a message to Emily."

Emily came to the door. "Letta, what is it? Come in."

The servant girl shook her head. "I can't ..."

Emily took her arm. "Nonsense. Henrietta has a pot of coffee on the stove."

Letta came in and handed the note to Emily. It was short and to the point: *Effective forthwith, Lucy will no longer be coming for French lessons. Mrs. Ingersoll.*

"What happened, Letta?"

"Yesterday, a Reverend Fowler came to see Mr. Ingersoll. They went into the parlor. I couldn't hear what they were saying, but Mr. Ingersoll was very loud and angry."

Emily shook her head in astonishment. "The reverend took the time to tell Ingersoll that I made a complaint against him, but he wouldn't take the time to investigate my charge."

Henrietta poured a cup of coffee for Letta. "It's just as Gaylord said."

The next day, as they were eating dinner, she got similar notes from the parents of three more students. "The word must be spreading," Emily said. "I'm a pariah." Tears welled up in her eyes. "I'm sorry, Michael. My foolishness has cost me four students. And with the baby coming we could really use the money."

"Don't worry about it," Michael said. "We'll be fine."

"What about your other student, Abigail?" Henrietta asked. "Do you think she'll stop coming as well?"

That question was answered the next day when Delia Hainsworth personally brought Abigail. While Henrietta was feeding Abigail cookies in the kitchen, Emily took Delia into the parlor.

"Delia, I want to thank you for having the courage to stick with me."

"Nonsense. I've always thought there was something wrong in that Ingersoll house. The fathers of your three students who left are all business associates of Ingersoll. He tried to pressure my husband and me, but I told him I will make my own decisions. But, as a friend, I must tell you, your actions were imprudent."

"I know. I was warned."

"Thaddeus Ingersoll is a powerful and well-connected man in this city. And there are many who are beholden to him. You're new to this city, but you must understand, the only thing that counts in this city is money and power and Ingersoll has both."

"Why is it he couldn't pressure you?"

"My husband is in banking. He's not part of that merchant class. Just be careful, Emily."

"What else can he do to me? He's taken away four of my students."

"I don't know. Just be careful."

CHAPTER SIXTEEN

The beginning of July was unusually hot and muggy. Anyone with the money and the wherewithal had already fled the city to live in the much cooler countryside. Those who couldn't leave because of circumstance or business obligations were forced to suffer the dreadful July heat and humidity and the ever-present stench of the city.

The heat was even more unbearable for pregnant women and Emily was getting close to her due date. It was two weeks since she'd lost her students, but she'd reconciled her decision to make the complaint despite the unpleasant aftermath. Delia had been right. She'd been imprudent. For days after Delia had warned her to be careful, she wondered what more Ingersoll could do to her. Then it hit her; *they were renting their house*. Did Ingersoll have any control over their landlord? They had a lease, but so far, nothing had happened and she began to relax.

It rained all day Tuesday, which only contributed to the discomfort she was feeling. Around four that afternoon, the doorbell rang. Letta was standing in the doorway, soaked to the bone, tears streaming down her cheeks.

Emily stretched out her hand. "Letta, come in out of the rain."

Seemingly oblivious to the rain, she didn't move. "Letta, what is it?"

"Lucy is dead…" she whispered in a hoarse voice.

Emily felt her legs buckle and if it wasn't for Henrietta standing next to her she would have collapsed.

She awoke on a couch in the parlor. At first, she thought she'd just had a bad dream, but when she saw an anxious and tearful Henrietta standing over her, she knew it wasn't a dream. Letta sat in a chair sobbing. "Letta, what happened?"

"She fell down the stairs and hit her head. The doctor came but there was nothing he could do."

"Did you see her fall down the stairs?"

"No. I was told."

Emily got up too quickly and the room began to spin. "That was no accident," she shouted. "That horrible man killed her."

"Now, now, Emily," Henrietta said, trying to calm her friend. "you don't know that."

"Are you telling me it's merely a coincidence? What about the bruises on her neck? The bruised eye? And now this? Am I to believe she accidentally fell down the stairs? No. I tell you he killed her."

Just then she felt a sharp pain and doubled over. Henrietta grabbed her arm. "Emily, what's the matter?"

"Oh, God … The baby… I think the baby's coming …"

"Come, Letta, help me get her up to her bed."

As soon as they got Emily into bed, Henrietta rushed down to the kitchen. She scribbled an address on a piece of paper and handed it to Letta. "This is where the midwife lives on Thirty-Ninth Street. Go and bring her here as quickly as you can."

It was just after seven when Michael came home. He was surprised to see Letta siting in the kitchen. She usually came to dinner on Sunday, her day off. "Hello, Letta, what are you doing—?" He stopped talking when he noticed her red eyes and her sad expression. A lump formed in his throat. "Where's Emily? Is anything wrong?"

"She's upstairs. The midwife is with her."

Michael bounded up the stairs and met Henrietta in the hallway. "Is she having the baby? Is she all right?"

"The baby hasn't come yet. It's a difficult birth. The midwife has been with her since four-thirty."

"I want to see her."

He tried to push past her, but she grabbed him and shook him. "Michael, listen to me. The midwife is doing everything she can. There's nothing you can do. Go downstairs. I'll call you when there's news."

He ran his fingers through his hair. "I don't understand. She wasn't supposed to have the baby for another two weeks."

"She's had a great shock today."

"What kind of shock?"

"Little Lucy is dead."

"Oh, my God. What happened?"

"She died in a fall down the stairs. Emily doesn't believe that. She thinks it was intentional."

"She thinks Ingersoll is responsible?"

"She does."

"And that shock brought on her labor?"

"It would seem. Now why don't you go down to the kitchen. There's a pot of coffee on the stove and there's cold chicken in the icebox."

In a fog, Michael went downstairs and hardly noticed that Letta was gone. He had no appetite, but he poured himself a cup of coffee. He didn't know how long he'd been in the kitchen staring into space when Henrietta came in. He jumped up. "Is the baby here?"

Henrietta nodded. "It was a difficult birth."

"Is Emily all right?"

"Emily and the baby are fine."

He rushed upstairs. The midwife, an elderly lady with her gray hair tied back in bun, was standing outside their bedroom. "Is everything all right?"

"Yes. She had a hard time, but they're both doing well." As he put his hand on the door-knob, the midwife cautioned him. "She's resting. Don't disturb her."

He tiptoed up to the bed. Emily was sleeping with a peaceful expression on her face, but the pillow was drenched with perspiration and her long auburn hair was a tangle of knots. Then he looked at the baby. It was bundled up in such a way that he could barely see its face. *It*? He'd forgotten to ask if it was a boy or girl. Just then, Emily opened her eyes. Michael gently brushed her hair back from her face.

"How are you doing?"

She nodded and tried for a smile. "I've been better," she said in a weary voice. "I thought the voyage across the Atlantic was bad …"

Michael moved the blanket away from the baby's face. "Emily, is it a boy or a girl?"

"It's a boy."

Michael felt light-headed and sat down on the edge of the bed. "A boy …" he muttered in almost disbelief. "We have a son … born in the New World ..." His expression hardened and he looked at his wife. "Emily, he'll never have to go through what we went through in Ireland. He'll have a better life."

Emily squeezed his hand. "Yes, he will. Our son is an American."

"What are we going to name him?"

The question caught Emily off guard. They hadn't bothered to play the name-the-baby game because they didn't know if it was going to be a boy or a girl. "I haven't really thought about it. Do you have anything in mind?"

"I'd like to name him Dermot."

Emily frowned. "Oh, Michael. You want to name the baby after your brother? He was such a troubled young man."

"I know. That's why I'd like to name him Dermot. My brother had such a short, unhappy life I'd like to think our baby could lead the kind of full life he never had." When he saw the doubtful expression on her face, he added, "We don't have to decide right now."

She nodded. "All right, let's think about it."

As he was going out the door, Emily said, "Lucy is dead."

Michael nodded. "I know."

That Sunday, Henrietta prepared a sumptuous meal of turkey, potatoes, and fresh vegetables. For dessert, she made apple and cherry pies. Letta, Gaylord, and Flynn were invited. With the birth of the baby, it was supposed to be a celebration, but the death of Lucy cast a pall over the day. All through dinner everyone tacitly agreed not to mention Lucy's death.

"So," Gaylord said, trying to stay upbeat, "Have you decided what you're going to name the little tyke?"

Michael was about to suggest the name Richard, which was Emily's father's name, but before he could speak, she said, "Dermot. We're going to name the baby after Michael's late brother."

Michael put his fork down. "Are you sure, Emily?"

She smiled back at him. “I’m sure.”

CHAPTER SEVENTEEN

By mid-August, Emily was feeling strong enough to resume her French lessons with Abigail. She sent word to Delia Hainsworth that she was ready.

On the day of the class, Delia arrived with Abigail and, much to Emily's surprise, the three girls who had dropped out earlier. Emily looked at Delia quizzically, but the woman whispered, "I'll tell you later."

As soon as the class was over, Emily brought tea into the parlor. She handed Delia a cup. "Well, what happened?"

"As I'd told you earlier, Ingersoll put pressure on the fathers of the girls to have them to stop coming to you. But then, when little Lucy died, suspicions were aroused and there was a lot of talk. No one will actually say it, but the consensus among some is that her death may not have been an accident."

Emily felt vindicated, but this matter couldn't be put to rest so easily. "Now will there be an investigation?"

Delia shook her head. "No. Despite what people may think of Ingersoll he's still a powerful man in this city."

"And powerful men can get away with murder?"

Delia looked down at her lap. "It would seem so."

"I can't believe that. I can't accept that. I *won't* accept that."

"Emily, I don't know how it was in Ireland, but New York is a wicked city. Most politicians are corrupt, most police are on the payrolls of wealthy criminals, most businessmen routinely lie, cheat, and steal to amass their fortunes. When it comes to the poor, we have young children dying every day from abuse, neglect, starvation, and disease. Young mothers routinely die in childbirth. I hope to God that someday all that will change, but in the meantime, that's the way it is and we just have to accept it."

One part of Emily told her that was unacceptable, but the more practical side of her told her that Delia was right. There was nothing she could do and she would just have to accept it.

Summer gave way to a wet and chilly fall. The beginning of November was especially cold, with biting winds whipping off the Hudson River and swirling through the streets of downtown Manhattan. It was late afternoon when Flynn, Michael, and a work crew huddled in the back of a wagon as they made their way back to the warehouse. Cully was waiting for them. He signaled for Michael to come into the office.

Without waiting for Michael to sit down, he said, "Well, I guess you know there's an election in a couple of days?"

Michael groaned and sat down heavily on a chipped wooden chair. The truth was, he hadn't thought about it. Between work and the new baby, he had precious little time to think about elections. He thought back to the tumultuous election last year. With a start, he realized that it had been over a year since they'd landed on Manhattan Island. Their first anniversary in Manhattan had come and gone without notice. The voyage … their night in the Five Points … their time in the boardinghouse … It seemed like a long, long time ago.

Michael looked at his boss uneasily. "What is it I'm to do?"

Cully tossed his eyeglasses on the desk and rubbed the bridge of his nose. "Same as last year," he said wearily. "You and the others will report to Tammany Hall. You'll get your marching orders there."

"Cully, I have a young baby at home—"

"Makes no difference, Ranahan. You owe your job to Tammany."

"No, Cully, I owe my job to you."

The old man shook his head. "I couldn't have hired you without Tammany's approval. If you don't show up on election day and do what you're told to do, you'll be out of a job the next day."

"But—"

"I'm sorry, Ranahan," Cully said, reaching for his glasses. "That's the way it is and there's nothing I can do."

As an angry Michael stormed out of the office, Cully called out, "Ranahan."

Michael turned. "What is it?"

"Be careful. This is going to be a vicious election. Tweed is running and he has no intention of losing a second time."

Remembering the violence of last year, Michael nodded glumly and left. He was going to go home, but he decided to stop by Coyle's boardinghouse to have a word with Gaylord.

Old man Coyle opened the door and scowled at Michael. He still hadn't forgiven him for leaving and depriving him of three cash-paying boarders. "What is it that you want?"

"Is Gaylord in?"

"He's in the parlor."

The reporter looked up from a newspaper and smiled. "Michael, what brings you here?"

"The election."

Gaylord's smile faded. "Ah, the election. And a mad one it'll be."

Michael sat down on the worn couch. "That's what I wanted to talk to you about. I'm to report to Tammany and I assume I'll be told to do what I did last year. Cully warned me to be careful."

"He gave you good advice. You know Tweed is running again?"

"So I've been told."

"This year the Democrats will field the usual band of shoulder-hitting ruffians, but this time they'll be led by one John Morrissey, a tough customer indeed. To counter the Democrats, the Whigs have employed one Bill 'the Butcher' Poole and his Bowery Boys gang."

"The Butcher?"

"He's a butcher by trade, but he's not adverse to carving up a human being as well. He's a nasty brawler, an eye gouger, and virulently anti-Irish. Mind you don't tangle with him."

"My God, is there no law and order in this city at all?"

"Very little. There's not a policeman in this city who will interfere with the shenanigans of this, or any other, election."

On election morning, those ominous words were ringing in Michael's ears as he entered Tammany Hall, which was crowded with other men such as himself, coerced into doing the bidding of Tammany.

He slid onto a bench next to Flynn. "Will there be trouble today, Flynn?"

Flynn's Adam's apple bobbed up and down and his face was pale. "I'm thinking there will be. Did you know—" He stopped when he saw a grim Bill Tweed step up to the lectern.

"Good morning, men," he said, gruffly. "Today is going to be an important day for Tammany. We must win this election for the Democratic Party—and meself," he added with a grin. "But there will be opposition. John Morrissey here wants to say a few words."

A stocky man with a full beard and a pugilist face stood up. "We got word that the Whigs and Know-Nothings are going to try to steal the ballet boxes in the Eighth Ward. They'll be sending Butcher Bill and his Bowery Boys to do the dirty deed."

At the mention of that gang, a howl went up from a group of men standing in the back of the auditorium. Michael turned to see a rough bunch of men wearing tall beaver hats and red stripes on their pantaloons pounding clubs into the palms of their hands. "They're a strange looking bunch," Michael whispered. "Who are they?"

"They're Morrissey's boys, the Dead Rabbits."

"All right, pipe down," Morrissey bellowed. "Save your energy for later." He looked over the seated crowd. "Some of youse will be going to the Eighth Ward office to defend it against all and any who wish to disrupt the election. The rest of youse will be assigned to election sites throughout the city. All right, off you go."

As the men shuffled up the aisle, several Dead Rabbits standing at the back of the auditorium were selecting men and shunting them off to the side. Michael and Flynn were among the seventy or so men selected.

Morrissey came up the aisle. "All right. Youse men will come with me to the Eight Ward headquarters. Pick up your weapons of choice and form up outside."

Michael, Flynn, and the others were led to a table where there were boxes filled with assorted clubs, axes, iron bars, bludgeons, and brickbats.

"What are these for?" Flynn asked a man with one eye and a long scar running the length of his face.

The man grinned a toothless grin. "To defend yourself with. What else?"

"Will I be needing something to defend myself with?"

Again, the smile. "I'm thinking you will."

Flynn sighed and picked up an iron bar.

"What's your choice?" the man said to Michael.

"None." He had no intention of becoming a street brawler for Tammany Hall.

The man grabbed his sleeve. "I wouldn't advise that, me boyo. If you don't take a weapon, you'll be the only one without and you won't stand a chance."

Reluctantly, Michael picked up a wooden club and weighed it in his hands. It was sturdy, but not too heavy. He hoped he wouldn't have to use it, but if there was trouble, he would defend himself.

En masse, the men, augmented by the Dead Rabbits, marched over to the building that was the headquarters of the Eighth Ward. It was an ornate building with six columns and a wide flight of stairs. Michael was relieved to see that, except for a steady stream of men leaving and entering the building to vote, there was no sign of trouble.

"All right, men," Morrissey said, "Spread out and keep a sharp eye on me."

For almost an hour, they milled about blocking the entrance. Anyone going in was searched for weapons. If anyone was recognized as a Whig, he was kicked back down the stairs.

Toward late afternoon, Michael was beginning to believe that there would be no trouble. Then he heard the roar of angry voices. From around the corner came a mob of thirty or forty men.

"Uh, oh…" Flynn whispered out of the side of his mouth, "here comes Butcher Bill and his Bowery Boys."

If Michael thought the Dead Rabbits dressed oddly, the Bowery Boys outdid them. They, too, wore tall beaver hats, but they also wore inordinately long black frock coats, loud, checkered, bell-bottomed pantaloons, floppy kerchiefs knotted under their collars, and their hair was plastered down with what looked to be lard. They advanced down the street armed with brass knuckles, knives, and lengths of iron pipes. A daunting sight. They were led by a man in a black stovepipe hat. He was powerfully built, about six feet tall and close to two-hundred pounds. Michael was struck by his eyes. They were the soulless eyes of a killer. He pounded an iron bar in his hand and shouted over his shoulder, "Come on, boys. We got a job to do."

"Is that Butcher Bill?" Michael whispered to Flynn.

"The same. And a more dangerous man you'll not find in this entire city."

As the mob moved toward the building, Morrissey, standing at the top of the stairs, said, "That's as far as you go, Bill."

Butcher Bill squinted up at Morrissey. "Stand aside, John, and nobody gets hurt."

Morrissey grinned down at him. "If you want to get into this building, you'll have to go through me and my men."

Butcher Bill grinned back. "Have it your way. You always were a stubborn man. Come on men," he called over his shoulder.

"Form a line," Morrissey bellowed.

Everyone, including Michael and Flynn, stood shoulder to shoulder at the top of the stairs. Michael felt his throat go dry as he watched the men start up the stairs.

Suddenly, he had a flashback of that terrible day the men of Ballyross had gone to Cork Harbor to protest the shipment of food out of the country. It was supposed to have been a peaceful demonstration, but some hothead from the village threw a rock striking the captain escorting the food wagons. As he fell from his horse, a frightened, undisciplined solider fired into the crowd and mayhem ensued. Many men from Ballyross died that day. Now, Michael wondered if there was going to be needless blood spilled over a damn fool election.

With a roar, the butcher and his men rushed up the stairs. In an instant, Michael found himself surrounded by howling men swinging axes, clubs, and iron pipes. Dodging an iron pipe aimed at his head, he swung his club, catching the man in the throat. The man, gagging, stumbled backward and tumbled down the steps.

Suddenly, time seemed to stand still and everything went into slow-motion. The howls of fury and the cries of pain blended into a dull cacophonous roar. As Michael fought to defend himself, all around him he saw heads bashed open, bodies stabbed, and blood splattered everywhere. The copious flow of blood made the steps slippery and more than once he almost lost his footing.

He didn't know how long they had been fighting, but suddenly, as if on some silent signal, the Bowery Boys disengaged and slowly retreated down the steps, dragging their wounded with them.

To the shouts and jeers of the Dead Rabbits, Butcher Bill and his Bowery Boys limped off the way they'd come.

At dinner that Sunday, Michael recounted the bloody battle, adding that he was lucky to come away with no more than a black eye and a superficial knife wound.

Gaylord nodded. "You were lucky. There were pitched battles at other sites throughout the city, but Tweed's Eighth Ward was the crucial location. The Whigs didn't get the ballot box and thus Tweed was elected to the United States House of Representatives. And as a reward for stopping the ballot box from being stolen by Butcher Bill, Morrissey and his Dead Rabbits have been allowed by Tammany Hall to open a gambling house without police interference."

Emily shook her head in disbelief. "What kind of lawless city is this?"

"What kind of lawless city indeed," Gaylord answered. "This kind of shenanigans has got to stop. And I pray to God it will end soon. Among the others who were swept to victory on election day were a saloon keeper, a stone cutter, a fishmonger, and a fruit vender. Most of these men have been elected to the Common Council which now has the deserved sobriquet 'The Forty Thieves.'"

CHAPTER EIGHTEEN

1852

January began with a snowstorm. By six in the morning, more than eight inches fell in the city making it difficult for horses to negotiate the frozen, rutted roads and for men to tread on icy sidewalks. Because of the frozen conditions, Michael was late for work. He barely had time to shake the snow off his clothing when Cully bellowed, "Ranahan, in my office. Now."

"Cully, I'm sorry I'm late, but the roads and sidewalks are treacherous. There are no omnibuses running on—"

Cully waved a hand in dismissal. "Never mind that. Sit down. Sit down."

Michael was relieved to hear that he wasn't going to be fired. Cully was a mercurial man capable of slapping a man on the back for a job well done one day, and the next day threatening to fire him for some minor blunder. But right now, the old man was more excited than Michael had ever seen.

"What's up?"

"Ranahan, I've just landed the biggest contract I've ever had."

"That's great, Cully. Where is the job?"

He slammed his fist on the desk, barely able to contain himself. "It's huge, Ranahan. We're going to be doing a construction project for William B. Astor."

Michael remembered something Flynn had told him about Astor. "Is he the one known as the landlord of New York?"

"The same. Ranahan, we'll be at this job for probably a year or more."

"For one mansion?"

"It's not a mansion. Astor is going to construct two hundred brownstone row houses, three to five stories tall."

"My God, that is huge. Where will they be built?"

"West Forty-Fourth, Forty-Fifth, and Forty-Sixth Streets."

"That's only four blocks from where I live."

"And it's too bad you don't own the house you're living in. All the homes in that area will greatly appreciate in value once this project is completed."

Michael agreed. But owning the house was out of the question. He simply didn't have the money. Realizing the enormity and complexity of such a project, he had a question. "Cully, how can we do a job like this? We'll need to hire hundreds of men."

Cully shook his head. "I won't be the only contractor. They'll be dozens and dozens of carpenters, land clearers, brick and stone men contractors. There's a lot of money to be made here, Ranahan. A lot of money."

Michael was glad to hear that. Construction in the city tended to be boom or bust, and winter months were traditionally slow. He lived with the constant fear that he wouldn't have work and he wouldn't be able to pay his rent. The bitter remembrance of him and his da being turned out of their cottage and watching it tumbled was seared in his memory. The mere thought of his family being thrown out into the street terrified him.

Shaking that thought from his mind, he said, "When do we start?"

"Right now, there are contractors clearing away the rocky outcroppings. Then the land has to be graded before construction can begin." He stood up. "Come on, I want to go to the site and see how things are proceeding."

"Today? With these road conditions?"

Cully rubbed his hands in anticipation. "I don't care. I've got to see what's going on."

Once Michael made sure that all the wagons were properly loaded and sent on to their respective work sites, he and Cully took the small wagon and headed up Sixth Avenue. The snow had stopped, but it still took them over an hour of slipping and sliding along the avenue to get to Forty-Fourth Street. As they approached the intersection, they saw a group of men preparing explosives to take down a thirty-foot high outcropping that ran half the length of Forty-Fourth Street.

"Who's in charge here?" Cully asked.

"I am." The contractor was a thin, red-faced man in his early fifties. Cully stuck his hand out. "I'm Cully of Cullinane Construction."

The man shook Cully's hand. "Tom Garrity."

Michael noticed Garrity's eyes were unfocused and he smelled of alcohol. As the two contractors talked, Michael wandered over to where the workers stood around a man kneeling over several sticks of dynamite and inserting a fuse. He looked up at Michael with that same unfocused look. And he, too, smelled of alcohol. "Who are you?" he demanded.

"Michael Ranahan. I work for Cullinane Construction."

"Well, there's nothing for you to do until I blast these outcroppings to Kingdom come," he snarled in a slurred voice.

With alarm, Michael noticed that the man's hands were shaking. He glanced at the other men. They, too, looked concerned, but they said nothing. One man, however, trying to make light of it said, "Noonan, mind you don't pack too many explosives this time and blow *us* all to Kingdom come."

"Mind your own damn business," Noonan muttered.

Michael didn't know much about explosives, but he knew that dynamite and alcohol were not a good combination.

Noonan stumbled to his feet and with two assistants in tow they went halfway down the block to plant the explosives. When they came back Noonan took a cursory look around to see if anyone was nearby. Then he connected two wires to a wooden dynamite plunger on which was written in large letters: CAUTION: EXPLOSIVES. He depressed the plunger and for a moment nothing happened. Then, there was an ear-shattering explosion. A great cloud of black dirt and rocks and boulders of all sizes erupted high into the air. Everyone stood with open mouth as one huge boulder that must have weighed four hundred pounds flew in a slow-motion arc through the air. As it started its descent, a horrified Michael saw that it was going to hit a house on Forty-Third Street. Helpless to do anything, he watched the boulder crash through the roof.

"Jasus..." Noonan mumbled, "I guess it was too much of a charge..."

Slipping and sliding in the snow, Michael ran toward the house, praying no one was home. The other men stumbled after him. When they got to the house, Michael saw that all the windows on the first and second floors were blown out. Dirt and dust bellowed out the windows.

He tried the front door but it was locked. Stepping back, he kicked the door open. Inside, the air was heavy with smoke and floating plaster and debris. He heard a faint whimpering in the parlor. As he started into the room, he stopped. The boulder was hanging precariously from the parlor ceiling held in place by two cracked beams. Apparently, the boulder had gone through the roof, the attic, the second floor and came to rest here. He saw a maid sprawled on the floor directly underneath the boulder bleeding profusely from the head. Heedless of the hanging boulder, he rushed in and dragged her to the safety of the entrance hall. Using her apron, he wrapped the hysterical maid's head to staunch the flow of blood.

"Is there anyone else in the house?" he asked.

"No … just me ..."

Michael was glad of that. He had no desire to go searching through a building that might be structurally unsound and could collapse at any moment.

Just then, Noonan and the others came in. Noonan glanced into the parlor and chuckled. "*Jasus*. Well, at least the stone didn't get into the cellar."

In a fit of rage over the man's lack of remorse for what he'd done, Michael lunged at him and floored him with a punch. He would have given the man a severe beating, but the other workers pulled him off.

Just then, Cully and Garrity arrived. "Hey, what's going on?" Garrity demanded.

"This man attacked me," Noonan said, getting to his feet and wiping his bloody nose.

"*You're drunk*," Michael shouted. "You could have killed this poor woman. You're just lucky no one else was in the house."

"What's the big fuss? It was an accident," Garrity said.

"It's not an accident when your explosives man is drunk. He's got no business handling explosives. And you've no business letting him."

Garrity pointed a finger at Michael. "Now don't you be telling me my business."

"He's right." Cully said. "Your man's drunk and so are you. Come on, Ranahan. Let's leave this lot to sort out the mess they've made."

Michael helped the maid to her feet. "Do you know where there's a doctor?"

"Yes. He's a couple of blocks away."

Michael and Cully helped the maid into their wagon and took her to the doctor's house. They waited in the parlor while he attended to her.

Five minutes later, he came out wiping his hands on a bloody towel. "She'll be all right. It's a nasty cut, but no serious damage. What happened?"

When Michael told him, the doctor frowned.

"It's not the first time something like this has happened. With all this new building construction going on in this neighborhood there are explosions going off from dawn to dusk. The noise, the dirt, and the danger have become intolerable. A few months ago, a huge boulder from an explosion crashed through the house of a colleague. Fortunately, no one was injured. But a month later, I treated a woman who was nearly killed when she was struck by a projectile from an explosion. We've complained to the authorities, but nothing has been done."

And Michael knew why. The "authorities" had no doubt received bribes from these same contractors.

On the way back to the warehouse, Cully was unusually silent. Finally, he said, "It's a bad business, Ranahan."

"What is?"

"I've always been the sole contractor on a job. I do things my way and with my men. I don't like the idea of having to work with the likes of a Tom Garrity."

"It's a big job, Cully, too big for us to handle alone. You said so yourself. What choice do you have?"

"I could turn the job down."

Michael's heart pounded in his chest. Only this morning he thought he was assured work for over a year. If Cully dropped out of the project, would there be enough work for them this winter?

"What will you do?" Michael asked quietly, almost afraid to

hear the answer.

Cully was silent for a moment, which seemed like an eternity to Michael. Finally, he said. "I can't turn the job down. It's worth too much money."

Michael breathed a sigh of relief.

When he got home, Emily was feeding the baby in the kitchen and Henrietta was cooking dinner. At almost six months, Dermot should have been fully engaged with the world around him, but he seemed strangely detached and uninterested in his surroundings.

Emily, who had fully recovered from the difficult birth and looking as lovely as ever, was trying unsuccessfully to get him to respond.

Michael kissed her. "How's he doing?

Emily frowned. "I don't know. When I take him to the park he doesn't really interact with the other children of his age."

"I'm sure it's just a stage." He sat down at the table. "I've got good news."

"Good news is always good to hear," Henrietta said.

"Cully has landed a big contract with Astor to build three blocks of row houses."

Henrietta's eyebrows shot up. "*The* William Astor?"

"The same. Emily, do you know what this means? I'll have steady work well into next year."

"Oh, that is good news. When will you start?"

"As soon as the land is leveled."

By March, the last of the outcroppings had been dynamited away and the land had been graded and prepared for building. During that time, there had been numerous overloaded explosive charges that caused considerable damage to surrounding buildings. But, fortunately, the only fatality was a careless and drunken Noonan who blew himself up in a premature explosion. Due to the increased workload, Cully had to hire more men and purchase three more wagons. Flynn, despite his fervent protests, was promoted to foreman again.

It was just after one o'clock when Michael got back to the warehouse.

Cully looked up. "What are you doing back so early?"

"There's been another delay."

"Who is it this time?"

"Nally and his plumbing crew. They're not finished installing the pipes. We can't put the flooring in until he's done."

"Goddamn it." The old man slammed his fist on the desk. "That's the fifth delay this month."

Cully's worst fears were coming to fruition. The Astor project was a massive undertaking involving dozens of contractors and hundreds of workers. Some contractors were competent, but many more were no better than Tom Garrity's crew. Cully had been clashing more and more with Nally who, because of his slipshod work, was holding him up by not completing the work on time.

"That's it. I'm fed up with that goddamn Nally. It's time to have it out with him."

"Is that wise? You know he's the brother-in-law of a Ward boss."

"I don't care if he's St. Patrick's brother. We don't get paid if we're not doing the work. Come on, I want to talk to that sonofabitch."

When they got to the job site, Cully jumped off the wagon before Michael could bring the horse to a halt. "Where's Nally?" he snapped at one of his workers.

"Where's he always?" the man said in disgust. "In the saloon around the corner."

Cully was so furious Michael decided he'd better go with him. They found Nally sitting on a bar stool talking to the bartender.

"Nally, why aren't you supervising your men instead of sitting here getting drunk?"

Nally turned and regarded Cully with bleary eyes. "And what's it to you, Cullinane?"

"You're holding me up. If you can't do the job, get off the site."

"Go to hell. I'll finish when I'm damn well ready."

Cullinane lunged at him. Although Nally was taller and younger, Cully was stronger. As they wrestled and crashed to the sawdust-covered floor, Michael jumped in to separate them. He pulled his boss off Nally. "Come on, Cully. This is no way to settle it."

The older man struggled to get free of Michael's grasp. "I'll kill the sonofabitch ... Let me go …" Suddenly, Cully grabbed his chest and groaned. At first, Michael thought Nally had stabbed him. But there was no blood. Cully sank to the floor clutching his chest and groaning in agony.

"Quick, give me a hand getting him into the wagon."

As soon as Cully was safely in the wagon, Michael drove to the house of the doctor who'd treated the maid. He and the doctor laid Cully on a bed. The doctor pushed Michael out of the way. "Wait outside while I examine him," he said curtly.

Fifteen minutes later, he came out. "He's had an attack of angina pectoris."

"What's that?"

"A syndrome characterized by constricting pain below the sternum, usually precipitated by exertion or excitement."

"Is he going to be all right?"

"I believe so, but he'll need plenty of bed rest."

"How long before he's back on his feet?"

"Could be months."

"Months? That's impossible. He has a business to run."

The doctor glared at Michael. "A dead man can't run a business."

Michael was stunned. "You mean he could die?"

"That's exactly what I mean."

After carrying Cullinane out to the wagon and making him as comfortable as he could, Michael made his way down Sixth Avenue trying his best to avoid potholes and ruts that would rattle the wagon.

Cully's house was only a couple of blocks from the warehouse, so Michael stopped there first to pick up Flynn and two other men.

The old man's house on Pine Street was a modest two-story building. They carried him upstairs to his bedroom and put him into bed.

"Cully, do you have a doctor?" Michael asked.

The old man winced in pain. "Yeah ... Dr. Foley ... He lives at 74 Water Street."

Fifteen minutes later, Flynn returned with the doctor, a rail-thin man in his early sixties with a no-nonsense demeanor.

"So, what seems to be the problem?"

"He's had an attack of…" Michael couldn't remember the name the doctor said.

"He wasn't talking to you," Cully snapped.

"Who said he had an attack?"

"A doctor uptown."

"He's a damn quack," Cully muttered.

"So, what do you think the problem is?" the doctor asked.

"I've had this terrific pain in my chest and it went down my left arm. Probably indigestion. I'm all right now."

Dr. Foley waved his arm. "Everybody out."

Michael sent Flynn and the others away.

Ten minutes later, the doctor came out. "It would seem that he did have an attack of angina pectoris."

"That's it. That's what the doctor said. An angina pectoris attack."

"I'm not surprised. I've told him repeatedly he must slow down. I've told him to avoid all extreme emotions and excessive passions and anxiety."

"But that's the way Cully is."

"Well, he's got to change if he wants to go on living. I've told him to slow down, but to no avail. The stubborn old coot never listens."

"The doctor uptown said he would need bed rest. He said it could take months."

"I agree. He needs to maintain a course of emotional and physical equilibrium."

"What's to become of his business?"

"*Ranahan*," Cully shouted from the bedroom. "*Get in here.*"

The doctor closed his bag. "I'll be back tonight to look in on him. You'd better go see what he wants."

Cully was sitting up propped by two fluffy pillows. "That quack says I had some problem with my heart."

"So did the other quack— I mean the other doctor. You've got to listen to him."

"I'll be damned if I'm going to stay in bed for a couple of months doing nothing. I've got the Astor project to consider, and ..." He winced and grabbed his chest.

"Should I get the doctor back here?" Michael asked in alarm.

"No, I'm all right. Just a little pain." He looked at Michael with squinting eyes. "If I must be laid up for a couple of days, do you think you could handle the business?"

"Me? Well, I don't know …"

"Of course you can do it, Ranahan. I've been watching you. I've seen how you handle the men." He grunted. "That troublemaker Larkin needed to be put in his place. And I liked your idea of loading the wagons in the proper order. I should have thought about it meself."

Michael was surprised that Cully had even noticed what he'd done. "Well, if you think I can do it…"

"You start tomorrow. They'll be extra pay in it for you. At the end of the workday, come back here and tell me what's going on."

As Michael started to leave, he said, "Cully, do you have anyone to take care of you while you're in bed?"

"No, but it doesn't matter. I'll be up and about a couple of days."

"That's not what the doctor said ..."

"That goddamn quack doesn't know what he's talking about. Just come back here tomorrow afternoon and tell me what's going on."

CHAPTER NINETEEN

To Michael's surprise he found that he was not only able to run the business efficiently, he enjoyed the challenge. Unburdened by Cullinane's impatience and short temper, he was able to deal more amicably with venders and fellow contractors. He was also grateful to the men, especially Larkin, who didn't challenge his authority. He suspected they knew it was in their own self-interest to see that Cullinane Construction remained a viable business.

As they sat down to Sunday dinner, Emily said, "It's been three weeks since his heart attack. How is your boss getting along?"

"As well as can be expected, considering how cantankerous he can be. Last week he tried to get out of bed, but a sharp pain in his chest made him collapse in pain."

"Who's taking care of him?" Henrietta asked.

"A woman who lives next door. She brings him soup and the occasional stew, but she's elderly and she won't be able to keep it up much longer."

"Does he have family?" Emily asked.

"Not that I know of."

"Well, then who's going to take care of him?"

"I'm sure I don't know."

"I could do it."

Michael and Emily turned to stare at Henrietta. "*You*?" they said in unison.

"Don't look at me like that. I took care of my infirmed father for over two years. I suspect I can handle Mr. Cullinane."

"I'm not so sure about that," Michael said. "He can be very irritating when he's healthy, but being a sick man confined to his bed hasn't helped his disposition."

"Well, I'm willing to give it a try, that is, if you can spare me,

Emily."

"That's not a problem, Henrietta. Dermot's not an infant anymore. We'll manage."

"Are you sure?" Henrietta knew that Dermot could be unmanageable.

"I am."

"Very well. I could go to his home in the morning, take care of him during the day, and be home in time to cook dinner."

"Oh, that's too much. I don't expect you to come home after taking care of an invalid all day and then prepare dinner."

"Well, who'll do it?" Michael asked.

"I will," Emily said.

Henrietta and Michael burst out laughing at that thought.

"What's so funny?" Emily asked, irritated by their mirth.

Michael patted his wife's hand. "Emily, remember the mutton dinner?"

"That was a long time ago. I've been watching Henrietta. I think I can manage in the kitchen."

"No," Henrietta said firmly. "I will continue to cook our meals."

"I agree," Michael said, slamming his hand down on the table.

Michael had his doubts about Henrietta taking care of Cully. He was a headstrong man and she was a headstrong woman. He envisioned them clashing on everything from soup being too hot to her bossy ways. He held out little hope that the arrangement would work. Still, despite his misgivings, he took her to meet Cully the next morning.

"Cully, I want you to meet Mrs. Henrietta Winslow. She has agreed to come here every day to tend to your needs."

The old man instinctively pulled the covers up protectively around his neck. He was not accustomed to seeing a strange woman in his bedroom, especially one eyeing him so critically. "I don't need a nursemaid, Ranahan. I thank you for your generous offer, Mrs. Winslow, but I'll manage meself."

Henrietta folded her arms and looked down her nose at him. "When I am introduced to a gentleman, it's customary for the gentleman to rise."

A red-faced Cully threw his covers aside and tried to get up, but the effort made him gasp in pain and he fell back onto the bed.

Henrietta pulled the covers back over him and smoothed them out. "Clearly, Mr. Cullinane, you cannot manage yourself. Now, let us have no more such foolish talk." She turned to Michael. "You can go. Mr. Cullinane and I will be just fine."

A wide-eyed and slightly terrified Cullinane croaked, "Ranahan, don't go ..."

"I've got to," Michael answered, barely suppressing a grin. "I have to get the men out on the jobs. I'll see you this afternoon."

As Michael went down the stairs, he realized that Henrietta had already won the battle of wits with Cully. He almost felt sorry for his poor intimidated boss.

Emily and Michael sat in their kitchen drinking coffee and enjoying a Sunday morning alone. With Henrietta off to tend to Cullinane and Dermot taking a nap, the house was quiet.

"So, how do you think it's working out with Henrietta and your boss?" Emily asked.

"Surprisingly well." Michael grinned. "Cully has become downright docile in the presence of our fearless and resolute Henrietta."

"From what I can see, she seems to be enjoying herself. She thrives on taking care of him and then coming home to take care of us."

"I've got to admit, she's a remarkable woman."

Emily opened the kitchen window and took a deep breath. It was still mid-April, but the red maple trees in their front garden was showing signs of blooming. "It's very balmy for mid-April."

Michael came up behind her and put his arms around her. "It is that. I have an idea. Why don't we take Dermot to see the Croton Reservoir today?"

"What's that?"

"It's a holding tank of sorts that supplies water to the whole city. Flynn said there's a great view from the top of the walls."

"That sounds like a wonderful idea. Dermot could use the fresh air. We both need to get out more. As soon as he wakes up, we'll go."

It was mid-afternoon by the time they stepped off the omnibus. Immediately in front of them was a huge construction site that ran the length of Sixth Avenue from Forty-Second Street to Forty-First Street. The cast-iron frame of what was to be a massive structure soared over a hundred feet in the air.

Looking up, Emily said, "This is so strange looking. What is it?"

"This is going to be the site of something they call the Crystal Palace." He chuckled. "We're not allowed to even utter that name in front of Cully."

"Why?"

He tried to get work here, but he was shut out by more, shall I say "influential," Tammany men.

"You mean they paid more in bribes?"

"Exactly. Flynn says he was madder than a wet hen over that one."

Emily gazed up at the massive structure. "Why does it look so odd?"

"Because the entire building is going to be all cast-iron and glass. Nothing like this has been built before in the city. I'm told they got the idea from the Great Exhibition Hall in London." He gazed up wistfully at the structure. "I'm sorry Cully didn't get the contract. I would have enjoyed watching this building go up."

Pushing Dermot's carriage east toward Fifth Avenue, they were awed by a second massive structure—the soaring fifty-foot brick walls of the Reservoir, which, indeed, did vaguely resemble an Egyptian tomb. Michael carried Dermot's carriage up a long flight of stairs that opened onto to the promenade.

They weren't the only ones taking advantage of the mild spring day. Dozens of men and women strolled along the walkways, some with perambulators, while young children ran with their hoops.

"Flynn was right about the view," Michael said. "It is spectacular." He pointed south. "Look, you can see the steeple of Trinity Church way down on Wall Street. And that land on the other side of the East River is Queens." He turned to look north. "Just look at all that rolling country up to Harlem and beyond."

Emily shook her head in amazement. She knew Manhattan was vast, but it was only from this vantage point that the vastness and wildness of the island could be truly appreciated. "There's so much land on this island, yet everyone's crowded into the lower end of the island."

Michael surveyed the surrounding panorama. "True enough. But look south. You can see the city is slowly moving north. There's going to be a lot of building in this city in the next ten years. And there's going to be a lot of money to be made. I've got to get my own business started."

"Well, we're saving where we can, Michael, but it'll take time."

"I know we're saving," he said, frustration creeping into his voice, "but I don't want to miss the building boom that I'm sure is coming. What are we saving, a dollar here, a dollar there? It'll take forever. I just wish there was some way to get hold of some real money right now."

"You mean like a loan?"

"That's what I was thinking, but it's not possible. I talked to a banker and he told me I'd need collateral. But I have nothing to offer."

As they strolled the promenade toward Sixth Avenue, Michael peeked into the carriage. "Too bad Dermot's asleep. He's missing a great view."

"Let him sleep. I can use the break. I've never seen a baby crawl so fast. When he's on the floor, I've got to watch him every second to keep him out of mischief."

"Do you miss Henrietta being around to help?"

"Only when Dermot's being rambunctious."

"And is that often?"

"Often enough."

Michael shot Emily a look of concern. "Maybe we should ask Henrietta to stop going to Cully's."

"No," she said emphatically. "It's a good thing she's doing and to tell you the truth, I think she really enjoys sparing with your boss."

Michael chuckled. "He pretends she's a great annoyance, but I think he likes having her around."

"And baking cookies everyday doesn't hurt either."

In silence, they stopped to look at the spectacular view across the Hudson River of the New Jersey palisades. As they turned to head back to the exit, Emily said, "I'm beginning to feel guilty taking Henrietta's five dollars a week. Do you think we could get along without it?"

Michael frowned. "I've been putting her money aside for my business. It's really the only way we've been able to save."

"I know. But it just doesn't seem right."

Michael watched little giggling girls engaged in a heated hoop race. "Well, I suppose we can do without her money. With the extra money that Cully's paying me to run the business, we're doing just fine. Of course, when Cully comes back to work, I'll lose that extra money."

"But when your boss comes back to work, Henrietta won't be needed any longer."

"True enough."

Emily pulled the blanket up around Dermot's neck. "It's starting to get chilly. Let's get the child home."

On the way to the omnibus, they stopped at the Croton Cottage, a popular destination for people visiting the reservoir. There was a huge sign on the side of the building that said "Billiards," but it also served ice cream and refreshments. Dermot woke up just in time to enjoy his first ice cream cone, which he managed to smear all over his face and clothing.

Emily studied him pensively. "You know, I do believe that's the first time I've seen him genuinely happy."

"Is that good or bad?"

"I don't know. I don't know."

When they got home, Henrietta was already at the stove preparing dinner.

"How's Mr. Cullinane doing?" Emily asked.

"As well as can be expected for a grumpy old man."

Michael shook his head. "I don't know how you put up with him. I have to work with him all day, but you don't."

"Ah, his bark is worse than his bite."

Michael waited until Emily took Dermot upstairs to change his diaper. "Henrietta, we've been thinking. Since you're spending so much time taking care of Cully, it isn't fair to go on charging you five dollars a week."

She stopped stirring the gravy and turned to him. "That's nonsense. I sleep here, don't I? I eat most of my meals here, don't I?"

"Well, yes, but—"

"I won't hear any more talk about my rent. Everything will remain status quo."

Her tone of finality told Michael it would be futile to argue any further with the headstrong woman. Changing the subject, he said, "So, how's Cully coming along?"

"His progress is slow. The doctor said his attack was worse than he'd thought. When he feels pain, I give him laudanum to relieve his physical pain. I also put mustard plaster on his chest. The doctor says it stimulates the internal organs."

"Did he say when Cully will be able to come back to work?"

She turned away from Michael, hesitant to say what she knew he didn't want to hear. "He said it could be weeks. It could be months."

Michael had mixed emotions about that. On one hand, he wanted Cully to be well enough to come back to work, but on the other hand, he appreciated the extra money he was making and he enjoyed being in charge. He wondered how he would handle it when Cully came back and he would become just a foreman again.

CHAPTER TWENTY

1853

It was February by the time Cully's doctor allowed him to come back to work. The old man's ruddy cheeks were now pale, the barrel chest deflated, and his clothes hung from his thin frame. Watching the frail old man, Michael was convinced the doctor had made a mistake in letting him come back so soon. But knowing Cully, he suspected the old man probably badgered the doctor into agreeing.

For the next several weeks, Michael's concern grew as Cully's condition continued to deteriorate. He never went out to visit the construction sites anymore, something he'd always done— to the great annoyance of the work crews. He stayed holed up in his cramped office and on more than one occasion Michael had caught the old man asleep at his desk.

A brutal snow storm brought all exterior construction work to a halt. Fortunately for Cullinane Construction, most of their work had moved indoors. Although it was bitter cold in the unheated buildings, at least the work could continue. But there were still friction and scheduling conflicts with other contractors. Windows were not installed on time. Gas lines were not connected properly. All these mistakes caused Cully's men to delay their own work. For the most part, Michael shielded Cully from the bad news. Usually, there was other work that could be done while they were waiting for the other contractors to finish their work. But now Michael was running out of side work for his men and there was no way to disguise the work crews coming back early.

With a scowl on his face, Cully stood in the doorway of his office watching the crews, one by one, coming into the warehouse.

“Ranahan,” he shouted in a hoarse voice, “into my office.”

Michael had been dreading this confrontation, but there was nothing more he could do to keep the men working.

“Why aren’t the men still on the job?” he asked accusingly.

“It’s the same old story, Cully. We’re waiting for other contractors to finish their work.”

Cully slammed his hand down on his desk. “I have a reputation to uphold, Ranahan. I’m the most reliable contractor in this city and I want it to stay that way. Goddamn it. I can’t let these slackers affect my business.”

Michael watched Cully’s face redden and the veins in his neck bulge. This was exactly what he was afraid of. As part of his agreement to let Cully come back to work, his doctor had made Cully promise to remain calm, but now, to no surprise of Michael’s, the old man was getting himself all riled up. He knew Cully could never stick to that promise.

“It’s going to be all right,” Michael said soothingly. “We’ll get the work done.”

“*How*?” Cully bellowed. “You can’t work around those bastards. You can’t—”

Suddenly, he grabbed his chest. ‘*Jasus, Mary and Joseph…*”

“Cully, are you all right?”

The old man began to slump in his chair and his face was turning blue. Michael ran to the door. “Flynn,” he shouted, “get the doctor here. Quick!” Then he remembered the laudanum medicine that the doctor had prescribed. He rushed to Cully’s side. “The medicine, Cully, where’s the medicine?”

“In the drawer…” Cully whispered, slipping out of his chair and onto the floor.

Michael yanked open drawer after drawer, but he found nothing but piles of architectural drawings and bills of lading. In a panic, he shouted, “Where is it, Cully? I can’t find it.”

But there was no answer from the old man, who appeared to be unconscious. Just then, he spotted a small black bottle under a pile of papers. With a shaky hand, he poured some of the medicine into Cully’s mouth. The old man coughed and gagged, but color began to come back into his face.

By the time the doctor arrived, Cully was breathing normally and color had returned to his face. The doctor shook his finger in

Cully's face. "I told you this could happen if you didn't control your temper. You've no business being back at work."

Cully wouldn't look his doctor in the eye. "The work's not getting done," he said, feebly.

"What's more important, the work getting done or you dying?"

Before Cully could answer, the doctor turned to Michael, "Get him back to his house. He's done here."

As February gave way to March and March gave way to April, there was no improvement in Cully's condition. Henrietta had come back to help and it was only her fierce determination to nurse him back to health that had kept him from slipping deeper and deeper into his illness.

As he had been doing since taking over again, Michael reported the work's progress to the old man at the end of the day.

Propped up by fluffy pillows, Cully sipped his hot tea. "Are we on schedule?"

"We are. The weather's been cooperating and we're all caught up. Things are going well."

For a moment, Cully said nothing, then, blinking away tears, he said, "The doctor says I can never go back to work."

"My God, Cully, that's terrible."

Cully stared into his cup. "It's probably time I packed it in."

Michael felt for the old man. He knew that Cullinane Construction Company was his whole life. But he felt a knot in his stomach as well as it also occurred to him that his own future was in jeopardy. He dreaded asking the next question, but he had to. "What will become of Cullinane Construction?"

Cully took a sip of his tea and he looked up at Michael with rheumy eyes. "I want to sell it to you."

It took a moment for Cully's words to sink in. Michael's heart pounded in his chest. At last, here was his chance to own his own business. Here was his chance to be in charge of his own destiny. But his joy at the thought of being his own master quickly faded when he realized his predicament. "Cully, I don't have enough money to buy the business."

"You could get a loan."

"No. I asked a banker about that. He told me I would need collateral."

The old man scowled. "Well, find a way, Ranahan, or I'll have to sell it to somebody else."

That night at dinner, Michael told Emily of Cully's offer.

She clapped her hands. "Michael, I'm so happy. This is the opportunity you've been waiting for."

"But I have no money, Emily. I would need a loan and a banker told me I couldn't get one without collateral."

"That's just one banker. I'm sure you can find someone who'll give you— Wait a minute, Delia Hainsworth's husband is a banker."

"Do you think he could help?"

"Delia is bringing Abigail over for a lesson today. I'll talk to her."

A week later, an anxious Michael Ranahan found himself standing in front of the Gotham Bank, an elaborately columned building on Rector Street. The office of Charles Hainsworth was on the second floor. Escorted by a soft-spoken elderly gentleman wearing a high, starched collar, Michael was led into an elegantly subdued office of paneled mahogany and rosewood, a space designed to convey the position and power of its occupant.

Hainsworth, a tall man in his early forties with a busy walrus mustache, rose to greet him.

"Mr. Ranahan," he said shaking Michael's hand, "Charles Hainsworth. Please sit down."

When Michael was seated, Hainsworth got right to the point. "So, Delia tells me you have an opportunity to purchase a construction firm."

"That's right. Cullinane Construction. I'm a foreman there at the present time."

"Did you bring the books as I requested?"

"I did." Michael slipped a large ledger across the highly-polished desk. "These are the records for the company."

The banker took his time, reading each page carefully. When he was done, he sat back and smiled. "It would appear that Mr. Cullinane has done an admirable job remaining not only solvent, but profitable as well; a feat that not every business in this city can boast of."

"Mr. Cullinane is a hard worker and I intend to make the

business even more profitable. But…" his voice trailed off.

"But what?"

"I've been told I don't have any collateral."

"Of course you have collateral," the banker said, tapping the ledger with his finger. "You have the Cullinane Construction Company."

Michael's heart leaped in his chest at hearing those magic words. "I do? I mean … I'm sorry, I don't understand ..."

"It's quite simple. When a bank loans money, it wants to make sure it will be made whole if the borrower defaults on the loan. That's what collateral is for. Clearly, Cullinane Construction is worth the value of the loan you would need to purchase the company."

"How much would I have to pay for this loan, Mr. Hainsworth?"

"The interest will be modest and we can work out a suitable payment schedule. You will pay the bank a certain amount every month until the loan is paid off."

"What if something happens and I can't pay the monthly payment?"

"Then I'm afraid we would be forced to call in the loan and request full payment."

"But I wouldn't have it."

"That's where the collateral comes in. The bank would be forced to seize Cullinane Construction and sell it to recoup its losses."

Michael's initial euphoria quickly gave way to despair. "You mean I would lose the company?"

"That's correct. But you needn't worry. According to the books, it's a sound company. I don't know if you're aware, Mr. Ranahan, but the building industry is growing in leaps and bounds in this city. A man who is willing to work hard can become very successful indeed. It's all up to you."

Michael's head was spinning. He'd come into this office expecting to be told that his desire to own his own business was but a pipe dream with no hope of coming true. But now, he was being told that his pipe dream could indeed become a reality. All he had to do was say yes.

"Mr. Hainsworth, I'd like to talk this over with my wife, if that's all right with you."

"Of course. It's a big decision and it's not something you want to rush into lightly."

Michael had invited Gaylord to dinner and explained the banker's offer to Emily and Gaylord.

"That sounds wonderful to me," Emily said, tears welling up in her eyes. "It would be a dream come true for you."

A grinning Gaylord slapped Michael on the back. "I most hardily concur. Mind, there is no shortage of unscrupulous bankers in this city, but the Gotham Bank is not one of them. It has an excellent reputation in the banking community. You would do well to heed your banker's advice."

"I don't know. I still have my doubts, and to tell the truth, fears."

"What are you afraid of?" Emily asked.

"What if something should go wrong? What if I fell behind on my payments? I could lose the whole business. We'd be penniless, Emily."

"As a newspaperman, I loathe to sound trite by employing tired clichés, but, as they say, 'Nothing ventured, nothing gained.'"

"Gaylord is right. Every successful businessman must start somewhere. I know it's a great risk, but I have faith in you. You can do this, Michael."

And so, three weeks later, on a bright, sunny April afternoon, a small group gathered on the sidewalk in front of the warehouse. Michael had insisted that Emily bring little Dermot to witness this momentous occasion. She had protested that he was too young to understand what was happening, but when he'd said with great emotion in his voice, "Emily, someday Dermot will come into this business with me. And someday, he'll own it. I want him to know that he was here at the beginning," she understood why it was important to him.

Michael, Emily, Dermot, Henrietta, Cully, Gaylord, Flynn, and all the employees gathered on the sidewalk in front of the warehouse to watch with a mixture of sadness and joy as the Cullinane Construction Company sign came down and the Ranahan Construction Company sign went up.

As the new sign was finally nailed into place, there was a loud pop that startled the group. Gaylord had brought with him a large picnic hamper stocked with several bottles of champagne and enough champagne glasses for everyone. He popped the second bottle and, grinning wildly, handed out champagne glasses. Except for Emily, and possibly Henrietta, no one assembled here had ever drunk champagne.

When the glasses were full, Gaylord raised his. "To the American dream," he said, in a voice choking with emotion. "Where else could a poor, uneducated immigrant come to our shores and in just three short years become the owner of his own business?"

Cully, clearing his throat and looking uncharacteristically uncomfortable, raised his empty glass, which would have been full but for the glaring, reproachful stare of Henrietta, who was meticulously supporting the doctor's order of no alcohol, and said, "I have an announcement to make." He turned to Henrietta with a shy smile. "Mrs. Winslow has consented to be my wife."

There was a moment of stunned silence, broken finally by the popping sound of another champagne cork. "This calls for more champagne," Gaylord said, beaming excitedly.

Emily raised her glass and there were tears of joy in her eyes. "To Henrietta and Mr. Cullinane, all the best and a long life for both of you."

A blushing Henrietta raised her glass. "I never thought I would marry again at this late stage of my life, but, well, there it is, and I couldn't be happier."

Cully held up his empty glass and turned to Henrietta imploringly. "Henrietta, I have one more toast. How about just a wee drop of champagne?"

She looked at him sternly. "Very well, Norbert, but just this once. Mind, don't fill the glass, Gaylord."

Flynn began to laugh. "*Norbert*?"

"It's my Christian name," Cully growled. "What's so funny?"

"I guess I didn't think you had a Christian name. Since I've known you, it's always been Cully."

"And it will stay Cully. I don't like my Christian name," he muttered.

"There's nothing wrong with your Christian name," Henrietta

said firmly. "And that is how I intend address you."

Cully scowled at everyone. "But you lot will continue to call me Cully. Is that understood?"

"Whatever you say," Michael said, suppressing a laugh.

Raising his half-filled glass, Cully said, "To the end of an era and the beginning of a new one." He turned to Michael with tears in his eyes. "Ranahan, I started building this city forty years ago, but, by God, you will finish the job."

Michael leaned over and whispered to a sleeping Dermot, "And you, my little man, will help me do that, won't you?"

That night, back at the house, as they prepared for bed, an amused Michael said, "I couldn't have been more surprised about Cully—*Norbert*—and Henrietta."

Emily ran a brush through her hair. "I wasn't too surprised. Didn't you notice she was off to see Cully every chance she got even after his doctor said he was out of danger? She was like a schoolgirl with a crush."

"On Cully? It just seems strange to me that that cantankerous old man and Henrietta, who can be cantankerous herself, would want to marry."

"I think they're a perfect fit, and I'm so happy for both of them."

When Michael slipped into bed, he pulled Emily close to him and kissed her. "Gaylord was right. Who would have thought that an illiterate immigrant like me could ever own his own business?"

She squeezed him. "You're not illiterate. You can read and write."

"Enough to get by, I suppose. You know, when we first got here and I walked those streets, and saw all those *No Irish Need Apply* signs, I'll admit, I was in despair."

"It was hard in the beginning, but now you have your own business, I've added five more students to my class, and we have Dermot."

"Speaking of the little rascal, are you going to miss having Henrietta around?"

"I will. He's a handful."

"What do you mean?"

"He doesn't listen. If he doesn't get what he wants he throws tantrums. Sometimes it's hard to get through to him. He can be quite sullen for a little boy."

Michael felt a chill go through him. She could have been describing his own brother, Dermot. He, too, was a handful and ended up dead because he wouldn't listen. "Maybe we should hire on another woman to take Henrietta's place."

"I might need someone sooner than you think."

"Why is that?"

Emily took Michael's head in her hands and kissed him. "Because, Mr. Ranahan," she whispered, "I'm pregnant."

Michael pulled her to him. "Emily, that's fantastic. When?"

"I'm thinking next January."

"What's it going to be— Oh, of course. We won't know till he comes."

"Or maybe till *she* comes."

Michael thought about that for a moment. "That would be grand having a daughter. Of course, she couldn't go into the business, but with the proper education you give her she'll marry well."

"Michael Ranahan, what kind of talk is that? If she wants to go into the business, she will."

"A girl? Preposterous, Emily. Construction work is no work for a girl or woman."

She snuggled close to him. "We'll see," she said, before falling into a deep, contented sleep.

The following Sunday, Emily invited Letta to dinner. Emily had kept in touch with Mrs. Ingersoll's parlor maid, but it had been months since they'd last spoken. It would be a good time to catch up. When Gaylord arrived, he was pleasantly surprised to see Letta helping Emily in the kitchen.

"Letta, it's so good to see you again. How have you been?"

"Well enough, Mr. Temple."

Emily thought she heard a certain evasiveness in Letta's tone, but she let it pass.

As soon as Henrietta and Cully arrived, they sat down to dinner.

As Gaylord passed the platter of chicken, he said, "Has anyone seen the new St. Nicholas Hotel?"

"I have," Michael said. "I wish I'd have had a hand in the building of it. It's quite grand."

"I tried to get in there when they started building it two years ago," Cully growled, "but that damn Tammany kept me out."

"They say it can accommodate eight hundred guests," Michael interjected, trying to divert Cully from a blood pressure raising tirade. "Is that true, Gaylord?"

"It is. I'm told they spent more than a million dollars on walnut wainscoting, frescoed ceilings, gas lighted chandeliers, hot running water, and central heating. It makes the Astor House pale in comparison. With its white marble façade stretching from Broome to Spring Street, it's quite a sight."

Henrietta angrily rapped her knuckles on the table. "There is something wrong with a society that builds extravagant palaces like that while there are people literally dying in the streets."

"I agree," Emily said. "Last winter a man froze to death less than two blocks from here. Is there nothing to be done?"

"I understand the police are taking in the homeless and letting them sleep in the precinct basements," Michael said.

"Maybe so, but there aren't enough precincts in the city to accommodate all the homeless."

"I fear for this city," Gaylord said, shaking his head. The cost of necessities has risen almost thirty percent this year alone. And it seems every day a new group of workers is going on strike. One day it's omnibus drivers, the next day it's hat makers, and on and on."

"What's City Hall doing about it," asked Letta.

Gaylord chuckled. "City Hall is part of the problem."

"That and Tammany," Cully muttered.

After dinner, the women went into the parlor for tea, leaving the men to talk politics and business. Cully wanted to stay and argue politics, but Henrietta insisted he was overtired and it was time to go. With barely a murmur of protest from the old man, they said their good nights and departed.

Emily brought a tray of tea and crackers into the parlor. When they were both served, Emily, remembering Letta's response to Gaylord, said, "How are things really going for you, Letta?

"It's not good. Since Mr. Ingersoll's death, Mrs. Ingersoll spends all her time in her room. I haven't been paid in over a month."

"That's terrible. What are you going to do about it?"

"I don't know. What Gaylord said earlier about the rising cost of necessities is true. I've talked to other servants in Gramercy Park. Some of the servants have been let go. Everybody's worried. I'm not happy where I am, but if I leave Mrs. Ingersoll's employ, I'm afraid I may not find another position."

"I'd be glad to hire you."

"You will?"

"Yes. Henrietta has been a great help with Dermot, but now that she's married, and me with a new baby on the way and French classes to teach, I'm going to need help. We have a spare bedroom for you."

Letta's eyes moistened. "Oh, Emily, that would be wonderful. You have no idea how dreadful it is to live in a house that's in perpetual mourning."

"I can imagine. When can you start?"

"I'll have to give my two weeks' notice."

"Of course." Emily embraced Letta. "Welcome to our home."

CHAPTER TWENTY-ONE

"That's not a good idea, Michael. Not a good idea at all."

Such was Gaylord's response to Michael's announcement that he was going to march in the Independence Day parade on July 4th.

They were eating at an oyster bar on Pine Street, where Gaylord was trying, one more time, to introduce his friend to oysters, the current rage of the city. But Michael would have none of it.

"And why is it not a good idea?" Michael asked, looking away as Gaylord slid another giant oyster into his mouth.

Gaylord wiped his mouth with a napkin. "You know there's bad blood between the Catholics and the Protestants nativists. Why would you want to march in their damn parade anyway? You're not even Catholic. You said so yourself. Are you sure you don't want an oyster?"

"I'm sure."

"You don't know what you're missing." Gaylord slid the plate of oysters toward Michael.

"I've gotten this far without eating an oyster," he said, sliding the plate back to Gaylord. "I imagine I can get through the rest of my life without them."

"Have you noticed all those oyster stands on street corners?"

"How could I not?"

"Some of the stands advertise all-you-can-eat oysters for six cents." He chuckled. "But here's the thing; if a customer eats too many oysters, the vender slips him a bad one to make him sick."

"Well, I'll never have to worry about that."

"Pity. You don't know what you're missing."

"About the parade, I'm a businessman now, Gaylord. I've got to make connections and that means keeping on the good side of the likes of Tammany and that other group—what's it called?"

"The Ancient Order of Hibernians," Gaylord said dryly.

"I've been told it's going to be a peaceful parade."

The newspaperman roared with laughter. "There is no such thing as a peaceful parade in Manhattan, my good friend. I'll give you an example. Back in '24, Irish Protestants marched to commemorate the anniversary of the Battle of the Boyne and they clashed with Irish Catholics who didn't take kindly to the Protestants celebrating Protestant ascendancy in Ireland."

"What happened?"

"As you can imagine, there was a real donnybrook with many smashed heads and broken bones, but only the Catholics were arrested and charged with disturbing the peace."

"Well, there are a lot more Catholics in this city today, some even in the police force."

Gaylord waved a hand in dismissal. "It doesn't matter. There's bound to be trouble. And you'd do well to be out of it."

"I've got to go. I gave the men the day off tomorrow to march."

"How generous of you," Gaylord said in a voice dripping with sarcasm. "I suppose you know that neither Astor, nor Vanderbilt, nor all the other truly wealthy men in this city have been so magnanimous."

"I said I would march with them."

Gaylord downed his last oyster, made a sign of the cross in the air toward Michael, and intoned, "May the Lord have mercy on your soul."

It rained all that night, but the morning of July 4th was sunny with temperatures expected to be in the mid-eighties by noon. A fine day for a parade. By nine in the morning, hundreds of New Yorkers were strolling down Broadway on their way to the annual military parade. The air was filled with the smoke and sounds of firing cannons and the popping, fizzing, and whirring of fireworks.

Michael Ranahan, Flynn, and the Ranahan Construction employees joined up with 500 other Irish marchers wearing green scarves and badges at the corner of Hudson Street and Houston Street.

The sorrowful and tragic events Michael experienced in Ireland during the five years of the famine had dampened his ardor for the old county, but seeing the smiling faces of all those Irishmen standing under an enormous banner depicting George Washington shaking hands with Daniel O'Connell made him swell with pride. Looking around him, Michael was happy to see that Gaylord was wrong. This was not an angry assemblage bent on fighting and destruction; it was a gathering of men who just wanted to express their pride in being a Catholic Irishman.

A great din of whistles, booming drums, and shrieking bugles signaled that the parade had begun. At first, the men shuffled slowly, heads bobbing out of sync, but as the line stretched out, they fell into a steady stride as they marched up Hudson Street. A few bystanders watching them pass clapped and cheered, while others jeered, yelling out *"mackerel snappers," "papal bastards," "bog runners,"* and worse.

A grinning Michael and other marchers cheerfully waved at them. If that was the worst they could do, it would be a good day.

The plan was for the Irish marchers to meet up with the main line of march at Abingdon Square in Greenwich Village. As they approached the square, Michael saw that there were perhaps a thousand marchers milling about. As the two groups converged, Hudson Street became clogged with a sea of men carrying a variety of banners and flags.

Seeing a motion out of the corner of his eye, Michael looked to his left and saw an omnibus coming out of Bank Street. He didn't know if the horses were spooked by the sight and roar of the men or if someone had prodded them, but for whatever reason the horses bolted into the ranks of the Hibernians, knocking down scores of men. To Michael's horror he saw a group of angry, bellowing men pull the driver down from his box and proceed to beat him with fists and flagstaffs.

As if this were some kind of signal, the Protestant marchers rushed the Catholic contingent. In seconds, hundreds of men were punching, kicking, and clubbing each other. The George Washington shaking hands with Daniel O'Connell banner was torn down. As Michael fought to defend himself, he noticed two groups that, moments before, had been standing on the sidewalks, seemingly not part of the marchers. But as the fighting started, they gleefully waded into the Catholic marchers punching and swinging clubs with abandon. Gaylord would later tell Michael that one group was a local gang called the Short Boys. The second group were volunteer firemen who rushed the marchers crying, "*Kill the Catholic sons of bitches!*"

Michael didn't know how long the battle lasted, but he was grateful to see a wedge of policemen rushing down Eighth Avenue toward them. Terrified and exhausted, he hoped they would put a stop to this madness. Then to his dismay, he watched as the policemen waded into the crowd clubbing anyone who was wearing the scarf and badge of the Irish Catholics.

Flynn had fallen to the ground after a vicious blow to the side of the head. Michael grabbed him by the scruff of the neck and pulled him up. "*We've got to get out of here, Flynn.*" He yelled to his men. "*Come on, men, follow me.*"

With renewed ferocity, Michael and his men clubbed and punched their way through the crowd and away from the advancing policemen. They broke free of the melee and kept running until they reached Houston Street. It was only then that Michael stopped to assess the damage to his sweating and panting men. All of them, including himself, were bleeding from head wounds. Two had superficial stab wounds, but nothing that required more than a bandage. Looking at his men, he again experienced the same flashback he'd had standing on the steps of the Eighth Ward Headquarters that election day. "*He'd led his men into a disastrous march to Cork Harbor, and now he'd done it again.*" Gaylord's stern warning rang in his ears. "*There's bound to be trouble. And you'd do well to be out of it.*" "I'm sorry, men," he said, his voice breaking. "I never should have allowed you to march today."

Flynn wiped his bloody nose with his sleeve. "It's not your fault, Michael. It's those damn nativists. They outnumbered us today, but one day ..." His voice trailed off.

"We can't keep fighting each other. For God's sake, we're all Americans, aren't we?"

Flynn shook his head. "No, Michael you're wrong there. There's *Irish* Americans, and there's *native* Americans. Two entirely different breeds all together."

Michael saw the other men nod in agreement. He was too tired, too sore, and too frightened to argue with them. "Go on home, men. I'll see you at work tomorrow."

As Emily dressed the gash on Michael's scalp, Gaylord read aloud from the *Brooklyn Daily Eagle*. "*Dozens of Irishmen were arrested for inciting the riot. They were solely responsible for the disturbance of the peace—*"

"That's a damn lie. We were attacked by *them*."

Gaylord continued reading. *"The marchers, armed with pistols, staves, and stones attacked anyone regardless of age or physical condition. The nativist spectators who joined in the riot were described as peaceful citizens who tried to reason with the Hibernians before being attacked and forced to fight to defend themselves. There was promise of serious results, but the riot was speedily quelled when a formidable body of police turned a corner at a double-quick, and the rioters scattered instantly. Happily, no person was mortally wounded in the encounter."*

Michael shook his head. "None of that is true. The police attacked *us*."

Gaylord folded the paper and tossed it on the table. "Just be grateful that neither you nor any of your men was killed or seriously injured."

"I agree," Emily said. "When are you going to learn, Michael? First, two elections, then this parade and you come home with your head busted open every time."

Michael grinned ruefully. "I guess it's a good thing I have a hard head."

For days, Emily, still shaken by what had happened at the parade, was curt with him and what conversation there was, was kept to a minimum. Michael tried to reason with her. "I got my head busted open, that's all. It wasn't so bad."

"*It wasn't so bad?*" she exploded. "What if you'd have been seriously injured or killed? What would become of me and Dermot and the coming baby? What would become of your business? You've got serious responsibilities, now, Michael." Tears welled up in her eyes. "You've got to think of us."

Michael was jolted by what she said. He hadn't given it much thought, but she was right. What if he'd been seriously injured, or, God forbid, killed? What would become of them? He'd been selfish. He'd put furthering his business interests above his family.

He would not make that mistake again.

He went to her and put his arms around her. At first, she pulled away, but he brought her back to him. "Emily, I'm sorry. You're right. What I did was stupid."

Emily buried her head in his chest. "Michael, I don't know what I'd do if you ... if you were ..."

He kissed her. "Put that out of your head. Nothing is going to happen to me." To lighter the mood, he said, "Remember back in April when we saw them building the Crystal Palace?"

"That strange looking building with all that cast-iron?"

"The same. Well, it opened last week. Let's go see it next Sunday. I'll ask Gaylord if he'd like to join us. I'm sure he can explain a lot of what we'll see there."

That Sunday afternoon, Henrietta took Dermot, who'd just turned two the previous month, to the park. Michael and Emily had agreed they would meet Gaylord at the Crystal Palace. At one in the afternoon, they stepped off the omnibus at Sixth and Forty-Second Street. Now that the Crystal Palace was completed, it looked even more magnificent than the cast-iron frame they'd seen under construction last April.

Gaylord came up behind them. "Magnificent, is it not?"

"It's beyond words," Emily said, gaping at the towering structure before them.

"It's officially called the *Exhibition of the Industry of All Nations*, and from what I've read it is not an exaggerated claim. Our own Walt Whitman has penned a poem about it called, *Song of the Exposition*. There is one stanza that stands out for me:

Mightier than Egypt's tombs,
Fairer than Grecia's, Roma's temples,
Prouder than Milan's statued, spired Cathedral,
More picturesque than Rhenish castle-keeps,
We plan, even now, to raise, beyond them all,
Thy great Cathedral, sacred Industry—no tomb,
A Keep for life for practical Invention.

Slightly embarrassed by his bombastic, theatric tone, he said, "Shall we go in?"

Although it was a sultry August afternoon, the interior was surprisingly cool. The glass and cast-iron frame gave the building a curiously light feeling, unlike the typically ponderous structures of brick and wood.

Once inside, they saw that the building was in the shape of a Greek cross with three entrances on Sixth Avenue, Fortieth Street, and Forty-Second Street. At the juncture of the four arms a 100-foot diameter dome rose 123 feet from the floor. The interior was so immense as to stagger the imagination, dwarfing even the imposing Equestrian George Washington statue in the center of the main hall.

Opening the guidebook, *How To See The New York Crystal Palace*, Gaylord read, "Two dozen cast iron columns support the dome, each sixty-two feet high. Thirty-two stained glass windows decorate the sides of the dome, each representing the arms of the individual states as well as that of the Union."

They followed the crowds wandering the building's halls past shimmering fountains and glaring clusters of gas-lights. They marveled at the miracles of the age, great and small: scales, meters, guns, lamps, safes, clocks, carriages, scientific instruments, agricultural instruments, a Fresnel lighthouse lens, telegraphy and photography equipment, fire engines, ships, and plans for an elevated railroad above Broadway.

To reach the second story, they climbed one of twelve broad staircases. The cast-iron fittings, the staircases, and railings were painted a rich cream color accented in red, blue, and yellow, giving it a gay, festive look.

An hour into their tour, Gaylord glanced at his pocket watch. "Come," he said, taking Emily and Michael by the arm. "There is going to be a demonstration of a steam-powered elevator. This is something we must not miss."

At the north end of the main hall, a crowd had already gathered around a curious structure—a tower thirty feet tall with a large platform at the ground level.

A young man with a full beard and wearing a top hat and a black frock coat stepped onto the platform. Pulling a lever, he activated the steam engine and the elevator jerked to a start. Up, up it went until it was suspended twenty-five feet in the air, a single strand of rope holding the elevator in place.

Then the man did a curious thing. He called out to his assistant, who was stationed at the top of the tower, "*Cut the rope*."

A gasp went up from the crowd. Without hesitation, the assistant swung his axe severing the rope. Some women averted their eyes, others turned away, some screaming, some swooning. The breathless crowd of onlookers waited for the platform to come crashing to the ground, but it dropped only a few inches, and then, amazingly, came to a stop.

Michael immediately grasped what had happened. "Did you see that?"

Emily and Gaylord shook their heads too dumbfounded to speak.

Michael explained. "When the hoist rope was cut, it released the tension on those clamping devices that grip the guide rails and they acted like some kind of brake."

Emily stared up at the grinning man on the platform who was tipping his hat to the crowd below. "Who is he?"

Gaylord consulted his guidebook. "That would be one Elisha Graves Otis. I do believe we will be hearing from this young man in the future."

Fascinated by what he had just seen, Michael couldn't take his eyes off the mechanism. "Do you know what this means? It means that with a safety elevator, we'll be able to construct buildings taller than four or five stories."

Gaylord nodded, finally grasping with Michael was saying. "Literally, the sky's the limit."

When they came out of the exhibit, Emily saw an odd, faraway look in her husband's eyes.

"What are you thinking, Michael?"

"Watching that elevator demonstration and looking at all those modern tools in there has convinced me that there is a great future in this city. We will not only build this city out, we will build it up."

CHAPTER TWENTY-TWO

With the birth of her child only two months way, Emily invited the midwife to tea to discuss arrangements. As the elderly woman sat across the table from her stirring her tea, Emily said, "I've asked you to stop by, Mary, because I'm pregnant and I want to—"

The old woman's eyes widened. "Oh, no missus. You must not be pregnant."

"Well, I am, and I'll need your help—"

The old woman shook her head. "Do you remember the terrible time you had with your delivery?"

"Yes, but everything's all right, isn't it?"

"I'm not a doctor, missus, but I've been a midwife for over forty years and I've seen a thing or two. It's my belief that you cannot, you *should* not, have this baby."

Emily felt a wave of dizziness overcome her. Not have the baby? What was her alternative, abortion? She couldn't even think of that possibility. "Mary, why won't you help me?"

The old woman's eyes focused on her teacup and both her gnarled hands grasped it tightly. "Things are changing in midwifery," she began slowly. "For as long as I can remember, male doctors wanted no part of the duties of a midwife. It was considered work fit only for a woman. Still, to protect our livelihood, we midwives take an oath that we will not reveal—" she cocked her head trying to remember the exact wording— "… any matter appertaining to your office in the presence of any man." She nodded firmly, pleased that she gotten it right.

"What does this have to do with my having a baby?"

"The doctors have invented a device—forceps, they call it. Now they're assisting us midwifes with difficult births. That was welcome help, but lately, they've been trying to take over entirely the work of the midwife."

Emily shook her head. "I still don't understand …"

"Don't you see, missus, they're watching us carefully. If I make a mistake and a baby or the mother dies, they'll hound me out of the business. They've done it before to others, I can tell you."

Emily was incredulous. "Are you saying you won't take the chance with my birth?"

The old woman's eyes teared up. "I *can't* take the chance, missus. It's the only work I know. I'm too old to work in a factory."

Sunday night dinner at the Ranahans had without premeditation become a tradition. It began with inviting Gaylord, then Letta, then Henrietta and Cully. It was so ingrained in everyone that they just showed up without the need of an invitation.

Half-way through dinner, a blushing Letta said in a soft voice, "I have an announcement to make."

"What is it, child?" Henrietta asked.

"I'm engaged."

Emily jumped up and embraced her young friend. "Oh, Letta, that's wonderful. Who is the lucky man?"

"His name is Otto Schmidt and he owns a beer garden in Kleindeutschland."

"We must meet this lucky man," Michael said.

Henrietta clapped her hands. "Yes, you must bring him to dinner next Sunday."

"I will."

Shortly after dinner, Letta left to meet her Otto. Emily pulled Henrietta into the parlor, away from the men. "Isn't that wonderful news about Letta?"

"It is. I was beginning to wonder when she would meet a suitable young man. I'm very happy for her."

Emily sat down. "Henrietta, I need your advice."

Seeing the concerned expression on her friend's face, Henrietta said, "Whatever is the matter, Emily?"

After Emily told her what the midwife had told her, Henrietta took Emily's hands in hers.

"You poor dear. Have you told Michael?"

"Yes, and he agrees with me. I can't—I *won't*—have an

abortion. But what am I to do?"

"What about another midwife?"

Emily shook her head. "Mary said that the way things are, no midwife will risk taking on a difficult birth."

Henrietta thought for a moment and then snapped her fingers. "Elizabeth Blackwell."

"Who's she?"

"She's the first woman to receive a medical degree in the United States. In fact, Gaylord wrote an article about her in the *New York Tribune*."

Emily jumped up. "Let's talk to him."

Emily barged into the dining room, breaking up a heated conversation between Cully and Michael over the need to buy a new wagon.

"Gaylord, what do you know about Elizabeth Blackwell?"

The newspaperman nodded at the mention of her name. "Ah, yes, quite an extraordinary woman. I wrote a story about her in the *Tribune*. She's originally from England. She came here and applied to over twenty medical colleges in New York and Philadelphia and they all turned her down. Finally, she was accepted at Geneva Medical College in upstate New York. It was a highly unusual process to say the least. The faculty couldn't decide whether to admit her, so they put it to the vote of the one hundred and fifty male students with the proviso that if one student objected, she would be rejected. It was an amazing outcome, considering the hostility men have toward women in the medical profession. Every male student voted for acceptance. She graduated first in class."

Henrietta clapped her hands. "That's marvelous. Where does she practice in the city?"

"Ah, there's the rub. Even though she's a certified medical doctor, the male doctors in the city have barred her from all hospitals and dispensaries."

Emily felt her hopes of finding a sympathetic doctor fading. "So, she has no practice?" she asked dully.

"She's not affiliated with any hospitals in the city, but she has opened a one-room dispensary on Seventh Street near Tompkins Square Park."

Emily took a deep breath. "Then I must go see her. She's my

only hope."

The next day, Emily took the omnibus to Avenue A and Seventh Street. She knew immediately where the dispensary was by the long line of women patiently waiting to get in. Judging from the way these women were dressed, it was apparent that they were the poor from the Five Points and surrounding areas.

Emily waited in line for almost an hour before she was admitted to the one-room clinic. The room, sparsely furnished, contained only a couple of old battered benches, a desk that had seen better days, and a cabinet containing medical supplies and equipment.

A young woman with large, kindly eyes came around the desk and offered her hand.

"Hello, I'm Doctor Blackwell," she said with a soft English accent. "And you are?"

"Emily Ranahan," Emily answered, slightly taken aback. She expected the doctor to be older and someone with the stern visage of a medical doctor. Instead, this woman was around her own age and was almost shy in her demeanor.

"What can I do for you, Mrs. Ranahan?"

"I'm pregnant," she blurted out.

The doctor smiled, looking at Emily's protruding stomach. "I surmised as much."

"I'm sorry, that was stupid. I mean I'm pregnant and I'm told I should not have this baby."

"Do you wish to have an abortion?"

Emily blanched. "No, no, nothing like that."

"Of course, it's your choice. But you should know that abortion is often safer than childbirth. The abortion rate in this city is about twenty percent. For some women, it's the only form of birth control available to them. Do you object on religious grounds?"

"No. I just want to have this baby."

"Very well. May I examine you?"

"Yes, of course."

When the doctor was finished with her examination, she said "Mrs. Ranahan, who said you should not have this baby?"

When Emily finished telling her about her conversation with Mary the midwife, Dr. Blackwell's soft brown eyes turned hard. "Your midwife is correct about one thing; doctors are encroaching on the occupations of midwives and I can understand her reluctance to take you on. On the other hand, she's wrong about your ability to have this baby. As you described your first birth, and my examination of you, there is no reason to believe you cannot deliver a healthy baby. Excessive bleeding is not uncommon, especially with the first child."

A wave of relief swept over Emily. "Oh, thank you, Doctor. Would you be willing to take me on as a patient?"

The doctor frowned. "It's not my usual business practice, Mrs. Ranahan. In this dispensary, I offer a wide variety of medical help to my patients, all of whom are desperately poor."

Emily was acutely aware that she did not fit the mold of the women with whom she had waited in line. It almost seemed selfish of her to take up the time of this doctor who had apparently decided to devote her life to the poor, but she was desperate. "Dr. Blackwell, I have no one else to turn to. I need you. I would be willing to pay whatever your fee is."

"It's not about the money, Mrs. Ranahan, it's about the time. I have only twenty-four hours a day to devote to my practice. I try to avoid anything that takes me away from that." When she saw the stricken look on Emily's face, she softened her tone. "I will, however, make an exception in your case. The birth will be at your home for, as you can see, I have no birthing facilities here. But you will come here for your prenatal care and checkups."

"Oh, thank you, Dr. Blackwell. Thank you."

The following Sunday, Letta brought her fiancé to dinner. Michael took one look at the heavy-set man with an enormous handlebar mustache and said, "You look very familiar … Oh ... now I remember. Weren't you a bartender at the Volksgarten Beer Garden?"

"I was. Now I own it," Otto said proudly.

"I came into the beer garden with a co-worker named Flynn."

"Flynn. Yes, of course. Do you still see my good friend?"

"Yes, he works for me."

Otto frowned. "I'm sorry to hear that. We both used to talk about owning our own businesses."

"Don't feel sorry for him, Otto. Since I made him a foreman he's sworn that he would never want to own his own business."

Otto shook his head in agreement. "It is a lot of headaches, but I manage."

A smiling Emily took Otto's arm. "Come with me, Otto. It's time for dinner."

January 15, 1854 was the third day of a vicious cold wave that gripped the city. The ominous gun-metal clouds rolling in low and fast from the northeast promised snow. Around noon, as Emily placed a bowl of soup in front of Dermot, she felt a sharp pain in her side. It wasn't all that unusual. For a month now, she'd been experiencing sharp pains and cramps. She sat down at the kitchen table to catch her breath. Letta poured her a cup of tea.

Suddenly, without warning, Dermot swept his bowl of soup off the table. "*I no want,*" he screeched.

Emily gripped the table to control her temper. "Dermot, you do not throw your food on the floor."

In response to her reprimand, he began screaming uncontrollably and banging his spoon on the table.

As Letta tried to calm him down, Emily bent down to clean up the mess. As she was getting up, she felt a wetness on her legs. "Oh, Letta, I think my water just broke." She pulled the screaming Dermot out of his chair. "Go to your room. Right now!"

Dermot knew from her tone of voice that she meant business. Sulking, he stomped upstairs.

A frightened Letta helped Emily sit down. "Is it time?"

"I think so. Michael must be told."

As had been previously arranged, Letta sent the boy next door to the job site to tell Michael what was happening.

By the time the boy found Michael it had begun to snow. "Mr. Ranahan, I'm to tell you your wife is going to have a baby."

Michael rushed over to a wagon being unloaded. "I need this wagon. Get everything cleared off, now!"

The men began tossing bricks and lumber into the street with reckless abandon. Almost before they finished, Michael was in the box with the reins in his hands and had turned the horse south, toward Seventh Street.

By the time he got to Dr. Blackwell's dispensary, the snow was sticking to the ground and the swirling wind and snow had reduced visibility to almost zero.

He rushed past the line of patiently-waiting women and into the dispensary. “Dr. Blackwell, my wife is going to have the baby.”

Calmly, the doctor pulled her assistant aside. “Mary, tell those waiting that I’ve been called away on an emergency. We will resume tomorrow.” Grabbing her medical bag, she said, “All right, Mr. Ranahan, let’s go.”

Ignoring the poor visibility and the stumbling horse and sliding wagon, Michael pushed the horse as fast as he could go. He drove north on Avenue A to Fourteenth Street, then turned west. At Sixth Avenue, he turned north and urged the horse forward. The visibility had grown so bad that at one point he almost ran into the back of a stalled wagon.

“Mr. Ranahan,” Dr. Blackwell said coolly, “I won’t be able to help your wife if I die before I get there.”

“You’re right, Doctor, I’m sorry.” Michael reined in the horse and proceeded up the avenue with greater caution. By the time they got to the house there was six inches of snow on the ground.

Emily was already in bed. Following Dr. Blackwell’s instructions, Letta had on hand plenty of clean towels and a kettle full of hot water. More water was being heated on the stove downstairs.

The doctor took Michael’s arm and led him to the door. “It looks like everything is under control, Mr. Ranahan. We’ll call you if you’re needed.”

Michael went to Dermot’s room, where his son was playing with two wooden locomotives.

Michael knelt beside his son and ruffled his hair. “Well, my little man, it looks like very soon you are going to have a little brother or sister.”

“I don’t want a brother or sister,” he hissed.

Michael was shaken at the vehemence in his son’s tone. “That’s no way to talk, Dermot. It’ll be fun having another little person around.”

“*No, it won’t. No, it won’t.*” As he repeated the phrase, he started to pound one locomotive into the other.

Michael pulled the toys out of his hand. “Stop that, Dermot, you’ll break your toys.”

“I don’t care.”

Michael got up and sat on the bed, unhappily studying his son. Emily had been saying for some time that Dermot was out of control and was given to sudden tantrums. Being at work all day he'd missed most of those episodes. He'd almost convinced himself that his wife was exaggerating. Perhaps the strain of the pregnancy had made her more irritable and less tolerant of a little boy. But seeing his son's behavior now convinced him that his wife had been right. Michael felt a chill. His son was acting just as his brother Dermot had acted as a little boy. He prayed that his son would not have the kind of short, tragic life his brother had.

After he put Dermot to bed, he went downstairs and made himself a cup of tea. For the next couple of hours, he heard moaning coming from the bedroom and the soft murmur of voices.

Around five o'clock, Dr. Blackwell came into the kitchen. "The birth went well, Mr. Ranahan. Your wife is resting comfortably. You can go see her."

Michael pumped the woman's hand. "Oh, thank you, Dr. Blackwell. Thank you."

Just as he was rushing out of the kitchen, he turned. "Oh, is it a boy or a girl?"

"You have a daughter, sir."

Letta was sitting next to Emily, wiping her forehead with a damp cloth.

Michael kissed his wife's clammy cheek. "How are you feeling?"

"Better than last time," she said in weak voice. "Dr. Blackwell was wonderful."

"You're wonderful, too," he said, brushing her damp hair away from her cheeks. Gently, he pulled back the blanket to view his new daughter "She's beautiful," he whispered.

Emily smiled and nodded.

"What will we name her?"

"Eleanor."

"Eleanor?"

"It was my mother's name."

Michael was only a child at the time, but he vaguely remembered her mother, a beautiful and graceful woman, but he never knew her Christian name. He recalled that her mother died in 1835. Emily would have been ten at the time.

"Eleanor, that's a nice name."

"Yes, isn't it …" she whispered, and slowly dropped off to sleep.

CHAPTER TWENTY-THREE

Early November was colder than usual, but with no snow in sight it was a good day for Ranahan Construction crews.

With genuine pride and satisfaction, Michael stood in the doorway of his warehouse and watched his seven wagons and thirty-five men start out for their respective sites. After eighteen months, he still could scarcely believe he was the owner of his own construction company. He was getting so much work that he was thinking of taking on a few more men and perhaps even another wagon. He would never tell Cully, but his ability to get along with real estate men, builders, and other contractors was largely responsible for the increase in new projects.

As Michael watched the last wagon disappear into the heavy traffic of Pearl Street, a heavy-set young man dressed in the ill-fitting clothing of a dandy approached.

"Is it Mr. Ranahan?" he asked with an oily smile.

"I am."

"Tommy Walsh says to say hello."

"Is it a job you're looking for?" Michael asked, dubiously eyeing up the chubby man. One look told him he wouldn't last a day in construction.

"Oh, no. Nothing like that. I have a position at Tammany Hall."

"So, what can I do for you?"

"You know election day is just three days away?"

Michael's stomach knotted. He knew this moment was coming, but it was not something he was looking forward to. Since that contentious election in 1851, when he stood on the steps of the Eighth Ward Headquarters to deny Butcher Bill and his Bowery Boys access to the ballot box, elections had been routine and uneventful. There was no need for the extra muscle of the working-class Irish. But this year was different. Fernando Wood was running for mayor and he was opposed by a determined coalition of nativists, Know-Nothings, and Whigs.

Michael turned around. "Come into my office."

He sat behind his desk and eyed the smiling young man. "What is it you want of me?"

"I'm sure you know this is going to be a very important election for Tammany. There's a bunch of people in this city that don't want Mr. Wood to be mayor."

"I'm aware of that."

"So, Tammany will require the services of you and all your men on election day."

Michael took a breath before answering. "I can't do that."

The young man's eyes bulged, as though Michael had said that he was personally running against Wood. His jovial mood suddenly changed. "What the hell do you mean, you can't do it? You have to."

"I'm sorry. I can't help Tammany this year. I have several contracts that are on deadline. If I don't complete the work by the contractual date, I face a financial penalty I can ill-afford."

The man's face reddened and he slammed his ham fist down on Michael's desk. "I don't give a flying fuck about your financial penalty."

"You don't have to," Michael said, trying his best to remain calm. "But I do."

The enraged man glanced around the warehouse. "It would be a shame if your warehouse should burn down."

Michael lunged across the desk and grabbed the surprised man by his lapels. "If that should ever happen," he hissed, "I will come looking for you and, I swear to God you will end up floating in the East River." He yanked the man to his feet. "Now get out."

As one of Tammany's men, he was unaccustomed to being treated this way. In confusion, he smoothed his gaudy suit and pointed a shaky finger at Michael. "I'll be sure to tell Tommy Walsh what you said."

"You do that."

For a long while after the man had gone, Michael sat his desk shaking with rage. After he calmed down, he glumly considered the ramifications of what he had just done. He had defied

Tammany and there would be a price to pay. The only question was: how big a price?

The election of 1854 was indeed violent and accompanied by the usual chicanery. In the end, Fernando Wood won by four thousand votes more than there were voters. It was rumored that the day before the election, the Dead Rabbits combed the city's cemeteries for names to add to the voter rolls.

Lying in bed on a cold blustery night in early March, Michael turned to Emily and said, "I'm thinking of expanding the business."

"Are you?"

"Yes. I'm getting more business than I can handle. I'm thinking if I buy a few more wagons and hire a few more men, I can really increase the value of the business. We've talked about buying our own home. If I can bring in more contracts, we'll be able to do that in a year or so. I'm going to talk to Mr. Hainsworth about getting another loan."

"It's funny that you should mention a loan. With all the additional students coming to my classes, the parlor isn't big enough. I think it's time to move to a location outside of the house. Do you think your loan could cover the expense of renovating the space and buying desks and chairs?"

"I don't see why not. Of course, we'll have to find a suitable location."

"I already have. I've found a wonderful location over on Sixth Avenue."

Michael squeezed his wife's hand. "Aren't you the resourceful one?"

She kissed him. "Well, I've got to keep up with you, don't I?"

Charles Hainsworth motioned Michael into a comfortable leather chair. "I haven't seen you since we negotiated the loan to buy your business. How are Mrs. Ranahan and your two children?"

"Actually, there are four now. Peter is two and Claire is almost six months."

"So, you have quite the growing family."

"I do."

"And how is your business coming along?"

"It's grand and I'm thankful for that. In fact, I have more work than I can handle. And that's why I've come to see you. I'd like another loan."

"Well, you certainly couldn't have picked a more propitious time. Our fair city is thriving. Manufacturing and transport sectors are expanding in leaps and bounds. As you are certainly aware, everywhere you look buildings are going up. New York City is quickly becoming the premier city in the world."

The banker opened a cigar humidor and offered Michael a cigar, which he declined.

Hainsworth sat back and exhaled a cloud of smoke that surrounded him like a blue halo. "What do you want the funds for?"

"Two things, Mr. Hainsworth. Right now, I have seven wagons and thirty-five men working for me. I would like to buy another three wagons and hire another fifteen men."

The banker nodded. "That seems reasonable given the building boom in the city. What was the other thing?"

"My wife's French classes have been taking on more and more students and there's not enough room in our house to accommodate them all. We found a suitable space in a building on Sixth Avenue. We would have to renovate the space to suit Emily's needs. And we would have to furnish it with desks and chairs."

"It sounds like you've thought this through."

"I have. But to tell you the truth, I'm terrified at the thought of taking on an additional loan. What would be your advice?"

"Of course, I will have to examine your books to ensure a loan is feasible. As I explained to you the first time, a bank wants to be assured that it's paid back. In the unlikely event of a default, the bank would be forced to seize your assets to recoup the cost of the loan. Having said that, it's clear that you are a responsible businessman. As for your wife's French classes, I hear nothing but praise from my wife and daughter, who, by the way, speaks French flawlessly now. My advice, Mr. Ranahan, is to take the loan."

When Michael got home, Emily was feeding baby Claire and the other three children were playing a game with Letta.

"How did it go?"

Michael kissed his wife. “He’ll have to look at the books, but he doesn’t see a problem. There’ll be enough money to buy the extra wagons and hire the men.”

“And my school?”

“That, too. He speaks very highly of you.”

Emily hugged him. “I’m so proud of you, Michael.”

Michael took a deep breath. “Mr. Hainsworth thinks it’s a good idea, but still, what if I can’t pay the loan?”

“You will, Michael, you will.”

CHAPTER TWENTY-FOUR

1857

Sunday breakfast at the Ranahans was always a raucous affair with four children needing to be fed at once. Usually, Letta was there to help, but she had gone with Otto to visit her parents in Kleindeutschland for the weekend. Emily stood over the stove preparing eggs and bacon. “Breakfast is ready.”

Michael scooped Claire up off the floor and placed her in her highchair. “Are you ready to eat?” he asked.

Claire banged her spoon. “Mama, mama …”

“I’ll take that to mean yes.”

Emily shot a worried glance at Michael. “She has no appetite.”

“Didn’t the doctor say she has a delicate stomach?”

Emily stroked her daughter’s wispy blonde hair. “I know, but she must eat. Look how thin she is?”

“She’ll do better as she gets older,” Michael said with more conviction than he felt. The truth was, Emily was right. Little Claire was unquestionably the sickliest of the four children.

That could not be said of two-year old Peter who scrambled up onto a chair next to his father. “I’m ready, Da,” he said in the serious way that he approached everything.

Michael tousled his son’s hair and grinned. “You’re always ready, aren’t you, Peter?”

“Yes, Da.”

As usual, Eleanor made her dramatic entrance. She had a stately way about her, almost regal, which Michael attributed to her mother’s lineage. For certain her imperial demeanor did not come from the Ranahan line of tenant farmers.

Emily studied her daughter and smiled, “My, my what a pretty frock."

"Thank you, Mother."

"Just think, Michael, she's only three and see how well she dresses herself."

"Like a little princess."

As Eleanor took her seat, Emily dished out the eggs and bacon. "Where's Dermot?"

"Late as usual," Michael said, trying to keep the frustration out of his voice. "*Dermot*," he bellowed, "*get down here*."

They heard the heavy footsteps of protest on the stairs. A sullen Dermot came into the kitchen and threw himself into a chair.

"Good morning, Dermot," Emily said, trying to ease the immediate tension that her son generally caused when he came into a room.

The boy stared at his plate in silence.

"Dermot," Michael said, "Your mother said good morning."

"What's so good about it?"

Michael was about to reprimand his son, but he saw the warning look from his wife and he refrained.

They ate in strained silence. Just as they were finishing up, Dermot jumped up.

"Where do you think you're going?" Michael asked.

"My room."

"You know you don't leave the table without permission."

It had all been Emily's idea. She had been raised in a refined household. Manners and proper decorum were to be adhered to at all times. At first, Michael thought it silly to impose such restrictions on young children, but when she explained that if children didn't learn proper manners at an early age, it might prove impossible to teach them later, he realized she was right. Looking at his surly son, he also realized there was a lot more to do in the manners department.

Dermot rolled his eyes. "Can I leave?"

Michael hesitated, trying to decide if he should punish his son for his rude behavior, but it was such a beautiful morning that he didn't want to ruin it for the rest of them. "You may leave," he said, curtly.

Taking advantage of the weather, Michael and Emily took the other three children out to the garden in the back. The advertisement for the house had promised a garden “filled with elegant forest trees,” but the few scrawny trees that had been planted died the first winter. It was only through the efforts of Emily that the garden looked as inviting as it did. Every spring, she planted new trees and shrubs and tenderly care for the existing ones.

When they’d first moved in here, Fortieth Street was mostly vacant lots with a few squatter’s shanties scattered here and there. But now, more and more residential and commercial buildings were going up all around them. The serenity that they’d enjoyed when they’d first moved here was shattered by the constant sounds of construction and traffic. It was only here in the garden that the outside sounds were muffled.

Michael and Emily sat in the shade of a young poplar watching their children play with their blocks and trucks and dolls.

After a long silence, he said, “What are we going to do with him?”

Emily shook her head. “I don’t know. He’s not like the other children. Look how well they play together.”

“What’s to be done?”

“I don’t know, Michael. I wish I knew.”

Although it had been almost seven years since Gaylord Temple had tried to get Michael to develop a taste for oysters, he hadn’t given up and today they were at an oyster bar on Rector Street.

“So, how’s business?”

“It’s grand. Purchasing those additional wagons and hiring fifteen more men was the best thing I’ve ever done.”

Gaylord shoved the plate of oysters toward Michael. “Are you sure you don’t want one?”

Michael pushed the plate away. “Positive. I’ll just drink my beer and watch you swallow those disgusting things.”

The newspaperman shrugged. “Suit yourself. You know, the city has gone quite mad.”

“Why do you say that?”

“Have you ever heard of a city with *two* police departments?”

“What city would that be?”

“New York City. Where else?”

“You mean *here*?”

"I do."

"How can that be?"

"It's all politics, as usual. Upstate Republican legislators believe there is massive police corruption under Mayor Fernando Wood."

Michael grunted. "Well, they're right about that. Do you know how much money I have to pay out to a non-ending stream of beat patrolmen and inspectors to keep from getting tickets for everything from blocking the sidewalks to overloaded carts?"

"Which is why the upstate Republicans passed a law called the Metropolitan Police Act. Among other things, it abolishes the Municipal Police Department and authorizes the creation of a Metropolitan Police Force under the supervision of five commissioners appointed by the governor; thus, cutting Mayor Wood out of control of the police."

"What does Wood have to say about all this?"

"As one would expect, he refuses to recognize the authority of the Metropolitan Police Department." The newspaperman rubbed his hands together. "Well, now it's getting hot. The new commission has ordered Mayor Wood to disband the Municipal police and turn over its property to the Metropolitans. Wood has refused to comply."

"Can he do that?"

"He's done it, and now the city is in chaos. Criminals arrested by the Municipals are set free by the Metropolitans. Both police departments are fighting over possession of station houses and equipment. It's all quite madcap."

"I can imagine."

Gaylord glanced at his pocket watch and stood up. "I've got to get over to City Hall. I have it on good authority that Metropolitan police captain George Walling is going to deliver a second warrant for the mayor's arrest.

"Second warrant?"

"Yes. The first time Walling attempted to serve the warrant, he was tossed out of City Hall by the Municipals. Do you want to come? It might be entertaining."

"Sounds like fun, but I've got an appointment with an architect."

When Gaylord arrived at City Hall dozens of uniformed

Municipals were already lined up on the top steps of City Hall. At the foot of the steps was a motley collection of rough looking men armed with clubs. Gaylord recognized most of them as Dead Rabbits.

A roar went up from the crowd as Captain Walling and a phalanx of uniformed Metropolitan policemen advanced toward City Hall.

Gaylord rushed out to meet the captain. With his barrel chest, dark eyebrows, and piercing blue eyes, the captain had all physical characteristics of a no-nonsense policeman.

"Good afternoon, Captain Walling. I'm Gaylord Temple from the *New York Tribune*. Why are you here today?"

"I am here to serve a warrant on Mayor Fernando Wood at the behest of the board of commissioners."

"Captain, how do you propose to gain entry to City Hall? As you can see, it's guarded by a rather large contingent of Municipal policemen. And the rabble on the lower steps, judging by the blue stripe down their pantaloons, are members of the Dead Rabbits."

Captain Walling looked at them with scorn. "That is precisely why the Municipals must be disbanded. Under Mayor Wood, corruption is rampant. When the Metropolitan police force is clearly established, there will be no consorting with the likes of the Dead Rabbits or their ilk. Now, if you'll excuse me, I have a warrant to serve."

As there were many more Municipals than Metropolitans, Gaylord assumed there would be no confrontation. But in an instant, the two groups converged and men on both sides started pummeling each other and swinging clubs with abandon. Men, knocked senseless, rolled helplessly down the steps only to be beaten again. Gaylord furiously took notes of the unfolding scene. He already knew what the headline of his story would be: *Police Riot in New York City.*

The battle between the two police forces raged for almost a half hour. Just when it looked hopeless for the outnumbered Metropolitans, a platoon from the Seventh Regiment appeared and advanced toward City Hall with fixed bayonets. With the soldiers outnumbering both groups, order was quickly restored. Captain Walling followed the soldiers into City Hall. Minutes later, a triumphant Walling escorted his prisoner, an infuriated Mayor

Wood, down the steps to a waiting police wagon.

As Wood was getting into the wagon, Gaylord called out, "Mr. Mayor, do you have anything to say?"

Recognizing the newspaperman, Wood said, "This is a travesty of justice. The state legislature is trying to turn New York City into a subjugated city. This will not stand."

CHAPTER TWENTY-FIVE

On a hot, sultry August day in 1857, one small, seemingly harmless event would explode into a world-wide crisis that would later be known as the Panic of 1857. It started when the New York branch of the Ohio Life Insurance and Trust Company suddenly closed its doors. Later investigations would reveal that the bank had been looted by its manager. Worse, the bank made reckless loans to stock market speculators. And the crisis widened. Many New York banks had made loans to the Ohio bank and now they panicked. They started calling in their outstanding loans. In the days that followed, hundreds of other firms would fail. By September, the panic had spread to Europe and banks in France and England were going bankrupt.

That Sunday night grim faces sat around the Ranahan table. As usual the children had been fed earlier and were up in their room playing.

"What does this mean?" Michael asked Gaylord.

The usually optimistic newspaperman was dour. "It's bad. Very bad. There have been fistfights on the floor of the stock exchange. Earlier this summer, my editor, Horace Greeley, wrote an editorial warning of a coming storm. 'For a long time now,' he wrote, 'it's been evident that our New York banks have been fiscally irresponsible.' He chided the luxury-mad New Yorkers for spending millions on houses and gaudy furniture. He predicted that the tremendous levels of speculation in stocks and real estate would create a crisis. Events have shown him to be right."

"I've always said the nouveau riche would destroy this city," Henrietta said emphatically. "There are simply too many ignorant people speculating in the stock market. It's all a bubble."

Letta paled. For over a year she had been depositing her savings in a bank downtown in preparation for her wedding. "Are the banks safe here?" she asked in a small voice.

Gaylord shook his head. "If the past is any guide, more banks will shut their doors, there will be massive unemployment, and building construction will come to a standstill. The economy will sink into recession. I see no other result."

Emily saw the stricken expression on Michael's face and squeezed his hand. "How long could this last, Gaylord?"

"I don't know, Emily. No one does."

"I think you're wrong about construction coming to a standstill," Cully said. "These rich people are pouring fortunes into their mansions. If I know them, they're not going to abandon their investments. Don't you agree, Michael?"

Like a drowning man, Michael was filled with gratitude for Cully's optimistic note.

"I do. I do. We're working on mansions that cost millions. We're installing fine marble from Italy and stained glass from Germany. Walls are covered with frescos painted by fine artists. I can't imagine they would walk away from that."

That night, as they were preparing for bed, Michael was uncharacteristically quiet. Emily put her arms around him. "What is it, Michael?"

The pent-up anxiety that had been building up since dinner finally exploded. "You heard what Gaylord said about building construction coming to a standstill," Michael shouted. "I agreed with Cully because I want what he said to be true. But I have my doubts. My God, Emily, what will I do? What's to become of the business? I have six mouths to feed. I have fifty men depending on me for their wages."

Emily rested her head on his chest. "We'll just have to take it one day at a time. That's all we can do."

The next morning when Michael got to the warehouse, a glum Flynn came into the office and handed him several envelopes. "These were hand-delivered."

Each letter, sent from various law firms representing his clients, said essentially the same thing: *Stop work on building immediately.*

Michael threw the letters on the desk. "My God, Flynn, half of my projects have been pulled."

"Are you going to let the men go?"

"Not yet. We still have projects to work on. As long as there's money coming in, I'll keep all the men working.

That wasn't the only bad news. Since the beginning of the panic, Emily had been losing students one by one until there was no one left. Reluctantly, she stopped advertising in the newspaper and surrendered her lease on her Sixth Avenue school.

As August gave way to September, the effects of the panic grew increasingly worse. All along Fifth Avenue mansions lay half finished. The rich were firing servants in droves and angry men were meeting in Tompkins Square Park weekly demanding food and work. On block after block, banks that had been thriving a month ago were boarded up.

With each passing day, Michael dreaded receiving another letter canceling another building project. But so far, none had come. He was working with his crew at a building on Sixth Avenue when a breathless youngster ran into the building. "Is there a Mr. Ranahan here?" he asked.

Michael's heart sank. This could only be bad news. "I'm Ranahan."

"I'm to tell you that Mr. Hainsworth wishes to see you immediately."

With mounting dread, Michael hurried to the banker's office. When he got there, the usually placid office was in a state of chaos. Men with worried looks on their faces were rushing about with arms full of papers. One old gentleman sat in a corner weeping.

A pale and drawn Charles Hainsworth ushered Michael into his office.

"You wanted to see me, Mr. Hainsworth?"

"I did. I suppose you've heard about the financial panic?"

"Yes. Some of my projects have been withdrawn, but I'm managing."

The banker nodded, distractedly. "The future is bleak, very bleak, indeed," he said, as though he were talking to himself. "Forty thousand unemployed and almost a thousand merchants have shuttered their doors. Losses are at a staggering one hundred and twenty million dollars."

"I didn't know it was that bad."

"It is. Oh, it is." He finally looked at Michael. "I'm sorry, but I have to call in your loan."

For a moment, Michael's mind went blank and his stomach clenched. "I … I don't understand …"

Hainsworth turned away from Michael's bewildered expression. "I told you that there might come a time when we would have to call in your loan."

"You said that would happen if I didn't pay. I'm current on my monthly note."

"It doesn't matter, we have to call in the loan."

"Then you mislead me, Mr. Hainsworth. You said nothing about calling in the loan as long as I was current in my payments."

"It's in the fine print," the banker pointed out.

"Well, I guess I didn't read the fine print," Michael snapped back. "Mr. Hainsworth, I can't afford to pay off the entire loan. You know I don't have that kind of money."

"Then you leave us no choice but to seize your warehouse and all your assets."

"But you can't do that—"

"We can and we will."

Michael slumped in his chair. He hadn't read the fine print, but he was sure the banker was within his rights. There was no use in arguing further. "When?"

"Tomorrow morning I'll send men to board up the warehouse."

"What will you do with it?"

"Try to sell it. Although, God knows that will be difficult, given the hard times that are upon us."

"So, you're telling me I have to go back to my warehouse and inform fifty men that they are out of work?"

"Look at it from our point of view, Ranahan. Gotham Bank has lent millions and millions of dollars to other banks as well as individual clients. One by one they're going bankrupt or defaulting on their loans. We're losing a fortune. In fact, we may go under ourselves."

Michael stood up. "You'll get no sympathy from me, Mr. Hainsworth." And on those words, he stormed out the office.

He got back to the warehouse just as the men were returning. He waited until everyone was there. Then he came out of his office. "Men, listen up. I have some bad news."

All conversation stopped and it was suddenly deathly quiet. Judging by the expressions on their faces, they knew what was coming. "I've just come from my banker. They've called in my loan."

"What does that mean?" Flynn asked.

"It means I have to pay the full loan amount, but I don't have the money."

"What does that mean for us?" asked one of the workers whose wife was about to give birth.

"It means," Michael's voice cracked, "that as of tomorrow morning, the bank owns Ranahan Construction."

"Do you think they'll keep us on?" someone asked.

"No. Banks don't know how to run a construction company. They'll try to find a buyer."

The men were too stunned to protest. One by one, they filed out of the warehouse in silence. Michael went back to his office.

Flynn stood in the doorway. "What's next, Michael?"

"I need to find a job. So do you."

"I'm not so bad off. I don't have a family to feed."

Dreading telling Emily about what had just transpired, Michael aimlessly walked the streets for hours and what he saw made him even more depressed. On almost every block a bank was shuttered or a business boarded up. Hollow-eyed and disoriented men wandered the streets, some of them trying to peddle the tools of their trade. But, of course, there were no buyers. Finally, it started getting dark and he went home.

"Did you work late tonight?" Emily asked when he came through the door. "Your dinner is on the stove, I'll—" She stopped talking when she saw the expression on his face. Tears welled up in her eyes. "Is it bad, Michael?"

His eyes filled with tears. "I've lost the business, Emily. It's gone. Everything I've worked for since we came here is gone. All gone."

She rushed to him and buried her face in his chest. "I'm so sorry, Michael."

"No, I'm the one who's sorry. I've let you and the children down."

"Don't say that. You've always done your best for us. No one has worked harder than you."

"If only I hadn't taken out that second loan. I was blinded by greed."

"That's not true. You did what any decent man would do for his family; you tried to give us a better life."

He clung to her. "Emily, I can't believe I've lost everything in the blink of an eye."

She led him to the table and they both sat down. "All right, let's look at the bright side. All the children are healthy. We've put enough money aside so we can afford to stay here for at least a year. You'll get a job and we'll just start over. In the meantime, I can make money by bringing in laundry."

Michael slammed his hand down on the table. "You'll do no such thing. Your father was a lord, Emily. You were a lady."

Emily took his hand. "Michael," she said softly, "all that is gone. Lost and gone forever. Now, I'm just Emily Ranahan."

Michael kissed her hand. "I'm so fortunate to have married you, but I'm afraid you got the sorry end of the bargain."

She stroked his cheek. "That's not true. I know of no finer man than you."

He stared off into the middle distance, a devastated expression on his face. "I just don't understand any of it. How could one man, or a handful of bankers, create such misery for so many undeserving souls?"

Emily said nothing. She had no answer.

Over the next several weeks, from sunup to sundown, Michael walked the streets searching for work. He didn't encounter many of the dreaded *No Irish Need Apply* signs, but it didn't matter. There was simply no work to be found anywhere.

Finally, in desperation, one dull October morning, he swallowed his pride and decided to go see Tommy Walsh.

Inside the Tammany Hall building, he went up to a desk manned by an elderly gentleman. "Who is it you wish to see?" he asked.

"Mr. Thomas Walsh."

"And your name is?"

"Michael Ranahan."

The man ran his finger down a long list of names and his finger stopped on one. He squinted up at Michael and his whole demeanor changed. "Mr. Walsh is not available," he said brusquely.

"Is my name on that list?"

The man opened a drawer and slid the list inside. "That's none of your business."

"I must see Mr. Walsh."

"I told you—"

Before he could finish, Michael bolted for the stairs.

"*Stop, you can't go up there without permission*—"

Breathing heavily, Michael stopped in front of Walsh's office and took a deep breath to get his breathing under control. Then, without knocking, he opened the door and went in.

Tommy Walsh was even more jowly than he remembered. His flaming red hair was now a more subdued auburn. Walsh glanced up over his newspaper. "You look familiar. What's your name again?"

"Michael Ranahan."

Walsh's face turned the color of his hair and he jumped to his feet. "Ranahan! Get the hell out of my office, you damn traitor."

"Please, let me explain."

"There's nothing to explain. We asked for your help and you refused. Tammany has a long memory. What the hell are you doing here anyway?"

"I need a job."

Walsh's eyes narrowed and then he sat back down and burst out laughing. "A job, is it? Aren't you the cheeky one? You turn your back on Tammany and now you expect us to help you find a job?" He waved a hand in dismissal. "Get the hell out of here."

"I couldn't let my men off work that election day, Mr. Walsh. As I told your man, I had several contracts that were on deadline. If I hadn't completed the work by the contractual dates, it would have been ruin for me and the loss of my business. Besides," Michael added feebly, "Mr. Wood won without my help."

Walsh lit up a cigar. "And no thanks to you. So, what happened to your fine business?" he asked, sarcastically.

"The bank called in my loan. I couldn't pay and I lost everything."

"Well, that's the way of the world, isn't it?" He picked up his newspaper and resumed reading.

A despondent Michael turned toward the door. It had taken all his courage to come here, but he'd hoped—prayed—Walsh might offer him a job. The knot in his stomach tightened. This had been his last hope. Where could he go from here?

As he opened the door, Walsh said, "Wait."

Michael stood riveted in the door while Walsh studied him. Then, pointing his cigar, he said, "Unlike you, Ranahan, I am a loyal man. I haven't forgotten what you did for my sister and because of that I'll find you a job."

Michael felt the crushing weight of the world lifting from his shoulders. "Thank you, Mr. Walsh. Thank you."

"You can show us how thankful you are the next time we come to you for help."

He wrote an address on a piece of paper and handed it to Michael. "It's not much of a job, but, considering the financial chaos going on in this city, just be grateful you have one. Be there at eight o'clock sharp."

Emily looked at the wall clock in the kitchen. It was just after seven. The kids had been put to bed, Letta had gone to see Otto, and the house was blessedly quiet. Normally, she enjoyed this quiet time alone—Dermot had been particularly raucous today—but now, instead of being able to relax, she was tense. Every night since he'd lost the business, Michael came home dejected from another fruitless day of searching for work. Her heart ached for him, but there was nothing to be done but wait for him to come home, offer him encouragement, and try to get him to eat something.

She stiffened when she heard the key in the latch. Then he was standing there with a big grin on his face.

Emily rushed to him. "Have you found work?"

He picked her up and twirled her. "I have."

"What kind of job is it?"

"I don't know."

"What—?"

"I went to Tammany Hall today and spoke to Mr. Walsh. He was understandably angry at me, but he remembered what we'd done for his poor sister and he took pity on me." He handed her the piece of paper. "Tomorrow morning I'm to go to this address."

Emily studied the piece of paper on which was written: *14 Water Street* and frowned. "And you don't know what kind of job it is?"

"It's a job, Emily, that's all I know and I'm grateful for that."

"You're right. It is good news. I can't wait to tell Henrietta and Cully. We've been invited to Sunday dinner."

"No," Michael snapped.

Emily was taken aback by the anger in his tone. "What's the matter?"

"I can't face Cully."

"Why not?"

"Emily, I lost the business. The business that Cully spent years building up. I just can't face him."

"He won't blame you. If he still owned the business, he'd have lost it, too. It wasn't you, Michael. It was the deviltry of a gang of dishonest bankers and speculators."

Michael turned toward the stairs. "You go, if you want. I'll stay home with the children."

A soaking rain further added to the gray grimness of the rundown warehouses fronting Water Street on the lower east-side. Michael, drenched by the rain, checked the addresses until he came to 14 Water Street. He took a step back in dismay. Fourteen Water Street was an ugly, drab warehouse with windows so dirty it was impossible to see what was inside. Over the door, a decaying sign said: *Clayton Coal Company*.

He stepped inside and immediately began to choke on the coal dust swirling around the dimly lit, cavernous room. Mounds of coal, piled fifteen feet high, covered the entire floor, save for small pathways, like rabbit runs, that snaked around the mounds. Michael watched grim men scurry along these rabbit runs pushing overloaded wheelbarrows of coal. At first, he thought the men's faces were just dirty from the coal dust, but on closer inspection, he saw that most of them were Negroes.

He spotted a tiny office in the corner. The sign on the open door said: J.T. Dunlap, manager. A small, wizened man with large, pointy ears that made him look like a gnome, looked up. "What do you want?"

"I was sent by Mr. Walsh."

He gave Michael the once over. "This is hard work here."

"I can do it. I was in construction."

The man guffawed. "Construction? That ain't hard work here."

"Whatever it is, I can do it, sir."

The man shrugged. "We'll see." He picked up a pen and opened a ledger. "Name?"

"Michael Ranahan."

"The pay is three dollars a day, Monday to Saturday."

Michael blanched. "Three dollars a day?" That was less than half what he'd been making when he was working for Cully.

"Take it or leave it."

Michael reminded himself of the fact that the city was in desperate shape and he should be grateful that at least he had a job, such as it was. "I'll take it."

Dunlap squinted at the wall clock. "You start at seven and you end at seven. It's after eight now. You'll be docked an hour's wage," he said, as he meticulously made an entry in the ledger. "*Kitch*," he bellowed, startling Michael, who didn't think the little man could be so loud. "*Get in here now*."

A moment later, a large Negro with broad shoulders and thick arms was standing in the doorway. "Yes, boss?"

"Show this man the ropes."

"Yes, boss." He looked Michael up and down as though trying to assess whether he would be up to the job. "Come with me," he said, with a deep, resonant voice.

The man towered over Michael. "I'm Kitch. What's yourn?"

"Michael."

"Mi-kill …?"

"Close enough."

"Well, Mikill, what you do to get sent to this hellhole?"

Michael shrugged. "I need a job."

Kitch nodded. "Don't we all. C'mon."

They walked to the far end of the warehouse and out through a large opening to where two large finger piers thrust out into the waters of the East River. Several steamships were docked at each pier. Men scurried up and down gangplanks pushing wheelbarrows full of coal.

"It be pretty simple what we do," Kitch explained. "We gets coal deliveries from steamships comin' up from Pennsylvania and whatnot. We stores it here till the steamships that run betwixt here and Albany need to coal up. And dats about it. The coal come in, the coal go out. Fo' the rest of the day you jest follows me and do what I do."

While some of the other men stopped to watch with great interest, Kitch began to shovel coal into a wheelbarrow. Michael followed suit. When both wheelbarrows were full, Kitch looked at Michael's load with a sly grin. "You 'bout ready?"

Michael shrugged. "Lead on."

With his powerful arms and shoulders, Kitch lifted the handles of his wheelbarrow and started for the pier. Michael did the same, but, inexplicably, his wheelbarrow seemed to suddenly have a mind of its own. It careened wildly to the right and then to the left. He tried mightily to get the wheelbarrow under control, but despite his best efforts it finally tipped over, spilling coal across the floor.

Kitch and the others roared with laughter.

"It's all 'bout balance, see?" he explained to Michael. "You best learn to control that barrow or you gonna find yourself in the East River."

Embarrassed, Michael began to furiously shovel more coal into his wheelbarrow. Kitch leaned over and whispered, "Don't put much in there till you learns to control it."

Michael did as he was told and by carefully paying attention to balance, he managed to get the wheelbarrow out to the pier. Now his next hurdle was negotiating the wheelbarrow up the gangplank, which was set at a precariously steep angle. Again, everyone stopped to watch.

Determined not to fall into the river, he gripped the handles tightly and made a run for the gangplank. He was wobbly and at times almost lost control of the wheelbarrow, but he made it. A grinning Kitch followed. "I thinks you got the hang of it."

It was after eight by the time Michael got home. When he came through the door he was almost unrecognizable. His hair was matted with coal dust and his face and hands were black. His eyes were red-rimmed from the coal dust-laden air in the warehouse and his throat was raw from coughing up coal dust all day.

"Michael, you look a fright. What kind of work did you get?"

"It's a coal company. I think I must have moved ten tons of coal today. At least that's what it felt like. God, my back is killing me."

"Will you go back tomorrow?"

"What choice do I have? It's a job."

"You can find another."

"I doubt that. It'll be all right. I'll get used to it."

"Go wash up. I'll fix your supper."

As Michael was going upstairs, Dermot came out of his room. When he saw his father's dirty face, he laughed and pointed. "You look like a nigger."

Without thinking, Michael backhanded his son, sending him crashing against a wall. "Don't you ever use that word in this house, do you understand?"

Through defiant and angry tears, Dermot shouted, "All the kids say it."

"I don't care. You will not use that word in this house or anywhere else. Do you hear me?"

"All right," he said, stomping back to his room.

The next morning, when Michael woke up he could hardly get out of bed. Every muscle in his body ached. With great effort, he dressed, kissed Emily goodbye, and set out for Water Street. As he walked to work, he stretched and loosened his muscles.

When he got there fifteen minutes before seven, most of the men were already there, milling about.

Kitch came over to Michael grinning. "How you feel today?"

"Like I got kicked by a dozen mules."

Kitch grinned. "You get used to it."

Little gnome-like Dunlap came out his office and consulted his timepiece. "Get to work."

In silence, men went to their respective wheelbarrows and began loading up the coal. For the first few trips, Michael's exhausted muscles screamed in agony, but after a while, they loosened up and he got into a rhythm—shovel, lift, push off, relax arms, move forward. As he developed a rhythm, he found he was fighting the wheelbarrow less and less. It helped that some of the men softly chanted songs whose words Michael couldn't understand, but whose smooth, rhythmic cadence seemed to make the task of pushing the wheelbarrow easier.

Around noon, Dunlap came out of his office looking at his timepiece. "Break time."

Without a word, the men gathered up the sacks they'd laid aside and hurried out to the piers. Michael followed and sat down next to Kitch.

As Kitch and the others opened their sacks, he looked at Michael. "We gets twenty minutes to eat. Where your food at?"

"I didn't bring anything. I never thought of it."

"You ain't gonna last here long you don't eat." He held out a piece of fried chicken.

Michael stared at it longingly. That piece of chicken certainly looked and smelled good and his stomach had been grumbling for hours now, but he saw that Kitch had only one other piece of chicken in his sack. "No, thanks, Kitch. I'm not hungry."

"Don't be shinin' me on. I knows you hungry. Who wouldn't, laboring likes we do? We have an old custom down south. You offer a body something to eat, it ain't polite to say no. So, c'mon, take it."

Hunger overcoming his embarrassment, Michael took the chicken. "Thank you, Kitch."

"It ain't nothin'."

When they'd finished eating, Kitch sat back with a satisfied smile on his face. "When the weather is tolerable, we all comes out here to get away from that damn coal dust. You works with that dust sunup to sundown it gets everywhere into your body—your hair, your eyes, your ears, your mouth. "I 'spect it gets in your stomach, too. It's so I can taste it."

"I know what you mean." Michael looked at hands. "Last night, I tried to wash it off, but, it's still there."

Kitch studied Michael. "You Irish, ain't you?"

"I am."

"I'm a freed slave myself," he said, matter-of-factly.

"You... *you* were a slave?"

"Why you lookin' at me like dat?"

"I'm sorry, I've never seen a slave before."

"*Freed* slave," Kitch corrected.

"Right. Free. I don't know much about slavery, but I didn't think a slave could buy his freedom."

"Well, I reckon I did."

"But how'd you get the money?"

Looking proud, he said, "Because I was an artist, that's how."

Before Michael could ask him to explain that, Dunlap came out. "Break's over. Back to work."

Michael came into the kitchen all excited. "Emily, I met a real slave today. I mean, a freed slave."

Emily turned from the stove. "Working with you?"

"Yes. And he told me he bought his freedom by being an artist."

"That sounds quite remarkable. How did he do it?"

"Before he could tell me how he did it, we had to get back to work."

"Speaking of work, how was it today?"

"Better than yesterday. Kitch says I'll get used to it."

"Kitch—?"

"The freed slave."

"Dinner's almost ready. Why don't you wash up and tell the children to come down?"

After the children were put to bed and the dishes done, Emily came into the parlor where Michael was reading the *Tribune*. It was Emily's idea. She'd told him if he wanted to learn to read better, a newspaper was good place to start.

"Anything good in the news?" she asked, plopping down on a sofa by the fireplace.

"Yes. You'll be interested in this. Dr. Elizabeth Blackwell has just opened her own hospital. It's called the New York Infirmary for Women and Children. The article says the hospital's mission is also to provide positions for women physicians."

"That's marvelous. I wonder how she managed to open it despite all those obstructionist male doctors in this city?"

"I'm not surprised. As I remember, she was a very determined woman. Here's another interesting article. Remember that elevator demonstration we saw at the Crystal Palace back in '53?"

"Yes. I believe the gentleman's name was Otis."

"Right. Well, he's just installed a passenger elevator in a building downtown." Michael put the newspaper aside and got that faraway look in his eye. "What I said that day is beginning to happen, Emily. With these elevator machines, the city is not just going to grow *out*, but it's going to grow *up*."

CHAPTER TWENTY-SIX

The Sunday dinner tradition at the Ranahans continued, but since the crash Michael and Emily couldn't afford to feed such a large crowd. The solution was that everybody brought something. Henrietta would bring a roast or chicken, Letta would bring desserts from her parents' bakery, Emily supplied the vegetables, and Gaylord always brought the wine.

"There is something peculiar going on in this city," Gaylord said, as he poured the wine.

"There is always something peculiar going on in this city," Henrietta pointed out.

"True, but this has nothing to do with sin, vice, or political corruption."

Michael grinned. "What else is there?"

"There is a religious movement afoot in this city. Last week I interviewed the Reverend Theodore Cuyler, pastor of Nineteenth Street Church. He told me he was pleasantly taken aback, if nonplussed, by the number of men suddenly attending his church—during the *week*, mind you!"

"During the *week*?" Cully said. "Well, that is peculiar."

"And it's not just the Reverend Cuyler's church either. Prayer meetings are popping up all over the city. Last Monday, Mr. Greely hired a horse and buggy and had me ride from one prayer meeting to the next to see how many men were praying. In two hours, I counted more than six thousand men at these noontime prayer meetings. And they were almost all businessmen, and, get this, most of them professed to having no religious affiliation."

Emily passed the platter of chicken to Henrietta. "That is remarkable. What do you think is going on?"

"Something similar happened at the beginning of this century. It was called the Second Great Awakening. What's going on now has all the hallmarks of that event."

"But why suddenly all this praying?" Letta asked.

"Let's look at our recent history. Up until this crash, there had been tremendous economic growth and prosperity in the United States. There's been a population boom, and, as Henrietta has noted on more than one occasion, many people have become quite wealthy."

"Nuevo riche," she corrected with a raised eyebrow.

"All of which has led to a steep decline in spirituality. Then came our economic crash. It forced thousands of merchants into bankruptcy, banks are failing, and railroad companies are going under."

"That's almost enough to send me back to church," Cully mumbled.

"But there is something else even more ominous on the horizon."

"And what is that?" Michael asked.

"The question of slavery. The abolitionists are growing louder and stronger every day. Mr. Greeley is an outspoken proponent of abolition and he often writes editorials condemning that 'peculiar institution.' There are some who believe the issue of slavery could eventually lead to civil war."

"I work with a freed slave," Michael said. "He bought his freedom."

"Well, he's in the minority. Most slaves, even if their masters are willing, would never have the wherewithal to buy their freedom."

"Then what's to become of them?" Emily asked.

Gaylord thought a long time. "I'm afraid the only answer to freeing the slaves is civil war," he said, finally.

"Well, that's quite extreme, isn't it?" Henrietta said.

"It is, but I don't see any other course."

And on that somber note dinner was finished in uneasy silence.

Every day Michael could hardly wait for their break so he could listen to Kitch tell of his life on a plantation. Listening to the freed slave describe his extraordinary experiences somehow made the drudgery and backbreaking work less burdensome.

It was a typically cold December day, but the men preferred to eat their meal out on the cold, windy pier rather than breathe in that coal dust, even if it was for only twenty minutes.

Kitch tossed a chicken bone into the river. "I growed up on Massa Tom's plantation in Virginia. It was a fine ol' house painted all white and standin' in a patch of oak trees. My mammy and pappy came over on the slave ships, but I was born on that plantation, me and my younger brother and sister. Did you grow up on a plantation, Mikill?"

Michael laughed. "Something like that, only they were called estates and they were owned by wealthy men—landlord's we called them. In exchange for growing crops for these landlords, we were allowed to build small cottages and grow our own potatoes."

"Was your landlord a good man?"

Michael nodded. "He was. I married his daughter."

Kitch grinned. "Ho, you did very well, my friend."

"It's not what you think. My landlord was murdered by brigands and eventually the estate had to be sold off to pay debts. My wife, Emily, and I came out here with only the proceeds she made from selling a ring."

"My Massa Tom, he weren't a bad sort, unlessen he got into the liquor. Lord, Lord, then he become a real rip-jack, sure enough. Anyways, when I was a child and still too young to go into the fields, I used to take a piece of coal and draw pictures on the back of an ol' shovel. I did that all day long. It was just somethin' to do, but I loved doin' it. Mammy used to say, 'Lord, child, don't let Massa see you doin' dat.'"

"Why not?"

"The slaves, they wasn't allowed to learn how to read or write. I guess she thought drawin' was like learnin' to read or somethin'. So I was real careful to stay out of sight. But one day Massa Tom's wife, she spys what I'm doin'. She was good woman. Always spoke soft and never gave a slave a whoppin'. She took one look at the back of that shovel and she brought me right up to the big house. Lord, I thought I was gonna get the whoppin' of my life. But she did no sech a thing. She sat me down at a table in the kitchen and gave me some paper and a pencil and told me to draw stuff. 'What stuff should I draw?' I asked her. 'Anythin' at all,' she says. Anythin' at all. Well, that puzzled me good."

Before Michael could ask him another question, Dunlap came out onto the pier and uttered the five words that Michael had come to hate: "*Break's over. Back to work.*"

The next day flurries came down, but, again, the men elected to take their break in the snow rather than sit in the throat-choking coal dust warehouse.

Pulling his collar up to ward off the bitter wind coming off the river, Michael began the questioning. "Did you become an artist as a child?"

"No. But the missus let me draw regular 'til I was old enough to go into the fields. But den, one day I be summoned to the big house and led to the kitchen. And there on the table was these little tubes of paints and brushes and canvasses and whatnot. I like to die. 'I want you to paint somethin',' she says. Again, I say, 'what should I paint' and she say, 'whatever you wants to paint. You can even paint outside if you wants.'"

"Well, I tell you, I was mighty puzzled by all of this, but, lordy, I had fun with them paints. It took me a little while to get the hang of mixin' colors and figurin' out what brush to use and whatnot, but pretty soon I was a paintin' fool. One day a week, she would bring me out of the fields and I would paint. There was so much to paint, I didn't know where to start. I painted the big house, I painted the barns, I painted the slave quarters, which was nothin' but long rows of cabins. I painted the one room where my whole family lived. I liked the bright colors, so I used the yellows and reds and oranges as much as I could. I didn't like the dark colors. I never used black or blue or purple."

"What did you do with the paintings?"

"They wasn't mine. The missus kept them or throwed them away, whatever. But one day, she calls me into the parlor and hands me some coins. I ain't never held coins in my whole life. I had no idea how much them coins was worth. She say, 'I sold one of your paintin's, Kitch. If I sell more, I'll give you more coins.' And then and there, looking down at those shiny coins in my hand I realized that if I got enough coins, I could buy my freedom."

"I had a similar experience," Michael said, excitedly. "When I was younger, I wanted to leave Ireland and come to America to get away from the tenant farmer's life. During the winter when there was no plowing or planting to do, I would trudge from village to village in the cold and the rain and convince merchants that I was a trustworthy lad and they could count on me to pick up and deliver their goods on time and in prime condition. I did that for three long years, saving a shilling here, a half-crown there, until I saved enough for passage to America."

"So, that's how you got to America?"

"No." Michael stopped to watch a steamship plowing up the river belching black smoke amidst swirling snowflakes. "Just as I was about to book passage, a disease killed all the potatoes. That was the start of the famine. I had no choice. I gave all my savings to my da so he could buy food for the family and seed for next year's planting."

Kitch scrambled to his feet. "Here come Mr. Dunlap, time to get back to work."

After work, Michael went home and recounted to Emily everything that Kitch had told him. Soon, she was as interested in Kitch's life as he was.

"Where does he live?"

"The Five Points."

"Oh, my. How dreadful."

"It's all he can afford. Besides, Negroes aren't welcome in many parts of the city."

"Does he have a family?"

"He had a wife and daughter, but they both died in a cholera epidemic that swept through the Five Points back in '52."

"How sad. Michael, why don't you invite your friend to dinner? I'm sure hasn't had a decent hot meal in quite a while."

"I don't know that he's ever had a decent hot meal in his life. But that's a good idea. I'll invite him to Sunday dinner."

"No. I don't think that's a good idea. He might be uncomfortable around so many strangers."

"You've got a point. Come to think of it, I'm the only one he talks to at the warehouse."

The next morning, Michael invited Kitch to dinner. He tried to refuse, but a grinning Michael reminded him of his old custom down south and the obligation to accept food offered.

By the time they arrived at the house the children, except

Dermot, were in bed. As usual, Dermot was giving Emily a hard time about going to bed early.

Michael brought Kitch into the kitchen.

"Emily, this is Kitch."

Emily bowed slightly. "I've heard so much about you, I'm glad that we finally get to meet."

Kitch swept his cap off his head. "Pleased to meet you, missus."

"Please, call me Emily. Oh, and this is our son, Dermot."

"Hello, young master."

A mortified Emily watched her son stare at Kitch as though he were a creature from mythology. "Dermot, say hello to Mr. Kitch."

"Hello," he mumbled.

Grateful that her son didn't say anything embarrassing, Emily took him by the shoulders and spun him around. "All right, off to bed with you."

Over a simple dinner of roasted chicken, dumplings, and vegetables, Emily and Kitch got to know each other. Kitch had a hard time making eye contact with Emily and generally stared at his plate. "So, Miss Emily, Mikill tells me you lived in the big house."

"I beg your pardon?"

"They call the plantation house the big house," Michael explained.

"Oh, I see. Well, yes, I guess you could say I lived in the big house. How'd you get a name like Kitch?"

"They tells me I was born in a kitchen. I guess that's it."

"I'm sorry, do you mind us asking all these questions?"

"No. Nobody ever showed no interest in me before."

"Tell us more about your art career?"

"Weren't much of an art career. I kept paintin' pictures and the missus kept selling them and she kept givin' me coins. See, I was thinkin' of buying my freedom so one day I ask Massa Tom what I was worth. He laugh and say, ''Bout five hundred dollar. But I ain't gonna let anyone buy you. You too valuable.' Well, that made me feel real bad."

"How much money did you have saved up?" Michael asked.

"I didn't know so I had a preacher count it. He said it come to three hundred and thirty-five dollars. I kept on paintin' and gettin' coins from the missus. I'm just burnin' to earn that five hundred dollars one way or the other. I remember being in the big house one time and hearin' a lady from the next plantation over sayin' how much she admired the picture I painted of Massa Tom's big house. Next day I say to the missus that maybe I oughta go to some neighborin' plantations and paint their big houses, too. She thought that was a high idea. She said they would probably pay good money for a picture of their own big house. Next day, she give me a pass and told me to go to Massa Jim's to paint his big house."

Emily frowned. "A pass?"

"Yes, missus. You couldn't leave the plantation unlessen the Massa give a pass."

"Like a permission slip to be away from the plantation?"

"Yes, missus. Slaves always had to get a pass to go anywhere off the plantation. If you got caught by the speculators, you show de pass to them. If you didn't have a pass, they strip you and beat you, and maybe sell you off to someone."

"Speculators?"

"They the ones that come around every now and then to buy and sell slaves. They come into the fields and pick out the slaves they wants to buy. Whenever the speculators come, we was all terrified of being sold off."

Michael and Emily exchanged stunned glances and they were both thinking the same thing: During the famine, life was horrific, but it was nothing like this.

"I was paintin' lots of pictures and gettin' lots a coin, but then one day I had a terrible accident out in the field. I guess I weren't paying attention, but I got my hand caught up in the cotton gin."

Michael looked down at Kitch's right hand. He hadn't noticed it before, but his hand looked more like a claw than a hand. How in the world, he wondered, was he able to hold on to a coal-laden wheelbarrow?

"It tore me up pretty bad. Lost two fingers. There weren't no doctor, so one a the old mammies who was born in Africa made up some kind of African mixture and rubbed it on my hand. I didn't lose it, but, as you can see, it ain't much good to me now. I tried paintin' with my left hand, but it weren't no good. The pictures didn't come out right. And that was that."

"Did your master want to sell you off?" Michael asked,

"He couldn't. After the accident, he cursed me good and called me a damaged goods nigger. He say no one would pay a decent price for me now. Massa Tom was a great drinker and a poor gambler. By and by, I finds out that Massa is in a whole heap of debt and is in danger of losin' the plantation. If that happen, me and the others gonna get sold off for sure and there no tellin' what kind of massa I get. So, one day I approach him. Massa Tom, I say, I would like to buy my freedom."

He laugh at me and say, 'you got five hundred dollars, boy?' 'No, sir,' I say. 'But it's like you said, I'm damaged goods. I ain't worth that kind of money no more.'"

He stared at me and there was real fire in his eyes. I'm thinkin' he's thinkin' that I'm some kind of uppity nigger and I'm gonna get a good whoopin' for sure. But instead, he say, 'how much you got?' I say 'I got three hundred and thirty-five dollars.' His eyes got real big. I know he could use that money to pay off some of those debts. Then he did somethin' he never did before. He shook my hand. 'You got a deal, boy. You give me that three hundred and thirty-five dollars and I'll give you your freedom.' And that was that."

Emily and Michael were staring at him with open mouths. Kitch's story was so fantastic that it seemed more like a fable than reality."

Finally, Emily was able to speak. "What about your family?"

"Didn't have none by that time. My pappy had run off a long time before. Then Massa Tom sold off my brother and sister…"

Emily gasped and tears welled up in her eyes.

"But he was decent about it. He sold them off together so they wouldn't be broke up. I 'spect the missus had somethin' to do with dat. She was always a kind woman."

"And your mother."

"She died shortly after the little 'uns was sold off. As soon as I got my freedom, quick as I could, I got out of the slave South and came north and ended up here in New York City." He gave Emily a sideward glance. "These dumplings are sure mighty delicious, missus. Might I have some more?"

Emily practically shoved the platter at him. "Have all you want."

When he left, Emily handed him a package. "Kitch, this is for you. Just some chicken and dumplings."

"Thank you, missus."

The end of 1857 saw increasing unrest among the unemployed and renewed efforts to organize themselves. The Kommunisten Klub, a group of German radicals, joined forces with James McGuire, an Irish labor leader, with a view toward uniting the unemployed. McGuire's rallying cry was: "If one man suffers, it doesn't matter whether he is an American or a foreigner—they all suffer."

Thousands of men gathered at Tompkins Square Park and marched on City Hall demanding a program of public works and jobs building the new Central Park and adding sewers to the city's streets. The next day they marched on Wall Street chanting "*We want work!*"

The newspapers, unsympathetic to the unemployed men's plight, lashed out at the marchers. The *Herald* editorial bellowed: *Shoot down any quantity of Irish or Germans necessary. Rioters, like other people, have heads to be broken and bodies to be perforated with ball and steel.*

Days later, men, now desperately hungry, poured into Tompkins Square Park. But this time the organizers couldn't control the men as shouts of "*bread, bread*" rose from the throng. The multitude, now a mindless organism of one, swarmed into the streets and began attacking bread wagons and food shops.

That night, Letta came home crying hysterically. Emily brought her into the kitchen and made her sit down. "Letta, what is it?"

Between racking sobs, she said, "I was at my parents' bakery … suddenly a dozen men broke the front window ... As hands snatched the bread and buns in the window, others barged into the shop with sticks and clubs ... They smashed everything ... They cleaned the shelves of bread and pastries ..." She buried her face in her hands. "When my father tried to stop them, they beat him with their clubs. Oh, Emily, it was terrible. Terrible."

"Is your father all right?"

"He has several cuts and severe bruises. I think he'll recover, but the shop is ruined. They destroyed everything, including his baking ovens." She looked up at Emily with red-rimmed eyes.

“Emily, he no longer has a bake shop. Everything he’s worked for his whole life is gone.”

CHAPTER TWENTY-SEVEN

1858

By mid-year, there were encouraging signs that the crisis was easing and the worst was over. The crisis wouldn't end for a couple of years, but business conditions were slowly improving, credit was easing, and trade was expanding. While this was happening, Michael, Kitch, and the other men who worked for Clayton Coal Company continued the mind-numbing drudgery of wheelbarrowing coal on and off steamships twelve hours a day, six days a week.

Michael had gotten used to the work. He no longer felt bone weary and exhausted at the end of the day. The work, nevertheless, was soul-deadening. The wages were poor and the conditions were dreadful. He had developed a hacking cough that wouldn't go away. And there were times when he became breathless struggling up a gangplank.

Henrietta extended an invitation to Michael and Emily to come to Sunday dinner. What was unusual about the invitation was that no one else was invited. While most Sunday dinners were at the Ranahans, Henrietta often hosted dinners for the group who usually gathered at the Ranahans on Sunday. But this time, she had specifically said only Emily and Michael should come.

As they sat down, Cully said, "How's the work going, Michael?"

Michael shrugged. "As well as can be expected. I thought construction work was hard, but pushing tons of coal on a wheelbarrow is a helluva lot harder."

Emily rubbed his shoulders. "At least it's keeping you in great shape."

"Aye, it is that."

Henrietta passed the platter of roast beef. "Will your school be starting up soon?"

"I don't know. I hear things are getting better, but so far no one has inquired about coming back."

"It'll happen."

"I hope so. We could use the money."

All through dinner, Henrietta and Cully had been acting strangely, sharing sideways glances at each other and smiling a lot.

As dinner was finishing up, Henrietta went into the kitchen and came back with a bottle of champagne.

Emily rubbed her hands together in glee. "What's the occasion, Henrietta? Good news for you?"

"No. Good news for you and Michael."

"I don't understand."

"Norbert, you tell them."

The old man had been uncharacteristically silent during dinner, but now he became fully animated. "I bought Ranahan Construction," he announced in a loud voice.

It took a while for Michael and Emily to absorb what he had just said. "You bought what …?" Michael asked.

"Ranahan Construction. Since the bank foreclosed on your loan, I've been keeping an eye on the property. Your man, Hainsworth, tried to sell it several times, but either the price was too high or the buyer pulled out at the last minute. I decided the time was right and I made him an offer. Cash on the barrelhead. No notes, no loans, no stocks exchanged. Cash. It didn't take him long to think it over. He took the cash."

"And why shouldn't he?" Henrietta interjected. "He's been sitting on a valuable asset that no one wanted or could afford. Banks are in the business of making money, not absorbing losses."

"So ... *you* own the company?" Michael asked, still not quite grasping what he was being told.

"I do. Lock, stock, and barrel. And, I might add, I bought it at a price that was considerably less than I sold it to you."

Michael was almost afraid to ask the next question. Cully had never said it, but Michael continued to harbor the belief that the old man had never forgiven him for losing the business. "Will I be able to go to work for you?"

Cully shook his head. "No."

Michael's heart sank. "Oh. Well … I understand…"

"It's *your* company.

"*My* …"

"Just as you paid the bank monthly, you will pay me monthly until I have received my money back. They'll be no cursed banks involved. This is a business deal strictly between you and me."

Emily was speechless. Michael wanted to say something, but a knot had formed in his throat that prevented him from speaking.

Henrietta thrust the champagne bottle into Michael's hand. "Well, don't just sit there. Open the champagne."

Cully picked up his glass and looked at Henrietta defiantly. "I'll have some."

She returned his defiant look. "All right, Norbert, just this once, but don't fill his glass, Michael."

When all their glasses were filled, Cully offered a toast. "To Ranahan Construction, may you continue to build this city."

Michael was about to add, *with the help of my son, Dermot*. But he suddenly had a terrible premonition that perhaps Dermot wouldn't be around to help him. Instead, he mumbled, "To Ranahan Construction."

The next morning, Michael arrived at the Clayton Coal Company just before seven. He went into the manager's office and announced he was quitting. Without a word, the taciturn manager opened his ledger and crossed Michael's name off the list of employees. He checked his timepiece and brushed past Michael.

Out in the coal room, he announced to the men those hated words: "Get to work."

Michael smiled as he realized he would never have to hear those words again. But his smile soon faded as he watched the men, like beasts of burden, begin their twelve-hour day by filling their wheelbarrows with coal. Thanks to Cully he would never have to do this sort of soul-destroying work again.

He looked around for Kitch, but his friend was nowhere in sight. He went back into the manager's office. "Mr. Dunlap, I don't see Kitch outside. Maybe he's sick. Do you know where he lives?"

The manager looked up with a mystified expression. "Why would I need to know that?"

"What if he's sick? How would you get his wages to him?"

"That is no concern of mine." He consulted his timepiece. "If he's not here by eight, he no longer has a job."

Michael decided he'd come back at quitting time to see if Kitch showed up for work. For most of the morning and early afternoon, he visited various old customers to see if they were ready to resume building. Most weren't, but he lined up enough customers so that his men would have work.

It was late afternoon by the time he got to his warehouse. He was grateful to see that the Ranahan sign was still over the door. Apparently, the bank couldn't be bothered spending the money to have it removed.

He walked into the darkened warehouse and into an eerie sight. It looked as though the workers had suddenly been snatched off the face of the earth. Stacks of lumber and piles of sand and bricks awaited loading onto the wagons. It was as Cully had said; besides selling off the horses, everything was as he left it.

He went into his office. Months of accumulated dust covered his desk and papers. He sat down behind his desk and closed his eyes. All those months of laboring for Clayton Coal seemed to fade as though it had all been a bad dream.

He opened his eyes and there was Flynn with his gap-toothed grin standing in the doorway. He had sent word to Flynn to meet him at the warehouse.

"Are we really back in business?"

"Yes, thanks to Cully."

"What's next?"

"Do you know where our men are?"

"Most of them."

"Good. Go find them and tell them I have work. In the meantime, I have to go buy some horses."

CHAPTER TWENTY-EIGHT

The Ranahan Construction Company slowly, but steadily, began its recovery. Michael still hadn't gotten all his clients back—some had gone bankrupt while those that didn't remained cautious about needlessly spending money. But the customers that had returned were enough to keep his crews busy. Determined not to make the same mistake twice, Michael promised himself that he would not overextend his business. He purchased seven horses and hired back 35 men, and that was enough to handle all his construction projects.

One sultry morning in mid-August, a messenger delivered a cryptic note. All it said was: *Your presence is requested at St. Patrick's Church at Price and Mott Street. 10 a.m. tomorrow morning.*

The next morning, when Michael arrived at the church there were about two-dozen men crowded into the pews toward the front of the church. He recognized some of them as contractors with whom he had worked before.

He sat down next to Angus Roy, a stonemason from Scotland. He had worked with the stonemason and his crew and admired their work, which was meticulous and workmanlike in every detail.

"What's this all about, Angus?"

"I've no idea, laddie. I received a message to be here this morning. That's all I know."

Just then a man wearing the red raiment of a bishop, accompanied by two priests and a well-dressed gentleman, came out onto the altar.

The idle chatter of the men in the pews stopped as the bishop put up his hands for silence. He was a man in his early sixties with a high forehead and gray piercing eyes that said they would brook no nonsense.

"Good morning, men," he said, with the soft brogue that Michael recognized as coming from the north of Ireland. "I am Bishop Hughes and I welcome you to St. Patrick's. I have asked you to come here today because I am about to embark on a most ambitious building project and I am led to believe that you contractors, stonemasons, and bricklayers are the best at what you do in this city."

"What is it that you want to build?" a man in the front row asked.

The bishop smiled slyly. "The biggest cathedral in New York City, nay, the whole of the United States."

"Where will you build it?"

"On Fifth Avenue and Fiftieth Street."

A murmur of shock and incredulity went up from the men in the pews.

"Way up there in the country?" another man exclaimed. "Why there's nothing up there but shanties, squatters, and pig farms."

The bishop smiled back defiantly. "Mark my words, one day Fifth Avenue and Fiftieth Street will be the center of the city."

Ignoring the laughs and guffaws from the men, the bishop pointed to the gentleman. "This is Mr. James Renwick. He will serve as the chief architect for the project."

Head nodded in the pews. Renwick's work was well known to them. He had designed the Grace Church downtown and the Smithsonian Institute Building in Washington D.C.

As he rose to speak, two priests carried two cloth-covered easels out onto the altar. Getting right to the point, Renwick, a bald man with a long aquiline nose and a full beard, said, "This project is expected to be completed by 1861 and there will be plenty of work for all who are qualified."

He walked over to the first easel and stripped away the cloth. Another gasp went up from the men. The rendering showed a magnificent gothic cathedral with two spires soaring into the sky. "This is what St. Patrick's Cathedral will look like." He pulled away the cloth from the second easel showing a floor plan of the building. "The cathedral will be four hundred feet in length covering an entire square block bounded on the east and west by

Fifth Avenue and Madison Avenue and on the north and south by Fiftieth and Fifty-First Streets. The two spires will be three hundred and thirty feet high."

Angus Roy leaned into Michael. "I'm thinking a completion date of 1861 is a wee bit ambitious. Look at the detail stone work alone. Still," he said, looking admiringly at the rendering, "however long it takes, I will be happy to work on such a splendid structure."

"How do we apply for work on this church?" Michael asked.

"You will be notified when and where to report for an interview. If you are deemed qualified, you will be hired."

A grim-faced Bishop Hughes stood up and pointed an accusing finger at the men. "I will tell you now. No graft of any kind will be tolerated. You will not give, nor will you receive, recompense from any source whatsoever, especially Tammany Hall."

The men glanced at each other uneasily. There was no such thing as construction in this city without Tammany having its hand in it. How could the bishop hope to keep them out?

That Sunday at dinner, Michael excitedly told everybody about the planned construction of the biggest cathedral in the United States.

"It sounds like a very ambitious project indeed," Henrietta said.

"It is," Gaylord agreed. "However, some doubters are calling it 'Hughes' Folly'."

"And no wonder," Cully added. "It's miles away from the real city. Who does he expect to get for parishioners? Pigs and chickens?"

"I'll say this, if anyone can pull it off, it's Dagger John."

Emily frowned. "Dagger John?"

"It's what they call the bishop because he always draws a cross after his signature. By the way, have you been to the site, Michael?"

"I have. Flynn and I went to take a look yesterday."

"Did you notice that great big house across the street from the proposed cathedral?"

"You mean the ugly five-story house? It wasn't very elegant, I can tell you that. Who lives there?"

"Madame Restell."

Henrietta almost choked. "You mean … *Madame Restell … the abortionist*?"

"The same."

"Good heavens," Emily exclaimed. "Why in the world would Bishop Hughes build his cathedral across the street from such an infamous woman?"

Gaylord chuckled. "It wasn't his plan. He tried to buy the site to build his official residence, but she outbid him. Some say—"

He was interrupted by angry shouts and crying coming from upstairs. Michael started to get up, but Emily saw the angry expression on his face and put her napkin down. "I'll see to it."

Embarrassed by the disturbance, Michael tried to get the conversation back on track. "It's certainly going to be an interesting project. I'm told they're going to import white marble from upstate New York and Massachusetts and granite from Maine. There will be massive bronze doors weighing twenty thousand pounds each and they say they will be so well balanced that they can be opened with one hand. It's going to be a marvel."

Gaylord poured more wine. "I've been told the overall building contract has gone to the Hall & Joy Company for the princely sum of eight hundred and fifty thousand dollars."

Michael nodded. "They are the biggest contractor in the city and they have a sterling reputation."

"It would appear that you can look forward to long-term and very profitable work," Henrietta said.

"I welcome the work. We're getting construction projects, but not like before. Even those who are building are building much smaller mansions. There's still fear about another crisis. But there is a problem with the cathedral project. The bishop has forbidden any contractor from dealing with the likes of Tammany Hall. I don't see how we'll be able to keep them out."

Gaylord grinned. "I wouldn't worry about that. I predict Tammany Hall will be no match for the pugnacious Bishop Hughes. Back in '44, anti-Catholic riots instigated by Nativist agitators threatened to spread to New York from Philadelphia, where two churches had been burned and twelve people died. The bishop ringed his churches with armed guards. Then he informed the nativist sympathizing mayor that if a single Catholic Church was burned in New York, the city would become a second

Moscow."

"What does that mean?" Michael asked.

"It was a reference to the Russian scorched earth policy. Before Napoleon's army got to Moscow, the Russian people burned their own city to the ground to deny it to the enemy."

"Let's hope that won't be necessary," Henrietta said with a raised eyebrow.

A grim-faced Emily returned just as dinner was finishing up. "Is everything all right?" Henrietta asked.

"As well as can be expected," Emily responded with a forced smile.

Later, as they were getting ready for bed, Michael said, "What was the ruckus all about?"

"As usual, Dermot took toys away from Peter."

"Sometimes I wish Peter would fight back."

"He's only four, Michael. It's Dermot I'm worried about. It seems that nothing I do gets though to him. I can punish him, send him to bed early, take away his toys… nothing seems to bother him. I'm at my wit's end."

"What do you think we should do?"

"I don't know. Thank God, the other children are no bother. Eleanor is her usual gentle self. Peter is the serious one and no bother at all. And Claire is, well, gentle little Claire."

"I'll talk to Dermot tomorrow after I come home from work."

"For all the good it'll do. Anyway, what's next with the church project?"

"I'm to get a message to report for an interview."

"Do you anticipate any problems?"

"Well, there's the foreclosure for one. And I might be too small a business for them. We'll see."

It had been a week since the meeting with Bishop Hughes, and Michael was beginning to worry that he would not receive an invitation. At last, and much to his relief, he received a notice to come to the offices of the Hall & Joy Company.

The Hall & Joy Company was housed in a huge warehouse on Hudson Street near City Hall. Unlike his small warehouse, this one was bustling with hundreds of workers sawing and cutting wood and loading up dozens of wagons with construction materials.

Michael was shown into a cramped office littered with architectural drawings and maps.

A slightly jowly man with thick spectacles that gave his eyes a strange magnification motioned Michael to sit down. "My name is Mason and I oversee hiring subcontractors," he said in a high-pitched voice. "And you are …?"

"Michael Ranahan of the Ranahan Construction Company."

"Ranahan Construction…" Mason consulted his notes. After a while, he looked up and frowned. "I see there was a bank foreclose on your loan."

Michael was expecting this question, but, still, it was a shock to hear someone actually say he had been foreclosed on. "Yes, sir. It was at the beginning of the panic. I was current with my payments, but the bank called in my loan anyway."

Mason grunted. "There was a lot of that going on in '57."

Michael thought he detected a note of sympathy in the voice, but perhaps that was just wishful thinking. The fact that he didn't ask Michael to leave immediately was at least encouraging.

"I see your company assets consist of seven horses and wagons and you employee thirty-five men. Is that correct?"

"It is," Michael answered, wondering where he got that information.

Mason continued to study his notes, making Michael nervous. He would have preferred to make eye contact so it would be easier to judge what the man was thinking.

"You are a very small company for our needs."

Michael's heart thumped in his chest. He was counting on getting in on this project. It would mean long-term employment for his men and a handsome profit for him.

"Sir, all my men are hard workers. They're reliable, sober, and… God fearing Christians," he added, hoping that would count for something

But it only elicited a mere grunt from Mason. After what seemed an eternity, he said, "All right, we'll hire you on probationary status."

"Probationary status…?"

"You will be watched to see if you perform up to our standards. If there are any signs of lateness, drunkenness, or slacking of effort, you will be terminated immediately."

"I can assure you, sir, there will be none of that."

"We'll see. You and your men will report to the Fifth Avenue site at eight o'clock Monday morning.

Michael couldn't wait to get home to give Emily the good news. But when he came through the door, he saw a tense look on Emily's face.

"What's the matter?"

"Dermot hit Peter with a toy and gave him quite a gash on his scalp."

Michael started toward the stairs, but Emily grabbed his arm. "Michael, he's only eight-years-old."

"I don't care how old he is. He attacked his younger brother."

"Before you see him, get your temper under control."

Michael took a deep breath. "All right."

Eleanor was waiting for him at the top of the stairs with a worried expression on her face. "Daddy, is Peter going to be all right?"

Michael embraced her. "Of course he will, sweetheart. He's a tough little Irishman, isn't he?"

"I guess ..."

Peter, with a bandage wrapped around his head, was propped up in bed surrounded by his toys.

"How's my little man doing?"

"Dermot hit me," he said, tears welling up in his eyes.

Michael sat down on the bed and held his son's hand. "I know. I promise you, he will never do that to you again."

Dermot was playing in his room when Michael came in. The boy didn't look up.

"Why did you hit your brother?"

"I don't know," he mumbled.

"Look at me when I talk to you," Michael snapped. "Why did you do it?"

Dermot looked up and his blank expression gave Michael a chill. He could have been looking at his own brother Dermot at that age.

"He wouldn't give me his wagon."

"So, you hit him?"

His son's utter lack of remorse infuriated Michael. He had to fight the urge to strike him. After all, wasn't that the way parents disciplined their children? He'd been given the back of the hand more than once when he was a lad and it had done him no harm. On the other hand, Dermot, too, had been given the back of the hand and worse, yet it never seemed to make any difference in his behavior. Again, he had that terrible thought: Was his son going to be like his own brother?

Michael sat down heavily on the bed. "That's not the way you've been brought up," he said softly. "We share in this family. And we don't hurt each other. Is that understood?"

Dermot barely nodded.

When he came into the kitchen Emily was pouring tea. "Is everything all right?"

"For now. I don't know what we're going to do with that boy."

"Nor do I." She handed him a cup. "When you came home you had a big smile on your face. Good news?"

"I've been hired for the project."

Emily kissed him. "That is good news. I know work has been slowing down."

"It has. This construction business is maddening with its up and down. I've had projects canceled because of an article in the newspaper or a wild rumor of a failing bank. This church project will be steady work. It won't be completed until 1861. If all goes well, that's three years of steady work."

"That is good," Emily said, looking away.

"Yes, it is," he answered, half-heartedly.

They sat silently drinking their tea. The good news of getting the church project was overshadowed by their son's inexplicable behavior.

Just before seven o'clock Monday morning, Flynn stuck his head in Michael's office door. "They're all here."

Michael came out and addressed the men. "We are lucky to be selected to be part of Bishop Hughes' project. This is a great opportunity for steady work over the next three years. We must show them that we are worthy of the job. I'll warn you now, people from Hall & Joy will be watching us. If anyone is caught drinking on the job or slacking off, we will all be sacked. Any questions?"

There were none. Everyone knew how important this job was and how lucky they were to get it. "Good, let's get started."

Michael led off in the lead wagon, followed by the other six wagons. The convoy rounded Washington Square Park and turned north onto Fifth Avenue. It was late August and the oppressive summer heat was dissipating and promising an early fall. It was a beautiful sunny morning and Michael was in good spirits. If all went well, he wouldn't have to worry about where the next project would come from for some time to come.

As the creaking wagons slowly made their way north, they passed the Harrington Manson at Fortieth Street. Michael smiled. That was his first construction job. It had been just eight years, but it seemed like a lifetime ago. At Forty-Second Street, they passed the Egyptianesque Croton Reservoir. On the next block, they passed the four-story Colored Orphan Asylum. Beyond that, formal structures began to give way to shanties, lean-tos, decrepit taverns, and pig farms.

As the convoy neared Fifth Avenue and Fiftieth Street, he heard the dull thud of explosives. Already the explosion men were beginning to dynamite the outcroppings on the site. He was glad that part of the job was underway. Actual construction couldn't begin until the land was leveled and graded.

There was a scrum of assorted wagons, horses, and men at the site. Michael liked what he saw. To the untrained eye, it looked chaotic, but he saw that wagons were assembled in certain areas and men with clipboards scurried from wagon to wagon assigning work. He glanced around at the men standing idly by while they awaited their assignments. Usually at this time, a whiskey bottle would be surreptitiously passed around. But there was not a bottle in sight. Apparently, Bishop Hughes' message had been taken to heart. Michael had a good feeling about this. This was going to be a good job site.

A man with a clipboard approached. "Who are you?"

"Ranahan Construction."

The man consulted his notes. "Take your crew down to Madison Avenue. Load up your wagons with the debris from the explosions, take it over to the East River, and dump it. Any questions?"

"No, sir."

As he was told, Michael led his men down to Madison Avenue and the men, shovels in hand and as happy as he'd ever seen them, waded into mounds of dirt and rock.

"I have examined your son and I don't find anything physically wrong with him, Mrs. Ranahan."

An anxious Emily listened to that diagnosis with a mixture of relief—and frustration. In desperation, she'd brought Dermot to Dr. Birney hoping he could explain her son's bizarre behavior. Of course, she was happy that there was nothing physically wrong with him, but that still left the question: why did he behave as he did?

"Doctor, can you explain his sudden tantrums, his explosive anger, his stubbornness, the uncooperativeness, the remoteness?"

"I'm afraid I can't, Mrs. Ranahan. In my examination of your son there appears to be nothing wrong with his eyesight or hearing. We don't know much about the brain, but there doesn't appear to be anything amiss there either."

"What should I do now?"

"I would advise you to allow time to run its course. There are many children who exhibit symptoms similar to your son's and many of those children eventually grow out of it. Give it time, Mrs. Ranahan. Give it time."

That night, Emily told Michael what the doctor had said.

Michael sipped his tea. "Well, I'm relieved that there's no physical malady, but what are we to do with him?"

"Let time run its course. Perhaps, he'll grow out of this. At least, that's what the doctor said."

"I guess that's all we can do."

CHAPTER TWENTY-NINE

1860

Michael and his crew had been working on the St. Patrick's site for almost a year and a half. For the first three months, they removed tons of detritus from the site. When that was done, they began hauling lumber, sand, marble, and granite from piers on the Hudson and East Rivers to begin the actual construction.

Now the church was beginning to take shape. The walls were up, the ceiling was in place. Some stonemasons fitted stones into the spires, while others worked on the immense columns in the interior. There was still much to be done in the vast interior space.

It was a cold and damp February afternoon and Michael was standing by while the stonemason, Angus Roy, inspected the stones that Michael's crew had just brought from the Hudson piers.

"How do they look, Angus?"

The stonemason squinted. "There are some wee blemishes here and there," he said, running his rough hand over a large stone, "but nothing that can't be chiseled out."

Michael looked up at the soaring twin spires. "Here it is February already. Do you think we will be done in another year?"

"Not 'a'tall. Och, all these architects are daft, are they not? Optimistic as the day is long. They draw pretty pictures of their buildings and announce some preposterous date when it's to be done. I suppose it pleases their clients, but it puts pressure on the likes of us to finish on time. Well, that won't happen this time, I'll tell ya that. We'll be lucky to finish the work by the middle of '64."

Michael grinned. "I don't mind the extra few years' work."

Angus winked at him. "Aye, and me as well."

While Michael was telling Emily of Angus's prediction of three more years of work, there was an insistent knock at the door. An excited Gaylord Temple was standing there.

"Come in out of the rain," Michael said.

"Michael, you've got to come with me tonight to the Cooper Institute."

"You mean all the way down to Seventh Street?"

"Yes."

"Gaylord, I'm tired. I've been loading and unloading stones since seven this morning. What's so important that I would be willing to go out on this miserably cold night?"

"Mr. Abraham Lincoln is going to give an address."

Michael shrugged. "Who is Abraham Lincoln?"

"He's a politician from Illinois and there's talk that he may run for president this year."

"Well, I wish him luck, but I have no intention of leaving my comfortable home on such an inhospitable night to see him or any other politician."

"You've got to come, Michael. I believe we'll be witnessing history."

"Why do you say that?"

"I've been reading his speeches. He's a brilliant man. I believe he's the only one who can address the problem of slavery in a coherent manner."

"Go, Michael," Emily said. "You need to get out of the house to do something other than work."

"Oh, all right. Let me get my coat."

By the time Michael and Gaylord arrived at the Cooper Institute, a striking five-story Italianate brownstone building located at Third Avenue and 7th Street, it had started to snow. The great hall, capable of holding fifteen hundred people, was already beginning to fill up. Michael was impressed. If so many people were willing to brave such an icy night, perhaps this Mr. Lincoln was indeed a great man.

They found two seats in the fifth row. Within half an hour the great room was filled to capacity.

An elderly gray-haired gentleman stepped up to the podium.

After a few brief words about the guest of the evening, he cleared his throat. "Ladies and gentlemen, it is my great privilege and honor to introduce our speaker tonight. I give you, Mr. Abraham Lincoln."

Lincoln had been hidden by the lectern. As he stepped up to the podium clutching a sheaf of foolscap papers, there was an audible gasp from the audience. He was a bizarre sight. Michael had never seen anyone so tall nor so angular and awkward. Over six feet, he was wearing a black frock coat that hung from his spare frame. Gaylord had said he was fifty-three, but his deeply lined, clean shaven face made him appear much older. What was impressive were the deep-set eyes which were both sad and hopeful at the same time. But all in all, the man did not present an impressive figure. Was this the great man that Gaylord had been talking about?

Lincoln stood at the lectern with his hands behind his back silently staring out at the crowd. For a moment, Michael thought the poor man had been taken with stage fright, but suddenly, the huge hands grasped the sides of the lectern and he began to speak in a startling high-pitched voice.

"The facts with which I shall deal this evening," he began, "are mainly old and familiar; nor is there anything new in the general use I shall make of them."

For the next half hour, he went on to speak of whether the National Government could regulate slavery in the territories. Later in his speech, he gently castigated the South for trying to demonize the Republican party. Finally, as he concluded, he explained why appeasement with the South would not work.

As Lincoln spoke, Michael forgot about the man's ungainliness, the high-pitched voice, the lurching mannerisms. Lincoln had transformed himself into a forceful man of conviction and purpose. What he said and the way he said it was completely mesmerizing. Michael turned around to see how the audience was receiving the speech. Every upturned face was in rapt attention. A few had tears in their eyes. In a hall of fifteen hundred people there was not a sound, save the high-pitched voice of Abraham Lincoln.

In concluding his speech, he said, "Let us have faith that right makes might, and in that faith, let us, to the end, dare to do our duty as we understand it."

For a moment, there was complete silence. Then the crowd that moments before was completely silent, sprang to their feet erupting in applause and wild shouting.

After the speech, Michael and Gaylord retired to McSorley's Saloon just down the street from the Cooper Institute. The potbellied stove was glowing red and the heat was a comforting barrier against the biting cold outside. The saloon was crowded with men who had just heard Lincoln's speech and everyone was engaged in animated conversation about what they had just heard and what it meant.

Michael and Gaylord squeezed into a spot at the end of the bar and ordered their ale.

"I have to say, Gaylord, when I first saw your Mr. Lincoln, I was not impressed."

Gaylord chuckled. "Nor was I. I have read his speeches, but I have never seen a photo of him. It was quite the shock."

"Still, I have never heard anyone so clear and persuasive before."

"Will he become president?"

"Lincoln is not yet the nominee for the presidency, but the Republican convention is scheduled for May. I'm confident he'll be selected."

"Will this mean war with the South?"

"Tonight Mr. Lincoln spelled out the problem quite eloquently. In the end, we cannot compromise the Constitution or our ideals to satisfy the South's insatiable appetite for their 'peculiar institution.' They demand nothing short of acceptance of slavery in all current and future states. We can never accede to those demands."

"So, it's war?"

"I'm afraid so."

CHAPTER THIRTY

Abraham Lincoln was elected the sixteenth president of the United States on November 11, 1860. Almost immediately secessionists made clear their intent to leave the Union before he took office in March. For the next several months, men of peace sought to find common ground for ways to avoid war between the states. All to no avail. On April 12, 1861, Confederate batteries opened fire on Fort Sumter.

The American Civil War had begun.

In a rush of patriotic fervor, thousands of young men in New York City signed up for the Union Army. By the end of May, more than thirty thousand men had volunteered for service.

These turns of events had an adverse impact on Ranahan Construction. Every day, one or more men failed to show up for work. They had joined the army. In April, the Sixty-Ninth Regiment, composed of mostly Irishmen, marched off to war with the blessing of Bishop Hughes.

Michael wasn't the only one feeling the loss of manpower. Every contractor on the building site was experiencing the same thing. Worried about the worsening manpower shortage, Michael, Angus Roy, and the contractors had a meeting with representatives of the Hall & Joy Company.

"Will work stop on the cathedral?" Michael asked.

The company spokesman, Willard Colgan, a balding man in his late fifties, was adamant. "Work will not stop. The bishop is well aware that many workers have gone off to join the army, but he insists we continue with the project."

"But how long can we go on?" Angus asked. "I've lost half of my men and there's talk among the others that they intend to join up soon themselves."

Colgan shrugged. "I have no other instructions. Continue your work until you receive instructions to the contrary."

In the first week of May, they did receive further instructions: Work on the cathedral was canceled until the war was over.

An anxious Emily read the notice from the Joy & Hall Company. "What will you do now, Michael?"

"If I can keep enough men, I still have a few small projects to keep us busy. But I don't know how I'm going to do even that. There's war fever out there, Emily. It seems like every Irishman in New York City wants to run off and fight Johnny Reb."

"Why the Irish?"

"Well, there are plenty of Germans, too. But many of the Irishmen hope that by showing their patriotism to this country, it will stop nativists from saying that Irish Catholics should be denied citizenship."

"And they're willing to risk their lives for this hope?"

"It's not just that. Some of these same men believe that the military training they'll receive will come in handy in the coming war of Irish liberation."

"Oh, my God, Michael. There's no way a ragtag band of Irish rebels can prevail against the might of England."

"Obviously, they think they can."

But it wasn't just the construction industry that suffered. New York City had always had a lucrative trading partnership with the South. The banking industry supplied much-needed loans to southern planters. For their part, the South believed in "King Cotton," a strategy in which the South convinced itself that the textile mills in the North couldn't exist without the South's cotton.

With the onset of the war, all trading with the South ceased, causing the city's manufacturing economy to crash. East River shipyards and iron works came to a standstill. Even the ice industry was crippled by a lack of orders from the South.

There was great unrest among the city's movers and shakers. Many New York businessmen, stung financially by the loss of trade, sympathized with the South. There was even talk of New York seceding from the Union. Mayor Fernando Wood proposed that if the union dissolved, the city should become a "free city"—

not subject to the laws of the Federal Government nor the meddling legislators in Albany.

Over the summer months, Michael's crew was reduced to less than a dozen men. The only reason he had any men at all was because they were too old to fight or had families to support. He struggled to find work even for this handful of men. In desperation, he signed a contract with the city to remove dead carcasses from the city streets. It was filthy, demeaning work, and not well paid, but it was work. It would have to do until the economy recovered. To reduce his expenses, he sold off half of his unneeded horses. At least they were easy to sell because the army had developed an insatiable need for horses.

Michael soon realized that the money from the animal removal contract was not enough to pay his men and keep the business running. As the fall approached, he was seriously considering shutting down the business.

But at the next Sunday dinner everything changed when Gaylord said offhandedly, "The economy is beginning to improve."

"Not from where I sit," Michael said glumly. "The only work I can get is hauling away dead animals." He laughed bitterly. "The only good thing about it is the city will never run out of dead carcasses so there'll always be plenty of work."

"Why do you say the economy is improving?" Emily asked.

"The war machine must be fed. It needs wheat to feed the troops and iron and steel to build and repair railway tracks and cannons and muskets. The war has cut off all traffic on the Mississippi and now goods must be transported by train. New York City has become a hub. The piers on both the Hudson and East Rivers are jammed with ships bringing in wheat from the Midwest and iron and steel from the mills of Pennsylvania."

Michael was listening carefully to what Gaylord was saying. "So, all this wheat and iron and steel has to be shipped to the army by train?"

"Exactly."

Emily was following her husband's train of thought and was one step ahead of him. "So, if Ranahan Construction can't do

construction, why not become Ranahan Hauling?"
Michael grinned. "That's what I was thinking."

He lost no time in signing contracts with several shipping companies to haul goods from the ships to the railroad yards on the west side of the city. Suddenly, he had more work than he could handle. He managed to hire a few more men and now he regretted selling his horses. With all the work available, he could have used them, but horses couldn't be bought in the city at any price. They had all been rounded up and shipped south for the war effort. But even without the extra horses, Michael and his men were guaranteed work as long as the war continued.

CHAPTER THIRTY-ONE

1863

As the war entered its third year, its appetite for more men, more guns, and more food became insatiable. Six days a week Michael's wagons made their daily round trip from the piers on the East and Hudson Rivers to the railroad yards. The steady wages were so good that Michael was able to increase his monthly payments to Cully. If he could continue at this rate, Emily calculated he would own the business outright within three or four years.

At Sunday dinner, the conversation turned to the economy. "Here's a thought-provoking fact I came across," Gaylord said, in his usual manner of bringing up interesting topics. "In 1860, there were fewer than a dozen millionaires in the city, but now, there are several hundred. Some of them worth over twenty million dollars."

"Why is that?" Emily asked.

"It's the war. The war has been a tragedy for the men who have to fight it, but for the men who supply the food, the uniforms, the guns and bullets, and everything else needed to keep the war machine going, it's been a godsend."

Michael nodded in agreement. "I'm a bit ashamed to say it, but I have been doing very well since the war started."

"You're not the only one."

"There's been talk of war profiteering," Henrietta interjected.

"No doubt there has."

"What exactly is war profiteering?" Letta asked.

"It's when an unscrupulous merchant overcharges for his merchandise," Gaylord explained.

"Or when he sells shoddy merchandise," Henrietta added.

"That's true. A shoe manufacturer in Albany has been arrested for selling inferior footwear to the army. Within days the boots fell apart."

"He should be shot for doing that to our boys," Cully said, slamming his hand on the table.

"I agree," Emily said. "Gaylord, how is the war really going? I don't think we're getting the complete story in the newspapers."

"You're not. The government and the military have cracked down on what kind of news we can write about. Even though I'm a newspaperman and completely opposed to any censorship whatsoever, I can understand the reason for it. It seems the Confederate generals are avid readers of our northern newspapers."

"I am going to volunteer as a nurse's aide," Emily announced, surprising everyone around the table, and no one more so than her husband.

"What brought this on?" he asked.

"I've read that more and more war wounded are being shipped north and there is a great shortage of staff to tend them. Isn't that true, Gaylord?"

"Regrettably, it is. Besides a fearful loss of life, there are thousands and thousands of wounded on both sides."

"Every day I see more and more men on the streets who have lost arms and legs. I just feel I have to do something."

"What hospital will you go to?" Henrietta asked.

"The Central Park Hospital."

Michael frowned. "All the way up on a Hundred and Second Street?"

"The army will provide transportation for all volunteers."

Henrietta patted Emily's hand. "My dear, have you thought this through? I have heard that in those hospitals there are dreadful sights of men with amputated arms and limbs and worse."

"I understand. During the famine, I volunteered at a fever hospital. I can assure you, I saw more than my shared of dreadful sights."

Michael was aware of that. But he also knew that she'd lasted only a few weeks in that deplorable place. He was worried about her. He was glad she wanted to contribute to the war effort in some way, but would she be able to do this? Rather than dwell on that possibility, he asked, "What about the children and their schooling?"

"I can still do that. It only takes a couple of hours to give the children their lessons."

"I'll take care of them the rest of the time," Letta offered. "Claire is seven now and can practically take care of herself. The others are no bother."

"There then," Emily said with a nervous smile. "It's settled."

It was a gray March morning and Emily stood at the corner of Fifth Avenue and Fortieth Street waiting for the wagon. Five minutes later, a covered army wagon pulled by a team of mules arrived. A sergeant jumped down and saluted Emily.

"Are you Mrs. Ranahan?"

"I am."

"Thank you for your service, ma'am," he said as he helped her into the back of the wagon.

Two women were already there. The first, an older woman with her hair in a tight bun, thrust her hand out. "Good morning," she said in a no-nonsense Irish brogue. "Milly Ambrose."

"I'm Emily Ranahan."

The second woman, a thin young woman in her twenties, smiled shyly. "Hi. I'm Martha Litton."

"What brings you here?" Milly asked Emily.

Emily shrugged. "I just want to do my part for our soldiers."

"Same as me. I've been a nurse for forty years. Retired last year, but from the newspapers it's clear they can use my experience."

"I'm sure they can. What about you, Martha?"

"My husband's in the army. I would hope that if my William was wounded, someone would tend to him."

"I'm sure they would, Martha."

They rode for a good while in silence. As they passed the unfinished St. Patrick's Cathedral, Emily said, "My husband was working on the cathedral before the war ended construction."

Milly grunted. "Hughes' Folly. That's a good name for it."

"You don't approve?"

"Look around you, child. There's nothing here but pigs and squatters. Where's his congregation to come from I ask you? The bishop could have put that money to better use helping the poor souls in the Five Points and other slums around the city. He should heed the words of the Holy Bible. 'Vanity, all is vanity.' That fits him right enough."

At One Hundred and Second Street, the wagon stopped. The sergeant came around to the back. "Here we are ladies," he said as he helped each one out of the wagon.

The three women looked up at a striking five-story structure located just inside the park. What used to be Mount St. Vincent's Academy had been taken over by the army in 1862 and converted into a military hospital.

When they came into the lobby, waiting for them was a tall, stiff-backed, dignified gentleman with gray mutton chop sideburns. Emily couldn't help but notice with alarm that the front of his white apron was stained with blood, but he seemed to take no heed of the way he looked.

"Good morning, ladies. I am Dr. Thaddeus Scott, a colonel in the Union Army and the medical director here. On behalf of the President and the army, I welcome you and thank you for whatever assistance you can offer. I must caution you that you are going to see and hear things that will be quite disturbing. You should know—"

"I've been a nurse for forty years," Milly interrupted. "There's not much that can disturb me."

With a disapproving look, Dr. Scott asked, "And where exactly where were you a nurse for all those years?"

"The Blackwell Asylum."

"Ah, you were a matron to lunatics in the madhouse," he said in a condescending tone.

"Well, I can tell you it was more than that," an indignant Milly responded.

"Very well. Follow me ladies."

They walked down a long corridor toward a set of double doors. As they approached, an eye-watering stench permeated the air. Martha faltered and Emily had to grab her by the arm. "It'll be all right," she whispered.

Dr. Scott threw the doors open and the full impact of the stench of putrefying flesh, blood, and moans struck them like a physical barrier. Lying in beds lining both sides of the long, rectangular room were the patients that Emily had come to help. As they followed the doctor, Emily was shaken by what she saw. Most of the patients were mere boys. Some had lost an arm, some had lost a leg, while others had lost a combination of both. One pale young man with a glassy-eyed stare had lost both his arms and his legs. Suddenly, Emily felt overwhelmed. What could she possibly do for them?

At the far end of the room, Dr. Scott explained the problems he was facing. "There are three deadly wound infections we are constantly fighting: tetanus, gangrene, and blood poisoning. We are finding that for every three soldiers wounded, two die of disease. These soldiers have come from battlefields in the south. Ambulances take them to field hospitals close to the battlefield. The field hospitals are strictly for emergency treatment, amputations and the like. From there they are moved by rail to hospitals such as these."

"What do you want us to do?" Emily asked.

"Mostly help change their dressings, give them sponge baths, and whatever else you can do to make them comfortable."

"Will we be assisting in the operating room?" Milly asked. "I am a trained nurse."

From the expression on the doctor's face, it was clear he was losing his patience with the irritating Mrs. Ambrose. "Have you ever assisted in an amputation?" he asked, pointedly.

"Well, no, but I'm sure I can do it."

"That won't be necessary. We have medically-trained personnel for that." He glanced at his pocket watch. "The wagon will leave at five o'clock to return you to your homes. Oh, one more word of caution. Do not establish a personal relationship with any of these patients."

"Why not?" Martha asked.

Dr. Scott's weary, bloodshot eyes swept over the ward. "Because many of these men are going to die."

Martha's eyes filled with tears. Emily put her arm around the young girl. "Her husband is in the army," she explained to the doctor.

"Young lady," Scott said, not unsympathetically, "if this is too much for you, I can have a soldier take you to your home right now."

Martha shook her head. “No. I’ll be all right. I want to do my part.”

“Very well.” Dr. Scott motioned to a young corporal who’d been standing to the side listening. “Corporal Berry will explain your duties.”

As the doctor hurried off, the corporal said, “Well, then, ladies, if you’ll follow me”

He led them to a table and a cabinet where a supply of bandages and towels were kept.

“Here is where you will find all necessary supplies.”

“Is that it?” Milly said with great disdain. “These are very meager supplies indeed.”

The corporal looked embarrassed. “There are shortages everywhere, ma’am. This is our procurement allotment and there’s nothing we can do about it.”

Just then a soldier thrashing in a bed near them cried out in terror. “*Oh, God ... they’re behind us ... look to the trees ... Run ... run ... run ...*”

The unconcerned corporal waved a hand in dismissal. “That’s Private Feeney. Pay him no attention. He has these nightmares all the time.”

Emily turned to look at the young man who appeared to be no more than eighteen. There was a bloody stump where his right arm used to be. Emily grabbed a towel and, rushing to his side, held his hand. “There, there,” she said, soothingly. “It’s all right. You’re safe here.”

The private’s eyes snapped open wide with terror. “*Run ... run ....*” He suddenly stopped screaming when he realized where he was.

Emily wiped the perspiration from the young man’s forehead. “You’re going to be all right.”

“Yes, ma’am. Thank you, ma’am.”

“My name is Emily.”

He nodded. “Thank you, Miss Emily.”

Assuming that he hadn’t had a real conversation since he’d been removed from the battlefield, she wanted him to talk, but she wasn’t sure if he’d want to or not. Overcoming her hesitation, she whispered, “It must have been terrible for you, Private Feeney.”

“Please, call me Caleb. It was, Miss Emily. The battle of

Thompson Station down there in Tennessee was the worst fight I've been in. We were whipping Johnny Reb real good, but then they surprised us by attacking our left flank. That was it. We broke and run and that's when I got hit with shrapnel from a cannon ball. Knocked me out cold. When I woke up it was night. I had lost so much blood I didn't have the strength to crawl toward our lines. My arm hurt real bad. I laid there for three days listening to our boys and them Johnny Reb boys moaning and dying. Finally, a burial party found me and carted me off to the field hospital. Lying out there in that field all that time didn't do my arm no good. Gangrene set in and they sawed it off."

Emily was astonished by the matter-of-fact way in which he told his story.

"The train ride up here was freezing cold," he continued. "There was no water and nothing to kill the pain." His eyes filled with tears.

Emily needed to change the subject. "Where are you from, Caleb?"

"Right here in New York City. You know where the Five Points is?"

"I know it all too well."

"I wanted so bad to get out of that place I thought the army would be my best bet. I guess I was wrong there."

She patted his hand. "When you're well, they'll let you out of the army. Please don't go back there, Caleb. There are other places in the city for you."

"Thank you, Miss Emily."

While Emily was tending to Caleb, she'd been watching Martha. For a good while the young woman just stood there with her arms folded, seemingly overwhelmed by everything around her. Then a man at the other end of the ward cried out for water. Tentatively, she picked up a water bucket and went to him.

Milly Ambrose, on the other hand, wasted no time in making her presence known. She paced up and down the aisle with her hands behind her back inspecting her surroundings. At one point, she stopped to roughly pull a bed back into the proper alignment. The man in the bed cried out in pain.

The corporal rushed over. "Ma'am, please don't do that. He's just had his leg amputated this morning."

"Order is important, corporal. An orderly ward is a happy ward," she declared and continued on her inspection rounds.

By the time Emily got home that night, she was physically and mentally drained. It was just as well the children had already gone to bed because the sight of her would have frightened them. The front of her dress was covered in blood and gore from changing dressings all day and her hair was in a tangle.

Michael went to her. "My God, are you all right?"

"I'm fine. It looks worse than it is." She went into the kitchen and slumped down on a chair.

"Can I get you something to eat?" Letta asked.

"No." After what she'd been through all day, the mere thought of food made her nauseous.

"A tough day?"

"Michael, you wouldn't believe what goes on in that place they dare call a hospital. The floors are slippery with blood. The bed clothing hasn't been changed since God knows when. There are not enough dressings for their wounds. Those poor boys, they're just not getting the attention they deserve. It's horrible. Horrible."

"Will you go back?" Letta asked.

Emily thought for a moment, remembering her dreadful experiences in the famine hospital. "I've made a commitment to go there three days a week. I'll go for as long as I can."

Two days later, the three women returned. Emily was surprised to see Martha in the back of the wagon. The poor girl had looked so unnerved at the end of that first day she didn't think she'd be back. On the other hand, she wasn't surprised to see Milly. The woman seemed to positively enjoy bossing the corporal and other aides around.

When they walked into the ward, Emily immediately noticed that there was another man in Caleb Feeney's bed. A feeling of dread washed over her. With a voice shaking with emotion, she asked Corporal Berry, "Where's Private Feeney?"

"Died yesterday morning. Blood poisoning."

The room began to spin and Emily had to grab the railing of a bed to steady herself. For a moment, she thought she was going to faint, but the feeling passed. It was her own fault, she chided herself. Hadn't Dr. Scott warned them not to get involved personally with the patients? She should have listened to his advice. But how could one not get personally attached to these poor frightened boys who were suffering so much?

Just then an orderly came rushing into the room. "*Emergency on the second floor*," he yelled. "Dr. Scott says he needs everyone up there right now."

Corporal Berry looked at the three women. They were all he had. "Come on, ladies. We're needed upstairs."

The frightful room that served as an operating room was even worse than the ward they'd just come from. New blood and copper-colored old blood stained the wooden floor. The sickening smell of blood and a sweet-smelling chemical permeated the air.

Dr. Scott was standing over a man stretched out on the table. Even though he was being held down by two orderlies, he was still thrashing about and screaming incoherently. He looked up at the three frightened women and wiped his hands on his blood-splattered apron. "I'm short staffed. I'll need your help. You two," he said, pointing to Emily and Martha. "Each of you grab an arm and hold him down. And you," he said to a wide-eyed Milly, "you're a nurse. You will assist me. Stand beside me and be ready to hand my instruments when I call for them."

As Emily grabbed the man's arm, she could see that the lower part of his leg had already been amputated. But the flesh just above the wound had turned a putrid black. It was gangrene.

The doctor nodded to an aide. "Administer the chloroform."

Emily breathed a sigh of relief. She'd heard that these operations were conducted without anesthetic. At least the poor man would be sedated.

The aide dripped the chloroform onto a piece of cloth that didn't look all that clean. At a nod from the doctor, he held it over the patient's nose. After a while, the man stopped thrashing.

Dr. Scott picked up a large single-edged knife. Without hesitation, he began to cut away the flesh four inches about the blacked skin. Using a circular motion, he deftly made a cut all around the circumference of the leg, cutting away muscle and skin, leaving a flap of skin on one side.

"Bone saw." A glassy-eyed Milly stared at him as though she were in a trance. "*I said, bone saw.*" When she didn't react, he snatched up an ebony-handled saw that looked to Emily very much like the kind of saw Michael used in his work.

"Even with chloroform," the doctor said calmly, "he's going to start thrashing about when I begin to saw. This part of the procedure must be done as quickly as possible. Any delay may cost him his life."

He paused for a just a moment as though rehearsing in his mind what he must do. Then he began to saw. With the first pass of the blade, the man let out a howl and began to buck. "Hold him, hold him."

"*Jasus, Mary, and Joseph …*" Milly shrieked. "*Sweet Jesus …*"

Without looking up, the doctor said, "Corporal, get this woman out of here."

The corporal took the dazed Milly by the arm and led her out the door.

As he continued to saw, Dr. Scott looked up at Emily. "You will assist me. Come stand by my side. Quickly now."

A frightened but determined Emily did as she was told. By the time she got to his side of the table, the doctor was done. He flung the severed piece of leg onto the floor.

Emily was too astonished at how fast he had sawed through the bone to be sickened by the sight.

"Sponge."

Emily looked down and saw a filthy sponge on the table. "This?"

"Yes."

As she handed it to him, it fell to the floor.

"Pick it up, quickly. Rinse it and give it here."

There was only a bucket with water stained red from someone else's blood. Without hesitating, she plunged the sponge into the murky water, squeezed it, and gave it to the doctor. After sponging the wound, he said, "Tenaculum."

Emily stared at an assortment of strange instruments on the table. "Tenaculum…?"

"The instrument with the hook."

Emily handed it to him wondering what in the world he would do with a large hook.

He shoved the hook into the open wound and pulled out a pulsating, bleeding artery. As he tied it off, he explained to the orderlies, "Notice, I've pulled the artery way out. When I tie it off, it will disappear up into the man's leg. When he gets his artificial leg, it won't press on the artery and there'll be less pain and discomfort. File"

Emily quickly handed him a long metal file. Aghast, she watched him scrape the end and edges of the bone smooth. Then he pulled the flap of skin he'd left across the open wound and sewed it up. Finally, he wrapped the stump with a bandage.

He looked up and for the first time Emily saw that his forehead was bathed in perpetration. Apparently, in spite of his calm demeanor, this operation was as nerve-wracking for him as it was for her.

"That's it. Thank you, ladies. You've done very well. I hope you never have to witness something like this again."

Emily and Martha wordlessly stumbled downstairs in a state of shock at what they had just taken part in. Corporal Berry was waiting for them with a sympathetic expression on his face.

"I suspect you both could use a strong cup of coffee. There's a pot in the backroom. Why don't you take a break before you begin tending the patients?"

Emily and Martha retired to the backroom and drank their coffee in silence, trying to absorb all that they had seen.

Finally, Martha broke the uneasy silence. "Emily, you were wonderful up there. I don't think I could have done that."

"Of course you could. I was watching you. You were very brave."

"The only thing that kept me from running out of the room in sheer terror was the thought of my William being operated on. I kept thinking—hoping—that some woman would be there to help him if necessary."

"I just hope we never have to take part in anything like that again." Emily put her tin mug down. "I guess we should get out to the patients."

When they came onto the ward, Martha asked Corporal Berry where Milly was.

"Gone. Dr. Scott said she's never to come here again. It happens. Some people just can't deal with what we do. That's understandable, but she did say she'd been a nurse for forty years. I don't understand that."

"She worked in a lunatic asylum," Martha said in defense of Milly. "I'm sure she's never witnessed anything like that. I feel sorry for her."

The corporal shrugged. "In any event, she won't be back here. The patient in bed four needs his dressing replaced."

For the rest of the afternoon Emily welcomed the ordinary routine of changing dressings and tending to the needs of the patients. Towards the end of the day, she sat down next to a man who had lost his left leg. He was much older than most of the others in the ward. She looked at his chart. "Sergeant Daily, is it?"

"'Tis ma'am," he said with a thick brogue. "Ordinance Sergeant with the Sixty-Ninth Regiment, now called the Irish Brigade."

"Where were you wounded?" She had stopped worrying about asking questions because she found that most of the men wanted to talk about what had happened to them or just to have a conversation with a woman.

"Chancellorsville. That was a dark and bloody battle, I can tell ya. We fought hard, but we was whipped by the rebs. I got hit by a mini-ball as we was movin' out. It tore up my leg pretty bad. When they got me to the field hospital, the doctors said the leg had to go and they cut it off." After a moment's pause, he said, "Funny thing, my leg has been gone for over three weeks now, but I still have pain. How can that be? Sometimes I wake up in the middle of the night and I feel the pain, and I think my leg is still there. I put my hand down there, but there's nothing there." He chuckled. "Funny thing, that."

Emily still couldn't get used to the matter-of-fact way these men talked about their horrific wounds. Hoping to make him feel better, she said, "I understand the army provides soldiers like you with prosthetic limbs and a pension of eight dollars a month."

He waved a hand in dismissal. "I'll have none of that," he said, disgustedly.

"But why not?"

"'Tis charity. That's all it is. I sacrificed my leg for the union. 'Tis an honorable scar I'll proudly wear. When people see me empty trouser leg, they'll know I fought for the Union."

Emily didn't know what to say. One would think that an amputee would jump at the chance for a wooden leg. But these weren't ordinary men. These were brave men who had gone through an ordeal Emily could only imagine.

CHAPTER THIRTY-TWO

The business of hauling freight had become so lucrative that Michael decided he had to hire more men. He didn't make that decision lightly. He hadn't forgotten how he'd lost the business the last time he'd hired additional men and tried to expand the business. But this time it was different. After the war, Gaylord had assured him, with all those newly minted millionaires, there would be a building boom. Michael certainly hoped that would be the case, but in the meantime, he needed more workers right now.

He was in his office only half listening to Flynn, whom he'd posted outside and assigned him to interview prospective new workers. Michael would have the final say on any man Flynn found acceptable.

Flynn was ruthless in his role. All day long, Michael heard him pass withering judgment on the unworthy: "You're too old." "You're too young." "Man, I don't think you could pick up a bag of sand." And on it went. But then, toward the end of the day, just as Michael was finishing up an interview, he heard Flynn say to someone, "We don't hire niggers. Off with you."

An angry Michael stood up. "All right, Cleary, you're hired. You'll start Monday." As the happy man was going out the door, Michael called out, "Flynn, get in here."

Flynn came in. "You wanted to see me?"

"Did I hear you tell someone we don't hire Negroes?"

"You did. Sure, the niggers are unreliable, Michael. They don't show up for work because they're too drunk or they got thrown into jail for beating their women. We don't need their likes here."

Michael slammed his hand down on the desk. "Flynn, what the hell is the matter with you? Those were the kinds of words that were thrown in my face when I first came to this country looking for work. Have you forgotten the No Irish Need Apply signs?"

Flynn hung his head. "I did not."

"All right, get back to work and know this: I'll hire any Negro who can do the work."

As Flynn got to the door, he turned, "Ach, it wouldn't have worked out anyways, Michael. The man's right hand was nothin' but a claw. How could he do a decent day's work, I ask ya?"

Michael jumped up. "*Claw*? Was he a big man?"

"Aye. He was that."

Without another word, Michael raced out of his office and into the street. He looked up and down, hoping to see a large Negro. But there was none in sight. He ran to the corner of John Street and there, about a block away, was the unmistakable gate of Kitch, lumbering up the street among a crowd of workmen and shoppers.

Michael raced after him, shoving pedestrians and peddlers aside. "*Kitch, Kitch,*" he shouted over the clatter of a thousand iron wheels grinding on the cobblestone street.

Kitch turned around and in an instant recognized Michael. "Mikill," he said, a wide grin spreading across his face, "my old friend!"

Michael, panting from the run, slapped him on his broad back. "Kitch, am I glad to see you. Come on back to my office. We need to talk."

In amazement, Kitch looked around Michael's office and shook his head. "So, you own all this?"

"Not exactly, I have a note to pay off first."

"When I came in here looking for work, I had no idea you were the owner. *Damn*!"

"Please forgive my employee when he said we don't hire Negroes. He was wrong and he shouldn't have said that."

"Mikill, I don't pay that no never mind. I hears that all the time."

"Well, you won't hear it here." After a moment's pause, Michael said, "You weren't there my last day at Clayton's. I went back several times looking for you, but no one knew what happened to you."

"I was mighty sick, Mikill. Some kind of evil ailment ran through my tenement sickenin' and killin' I don't know how many. I was vomitin' for days and my legs, Lordy, how my legs hurt. I thought I was gonna die for sure, but somehow, I didn't. After, some people from somethin' called the sanitation commission paid a visit to the buildin'. They said it was cholera. They said we shouldn't be drinkin' bad water. Well, how's I supposed to know good water from bad water? Best I can tell, *all* the water in the Five Points is bad."

"Well, I'm just glad you're all right. How would you like a job?"

"You mean, here with you?"

"Here with me."

Kitch's face widened in a broad grin. "Well, I reckon I would."

At Sunday dinner, the talk was all about the unpopular draft laws enacted in March of 1863.

"Who does this draft law affect?" Letta asked.

"Every male citizen between ages twenty and forty-five," Gaylord responded.

"I had to sign up," Otto said glumly.

"I had to sign up myself," Michael said, indignantly. "I'm forty-two with a wife and four children and they want to send me off to war?"

"I don't think you have to worry about getting drafted," Henrietta said. "I believe they want the young men."

"That's almost as bad. Am I going to lose all my men again? I'll be ruined."

"You won't be able to stop your young workers from being drafted," Gaylord agreed. "However, what I find most troublesome is the provision that allows a man to buy his way out of the draft for three hundred dollars."

Cully was aghast. "That's outrageous. Why, that's a years' wages for most men."

"True enough, and Andrew Carnegie and JP Morgan have already availed themselves of the provision and hired substitutes."

"Aye," Michael said bitterly. "That's what it's all about—a way out for the rich."

"And speaking of the rich, "Gaylord added, "what could Secretary Chase have been thinking when he ordered a three-thousand-dollar shawl from A.T. Stewart's for his daughter in a time of war?"

"My God," Emily exclaimed, "that represents the price of ten men's lives,"

"I doubt he gave it much thought," Michael added.

Gaylord poured more wine into his glass. "It's not just the three-hundred-dollar clause that's provoking the people. The draft also excludes Negroes."

Michael shook his head in agreement. "Just yesterday, I heard a man up on a soap box complaining about that very thing. His point was why should white men go fight to free Negroes so they can come north and take their jobs away from them."

"It's a sore point," Gaylord admitted. "As far as the draft is concerned, I think we'll have all the answers soon enough. The lottery is to begin next Saturday."

"Where?" Cully asked.

Gaylord chuckled. "The Ninth Ward headquarters up on Third Avenue and Forty-Seventh Street."

"Why that's an area of nothing but vacant lots and the odd building," Otto noted.

"Exactly. And I do believe that is intentional. This draft lottery is a touchy business. They want to stay away from the crowds downtown."

The following Saturday morning, at Horace Greeley's instruction, Gaylord went up to the Ninth Ward to cover the proceedings. In spite of the desolate location, a large crowd had gathered, but they were mostly curious rather than angry. The provost marshal began reading off names drawn from a large barrel. By the end of the day, twelve hundred thirty-six names had been selected. Gaylord was relieved that there had been no disturbance.

The next day, Sunday, he toured the city's bars and taverns. Everywhere he went, men and women were pouring over the names listed in the newspapers. Getting drunk on whiskey and beer, they denounced the draft in colorful, if angry, words.

CHAPTER THIRTY-THREE

Monday morning was miserably hot and muggy. At six o'clock, Gaylord joined hundreds of men and women streaming north along Eighth Avenue beating on copper pots and waving NO DRAFT signs as they marched to the Ninth Ward headquarters.

At 10:30, a nervous provost, guarded by 60 equally nervous policemen, and watched by an angry crowd, began to draw more names from the drum.

Just then, Gaylord spotted the Black Joke Engine Company in full regalia, marching up Third Avenue. He was not surprised to see them. Sunday night he'd spend the evening in a saloon frequented by the volunteer firemen. They were furious because they'd been led to believe they were exempt from the draft. But that turned out not to be true and several of their men had been selected on Saturday. As the night wore on and they got drunker and drunker, some of the more vocal members bellowed that they should march on the draft location in the morning to not only halt the draft proceedings, but to destroy all evidence that their members had been selected.

As soon as the firemen got to the site, they began to stone the building. The undermanned police were no match for the angry men and were driven off. The firemen smashed the draft wheel, swarmed into the building and poured turpentine everywhere, and set fire to the building. Then they waited outside to drive off any fire company that would dare show up to put out the fire.

Encouraged by the actions of the firemen, the crowd quickly became a witless mob. Women, using sticks, began tearing up cobblestones that the men hurled through windows. While this was going on, a man in a buggy came galloping up Third Avenue. Gaylord recognized Superintendent of Police John Kennedy. What in the world, he wondered, did he think he was going to accomplish against this mob?

He had barely stopped his buggy when someone recognized him. "*It's Kennedy,*" a man shouted. "*That sonofabitch is with the police. Let's get him.*"

The crazed mob swarmed the buggy, pulling Kennedy down to the ground. Dozens of men and women attacked the helpless man with sticks, bricks, and knives. When they finally left him, he was unconscious and almost unrecognizable. His clothes had been ripped from his body and he was covered in blood and mud. Gaylord dragged the superintendent to the buggy and lifted him inside. Then, taking the reins, he turned the wagon around and sped south for the police station on West Thirty-Fifth Street.

The newspaperman galloped past a band of rioters who were tearing up tracks and cutting telegraph lines that connected local police precincts to the central office. Another mob shouting "*Kill all niggers*!" pulled Negro men and women off omnibuses and beat them. A fringe group, standing in the middle of the street, tried to stop the buggy. Gaylord, realizing that if they stopped him they would beat him to a pulp, put the whip to the horse and anyone who tried to grab the reins. As he scattered the mob, a rock crashed into the side of his head. Brushing the blood out of his eyes, he continued down Third Avenue.

After he handed off the unconscious Kennedy to a squad of policemen, he went directly to Michael's house.

Emily opened the door and was shocked at the sight of Gaylord. He was deathly pale. Blood streamed down his forehead and the front of his coat was smeared with blood. "My God, what's happened to you?"

"All hell is breaking lose in the city. There are mobs roaming the streets attacking Negroes and anyone they think is rich. They almost killed a superintendent of police. Buildings are being set on fire. Where are your children?"

"Upstairs."

"Good. Keep them in the house. No one is safe on the streets."

"I will. Let me get you cleaned up."

"No time. I've got to get back out there."

"In the name of God why?"

"Because I'm a newspaperman. I'm scared to death, Emily, but it's what I do."

"Well, for God's sake be careful."

"I will. Remember what I said. Under no circumstances allow the children to leave the house."

"I won't." As soon as he was gone, she bolted the door.

She called all the children into the kitchen. "Mr. Temple was just here. No one will go out of this house today. There are some very bad things going on in the streets."

"What's happening," Eleanor asked.

"People are rioting."

"Why?"

"It's complicated, but it has something to do with men not wanting to get drafted."

"Are they burning down buildings?" Dermot asked, his eyes bright with excitement.

"That's none of your concern."

"I smell burning outside. They must be burning buildings nearby. Why can't me and my friends just go see what's going on?"

"Because I told you. It's too dangerous. We will all remain in this house until we are told that it's safe to go out."

"How long will that be?" Dermot persisted.

"I don't know."

With a look of concern on his face, Peter said, "Where's Da?"

"I don't know, Peter. I'm sure he's safe and he knows enough to come home if he thinks it isn't. Now, all of you, go to your rooms and play."

Michael and his men were at Hudson River pier loading wagons when a mob appeared at the top of the street. Carrying torches and chanting, "*Down with the draft…Burn down the rich man's warehouses …* "*Kill all the niggers …*" as they advanced toward the pier.

Michael whispered to Kitch. "Get inside."

Kitch tensed. "I ain't 'fraid of dem, Mikill."

"Kitch, do as I say. Get inside the pier and out of sight."

As Kitch did as he was told, the mob, seeing the pier, broke into a trot, chanting, "*Burn it down … Burn it down …*"

Michael turned to his men and said calmly, "Grab a tool and

spread out."

Silently, the men picked up axes and hammers and formed a line in front of the wagons. As the mob reached the pier, Michael shouted out, "Move on, the lot of you. Any man who tries to put a torch to this pier will answer to me and my men."

A large, burly drunk, apparently the leader of the mob, stepped forward. "Get the hell out of the way, damn you. Why are you protecting the rich man's property?"

Michael took a step forward and pointed his axe at the man. "You take one more step and I will split your skull with this axe." As he said that, his men inched forward, itching for a fight. They knew that if the mob had its way, they would burn the pier and their wagons, the source of their livelihood.

The mob leader, realizing that these wagon drivers couldn't be intimidated, turned away. "Come on," he shouted to the others, "there's plenty more that can be burned down."

After they'd gone, Kitch came out and there were tears in his eyes. "Mikill, I will never hide from white trash like dem again."

"You won't have to. I think this might have something to do with the draft. I want you to go to my house now and stay there till this madness blows over."

"I can go to my room in the Five Points."

Flynn, who'd been listening to the conversation, shook his head. "Too dangerous, Kitch."

"All right, Mikill. I'll go to your house after the day's work is done."

"You'll go now. I don't know what's going on, but I want you off the streets."

As Kitch started up the street reluctantly, Michael shouted after him, "Be careful, Kitch."

Kitch waved and disappeared around a corner.

After Michael and his crew unloaded their cargo at the rail yards, Michael said, "Let's get the wagons back to the warehouse."

As they moved through the streets of downtown Manhattan, they encountered robbing bands of drunken men and women setting fire to buildings.

When they got to the warehouse, Michael said, "Everybody go home. It's too dangerous to continue working."

"What are you going to do?" Flynn asked.

"I'm going to stay here. If a drunken mob has a mind to burn down my property, they'll have to go through me."

"I'll stay with you," Flynn said without hesitation. He turned to the other men. "What about you lot?"

Without a word, every man raised his hand.

The men barricaded the doors and windows and formed a line outside. The air was thick with smoke and the smell of burning wood. To Michael's relief, Pearl Street was deserted. But how long would that last, he wondered?

While rioting occurred in many parts of the city, none of it was coordinated. The central cause of the riots was opposition to the draft, but each individual mob selected individual targets. Homes of wealthy men were looted and burned by some. Others attacked businesses and warehouses. While still others roamed the streets looking for Negroes.

Around four in the afternoon, Gaylord caught up with a mob of several hundred men, women, and children all armed with sticks and cobblestones and streaming up Fifth Avenue. When they got to the Colored Orphan Asylum at Fifth Avenue and Forty-Third Street, the leader of the mob stopped in front of the large four-story building surrounded by grounds and gardens. Raising a torch, he cried out, "*Look, the nigger kids' home is right here. Let's burn it down.*"

Knowing that there could be hundreds of children inside, Gaylord watched in horror as the mob hurled themselves against the building. Three swings of an axe and the front door came crashing down. Gaylord followed a stream of wild-eyed men, women, and children as they swarmed into the building. A dismayed Gaylord watched as they proceeded to ransack the building and set it on fire.

While the mob was busy looting and setting fires, Gaylord made his way through the building looking for the children. He found about two hundred of them huddled in the basement, protected by the superintendent of the asylum and his assistants, who, pathetically, considering who they were up against, had armed themselves with brooms.

"What are you doing here? You must get the children out of here."

"We're afraid to take the children out into the street," the terrified superintendent said.

"But you can't stay here. They're burning the building."

Gaylord opened the back door. "Come. Right now, the mob is busy looting upstairs, but if they come down here …" He left the rest of the sentence unsaid, but the superintendent understood exactly what he was getting at.

"Where can we go?"

Gaylord thought for a moment. "The safest place is a police station. There's one on West Thirty-Fifth Street. Quickly, we have no time to lose."

With the entire mob inside the building, there was no one on the street. Gaylord and the other adults quickly and quietly shepherded the children down Sixth Avenue to the police station, which was already crowded with frightened Negroes and whites who had been taken for "three-hundred-dollar men."

By the time Gaylord got back to the asylum, multiple fires had taken hold and the building burned to the ground.

At about the time the orphanage was burning, Emily went upstairs to check on the children. Eleanor and Claire were playing with their dolls in their room, but when she went to the boys' room, she found only Peter.

A wave of dread washed over her. "Where's Dermot?"

Peter pointed to a window. "He went out that way. He said he was going to go play with his friends."

A frantic Emily rushed headlong down the stairs and grabbed her coat. As she opened the front door, she collided with Kitch, who was about to knock.

"Whoa! What be the trouble, Miss Emily?"

"It's Dermot…" she answered in a voice constricted by fear. "He's gone out. Gaylord told me the city has gone insane with rioters. I told that boy specifically not to go out. Now I've got to find him."

Kitch put his big hands on her shoulders. "You caint do that, Miss Emily. It's too dangerous for a woman to go out on the streets. There be crowds of crazy men, women, and even young chil'en wanderin' about lookin' to do mischief. Mikill say I should come here to stay. It took me 'bout an hour to get here from the

Hudson piers on account of I had to keep hidin' myself from those riff-raffs on the prowl."

"I agree with Michael. It's best you be off the streets. Go into the house. I'll find my son."

"No, I'll do it. You needs to stay here with your own chil'en."

"But you can't go out there either. Gaylord told me they were attacking Negroes."

"Don't you worry 'bout that. I can take care of myself. Where should I start lookin'?"

"He has some friends over on Thirty-Eight Street. I was going to start there, maybe—"

"You jest go back inside and lock the door. I'll find that child and bring him home, don't you worry none."

Kitch headed down Thirty-Seventh Street toward Sixth Avenue. Luckily, night has fallen and the street was deserted. But when he got to Sixth Avenue and turned the corner, he saw a crowd at the corner of Thirty-Eighth Street. Women were digging up cobblestones, which men and boys hurled through the windows of a four-story mansion. Others were chanting, "*Burn down the rich man's mansions …*" and "*a three-hundred-dollar man lives there …*"

Staying in the shadows, he crept closer to the mob. When he was about fifty feet away, he saw Dermot among a group of young boys. With grins of delight, all of them, including Dermot, were throwing stones at the house. Kitch backed into a darkened doorway, wondering how he would get the boy's attention without being seen.

Unexpectedly, Dermot started walking toward him, his eyes on the ground, looking for more rocks. When he was about thirty feet way, Kitch whispered from the doorway. "Dermot, c'mon home, now. Your mama's worried sick."

A startled Dermot looked up. Seeing Kitch, he backed away, shaking his head. Kitch stepped out of the doorway. "Dermot," he said, more insistently, "you hear me? Your mama wants you to come home right now."

Someone in the crowd spotted Kitch. "*Look, there's a nigger … Let's get him …*"

Kitch started to run. His thought was that if he could get to the

Ranahan house, he'd be safe. But as he reached the corner of Thirty-Seventh Street, it occurred to him that he couldn't go there. The mob would follow and surely burn their house down and harm Emily and the children. With no other choice, he continued running down Sixth Avenue, hoping to outrun the mob of mostly drunken men and women.

He was putting distance between himself and the mob, when at the corner of Thirty-Fifth Street, a dozen men burst out of a saloon and surrounded him. Slowly, they circled him, wary of the big man's size. Within moments the mob caught up. Three men swinging clubs crashed into Kitch beating him to the ground. Doing his best to ward off the blows, he swung his massive fists, breaking noses and ribs. He kicked out, slamming his big boots into testicles, shins, thighs, and stomachs. But they were relentless and continued raining down blows on him. The pain reminded him of the many times he'd been flogged by the Massa. But the floggings stopped eventually. Here, the pain from the blows of clubs and cobblestones seemed to go on forever. As he was losing consciousness, he was vaguely aware of being doused with kerosene.

Then there was a lit match. And excruciating pain.

And then there was nothing.

As the dead body of Kitch burned, the mob continued to pummel him with clubs and sticks. Then a man appeared out of the crowd holding a rope. "Let's string the sonofabitch up."

And a chant went up. "*String him up .... String him up ... String him up ...*"

A noose was fitted around Kitch's neck and he was dragged to a nearby lamppost. The end of the rope was thrown over the top of the lamppost and three men pulled on the rope until Kitch's body was ten feet in the air.

Just then, it started to rain hard. The downpour seemed to bring the mob to its senses. Clubs, sticks, and cobblestones were cast aside and, one by one, the mob dispersed, barely giving a second glance to Kitch's smoldering body swaying from the lamppost.

When Michael got home around midnight, Emily rushed to him and threw her arms around him. "Oh, Michael, I was worried sick about you. Where were you?"

“Me and my men stood guard at the warehouse. Emily, they’re burning the city to the ground. It’s madness out there. When it started to rain, I decided the rioters were finished for the night. Are you all right?”

“Yes.”

Michael heard the hesitation in her voice. What’s the matter?”

Tears welled up in her eyes. “Dermot went out tonight even though I told him not to.”

“Damn that kid.”

“It’s all right, Michael. He’s home now.” She started to cry.

“So, what’s wrong?”

“Kitch was here. He went out to look for Dermot. He hasn’t come back yet.”

“Oh, Jesus … I’ve got to go look for him.”

“No, please don’t go out there again. I beg you.”

“I have to. I’ve seen what they do to Negroes. I even saw one hanging from a tree on Canal Street. If he’s hurt, he’ll need my help.”

Just then there was a knock at the door. Emily breathed a sigh of relief. “Thank God, he’s back.”

Michael opened the door, expecting Kitch, but instead a pale and disheveled Gaylord was standing there.

“Can I stay the night here? I’m too exhausted to go back to the boardinghouse.”

“Of course. Come in. I’m going out, but Emily can make you a cup of tea.”

“Whiskey would be better,” he said, shaking the rainwater off his coat. “Where are you going?”

“To look for Kitch. He went out to find Dermot and he hasn’t come back.”

“I don’t like the sound of that. I’ll go with you.”

“No, it looks like you’ve done enough for one day. Stay here.”

“No. We’ll find him together.”

“All right. Come on. The wagon’s in the backyard.”

Michael led the horse down to Sixth Avenue. It was still raining and the avenue was deserted, but flames were still shooting out of the mansion’s windows on Thirty-Eighth Street. They went to take a closer look. The street was littered with cobblestones and sticks, and there were potholes where the cobblestones had been dug up. The air was thick with the smell of smoke and burning wood.

"Why aren't the firemen here to put out the fire?" Michael asked.

"They're probably too busy putting out fires in other parts of the city. Did you know these fiends burned down the Colored Orphan Asylum today?"

"I did not. What in God's name is the matter with these people?"

"What they are doing is inexcusable. But for too long, these poor wretches have been a simmering volcano of resentments. You've seen the filthy conditions under which they live with the rats and the vermin. Their children died regularly and they don't know why. They're poorly paid, assuming they can find employment. Their politicians are too busy dealing in graft to pay attention to their plight. And now, there's the draft. They've been asked to fight to free slaves who they're afraid will take their jobs. For some of them that was the last blow and the result is all this," he said bitterly. "Although the madmen who did this are to blame for this destruction of life and property, so, too, are the city's politicians, damn them."

Michael turned the wagon around. "Let's go down Sixth Avenue. Maybe—" He stopped talking when he saw something hanging from a lamppost a few of blocks away. With a sickening feeling, he said, "What do you think that is?"

Gaylord squinted. "Where—? Oh, good God. That's a body hanging. I've seen it more than once tonight."

Michael led the horse down the avenue carefully skirting piles of cobblestones and potholes. He pulled the wagon up in front of the body, which was burned beyond recognition.

"I can't tell if he was black or white," Gaylord whispered. "I wonder who the poor soul was?"

"I don't know—" Then Michael noticed the dead man's claw-like right hand. "Oh, Jesus, it's Kitch."

Michael maneuvered the wagon under the body, then they untied the rope and slowly lowered the body into the wagon.

"Where will we take him?" Gaylord asked.

"To my house."

Gaylord came into the house first to warn Emily, who was anxiously pacing around the kitchen.

"Did you find Kitch?"

"We did ..." Gaylord said, choking back tears.

"He's dead?

"I'm afraid so."

Emily sat down heavily "Where is he?"

"Michael's bringing him in. I don't think you should see him. It's a ghastly sight. They burned and hanged him."

"Oh, dear God. Bring him in here. He'll have to be cleaned up."

Michael laid the body on the table. In the light of the kerosene lamps he looked even worse. The skin was charred and most of the clothing had been burned a way. Looking at the body, Emily realized there was no point in cleaning him up. He was no longer recognizable as a human body.

"Is there a next of kin?" Gaylord asked.

Michael shook his head. "No. His wife and daughter are dead."

"Then, we'll have to bury him," Emily said in a dull voice.

"Where?" Gaylord asked. "We can't bury him in a whites only cemetery."

"Are there no Negro cemeteries?" Michael asked.

Gaylord shrugged. "None that I know of."

"The Hudson River."

Both men looked at Emily. Then, Gaylord snapped his finger. "You're right. It's the only thing we can do. With the mood this city is in now, even if we found a Negro cemetery, I wouldn't put it past some fiends to dig him up and further desecrate the poor man."

Michael shook his head. "But not the Hudson River. We'd need a boat. But I know where we can put him into the East River."

The two men carried the burlap-wrapped body outside and slid it into the back of the wagon.

Michael turned to Emily. "We'll be back shortly."

"I'm coming with you."

"This is not something you need to see."

Emily climbed up into the seat. "I'm coming."

It was almost one in the morning by the time they reached the Clayton Coal Company warehouse. The rain had stopped, but the moisture in the air made for a muggy, sticky night.

"There are finger piers behind the warehouse," Michael explained. "They jut out into the river about sixty feet. The tide runs swiftly here. If we weight the body down, it'll disappear from sight and wash out to sea."

"What'll we weight the body down with?" Gaylord asked.

Michael pointed at the warehouse. "Coal."

After they carried the body out to the end of the pier, Michael jimmied a backdoor lock and slipped inside. A couple of minutes later, he came out to the pier with a wheelbarrow full of coal. As he shoveled coal into the burlap sack, tears stung his eyes as he remembered the first time Kitch had showed him how to properly load a wheelbarrow. When he was finished, they closed up the sack.

The three stared down at it.

"We should say something," Gaylord said.

"Do you know any prayers?" Emily asked.

"You ask this of an atheist?"

In spite of the circumstances, Emily giggled. "Well, we're atheists as well. So, now what?"

Michael gazed out at the dark Queens shoreline on the other side of the river. "Isn't it sad? Kitch survived being a slave and was able to buy his freedom only to come here and die in New York City at the hands of a murderous lynch mob."

"It's a cruel city," Gaylord said softly.

"It is that."

Emily said nothing, but the same dreadful thought kept running through her head: *Kitch was dead because of Dermot.*

The two men picked up an end of the sack and gently let it slip into the black swirling river. They watched as it quickly sank out of sight and then silently returned to the wagon.

The next morning, as Michael was dressing for work, Emily brought up the subject that had kept her awake all night. "Michael, you know our son is responsible for Kitch's death."

Michael sat down on the edge of the bed. "I know. Should we talk to him about it?"

"What would be the point? Would he even understand what he did?"

"He's twelve-years-old."

"Michael, both you and I know he's not a normal twelve-year-old."

"I suppose you're right. If he doesn't already realize what he's done, we'd only put the weight of guilt on him for the rest of his life. I guess we should leave it alone."

"I agree."

Sunday dinner was a somber affair. The upheaval and devastation of the past week had left everybody in a state of numbed shock.

"Was there any damage to your beer garden?" Michael asked Otto.

"No. I stood guard with a shotgun."

"How about you, Michael," Cully asked. "Was there any damage to your warehouse?"

"No. Like Otto, me and my men guarded it until the riots were over."

"You were very lucky," Gaylord said. "Those barbarians tried their best to burn the whole city down."

"What finally stopped them?" Henrietta asked.

"The army—six thousand of them, fresh from fighting on the battlefields of Gettysburg. It ended in a bloody confrontation near Gramercy Park between the mob, the police, and the army. Troops set up howitzers and cannons. Twelve people were killed, including two soldiers."

"How many people died all together?" Emily asked.

"The best estimate is around a hundred and fifteen, including nearly a dozen Negroes who were lynched."

The group became silent as they thought about Kitch. Then Gaylord continued. "Hundreds of buildings have been damaged. I hear as many as fifty burned to the ground. There's millions of dollars in damage."

"Will the city ever recover?" Letta asked.

"It will. But the memory of what went on for those four days, the deaths and the destruction, will never fade."

CHAPTER THIRTY-FOUR

1865

The war years created an economic boom in New York City that allowed countless thousands of men to move up into the middle class and the middle class to move up to the upper class. Michael Ranahan was one of those who moved up to the middle class. Since the start of the war, he'd been adding more men and more equipment. Now the Ranahan Construction Company employed 75 men with a fleet of 17 wagons. In addition to hauling freight for the government, a building boom offered him the opportunity to get back into the construction business. Not content to simply frame out houses and lay brick, he hired skilled carpenters, stone workers, and artists. Now, instead of merely being a sub-contractor, he could build a house in its entirety from the foundation to the chandeliers in the ballroom.

The boom was prosperous for Otto Schmidt as well. He and Letta had saved enough money to get married that spring. The wedding was held at the Volksgarten and everyone was invited. He almost ran out of beer, but a good time was had by all.

It was a crisp Sunday afternoon in March when Michael looked at his pocket watch and offhandedly said to his wife, "Why don't we go for a walk?"

She looked at him quizzically. "We haven't taken a walk in years."

"I know, but it's such a beautiful day."

"All right. Where do you want to go?"

"I thought we'd take a stroll along Seventh Avenue. It's really becoming a prosperous and fashionable thoroughfare. And there are a lot of buildings going up, maybe I can find some work there."

As they approached Fifty-First Street, admiring the new brownstone houses that were springing up seemingly everywhere, a man came down the steps of a new and handsome brownstone with a broad smile on his face.

"Ah, Mister Ranahan, good to see you again. And do I have the pleasure of meeting Mrs. Ranahan?"

"Emily, meet Mr. Fox."

Emily offered her hand, wondering what this was all about.

"Shall we go in?" Fox asked.

Emily shot her husband a questioning look.

"Mr. Fox is a real estate man," Michael explained. "I've asked him to show us this brownstone."

"What on earth for?"

"Because I want to buy it."

"But—?"

"Emily, I'm tired of living in a rented house. We deserve something better."

Before Emily could offer an objection, Fox interjected, "Why don't we begin at the garden level?"

Once inside, Fox pointed to the backyard. "Out there is a splendid garden. I understand you enjoy gardening, Mrs. Ranahan?"

"I do." Emily shot a glance at her husband, wondering what else he had told Mr. Fox.

"This spacious and airy room could be a study or a library."

"Or a classroom," Michael added, glancing at his wife.

"That, too, I guess." Fox led them into the kitchen. "And here is the kitchen. Note the cast-iron stove, Mrs. Ranahan. It's the very latest in modern kitchens. Shall we go upstairs?"

At the top of the stairs, he said, "And here is a spacious parlor. Note the sixteen-foot ceilings. Now on the next level—"

"I've seen enough."

The real estate man frowned. "Oh, dear, you really should see the two floors above, Mrs. Ranahan. There are two spacious bedrooms on the third level and three more bedrooms on the fourth and—"

"I'm sure it's lovely. How much does this house cost, Mr. Fox?"

"Only forty-five hundred dollars."

"What—?"

"And a steal at that price, I might add."

Emily turned to her husband. "Michael, what could you be thinking?"

"I should point out," Fox added hastily, "that the home has indoor plumbing, Croton water, gas light, and plaster walls."

When he saw that wasn't making much of an impression on Emily, he started down the stairs. "I'll let you two talk. If you have any further questions, I'll be right outside."

When the real estate man was gone, Michael said, "We can afford this, Emily."

"Not only is it a ridiculous amount of money, it's far too large for us."

"It's nowhere close to the size of your manor house back in Ireland."

"Michael, that was a lifetime ago. I don't even think about those days anymore."

"You know business has been good. I'm winning bids on mansions that I could only dream of building a couple of years ago. I've paid off Cully. I own the business outright and we have no debt."

"But what if there's another downturn and the construction work stops? Then what?"

"It's a risk, I'll grant you, but I've learned that if you are to succeed in this city you have to take risks. Didn't we take a risk coming out to America when we knew nothing about it?"

That gave Emily pause. What he'd said was true. Yes, conditions in Ireland were bad, and there was no question that they had to leave, but they could have gone to England, which was much closer and a country she knew well. Why did they choose to go to America? It was the adventure, the excitement, and, yes, the risk, she decided.

She looked around. "It is a lovely house."

Michael studied her. "It is. And it has plaster walls."

Emily turned to the stairs and smiled. "Let me see that room again that could become a classroom."

When they came outside, Mr. Fox was pacing nervously. He stopped when he saw them. "Well, are there any questions I can answer for you?"

"How soon can we move in?" Emily asked with a grin.

They moved in to their new home on the 15th of April, the day before Easter. While Michael and Cully carried boxes upstairs and Emily and Henrietta loaded dishes into the kitchen cupboards, the children raced through the house exploring all the nooks and crannies.

Fifteen minutes later, the four children stormed into the kitchen. From the grim expressions on their faces, Emily knew something was amiss.

"What's wrong?"

"I want the bedroom on the top floor," Eleanor said, "but Dermot says it's his."

Emily looked at Peter. "And what bedroom do you want?"

He rolled his eyes. "It doesn't matter, Ma. You only sleep in the room anyway."

"And what about you, Claire?"

She shrugged. "I don't care."

"Which bedroom do you want, Dermot?"

"The one in the back of house."

"Very well. It's yours. Eleanor, you can have the bedroom on the second level."

The drama over, the kids went off to finish exploring the house, but Eleanor stayed behind. "Mother, it's not fair. Dermot always gets what he wants."

Emily took her daughter's hands and in a conspiratorial tone whispered, "Eleanor, your bedroom is much larger than his and the view is better." She winked at her. "Don't tell your brother that."

Eleanor grinned. "I won't," she said, racing off to find the other children.

"You handled that well," Henrietta said.

"When it comes to Dermot, I always have to be careful."

"Does he still have tantrums?"

"Oh, God, yes. He's fourteen now. I keep hoping he'll grow out of it, but so far that hasn't happened."

Michael and Cully came into the kitchen. "I heard all the shouting. Is the crisis solved?"

"For the time being."

It was mid-afternoon when an ashen-faced Gaylord came rushing into the kitchen as the four were having lunch. "Have you heard the news?"

"What news?" Michael asked.

"President Lincoln was assassinated last night. He died early this morning."

Emily put her cup down so hard it cracked. "Oh, my God…"

Michael shook his head. "Dead? Remember, when we saw him at the Cooper Institute back in '60? I was so impressed. There was something about that man…" His voice trailed off.

"He was a great president," Cully added, shaking his head. "He got us through the war and held the country together."

"Was it the Confederates that did the dastardly deed?" Henrietta asked with raised eyebrow.

"No, some actor named Booth."

Michael went to the sink to get a drink of water for Emily who'd gone pale. "What now?"

Gaylord shrugged. "Andrew Johnson is our new president. No one seems to know anything about him."

Emily took a sip of water. "I hope this doesn't mean that the war will break out again."

Gaylord shook his head. "No. The South is finished, but there's much to be done down there. I would have preferred that Mr. Lincoln be in charge."

"Where will he be buried?" Henrietta asked.

"Springfield, Illinois, but the funeral train will stop here on the 24th. The body of Mr. Lincoln will lay in state in City Hall."

"I must see him one more time," Michael said in a voice constricted with emotion.

The brilliant sunshine of April 24th was in stark contrast to the deep feelings of mourning that gripped the city. There was scarcely a building in Manhattan that was not draped in black crepe.

Michael and Gaylord stood among the crowd outside City Hall waiting for the cortege to make its way up Broadway. Dozens of men had climbed trees to get a better look.

City Hall was covered in black mourning drapes while flags flew at half-mast. Over the entrance to the building, the words

"THE NATION MOURNS" appeared in giant white letters placed on a backdrop of black.

A murmur of anticipation went up from the crowd at the sound of muffled drums reverberating off the surrounding buildings. Leading the solemn procession was a detail of mounted police, followed by high ranking generals and their staffs. The hearse came next, followed by approximately eleven thousand soldiers marching in solemn cadence to the muffled drums. The crowd fell into awed silence at the sight of President Lincoln's enormous glass-sided hearse that was so heavy that it required sixteen matching gray horses to pull it.

As Michael watched with tears in his eyes, Gaylord furiously scribbled in his notepad. All around them, men silently removed their top hats and ladies burst into tears. A few boys, mesmerized by the scene, forgot to remove their caps. Embarrassed parents scolded their offspring as they snatched the caps off their heads.

After the casket was carried into City Hall, Gaylord said, "Come on, I want to view the body."

Michael pointed at the thousands of people who had already lined up to enter City Hall. "I do as well, but look at all those people. We'll never get in."

"Follow me."

Gaylord led Michael around to the back of the building. A rear door was guarded by a squad of burly policemen. The newspaperman approached a sergeant with large mutton chops.

"Sergeant Carroll, this is a sad day, is it not?"

"Aye, it is that, Mr. Temple. The president was a pure man and he'll be greatly missed."

Gaylord pulled the sergeant aside and whispered. "Later tonight, I plan to be at McSorley's. I'd be privileged to buy you a pint in honor of our deceased president."

The sergeant licked his lips. "I think I'll take you up on that, Mr. Temple. A pint after this day's melancholy duty would be a welcome thing, indeed."

Gaylord looked over his shoulder. "I wonder if we might slip in and have a look?"

The sergeant frowned. "I'm sorry, but I can't do that, Mr. Temple. My orders are to let no one through this door."

"Of course, of course. I understand. But my editor, Mr.

Greeley, has sent me here to get the story. I can't go back without being able to describe what's going on inside."

"Well, I don't know…" He gave Michael a stern look, as though seeing him for the first time. "And who is this?"

"A new man at the paper. I'm breaking him in. Sergeant, we'll be quiet as a church mice, my word of honor."

After a thoughtful pause, the sergeant said, "All right. Rafferty," he said to a policeman standing in front of the door. "Let these two in. Official business."

The president's casket had been placed at the top of the magnificent curving double staircase in the City Hall rotunda. Despite the hundreds of people slowly climbing the stairs, there was complete silence, the only sound the scraping of feet on the marble steps.

At either end of the casket stood an admiral and a general. As they passed the casket, Michael gazed at the president. In peaceful repose, the deep-lined face masked the horror of his death. Michael, recalling the soaring words of his speech at the Cooper Union Institute, wondered what manner of man would end the life of such a great man.

It was just over a month since Lincoln's death. Emily and Letta were in the kitchen preparing Sunday dinner while Michael, Gaylord, and Otto were in the parlor chatting.

"Where's Henrietta and Cully?" Gaylord asked.

Michael looked at the clock on the mantle. "I don't know. They're usually here by this time." Just then there was a knock at the door. "Here they are," Michael said, heading for the door. Instead of Henrietta and Cully, a young boy wearing the livery of a Western Union messenger was standing there. He tipped his cap and glanced at the envelope in his hand. "Are you Mr. Ranahan?"

"I am."

He handed Michael the telegram. Knowing that telegrams were seldom good news, he immediately tore it open and gasped when he read the contents. "Go*od Lord ...*"

Gaylord came to the door. "What is it?"

"It's from Henrietta. Cully has had another heart attack."

Emily came out of the kitchen wiping her hands on her apron. "Is it serious?"

"She says he hasn't much time."

"Oh my God ..." Emily stripped off her apron and handed it to Letta. "We must go to them. Letta, can you finish making dinner and feed the children?"

"Of course. Otto and I will manage. Go."

Emily, Michael, and Gaylord piled into his wagon and, moving as fast as they could through the crush of Sunday traffic, made their way downtown to Cully's house.

An ashen-faced Henrietta met them at the door. "The doctor is with him."

They sat down in the parlor, grim-faced. "When did it happen?" Emily asked.

"This morning. As he was getting out of bed, he just fell back and clutched his chest. I sent for the doctor. After examining him, he said Norbert had had a heart attack."

"Well, he's had them before," Michael said, trying to sound optimistic. "I'm sure he'll make it through this one."

Henrietta shook her head sadly. "The doctor doesn't think so."

Just then the doctor came into the parlor. "There's nothing more I can do for him, Mrs. Cullinane. You should go in and see him."

"We'll wait out here," Emily said."

"No. You're his friends. He'll want to see you."

"Emily, Michael, and Gaylord quietly followed Henrietta into the darkened bedroom. A sunken-faced Cully, propped up by pillows, weakly waved his hand. Henrietta took his hand and sat down on the bed. "Norbert, is there anything I can do for you?"

"Yeah," he whispered in a hoarse voice, "you can stop calling me Norbert."

Henrietta squeezed his hand and smiled. "You old fool—I mean ... Cully."

Cully tried for a smile. "Thank you, Mrs. Cullinane."

"Your friends are here."

Cully looked at them, but Michael wasn't sure he recognized them.

"Thanks for coming ..." He closed his eyes and was quite still for a moment. Then he gave a slight shudder and a gurgling sound came from his throat. Then he was still again.

The doctor, who had been standing in the doorway, stepped up to the bed and placed the stethoscope on Cully's chest. He turned to Henrietta and shook his head. "He's gone. I'm so sorry."

Henrietta bit her lip and nodded. Emily threw her arms around her. "Henrietta …"

Henrietta embraced her friend. "It's all right. We had some good years together. I'm grateful for that."

For the next three days, seemingly every contractor in Manhattan came to pay their respects to Cully, who was laid out in the parlor. Although he'd had a rocky relationship with Tammany Hall, several officials also came to pay their respects.

The next morning was rainy and blustery. Henrietta, Emily, Michael, and Gaylord followed the casket into St. Mark's Church-In-The-Bowery cemetery located at the intersection of Second Avenue and Eleventh Street.

At the end of the service, Henrietta stepped forward and dropped a rose into the grave. She turned to Michael. "You probably didn't know it, but Norbert … I mean, Cully, thought of you as the son he never had. He was a man of few words, but he was proud of the way you expanded the business. I know you think he blamed you for losing it, but he never did. Above all else, Cully was a businessman. He understood why the bank foreclosed on you and he never held it against you." She was silent for a moment and then looked at the others. "Most of you remember Cully as something of a gruff old curmudgeon. But I got to know the real Cully. He was a gentle, sweet man and I am so grateful that we had the time together that we did."

As Emily embraced Henrietta, Michael spoke up. "I would like to say a few words as well." He stepped forward and dropped a rose into the open grave. "I owe so much to Cully I don't know where to begin. But I'll just mention a couple of things. It was Cully who gave me my first job in America. It was Cully who gave me the opportunity to own my own business. And it was Cully who sold the business back to me after I'd lost it in foreclosure. He was a very generous man and I'll never forget what he did for me and my family."

As they were leaving the cemetery, Gaylord pointed to a grave with a weathered tombstone. "That's where Peter Stuyvesant, the last Dutch director-general of the colony of New Netherlands, is buried.

At the beginning of September Emily placed notices in the *Evening Mirror*, the *Tribune*, and the *Daily Express* advertising *Emily's School for Young Ladies*. Within a week, she was receiving inquires. By the beginning of October, she had signed up a classroom full of young ladies who had come to study not only French, but grammar, penmanship, geography, and arithmetic—subjects not usually taught to young women.

When Michael came home the night after the first class, he asked Emily how it had gone.

"Exhausting, but very exciting. I've decided to dedicate certain days to certain subjects so as not to overtax the girls."

"Are they good students?"

"Very good. Most of them have a foundation in writing and arithmetic, but they still have a lot to learn."

"Are our children part of the group?"

Emily rolled her eyes. "All except Dermot. He refuses to sit in a classroom full of girls."

"What about Peter?"

"He loves it and, I might add, the girls love him. He's quite the center of attention."

"And Claire?"

"At nine she's still a bit young for some of the lessons, but, as usual, she loves it when we read poetry."

He took her in his arms. "You don't think this is too much for you, Emily?"

"Not at all. I really enjoy interacting with the girls. But what saddens me is how timid most of them are. They're bright and smart, but so reticent to express an opinion."

"Why is that?"

"I think it's because of the way society is today. Children are to be seen and not heard, especially girls."

Michael laughed. "Why do I have a feeling you're going to change all that?"

"I will. These young girls will grow up to be young women. I want them to be assertive and feel free to express their opinions."

"Well, I certainly want that for Eleanor and Claire."

CHAPTER THIRTY-FIVE

1869

In the four years since the war ended, Michael Ranahan's Construction business continued to grow due to two factors: One, the wealthy, chased by the creeping incursion of commercial stores and merchants into their lower Manhattan neighborhoods, fled to the north of the city. And two, wealthy men who were already living uptown simply tore down their old mansions to build bigger and more ostentatious ones.

To keep up with the increased workload, Michael now employed one hundred and fifty men and a fleet of horses and wagons. He also increased the number of skilled craftsmen, stonemasons, finish carpenters, and artists who worked for him. As a result, Ranahan Construction had become one of the biggest contractors in the city.

Michael looked forward to Sunday morning breakfast with his family because it was the only time he got to see all his children at the same time. Now, as he sat at the kitchen table reading the newspaper, Emily was making breakfast. She cracked an egg into the skillet. "Call the children, Michael. We're about ready."

He went to the foot of the stairs and shouted, "*Breakfast. Come and get it.*"

At thirteen, Eleanor was on her way to becoming an attractive young lady and she was looking more and more like her mother. She took her usual place next to her father.

Michael bowed. "Good morning, Eleanor."

She bowed back. "Good morning, Father."

Michael and Emily exchanged amused grins. All the other

children called them Da and Ma. Only Eleanor called them Father and Mother and had done so since she'd learned to talk.

Peter came in next and as usual he was carrying a book. He was twelve now and the most studious of the children. Emily often told Michael that Peter looked just like him, but he didn't see the resemblance.

"What are you reading now?" Emily asked.

"*Ragged Dick.*"

Emily nodded approvingly. "Horatio Alger Jr. is a very good author, isn't he?"

Peter nodded, sliding into a chair opposite his sister.

"What's it about?" Eleanor asked.

"A poor bootblack in New York City. I haven't gotten very far into it, but so far I like it."

Next came little Claire. Michael and Emily had hoped that over time she would gain a little more vigor and a decent appetite, but at eleven, she was still pale and delicate.

She sat down next to her sister. "Ma, I'm not hungry. I don't want bacon and eggs."

Emily shot a troubled glance at Michael, who nodded in understanding. "What will you eat?"

"Maybe a little toast."

Michael was about to call out to Dermot, who was always the last one to come to the table, but he appeared and sullenly slid into a chair.

Halfway through breakfast, Michael said, "I have some exciting news."

Eleanor, who always enjoyed hearing about her father's business, said, "What is it, Father?"

"Has anyone ever heard of a Mrs. Winifred Eldridge?"

"Isn't she a very wealthy and eccentric woman who lives downtown?" Emily asked.

"She is. And I may be building her new home."

"Where?" Peter asked.

"Fifth Avenue and Fifty-Seventh Street."

Peter frowned. "But that area is filled with shantytowns and slaughterhouses and—"

"The unfinished cathedral," Dermot interjected, smirking at his father.

Michael didn't know why, but Dermot never passed up the opportunity to be sarcastic with him. It was as though he believed that the unfinished cathedral was his father's fault.

"It's true the cathedral is incomplete, but construction will resume soon," Michael explained patiently.

"Then why don't you go back to working there instead of building a stupid house for some old lady?"

Michael forced himself to remain calm. "Because this project is more prestigious and it will pay a lot better. Instead of being just one of several construction companies working on the cathedral, I will be the sole contractor on this project."

"Your father has developed quite a reputation as a builder in this city."

"That's because you do good work," said Eleanor with the conviction of an admiring daughter.

"Thank you for your vote of confidence, young lady."

"When will you start?" Emily asked.

"The architect, Robert Mercer, and I are going to meet with Mrs. Eldridge at her home tomorrow."

"Where did you meet Mr. Mercer?"

"Funny thing is, I haven't. I received a letter from his office briefly outlining what he was planning and asking me to meet him at Mrs. Eldridge's home."

Emily patted her husband's hand. "We're all very proud of you, aren't we, children?"

Everyone nodded in the affirmative, except Dermot.

The next morning was colder than usual for April. Michael waited outside Mrs. Eldridge's elegant Italianate façade brownstone on Waverly Place in Greenwich Village for the architect to arrive. His shivering was not from the cold wind whipping off the Hudson River, but from excitement and apprehension. On one hand, landing such a prestigious project would be a real feather in his cap. On the other hand, what if he didn't meet with the approval of Mrs. Eldridge?

Just then, the architect pulled up in a hansom cab. Alighting from the cab and carrying a large canvas portfolio, he said to the driver in a commanding voice, "Wait here for me."

The driver tipped his hat. "Yes, sir."

Robert Mercer, a tall, trim man in his fifties, exuded an air of confidence, no doubt due to him being one of the most sought-after architects in the city.

He put out his hand. "Mr. Ranahan, I presume?"

Michael shook his hand. "Yes, sir."

"Do you have any questions before we go in?"

"Just one. Why did you select me?"

"I've seen your work, Ranahan. Nothing shoddy. First-rate," he said in a clipped tone. "Furthermore, I have not heard a whisper questioning your honesty or integrity. That's the only kind of man I can work with. Shall we go in?"

The expansive, high-ceiling foyer was clad in tessellated marble and lined with mirrors. A liveried maid dressed in black and purple led them into a drawing room filled with expensive French furniture and florid tapestries. In the style of the day, the room was crammed with a bewildering array of chairs, couches, tables, and assorted priceless pieces. An ornate mahogany cabinet against a far wall was jam-packed with what Michael assumed was very expensive porcelain China.

A moment later, an imperious woman swept into the room. Heavy-set with black hair plastered down and parted in the middle, Mrs. Winifred Eldridge appeared to Michael to be in her mid-sixties.

"Gentlemen, thank you for coming," she said in a deep, throaty voice. She studied Michael through a pair of pince-nez glasses perched at the tip of her nose. "Before we begin, Mr. Mercer, please introduce me to this young man."

"Mrs. Eldridge, may I present Michael Ranahan of Ranahan Construction. Subject to your approval, of course, I propose to use him as my contractor."

"Young man, what are your credentials?"

An intimidated Michael swallowed hard. This was the first time he had ever met the person for whom a house was to be built. Usually, he dealt with architects and contractors. He'd worn his best suit, but it looked positively shoddy compared to Mr. Mercer's tailored suit and Mrs. Eldridge's elaborate gown.

"Ma'am, I've been in the construction business for seven years now. The last four as sole proprietor. I worked on the Astor project back in '52 and—"

"Ah, Willy Astor. A delightful man. Do you know him?"

"Not personally, ma'am. I've also worked on St. Patrick's Cathedral before the war interrupted construction. Then—"

"That's quite enough," she said, silencing him with a raised gloved hand. "If Robert recommends you, that's good enough for me. Do you have any questions for me?"

"I understand the house will be built on Fifth Avenue and Fifty-Sixth Street."

"That's correct. Robert, have you made your renderings?"

"I have, ma'am." The architect pulled several renderings from his portfolio and spread them out on the floor.

Michael was flabbergasted. He was expecting the usual renderings of a typical drab brownstone mansion with a high stoop. But Mercer's sketches showed something very different—a magnificent house clad in white marble with a two-story mansard roof covered in gray slate with green copper trim. The rendering of the house was like something he'd never seen before in New York City and he wondered if he and his men had the skill to build such an extraordinary structure.

Mrs. Eldridge, closely studying the renderings, clapped her hands in delight. "Robert, you have captured my wishes on paper."

The architect nodded in appreciation. "Well, you did suggest I look at the residential designs of Paris and the French country palaces for inspiration." He swept his hand across the renderings. "This is the result. As you can see, the mansard roof is in the style of France's Fontainebleau."

Her eyes glistened. "It will be magnificent. When can you start?"

The architect gathered up his renderings. "First, I have to draw up a complete set of blueprints. That process should be completed by May. I estimate construction can begin in early June."

"Splendid. How long will it take to build?"

Mercer looked at Michael. "Two years at the most."

Michael solemnly nodded in agreement. He wasn't quite as certain as the architect that it was enough time to build such an edifice, but he wasn't about to disagree with him.

Seated around the Sunday dinner table, the family, Gaylord, and Henrietta listened as Michael described the building he was going to construct.

A doubtful Gaylord shook his head. "I don't know, Michael. There are some who are already calling Mrs. Winifred Eldridge's project 'the wasteland.'"

"Why would they say that?" Eleanor asked.

"Because of where it's to be built. So far uptown."

"Isn't that what I said, Da?" Peter chimed in. "There's just shantytowns and slaughterhouses up there."

"It's not as bad as all that," Michael said. "It's only a couple of blocks away from St. Patrick's Cathedral."

"The *unfinished* cathedral," Dermot muttered with a smirk.

"It's true the area is quite desolate now," Henrietta said firmly. "But Mrs. Eldridge is a woman of vision and great wealth. If she moves there, others will follow. Mark my words."

"She *is* a most remarkable and adventuresome woman," Gaylord conceded.

While the others were speaking, Michael studied his eldest son with a look of concern. The children were growing up. For some time now, he and Emily had been discussing their children's future. They'd come to accept that Claire would always be of a delicate disposition. Fortunately, she'd become completely enamored of poetry and spent countless hours reading the books of poetry that Gaylord gave her.

Unlike Peter and Eleanor, who excelled at academics, Dermot was a poor student. With no prospects of a college education in his future, they agreed it was time for Dermot to seek gainful employment.

"Dermot, there's going to be plenty of work on this site," Michael said hopefully. "Would you like to come work with me?"

Dermot shook his head emphatically. "No. I don't want to work for you," he mumbled.

Michael felt the blood rising in him, but he also saw Emily's warning glance and checked himself. "Son," he said patiently, "you're eighteen. It's time you found real employment, not the odd jobs you pick up here and there."

Before Dermot could respond, Eleanor interjected. "I'll do it. I'll work for you, Father."

Michael smiled. His daughter's unbounded enthusiasm always delighted him. "Thank you for the offer, Eleanor, but construction work is not suitable work for women."

"Why not? I'm strong. I can do it."

Emily patted her daughter's hand. "For one thing, Eleanor, you're only fifteen. And your father is right. Construction is no work for a young lady. You're bright and intelligent. You'll be going off college in a couple of years."

"Where will she be going?" Henrietta asked.

"We're thinking Vassar."

Eleanor made a face. "Mother, that's way up in Poughkeepsie!"

"It's not that far away. Besides, there aren't many colleges for young ladies."

"It *is* a fine college," Gaylord said.

Henrietta raised her eyebrows. "And expensive."

"We can afford it," Emily said. "Michael's business has been very good and we've been able to put some money aside for the children's education."

Changing the subject, Gaylord said, "When do you start construction?"

"Mr. Mercer thinks early June."

"That's just a couple of months away. Pity. I suppose this means you won't be able to take part in Mr. Roebling's huge undertaking."

"Who's Mr. Roebling?" Eleanor asked.

"He's a bridge builder," Peter piped in. He's built suspension bridges over the Ohio River and the Delaware River."

"How do you know so much about it?" an amused Michael asked.

"I read the newspapers," he answered as though that should have been perfectly obvious.

Emily beamed at her son. "Our future newspaper reporter. She looked at Gaylord with mock sternness. "You know you're to blame for that."

"Guilty as charged. Newspaper reporting is an honorable profession and I believe young Peter here will make an excellent reporter."

"He certainly is nosy enough," Michael said.

"Inquisitive, Da" Peter corrected. "Inquisitive."

"I stand corrected."

"What kind of bridge does Mr. Roebling propose to build?"

Emily asked.

"A suspension bridge over the East River connecting the cities of Brooklyn and New York," Gaylord answered.

"My God," Emily exclaimed. "It would have to be a very high bridge indeed to allow ships with tall masks to sail under it."

"It appears he's taken that into consideration. I've heard it will be two hundred and seventy-seven feet above mean high water. The tallest sailing ship should be able to pass underneath without any trouble."

"It's going to be interesting to watch it constructed," Peter said with a gleam in his eye.

Gaylord nudged Peter. "Maybe you and I can report on it together."

Peter nodded solemnly. "I would like that, Uncle Gaylord.

Claire, who had been silent all through dinner, said quietly, "Maybe one day Mr. Whitman will write a poem about the bridge."

There was a stunned silence. All the adults sitting around the table were aware that critics had berated the poet for being too descriptive in writing about the delights of sensual pleasures.

Henrietta raised her eyebrows. "Child, what do you know about Walt Whitman?"

"I've read *Leaves of Grass*, Aunt Henrietta. I didn't understand all of it, but most of it was beautiful."

Henrietta was scandalized. "Wherever did you get hold of that book?"

"Uncle Gaylord gave it to me."

Gaylord reddened. "Despite what you may have heard, Henrietta, Mr. Whitman is a splendid poet."

"Be that as it may, I question the suitability of a child reading such … '*poems*.'"

"I think he's a fine poet," Claire said quietly.

"Then it's settled," Emily said, trying not to smile. "He is a fine poet."

That night, as Michael climbed into bed, he said, "I know I've said it before, but I ask the question again—what are we to do with Dermot? He's eighteen. When I was his age I'd been working for eight years."

Emily touched her husband's cheek and smiled. "Michael, he's not the son of a tenant farmer."

"True enough. But he's not the son of a landlord either. It's high time he earns his keep."

Emily sighed. "He does worry me. I don't like the young men he's consorting with."

"*Young men*? They're hooligans, Emily. Pure and simple."

"I guess they are. One of his friends was arrested last week for pick-pocketing."

"And will Dermot be next? Will we be bailing him out of a police court?"

"God, I hope not. Have you tried talking to him?"

"You know that does no good. The slightest criticism and he becomes a wild man. There are times I thought I would have to physically restrain him."

As Emily slipped into bed, tears welled up in her eyes. "We can't lean on him too hard. I'm afraid we'll drive him away. He'll leave the house and we may never see him again. I can't bear the thought of him wandering the streets like some… street ruffian."

Michael kissed his wife. "Neither can I."

For a long time, they both lay awake unable to sleep and unable to decide what to do with their troubled son.

CHAPTER THIRTY-SIX

Work began on the Eldridge site in mid-June. In preparation for such a huge undertaking, Michael hired more men and bought more wagons. The weather cooperated and he was able to clear the site of rock outcroppings by the middle of August.

One day towards the end of the month, at Eleanor's insistence, Michael brought her to the site. She was full of questions about costs, timelines, and why wood was used instead of stone.

Just then, Flynn approached. "Michael, do you have a minute?" He rolled his eyes. "You're needed to settle a dispute between the stonemasons and the carpenters."

"Again?"

"Aye. Again."

"Eleanor, you stay here and don't get into trouble. I'll be right back."

When Michael returned, he saw that his daughter was deeply engrossed in watching a carpenter cutting wood. "What are you looking at, Eleanor?"

"That man. The one cutting wood. Do you see what he's doing?"

Michael nodded. "He's cutting wood."

"Yes, but watch what he does. He picks up a piece of lumber from the lumber pile. Then he walks all the way over there and cuts the wood. Then he brings the pieces back to the pile of lumber."

Michael shrugged. "So?"

"It's a waste of time, Father. Why doesn't he just cut the wood at the wood pile instead of waking back and forth?"

Michael immediately saw what she was getting at. "You're right," he said, impressed by his daughter's sharp observation. "He is wasting a lot of time. Flynn," he called out to his foreman.

Flynn trotted over. "You called?"

"Go tell young Farley there to cut the wood at the pile and stop flitting about the work site like some silly gobdaw."

"Will do."

As Flynn left to instruct the worker, Michael said, "Eleanor, thank you for that good observation. Time is money in this business."

Eleanor's eyes shone as she looked around the busy work site. "Father, I love all this. The excitement, the chaos, the dust of the bricks, the smell of newly-cut wood. Can't I work for you when I'm older?"

Michael kissed his daughter. "We discussed this before. Your mother and I have decided to send you to college. You're far too smart to be working with the likes of me."

Before Eleanor could protest, Gaylord called out from the street. "Ahoy, there. Permission to come aboard the work site?"

Michael grinned. "Permission granted."

Gaylord bowed to Eleanor. "Have you finally convinced your father to let you work with him?"

Eleanor frowned. "We were just discussing that, but he said no."

"Gaylord, what brings you up to the wilds of uptown New York?" Michael asked.

"I just wanted to see how you're progressing."

Michael's eyes swept over the hundreds of busy men working on the site. "We're ahead of schedule. As you can see, we're laying the foundation. Soon the walls will be going up."

"Good to hear. Listen, Michael. John Roebling is going to be at the Cooper Institute tonight to discuss his bridge. Do you want to come?"

"Why not? It might be interesting."

The muggy sticky day had turned into a muggy sticky evening. Michael, Gaylord, and dozens of curious architects, builders, and members of the press filed into the Cooper Institute building. As they took their seats, Michael realized that this was the same auditorium where he'd heard Abraham Lincoln give his speech nine years earlier. The thought of the dead president still saddened him.

A group of men came out on the stage and took seats. Of all the men on the stage, Michael recognized only William Tweed, whom the newspapers were now calling, "Boss Tweed." He looked a lot different from the young man he remembered running for assistant alderman back in 1850. His sparse hair was now dark reddish-brown, but his eyes were still bright blue. He had gained considerable weight in the intervening years. Michael judged him to be at least three hundred pounds.

He nudged Gaylord. "Who are the others?"

"John Roebling and his son Washington, Mayor Abraham Oakey Hall, and Martin Kalbfleisch mayor of Brooklyn. I don't know the others, but I presume they're directors of the Brooklyn Bridge Company."

A stern-visaged John Roebling stepped up to the lectern and pinned the audience with his sunken blue eyes in his deeply lined face. "I have been asked by the directors of the Brooklyn Bridge Company to say a few words about the bridge I propose to build."

With an unmistakable German accent, he proceeded to explain in great detail how the bridge would be built. When he finished, he said, "Are there any questions?" His tone said he did not welcome questions. Nevertheless, several hands shot up.

A reluctant Roebling pointed to Gaylord. "Mr. Roebling, Gaylord Temple from the *New York Tribune*. You mentioned caissons. Could you explain what they are?"

Coming to his father's rescue, Washington Roebling quickly stepped up to the lectern. He knew his father was uncomfortable addressing large audiences. The young Roebling was about thirty years old with a determined square chin. Unlike his stone-faced father, there was a pleasant expression in his light gray eyes.

"I can answer that. When we talk of a caisson, think of a large wooden box with no top. Now invert it and you have a caisson. In this case, the box will be quite large—an area of some seventeen thousand square feet—with walls almost ten feet high. We'll position the caisson exactly where we plan to place the tower on the Brooklyn side. As we load granite blocks onto the roof, the caisson will slowly begin to sink toward the bottom. To keep the water out, we will pump compressed air inside. When the caisson strikes sediment, we will send men down to begin digging away the sediment and rock, allowing the caisson to sink lower and lower until it hits bedrock. When we're sure the caisson is on firm footing, we'll fill it with cement. Then we will do the same on the New York side. Are there any further questions?"

Another hand shot up. "Mr. Roebling, how do the men get inside the caisson?"

"By the use of airlocks. As the container—an elevator, really—in the airlock descends carrying the men, it, too, will be filled with compressed air."

"Who will supervise the work of building the bridge?"

"I will. There must be someone at hand to say yes or no, and it often makes a great difference which word they use," he added with a smile.

The whole thing sounded so preposterous that the audience had nothing more to ask, except Gaylord. "One last question, Mr. Roebling. When do you plan to launch the first of these caissons?"

"We're targeting next May."

After the meeting, Michael and Gaylord retired to McSorley's to discuss what they'd just heard. Stepping up to the long bar, Gaylord ordered two ales. "Well, what did you think?"

"A suspension bridge over the East River sounds almost too fantastic to be true. It will be an enormous undertaking."

"And a dangerous one at that. Some of these bridges have been known to collapse. I can think of two. In '31 a bridge collapsed in England. Then in '50, a French suspension bridge collapsed while a battalion of soldiers was marching across it. Over two hundred were killed. Can you imagine how many people would die if the Roebling bridge collapsed loaded with pedestrians and traffic?"

"It would be terrible," Michael agreed. "But I'm thinking about those caissons. That sounds like very dangerous work indeed. I wouldn't want to work down there with all that water surrounding me."

Gaylord chuckled. "Fortunately, that's not the kind of work neither you nor I will ever have to do. Still, I pity the poor blighters who will do the work."

Three weeks later, an ashen-faced Gaylord appeared at the

door. Emily took his arm. “Gaylord, whatever is the matter?”

“Mr. Roebling is dead.”

Michael came to the door. “Gaylord, come in. Which Mr. Roebling?”

“The father.”

Seated at the kitchen table, Gaylord explained. “It was a freak accident. Mr. Roebling was standing on a piling at the Brooklyn pier taking compass readings. As a ferry approached the dock he tried to back off the piling, but his boot got caught and the ferry crushed his foot. That was three weeks ago. He died today of tetanus.”

“Oh, my God, that’s terrible. What’s to become of the bridge now?” Emily asked.

“His son, Washington, will take over as chief engineer.”

“Will he be able to do it?” Michael asked.

“Apparently. They say he’s been working closely with his father and understands what must be done.”

“I’m not surprised. When we heard him speak, I was certainly impressed with the young man. So, the construction of the bridge will continue.”

“That’s what I’m told.”

CHAPTER THIRTY- SEVEN

1870

At Sunday dinner, the topic of conversation was the Roebling bridge.

"The Brooklyn caisson will be towed into position tomorrow," Gaylord announced.

"Will you be there to report it?" Emily asked.

"Indeed, I will. Mr. Greeley is very keen on seeing this bridge built. He's written several editorials declaring that the cities of New York and Brooklyn must be united, pointing out that Brooklyn is the third-largest city in America."

"Can I go with you tomorrow?" Peter asked in a voice high-pitched with excitement.

Gaylord looked from Emily to Michael. "Only if your parents agree."

"Of course he may go," Emily said, laughing. "I don't think we could keep him away."

"But mind," Michael warned his son, "if Uncle Gaylord should manage to get a ride on the caisson, you will not go with him. Is that understood?"

"But why not?"

"Because I don't trust the whole enterprise. Mr. Roebling described the caisson as a giant inverted box. The currents in the East River can be fierce. What if it should tip over? The whole thing would sink like a rock."

"No need to worry on that account," Gaylord said. "I have no intention of being carried down the East River on, as you say, a floating box. However, I am ashamed to say that in spite of my misgivings, Mr. Roebling, Mr. Kingsley, the project coordinator of the bridge, and several others plan to ride on the caisson"

"I want to work inside the caisson," Dermot said, with unaccustomed excitement in his voice.

"You will do no such thing," Emily said, startled by the very idea of her son imprisoned in a box beneath the East River."

"Why not? You're always telling me I need to find employment. I hear they're going to pay more than two dollars a day for the work. That's more than Da pays his men."

"They're paying more because it's dangerous and dirty work," Michael pointed out.

"I don't care. It's a lot of money," Dermot muttered.

"When will they begin to lower the caisson, Uncle Gaylord?" Eleanor asked.

"Probably within the next two weeks."

Emily noticed Gaylord had suddenly gone pale. "What's the matter, Gaylord? Are you ill?"

The newspaperman swallowed hard. "When the caisson reaches the sediment, the Brooklyn Bridge Company is going to offer a tour of the caisson for the press."

"That sounds exciting," Eleanor said.

"Not, my dear, if you are claustrophobic."

"Oh, goodness," Emily said. "Is there any way to get out of it?"

"I'm afraid not." Then he looked sideways at Peter. "Unless, young Peter here would like to take my place."

"Yes, please. Please."

"Calm down," Michael said. "Your Uncle Gaylord is only jesting with you."

"But I would do it," Peter said confidently. "What a story it would be!"

Gaylord tilted his wine glass toward the young man. "I'm sure you would make an admirable job of it, Peter. But, alas, if I hope to retain my position of employment, *I* will have to descend to the depths of the roiling East River."

"Do you think *I* might go with you?" Michael asked impulsively.

Emily put her fork down. "Michael, it sounds dangerous down there. Gaylord has to go, but there's no reason for you to risk your life."

"This wouldn't be some kind of lark, Emily. The Eldridge

mansion is almost done. It's time I started looking for new work."

"And you'd like to work on the bridge?" Eleanor asked, her eyes aglow at the possibilities.

"Why not? I hear there's plenty of work. Do you think you can get me down there, Gaylord?"

"I don't see why not. I got you into City Hall posing as a new reporter to view President Lincoln's body, didn't I? I don't see why we can't use that ruse again."

On a drizzly April morning, an apprehensive Gaylord reluctantly made his way to the Brooklyn pier. When he got there, Michael and a small crowd of reporters representing the dozens of newspapers in the city were already milling about. Gaylord recognized several of the reporters from the *New York Times*, the *World*, the *Police Gazette*, and the *National Intelligencer*.

Michael grinned at his friend's pale and serious demeanor. Usually one with a witty joke, he looked positively funereal.

"Gaylord, you look like you're on the way to the gallows."

"I think I'd prefer that to drowning in the East River like a wharf rat." He turned to a reporter from *Harpers Weekly*. "What do you think, Harry, are we all going to die down there?"

Harry, a rotund man with bushy muttonchops, laughed. "Not at all, Gaylord. Besides, this is what we get paid to do."

Gaylord gave him a sickly grin. The man sounded confident, but, although it was only seven in the morning, his breath smelled of whiskey.

"Apparently," Gaylord whispered to Michael, "my friend Harry has had a couple of drinks to give him Dutch courage."

A serious looking young man, no more than twenty-one, with a high starched collar and a handlebar mustache stepped out of the construction shed.

"Gentlemen, please gather around." When they were in a group, he said, "My name is George McNulty. I'm one of the assistant engineers on the project. I will be leading you down to the caisson in groups of five."

There was a murmur of disappointment. The reporters assumed that Washington Roebling himself would lead the tour. While McNulty explained the procedures to be followed, two assistants handed each man a pair of rubber boots.

"Are these necessary?" Gaylord asked.

The man laughed. "If you want to come out of the caisson with your shoes, I'd advise you to put on the boots."

McNulty pointed at Michael, Gaylord, and three other reporters. "You five will be first. Please follow me."

He led them out onto the caisson past swarms of men moving and positioning granite blocks to an opening in the caisson. Gaylord looked down into the dimly lit round hole and swallowed hard.

"This is the airlock. We will climb down the ladder one at a time." McNulty pointed at Gaylord. "Sir, you will go first."

With shaky hands, Gaylord went down the ladder into the cast iron airlock lit only by a calcium lamp.

Gaylord was startled to see a man already there. "Who are you?"

"I'm the operator."

"Is this apparatus safe?"

"Of course. Haven't I been operatin' it for a week now?"

The airlock, made of half-inch boilerplate, was six feet in diameter and seven feet high. The confined space made Gaylord's heart pound in his chest.

When the others were all in the airlock, McNulty pulled down an iron hatch on the ceiling and locked it. The operator turned a valve and compressed air flooded the elevator.

Gaylord stuck his fingers in his ears and winced. "Ow! My ears hurt. Is that normal?"

McNulty nodded. "It is. We don't begin a descent until the gauge shows that the air pressure inside the airlock is the same as the air pressure inside the caisson."

When the air pressure was equalized, the operator began the slow descent as the airlock bumped against the sides of the cylinder. When the airlock stopped, the operator opened a hatch in the floor. Immediately, warm, muggy air smelling of rotten eggs, the sea, and unidentified decaying organisms rushed into the capsule.

One by one they climbed down a ladder into the caisson, blinking to adjust to the dim light of calcium lamps. The ceiling was less than ten feet high, making the space all the more claustrophobic. The huge space was partitioned off with wooden walls and wide doorways to permit workers to move from one area to another.

The wall and ceilings were covered with a glistening coat of mud and there were standing puddles of water. All the workers wore rubber boots and Gaylord realized why they were necessary. With every step he took the mud threatened to suck the boots off his feet. When he saw the workers walking on planks over the mud, he did the same.

McNulty led them to the outside wall where the workers were digging out a huge boulder that was preventing the caisson from sinking. "We try to dig out the boulders, but if they're too big, we use explosives to break the rock into more manageable pieces."

The men chuckled at the high and thin sound of his voice that down there made him sound like a girl.

"How much progress do you make in a week of digging?" Michael asked.

"About six inches a week."

"Only six inches?"

"We're boring down through basalt and trap rock. It's quite time consuming."

Gaylord glanced uneasily at the ceiling, which was dripping water, and tried not to think about the tons of granite and water over his head. "Are there any ill-effects from working down here?" he asked the young engineer.

McNulty shrugged. "Some complain of headaches, itchy skin, bloody noses, and slowed heartbeats." Then grinning, he added, "But there are some who claim they have an increase in appetite."

"Is it always this hot down here?" Michael asked.

"Yes. Even on the coldest winter day the temperature down here is in the upper eighties."

Michael looked around at the scores of men shoveling sediment into wheelbarrows. "Mr. McNulty, I don't understand something. What makes the caisson sink deeper into the sediment?"

"You see it right there," McNulty said, pointing to a man filling a wheelbarrow with sediment. "Shovel full by shovel full as we remove more and more sediment, the caisson will slowly sink to the bedrock. Now, if there are no further questions, we can go back up."

Glad to be at the surface again, Gaylord was the first to scramble up the ladder. As soon as they stepped off the pier, Gaylord grabbed Michael's sleeve. "Let's find a saloon. I need a drink."

Michael glanced at his pocket watch. "It's only after eight."

"I don't care. I need a drink."

They found a saloon a couple of blocks away from the pier. Apparently, Gaylord wasn't the only one who needed to steady his nerves. Several of the reporters who'd gone down into the caisson were there as well.

Gaylord ordered whiskey, which he promptly knocked down in one gulp. Slapping the bar with his palm, he said, "I'll have another, bartender."

Michael grinned at his friend. "Besides being terrified, Gaylord, what did you think?"

"That's a terrible, terrible place. I'll never go down there again. I don't care if Mr. Horace Greeley fires me."

"It was pretty bad." All the while they were down there, Michael had been thinking of his son. He wished he could have brought Dermot down there so he could see for himself the terrible working conditions. He was sure the experience would have banished from his mind any thought of working in a caisson.

Gaylord downed his second whiskey and shook his head. "Who would want to work in that ghastly environment?"

"A man who needs money, or a man who needs a job, or—" He suddenly thought of his son. "A man who thinks he has something to prove."

Gaylord grunted. "Well, I'll tell you one thing. There's not enough money in the whole wide world to make me work in that ghastly hellhole."

Two weeks later, Gaylord appeared at the Ranahan's door. "A terrible thing has happed at the Brooklyn Bridge," he told Emily.

Seated at the kitchen table, he recounted to Emily and Michael what had happed. "It seems that a fire broke out in the caisson. Washington Roebling went down into the caisson to direct the efforts to extinguish the flames. Best as I can ascertain, working down there in the compressed air for so long caused him to develop what they call 'caisson disease.'"

"What is that?" Emily asked.

"It's a mysterious illness that affects men who work down in the caissons. The symptoms are excruciating joint pain, paralysis, convulsions, numbness, speech impediments, and, in some cases, death. Mr. Roebling is partially paralyzed and is confined to bed. They say he will never be able to visit the worksite again."

"No man should have to work in those conditions," Michael said, remembering his trip down into the caisson. "What will happen to the bridge now?"

"It seems he's married to quite a remarkable woman. Although he'll be confined to his apartment in Columbia Heights, he will continue to direct operations by observing with field glasses and sending messages to the site through his wife, Emily Warren Roebling,"

"She does sound like a remarkable woman," Emily agreed.

"I don't believe in such things," Michael said, "but with John Roebling dead and now his son paralyzed, it makes me wonder if the bridge is cursed."

Gaylord shook his head. "You're not the only one to think that, Michael."

CHAPTER THIRTY-EIGHT

1871

The Eldridge mansion was completed in May of 1871, on time and under budget. As a result, Michael's reputation in the building community had become greatly enhanced. The mansion was no longer derisively referred to as "the wasteland." It was now known throughout the city as the "Marble Palace."

Now that the mansion was finished it was time to find new work for his company. He made an appointment to see William C. Kingsley, Brooklyn's leading contractor. Kingsley came with a sterling reputation. He was only thirty-eight, but he'd already built Prospect Park and the Hempstead Reservoir, and now he was the general contractor of the Brooklyn Bridge. Construction on the bridge had begun a year ago, but there was still much to be done and Michael was sure he could find work here.

On a bright, sunny Friday morning in May, Michael hurried down Water Street in Brooklyn and stepped into the offices of Kingsley & Keeney Construction Company. An elderly man with green eye shades sat at a high desk. He looked up at Michael with a questioning look.

"My name is Ranahan, I have an appointment to see Mr. Kingsley."

"Wait here," he said, and without another word scurried down a hallway.

A moment later, a man over six feet tall, powerfully built, with broad shoulders and a deep chest came down the hall and stuck out his hand. "Bill Kingsley."

Michael shook hands. "Michael Ranahan."

"I know. I know. Your reputation precedes you. Come, let's

talk in my office.

As Michael settled into a comfortable chair in front of Kingsley's desk, he took a moment to study the big contractor. He had an honest-looking face that was set off by a fine head of wavy dark-red hair and a neatly trimmed beard. Michael liked what he saw.

"So, what can I do for you, Ranahan?"

"I've just finished the Eldridge mansion and—"

"I know. I took a ride by it just yesterday. They're calling it the Marble Palace. You did a fine job of it, Ranahan.

"Thank you. I was wondering if there was a place for my company on your project."

"Of course there is," Kingsley said without hesitation. "I have dozens of subcontractors working on the bridge. Unfortunately, I'm forced to let several go a week. Neither I nor Washington Roebling will countenance shoddy workmanship."

"Mr. Kingsley, I can guarantee that you will see no shoddy work from my men."

"I know. That's why I'm hiring you."

Michael was taken aback by Kingsley's directness and how quickly they'd come to an arrangement. He'd expected more give and take. "When do we start?"

"Monday morning. Seven sharp."

Monday morning Michael and his crew arrived and were quickly put to work. Half his men were assigned to haul the tons of stone that would form the bridge. The limestone was quarried at the Clark Quarry in Essex County, New York. The granite blocks were quarried and shaped on Vinalhaven Island, Maine and delivered from Maine to New York by schooner. The other half of Michael's men were put to work constructing wooden scaffolding for a small army of stone-cutters and masons.

By the time Michael got home from work that first day, it was after eight. Emily had a hot supper waiting.

"So, how did it go?"

"I'm impressed. Although there are hundreds of carpenters, stonemasons, mechanics, and riggers swarming all over the site, the work goes surprisingly well, thanks to Roebling's disciplined and professional assistant engineers."

"Do you know any of them?"

"No, but two of them, Francis Collingwood and Charles Martin are graduates of Rensselaer College. Martin is second in command to Mr. Roebling. Another fellow named Wilhelm Hillenbrand has recently migrated from Germany. Each has a specific area of responsibility which makes it easier for subcontractors like me to know who to go to for specific problems and issues."

"So, do you think you're going to like working there?"

"I do. Emily, if this bridge gets built, it will be the wonder of the modern world. I'll be so proud to be a small part of that."

"It will be something." Emily put his dinner in front of him and called up the stairs, "Children, come say goodnight to your father."

Eleanor, Peter, and Claire came running into the kitchen.

"Da, did you go down in the caisson?" Peter asked excitedly.

"No, son. I was down there once and that's enough for me."

"I'd like to go down there. Just to see it."

"It's a very nasty place for anybody, but especially a young boy."

"Da, I'm sixteen," Peter protested.

Emily pushed the hair back from his eyes. "Why don't you concentrate on being a newspaperman like your Uncle Gaylord?"

"I am. That's what newspaper men do. They go down into places like that."

Michael laughed. "You might want to talk to Uncle Gaylord about that."

"Father, did you climb up on the towers?"

"No, Eleanor, that's not my job."

"What *do* you do?" Claire asked.

"We build scaffolding and transport great big granite and limestone boulders. The granite comes from all the way up in Maine."

"Enough with the questions," Emily said. "Let your father eat his supper in peace."

After he kissed them all good night, they went back upstairs to their bedrooms.

"Where's Dermot?" Michael asked.

"Where is he always? Out with his friends."

"That boy has got to get a steady job, Emily. He can't go on—"

Just then, they heard a key in the latch and then footsteps on the stairs.

"Dermot," Michael called out. "Come here."

Dermot came into the kitchen. "What?"

"Where were you?"

"Out with my friends."

Michael studied his son closely. His eyes were bloodshot and he smelled of alcohol. "You've been drinking."

Dermot shrugged. "I had a couple of beers. So what?"

"Judging by the smell of alcohol, I'd say you had more than a couple."

"I'm twenty years old," he exploded. "I can drink if I want to."

Michael felt the anger rising in him. "Where do you get the money? You don't have a job."

"I manage."

Michael pointed a finger at his son. "You will not come into this house drunk again. Do you understand?"

"You can't tell me what to do."

Michael slammed his fist on the table. "I can damn well tell you what to do as long as you live in this house."

Dermot's face reddened. "Well, I don't have to live in this goddamn house."

"Watch your language," Emily said quietly.

"The both of you are always telling me what to do. I'm sick of it."

"We only want what's best for you," Emily said in a still voice that she hoped would calm her son.

"Then just leave me alone."

"If you were halfway responsible, we would leave you alone." Michael waved a hand in dismissal. "You're drunk and you're slurring your words. Go to bed. We'll talk about this in the morning."

"I'm sick and tired of you treating me like a child."

"Then stop acting like one," Michael snapped back.

"*I don't have to take this from you!*" Dermot screamed, as he headed for the door. "*I'm getting the hell out of this house.*"

Michael rose to stop him, but Emily grabbed his arm. "No,

Michael, let him go. When he cools down, he'll come home."

"I'm not so sure of that, Emily. I'm not sure of that at all."

Emily started every time she heard a key in the latch, hoping that it might be Dermot. But it never was. It had been two weeks since their son had stormed out of the house and they had not heard a word from him. Michael asked Gaylord to check with his sources to see if he could find out where he'd gone. Gaylord reminded Michael that New York was a big city, but he promised to do what he could.

The weeks turned into months and still no word from Dermot. As best they could, the Ranahan family went on with their lives. Emily continued teaching classrooms full of young ladies, although from time to time her mind often drifted from her lesson plan to thinking about where her son might be. Eleanor had gone off to Vassar to pursue a degree in art and literature. Gaylord had gotten Peter a job as an office boy at the *Tribune*. And Claire continued to immerse herself in her poetry books.

CHAPTER THIRTY-NINE

1872

It was a bitter cold January morning with a biting wind so strong it was whipping up whitecaps in the East River. Michael was supervising the unloading of granite blocks at the New York City-side caisson. As he idly watched his men, he turned his attention to the forty-man work crew coming out of the caisson at the end of their shift. The poor bedraggled devils barely looked human. Their faces were blackened and their eyes were bloodshot. Their trousers and boots were covered with stinking mud. Although it was barely twenty degrees, they were bathed in sweat. Michael was reminded of what the engineer McNulty had told them: "*Even on the coldest winter day the temperature down here is in the upper eighties.*"

As the exhausted men shuffled off the caisson, Michael's eyes focused on one young man's gait and with a start recognized it immediately. "*Dermot,*" he called out.

Dermot looked over his shoulder, but kept walking.

Michael ran toward him. "Dermot, wait."

Dermot spun around. "What do you want?"

Up close, Michael was shocked by his son's appearance. His face was gaunt, his bloodshot eyes were sunken into his face, and his hair was plastered down from sweat. Since Dermot had stormed out of the house eight months ago, Michael had never given up looking for him. Every time he saw a young man around Dermot's age walking down the street, he'd rush up to him only to find he was mistaken. He rehearsed in his mind exactly what he would say when he did meet his son, but now he couldn't remember his carefully worded speech.

"How are you?" he blurted out.

"I'm all right."

"Your mother misses you. I miss you. Your brother and sisters miss you."

"I gotta go."

"How long have you been working down there?"

"A few months."

"My God, Dermot, you could work for me. You wouldn't have to work in that hellhole."

Dermot shrugged. "It's all right."

Suddenly, his nose started to bleed, but he didn't seem to notice.

"Dermot, your nose is bleeding."

"Huh? Oh." He quickly wiped his nose with his dirty sleeve. "It happens all the time down there."

"Dermot, please don't go down there anymore."

Dermot smirked. "Still telling me what to do."

"Don't do it for me. Do it for your mother?"

Suddenly, Dermot's face contorted in pain. With an animal-like groan, he doubled over and fell to the ground writhing in agony.

Several men ran over. "It's the caisson disease," one of them whispered knowingly.

Another young fellow knelt beside Dermot. "He's my roommate. Someone help me get him to our boardinghouse."

"Where is it?" Michael asked.

"One Thirty Front Street. It's only a few blocks from here."

Michael called out to Flynn, whose crew had just finished unloading the wagon. "Flynn, get the wagon over here right now. Fallon, go fetch a doctor and bring him to 130 Front Street. Hurry, man."

Michael was relieved to hear that his son wasn't living in the Five Points, but the decrepit boardinghouse on Front Street would not have been out of place in that slum.

They carried Dermot upstairs to the windowless room he shared with his roommate. Michael was appalled at the conditions under which his son lived. The cramped, dark room wasn't much bigger than a good-sized closet. The only furniture was two cots.

They laid him on top of dirty sheets that looked as though they hadn't been washed in months.

A moment later, Michael heard footsteps on the stairs. The doctor, a middle-aged man in a black frock coat and a stiff white collar, appeared in the doorway.

"What seems to be the problem?"

"It's the caisson disease," the young man said.

The doctor looked at him sharply. "Who are you?"

"I'm his roommate, sir. He's had this before, but not this bad."

"All right, everybody out while I examine this man."

"Doctor, I'm his father."

"Very well, you can stay. Everybody else out."

The doctor listened to Dermot's heart with his stethoscope. "He has an irregular pulse and there's lung congestion. How long has he been like this?"

"I don't know."

The doctor gave him a puzzled glance.

"We've been alienated for some months now," Michael explained. "I only just saw him again less than an hour ago."

"Does he work in the caisson?"

"He does."

"I thought so. That young fellow was right. He has caisson disease. I've treated cases like this before. There's something about working down there that causes this."

"What *is* the cause?"

"No one knows. All I know is that it's criminal to allow men to work in those conditions. Washington Roebling himself has been struck down by the disease and now he's a paralyzed cripple. It's all madness, trying to build such a massive bridge. I predict the whole enterprise will come tumbling down one day—if they even finish it."

"Will my son be all right?"

The doctor returned his stethoscope to his bag. "It depends. The disease can manifest itself in excruciating joint pain, paralysis, convulsions, numbness, speech impediments, and—" he turned to look Michael in the eye— "in some cases, death."

Michael sat down heavily on the adjoining cot. "What can I do for him?"

The doctor looked around the shabby room. "For one thing,

get him out of this disease-ridden hovel."

"I will. I intend to take him home."

"He needs bed rest, plenty of fluids, and a decent meal. It looks as though he hasn't had a decent meal in quite a while."

Flynn helped Michael carry Dermot down to the wagon. As they rode to his house, Michael wondered how he would break the news to Emily. He knew she would be glad to see him, but on the other hand, she would not be happy to see him like this.

When they got to the house, he went in first. Emily was in the parlor. She looked up from her knitting. "You're home early." Then she noticed the stricken expression on his face. "My God… is it Dermot? Is… he—"

"He's not dead, but he's a very sick young man. He has the caisson disease."

"Oh, my God. Where is he?"

"In the wagon outside. Prepare his bed. Flynn and I will bring him up."

Emily let out a cry when she saw her son. She took his hand. "Dermot, it's your mother. Can you hear me?"

"He's been going in and out of consciousness," Michael explained.

Tears welled up in her eyes. "I must clean him up. Get his filthy clothing off. I'll get hot water and towels."

To save time, Michael took out his knife and cut away Dermot's clothing. By the time he was finished, Emily was back with a pail of hot water.

As she was washing the dirt and mud off him, he came to and grimaced in pain. "My shoulder… oh, my God …" he mumbled. "My elbows … I can't stand the pain ..." Then he lapsed into merciful unconsciousness again.

One by one Eleanor, Peter, and Claire slipped into the room.

"Is he going to get well?" Eleanor asked.

"We hope so," Emily said.

Peter looked at him with eyes wide with wonder. "He was working down in the caisson, wasn't he?"

"Yes."

"And now he has the caisson disease. You were right, Da.

That must be a terrible place."

"It is, Peter. It is."

After the children went to bed, Emily continued to sit with Dermot. Michael came into the bedroom. "Emily, I'll stay with him. You get some sleep."

"No, I'm all right," she said, wiping blood that was trickling from Dermot's nose.

Michael sat down on the edge of the bed. "Then I'll stay with you."

"No. Go to bed. You need your sleep. You have to go to work tomorrow."

"I'm not going to work. Flynn can handle it."

They sat there in silence, Michael on the bed, Emily in a chair, dozing on and off for several hours. Around three in the morning, Dermot curled up in a fetal position and began to moan.

Emily jumped up. "Dermot, are you all right? Can I get you something?"

Suddenly, without warning, he vomited. As Michael tore the soiled sheets away, Emily went to get clean ones. When she came back, she wiped away the vomit from his face. "Dermot, can you hear me?"

He remained in a tightly curled fetal position, giving no sign that he heard her.

"Should we send for the doctor, Michael?"

"What could he do? The doctor who examined Dermot at his boardinghouse said he didn't even know what causes this. He advised bed rest and plenty of fluids." Michael looked closely at his son. "He seems to be sleeping. There's nothing we can do but keep vigil."

It was dawn and the sun was just beginning to penetrate the tightly drawn curtains. Suddenly, Dermot began to shake uncontrollably and his body jerked with muscle spasms. The motion of his body grew more and more violent. His nose started to bleed again. Then he started to foam at the mouth.

Emily cried out, "Oh, my God … I think he's having a seizure. What should we do?"

Michael tried to hold Dermot down, but the violent jerking of his body made it impossible. Suddenly, the motion stopped as quickly as it had begun and he appeared to be sleeping again.

Exhausted, Michael and Emily sat down to resume their vigil and occasionally dozed off. It was almost six when Dermot suddenly cried out. He was silent for a moment, then there was a slight gurgle in his throat and he became completely still.

Michael and Emily froze. Then, hesitantly, Michael got up and put his ear to Dermot's chest. He pulled himself up to his full height and began to sob. "He's dead, Emily," he said, his voice choking with emotion. "Our son is dead."

Emily tried to sit down, but the room was spinning. Then everything went black.

"Caisson disease" or, as it was also called, "the 'bends," was not a well-understood phenomenon in 1872. It would be thirty-five years before the etiology of decompression sickness would be fully understood.

Dermot didn't die because he worked down in the caisson. He died because he, and all the other workers who got sick, ascended too quickly. Scientists now know that when a body descends to depths of more than sixty feet and breathes compressed air, nitrogen bubbles begin to form in the blood steam. A slow, controlled ascent allows the nitrogen bubbles to dissolve. A quick return to the surface doesn't give the nitrogen time to dissolve and the bubbles usually migrate to the large joints of the body, which can cause excruciating pain in the joints, and sometimes, as in Dermot's case, death.

Roebling hired a doctor to investigate the cause of caisson disease. He never did find the cause, but he stumbled on a possible solution. He recommended that the men take five minutes to ascend the caisson. Unfortunately, his recommendation was far short of the twenty minutes that was actually necessary.

Before the Brooklyn Bridge would be completed one hundred and ten men would be afflicted by caisson disease. Three, in addition to Dermot, would die.

On a frigid January morning, Dermot Ranahan was laid to rest in the cemetery of St. Mark's Church-In-The-Bowery, the same churchyard where Cully was interred. As a dull winter sun struggled to break through gray-metal clouds scudding across the wintery sky, the Ranahan family, Flynn, Henrietta, Gaylord, Letta, and Otto gathered around the open grave.

Michael saw a young man standing off to the side whom he recognized as Dermot's roommate. "Son," he called out. "Please stand here with us."

"I don't want to intrude, sir."

"No, please." He shook the young man's hand. "I'm sorry, I didn't get your name when last we met."

"It's Liam, sir."

"Emily, Liam was Dermot's roommate."

Emily shook the young man's hand. "Did you know my son well?"

"Only a couple of months, ma'am."

"Thank you for coming."

A corpulent priest, tightly wrapped in his black frock coat to ward off the cold, began to intone the prayers for the dead. From time to time he glanced at a piece of paper tucked in his missal whenever he had the need to refer to Dermot by name. Concluding the ritual, he said, "Eternal rest grant unto him, O Lord, and let perpetual light shine upon him. May the souls of all the faithful departed, through the mercy of God, rest in peace. Amen."

He shut his missal with great finality, grateful that he would soon be out of this biting cold. "And that concludes our service."

Claire spoke up in a soft voice. Holding up a book of poems, she said, "Would it be all right if I read a poem?"

The priest glared at her. "It's highly irregular young lady for—"

"Claire," Emily said, interrupting the priest, "we would love to hear your poem."

In a soft, but clear voice, she said, "This is a poem by Christina Rossetti, one of my favorite poets." She cleared her throat and read:

Remember me when no more day by day
You tell me of our future that you planned:
Only remember me; you understand
It will be late to counsel then or pray.
Yet if you should forget me for a while
And afterwards remember, do not grieve:
For if the darkness and corruption leave

A vestige of the thoughts that once I had,
Better by far you should forget and smile
Than that you should remember and be sad.

With tears streaming down her cheeks, Emily embraced her daughter. “Claire, that was a beautiful poem. Thank you.”

That night as Emily and Michael were getting ready for bed, Emily said, “That Liam is a nice young man. It comforts me to know that in the end Dermot had at least one real friend.”

Michael buried his face in his wife’s hair. “Will we ever understand what happened to him?”

“I don’t know, Michael. I don’t know.”

As they got into bed, Michael blew out the candle. “Well, at least he’s in peace now. That’s comforting.”

Emily turned toward the wall to prepare for a long sleepless night. “Yes, it is.”

For the next three days, Michael, unable or unwilling to go back to work, stayed home, sunk in a deep depression. Emily empathized with his grief for she, too, was grieving, but on the fourth day she decided it was no good for him to continue wallowing in sorrow and self-pity.

When he came down to breakfast, as she poured him a cup of coffee, she said casually, “When do you plan to go back to work?”

“I don’t know.”

“You have a hundred and fifty men working there.”

“Flynn can handle it.”

“I don’t think he can. Every day there are major decisions that have to be made. It’s not fair to put that burden on him.”

Michael looked up at her with bloodshot eyes. “Emily, I don’t think I can ever go back there.”

“Why?”

“That bridge killed our son. I never want to see it again.”

Emily sat down and took her husband’s hands in hers. “It was a terrible accident, Michael, but you can’t blame the bridge.”

“Well, I do. I’m thinking of pulling out of my contract with the Brooklyn Bridge Company.”

“Michael, you can’t do that. You’ll put a hundred and fifty

men out of work."

Angry at her unreasonable nagging, he bolted from the table and stomped up the stairs to their bedroom and threw himself on the bed. *Why couldn't she understand?* he asked himself. His eldest son, the one he thought would come into the business, was dead. If it hadn't been for that goddamn bridge he would still be alive. There was no way he could go back to that cursed bridge. But after a while he calmed down and slowly began to realize she was right. In his grief, he'd forgotten his responsibility to his men and to his company. These people depended on him. How could he have been so selfish as to even consider pulling out of his contract?

He came back downstairs. Emily was at the kitchen table drinking coffee and staring out the window.

He came up behind her and put his hands on her shoulders. "You're right," he said, softly. "I have to go back. I'm sorry I put you through all this."

She stood up and embraced him. "I know how you feel. He was my son, too. But life must go on. *We* must go on."

The next morning Michael went back to work and Flynn was very glad to see his boss. "There's been trouble afoot," he whispered.

"What is it?"

"Since Dermot died, the men working in the caisson have been grumbling about the terrible conditions down there. They went on strike demanding to be paid three dollars for a four-hour stint."

"Did Kingsley give it to them?"

"He did not. He threated to sack the lot and the strike collapsed."

CHAPTER FORTY

On a balmy morning in May, Assistant Engineer George McNulty called a meeting of the contractors. As they gathered in front of the construction shed, Michael came along side Angus Roy. "What's this about?"

"I dunno, laddie. Maybe there's another strike in the offing."

McNulty stepped out of the shed and raised his hands for quiet.

"Gentlemen, I have an announcement to make. Mr. Roebling has decided to halt further digging in the caisson."

A murmur of disbelief rippled through the assembled men. "Have we hit bedrock?" a contractor asked.

"No, but Mr. Roebling has decided that the sand it is resting on will be sufficient."

Michael spoke up. "Mr. McNulty, are you saying Mr. Roebling is willing to risk piling tons and tons of granite on this foundation?"

"He is."

"What if the caisson continues to sink? The bridge will come down."

"And your name, sir?"

"Michael Ranahan."

"Are you an engineer, Mr. Ranahan?"

Michael reddened. "No, I am not."

"Then I suggest you let the engineers concern themselves with the integrity of the bridge. Thank you, gentlemen."

Later, Michael met Gaylord, who had just come from interviewing George McNulty, in a saloon on Water Street.

They took their beers to a table in the back away from the

noisy bar.

"Why did they stop digging?" Michael asked.

"The Brooklyn caisson hit bedrock at forty-four feet, but the New York caisson is at seventy-eight feet and still has not hit bedrock. Mr. Roebling was becoming more and more concerned with the increased cases of caisson disease, so he made a decision that the New York caisson, which is sitting on sand, was safe right where it was."

"My God, what if he's wrong?"

Gaylord drained his mug. "Only time will tell."

As the work continued in a steady pace, the bridge began to take shape. The Brooklyn anchorage was started in February 1873, the New York anchorage in May 1875. The Brooklyn tower was completed June 1875. And so, it went.

On a Friday morning in August of 1876, Michael made sure he got to work early so he could witness the spectacle. The press had been notified in advance that one E. F. Farrington, master mechanic, was going to ride a cable spanning the Brooklyn and New York towers. He would be the first man to use the bridge to cross the East River from Brooklyn to Manhattan.

Although the purpose of the trip was to demonstrate to New Yorkers that the cables that spanned the East River were safe, thousands of curious spectators crowding docks and ferry boats had come to watch. Scores of ships of every description anchored in the East River to observe this unprecedented event.

At one in the afternoon, a boatswain's chair was attached to the traveler at the Brooklyn anchorage and the fifty-year-old Farrington climbed into it. The boatswain chair, pulled by an engine, set off on its journey as cannons fired and whistles blew from ships below. A surprised Farrington, who hadn't expected a crowd to witness his journey, waved his hat to the throng below. The journey from the Brooklyn side to the New York side took twenty-two minutes.

When Farrington came down, he was mobbed by bridge workers who congratulated him and slapped him on the back. Bottles of whiskey were surreptitiously passed around. And then it was back to work for everyone.

Michael and Emily were having lunch at home on a crisp afternoon in March of 1877. As they were finishing, Peter came home.

"What are you doing here?" Michael asked. "Don't you have classes?"

"Something's come up that's more important."

"What's more important than school?" Emily asked.

"I am going to walk across the Brooklyn Bridge today," he announced proudly.

"You mean on that footbridge that was put in place for the use of the bridge workers?" Michael asked.

"The same."

Emily was shocked. "You can't do that, Peter, it's too dangerous."

"Ma, the bridge workers use it every day."

Emily looked at her husband for support, but he merely shrugged. "He's right. Workers cross that footbridge every day."

"But Peter is not a worker," she pointed out emphatically. "That footbridge sounds dangerous and our son should not be risking his life for… for… Why *do* you want to cross the bridge?"

"I'm going to write an article for my college newspaper."

"You need special permission to walk that bridge," Michael said. "How did you get it?"

Peter grinned. "Uncle Gaylord."

Emily shook her head. "I might have known. Is he going with you?"

"No, he's afraid of heights."

"And depths," Michael added.

"Do you want to come, Da?"

"Absolutely not," Emily said. "Your father is too old to be doing anything that reckless."

"Emily, I'm only fifty-six. I think I can still walk across a bridge."

"Well, not this one and that's final."

At two that afternoon, Michael and Peter reported to the construction shed on the Brooklyn side of the bridge.

A rail-thin man of indeterminate age with several missing

teeth greeted them. "What can I do for you, Mr. Ranahan?"

"My son is here to walk the bridge, Barry."

"Does he have a letter of permission?"

Peter showed him the letter.

"So, you want to cross the bridge?" he asked, stating the obvious.

"I do."

"And are you going along, Mr. Ranahan""

"I am. I've been watching men crossing that bridge and I think it's high time I got a look at the view from up there."

"All right. Come with me."

He led Michael and Peter up a long ladder to a platform almost at the peak of the tower.

Michael looked around. "My God," he exclaimed. "I thought the view from the Croton Reservoir was spectacular, but this is even better. Look, Peter you can see New Jersey, and there's Harlem all the way north."

But Peter wasn't interested in the sights. He was staring wide-eyed at the flimsy footbridge made of rope and wooden planks. To his consternation, he saw that the walkway was swaying in the stiff breeze. He looked down at the swirling waters of the East River and gulped. "How high are we?'

"More than two hundred and fifty feet above the water," Barry said.

"Is this bridge safe?"

Barry scratched his chin. "Well, it hasn't fallen down yet."

Michael saw the look of terror in his son's eyes. "Peter, you don't have to do this if you don't want to."

"There's no shame in that," Barry added. "Lots of folks come up here, take one look at that bridge and turn around and come right back down."

"No. I came here to cross the bridge and by God, I will."

"A word of caution," Barry said. "Don't walk in lock-step like soldiers. If you do, you'll make that bridge really start to swing and it won't be pleasant."

"Barry, what do we do when we get to the other side?" Michael asked.

"There's a ladder you can climb down or you can turn around and come back. It's up to youse."

Michael went first, followed by his son. By the time they got to the center of the bridge, the view was even more spectacular. Michael pointed. “Look, there’s Governor’s Island, and there’s Fort Hamilton, and there’s the Navy Yard.”

Peter had a white-knuckle grip on the rope railings. “Yeah, it’s great. Can we keep moving?”

When they got to the other side, Peter grinned for the first time since he’d set foot on the bridge, grateful that he hadn’t plunged two hundred and fifty feet to his death. “Wow, that was great.”

Michael patted his son on the back, knowing it took all his courage to cross the bridge. “Well done, son. Shall we go down the ladder?”

“No. I want to walk it again.”

“Are you sure?”

“I am.”

Michael nodded. “After you.”

Peter wrote his first-person account of crossing the Brooklyn Bridge to great acclaim from his fellow journalist students at the college. Gaylord also had the article reprinted in the *Tribune*.

CHAPTER FORTY-ONE

1883

It had taken twelve years to finish the Brooklyn Bridge, which was twice as long as expected and at a cost of 15 million dollars, which was twice the original cost projections. But it was finally done and today was its grand opening.

Michael and Emily were at the kitchen table having coffee and reading their newspapers when Peter came rushing in and poured himself a cup. At twenty-eight he looked even more like his father, although Michael could never see the resemblance. After graduating from college he'd gone back to the *New York Tribune* as a reporter.

"Are you two going to the opening of the bridge?"

"No," Michael said a little too quickly.

If Peter noticed the almost angry tone in his father's voice he didn't let on. "Why not? It'll be the event of the century. Do you know the bridge's roadway is eighty feet wide? Why, that's as spacious as Broadway itself."

"I know, Peter. I worked on the bridge for twelve years, but I've seen enough of it."

Peter gulped down his coffee. "Well, I'm off. I'm covering the opening for the *Tribune*. Uncle Gaylord says I'm to write the lead story."

"That's wonderful, Peter," Emily said. "I'll be sure to read your story tomorrow."

"You two really should go. They're going to set off fourteen tons of fireworks. That's going to be spectacular."

"I'm sure it will be." By force of habit, Emily inspected her son to make sure his shoes were shined and his tie was on straight.

"You'd better be on your way. I hear very large crowds are expected."

"That's what they say."

As he was going out, Peter almost collided with Eleanor, who was coming into the kitchen.

"What's his big hurry?"

Michael chuckled. "He's on his way to the Brooklyn Bridge. He's going to write the lead story."

"He's doing very well at the newspaper, isn't he?"

"He is," Emily agreed. "Gaylord says he's a natural."

"How does Uncle Gaylord feel about being promoted to editor?"

Michael grunted. "He doesn't like it. He hates being cooped up in an office."

"Well, he is getting a little old to be chasing stories all over town."

"Don't let him hear you say that."

"My lips are sealed."

"Are you going to the bridge opening?" Emily asked.

"I wouldn't miss it for the world. I feel like I built that bridge."

"That's close to the truth," Michael agreed. "You made me take you there so many times I should have put you on the payroll."

"You still can, Father," she said with an impish grin.

Michael shook his head. "How many times have I told you, Eleanor, construction is no business for a woman?"

"Father, I don't want to be a laborer hauling bricks up a ladder. The whole construction trade is getting more and more scientific. The days are gone when you could just load a wagon with bricks and go build a house."

Michael had to agree with her. Architects were using so many different types of materials to build that it was getting difficult to keep track of everything needed to construct a modern building.

"When is that architectural firm you're working for going to allow you to design a building?" Emily asked.

"Not soon enough, as far as I'm concerned."

"What's the problem?"

"My biggest problem seems to be that I'm a woman."

Michael frowned. "That doesn't seem right."

"It isn't. I guess I'm going to have to work a little bit harder than the boys."

"Is David going to the bridge opening with you?" Emily asked.

Eleanor blushed. "Yes, he is, if you must know."

"When is that fellow going to ask you to marry him?"

"Father, really."

"What? He's been courting you for almost two years now."

"I'm not in a rush to get married."

Michael was taken aback. "You're not getting any younger you know. Don't you want to have children?"

"I'm only twenty-nine for goodness sake. All in good time. Right now, I want to concentrate on my career."

Michael studied her. "*Career*? Women don't have careers."

Emily patted her husband's hand. "Michael, you are so old fashioned."

"No, I'm not, it's just that—"

Eleanor gave him a kiss on the cheek. "You *are* old fashioned, Father, but I love you anyway. Bye, I've gotta run."

Emily sighed. "Well, it looks like all our children are off to see the opening of the Brooklyn Bridge."

"Where's Claire?"

"She left hours ago."

"Why so early?"

"She said she wants to write a poem about the bridge as the sun is coming up."

"She's really serious about this poetry business, isn't she?"

"She is, and she's written some beautiful poems. Some have been published in literary magazines."

"I know." Michael shook his head in amazement. "Imagine, a daughter of mine writing poetry."

"At least she's not pestering you to work in the construction business."

"I guess I should be grateful for that."

Emily poured them another cup of coffee. "Why don't we go to the opening?" she said casually.

Michael put the newspaper down. "Emily, you know how I feel about that goddamned bridge."

"I do, but you're being irrational."

"Oh, so now I am not only old fashioned, I'm irrational as well."

Emily took both of his hands. "Michael, the bridge didn't kill Dermot."

Tears welled up in his eyes. "If only he hadn't gone down into the caisson—"

"That was *his* choice. There's not a day goes by that I don't think about him and how things might have been, if only he'd made better choices. But they were *his* choices. And remember, Dermot wasn't the only one to die constructing the bridge. John Roebling died even before construction began and his son was paralyzed by the caisson disease. I read somewhere that twenty-seven men lost their lives during the construction of the bridge.

"Michael, you should be proud of the work you did there. It's truly a wonder of the modern world. No one has ever built a bridge like the Brooklyn Bridge."

Michael sadly shook his head. "Roebling stopped the caisson digging in May. Dermot died in January. Five months. If only Roebling had made that decision before Dermot …" His voice trailed off.

"Michael, did you ever consider that Dermot's death might be the reason Mr. Roebling made that decision? If that's true, Dermot didn't die in vain. Through his death he may have avoided countless future deaths."

Michael went to the sink and rinsed out his cup. Looking out the kitchen window, he watched two squirrels chasing each other. Then, after a long silence, he said, "All right, we'll go."

"Wonderful."

"Should we invite Henrietta to come along?"

"I think not. Her arthritis has slowed her down and I don't think she would do well in the crowds the newspapers are predicting."

"All right, then it's just you and me."

It was a crystal-clear day with not a cloud in sight. The *Tribune* had reported that South Street would be the best vantage point for viewing the festivities. Seemingly, everyone in New York City had taken that advice. Emily and Michael shuffled along with the excited crowds of men, women, and children slowly streaming toward South Street.

Hundreds of vendors energetically hawked their wares. Pictures and commemorative medals could be had for ten cents. Sheet music extolling the bridge cost twenty-five cents. American flags of all sizes and shapes were on sale for prices ranging from ten cents to five dollars. Every grog shop along South Street was bursting with thirsty customers. A large banner across the front window of one saloon proclaimed: *Babylon had her hanging garden, Egypt her pyramids, Athens her Acropolis, Rome her Athenaeum; so Brooklyn has her Bridge.*

The waters of the East River were a dazzling cerulean blue. Ferries and lighters and other small craft made way around a virtual armada of ships. Everything from frigates to schooners to steamships were anchored in an area that extended from the bay to several miles upriver beyond the bridge. Every ship with a mast flew colorful flags and streamers, adding to the festive atmosphere.

Just before noon, as guns boomed at Fort Hamilton and the Navy Yard, the Atlantic Squadron, with the flagship USS Tennessee in the vanguard, came steaming up from the bay and into the river below the bridge.

Emily Roebling was given the honor of taking the first ride over the bridge with a rooster—a symbol of victory—in her lap. Next came President Chester A. Arthur and New York Governor Grover Cleveland. As they walked toward the center of the bridge, a flag signal was sent to the fleet below. Instantly, there was the boom from a gun on the Tennessee. Then the whole fleet commenced firing. Steam whistles on every tug, steamboat, ferry, and every factory along the river, began to scream. Bells rang and Emily and Michael, along with the crushing throng, began cheering wildly.

They didn't stay for the fireworks display, but it took some time to get free of the crowds and they didn't get home until after six. While Emily kicked her shoes off in the parlor, Michael disappeared into the kitchen. A minute later he came into the parlor carrying a bucket of champagne and two champagne glasses.

"My, my, what's the occasion?" Emily asked.

“Why, the opening of the bridge.”

“The way you feel about the bridge, I didn’t think—”

He popped the champagne cork. “I never wanted to see the bridge again, but it is something to celebrate. You said this morning that I should be proud of the work that I did there. Well, I am proud, Emily. Something magnificent has been done here and I’m glad I was a part of it.”

He raised his glass. “To the genius of John and Washington Roebling.”

“And don’t forget Emily Roebling,” Emily reminded her husband. “She took over his duties after he was no longer able to get to the construction site himself.”

Michael nodded. “Duly noted. To Emily Roebling.”

Michael sat down next to his wife. “Are you happy?”

Emily looked at him. “Do you mean happy about today?”

“No. With your life. Our life.”

She kissed him. “I couldn’t be happier. You?”

“I am, but I’ve always thought that somehow I’d let you down.”

“What are you talking about?”

“Look where you came from and look where I took you.”

“Michael, I thought that silly notion was out of your head by now. I told you before, Ireland and that life—*my* life—was a long time ago. I’m happy with the life you and I have forged here in the New World.”

He smiled. “I remember the first time I saw you in your father’s carriage when you came back to Ballyross. I thought you were the most beautiful girl in the world. I still do.”

“Thank you, kind sir.”

“When you passed by that day you looked right through me. It broke my heart.”

“Nonsense. I was looking directly at you.”

“You were?”

“I thought you were a most handsome young man.”

“But you never let on.”

“I’m afraid I was quite full of myself back in those days.”

“It seems like such a long time ago.”

“Thirty years.”

Michael poured more champagne. “Remember our first night

in New York?"

"The Five Points? Who could forget?"

Michael sat back and put his feet up on the hassock. "All in all, we've had a good life, haven't we?"

"We have. Despite being treated like a mere 'woman,' Eleanor really enjoys her work. She'll get her chance. Peter has found his calling as a newspaperman. Who knows, perhaps one day he'll own his own newspaper."

"And how is Claire doing at your school?"

"I'm thinking of letting her take over for me."

"What brought that on?"

"Well, I am getting on in years."

"You're only fifty-seven."

"The school is busier than ever. I have over a hundred girls now with four teachers, including Claire, who's been doing a wonderful job. I'd like her to take over for me. What about you? Any thought of retiring?"

"On bad days, I think about it. Ranahan Construction has over a hundred and fifty men. We're working on several projects at the same time. I've been thinking about what Eleanor said this morning. The construction business has gotten more complicated since I first went to work for Cully. I'm sixty-two now. Maybe it's time to slow down."

"Anybody in mind to take your place?"

"Actually, I'm thinking of Eleanor."

"Really? What about women in construction?"

"She made a good point this morning. I don't need another laborer to haul bricks, but I could use someone with a sharp eye for detail, someone with good administrative abilities. I still remember that time I took her to the Eldridge Mansion worksite and she pointed out how a carpenter was wasting time. She was only fifteen at the time. Eleanor could do the job, but, as you said, she really likes what she's doing."

"Michael, she would drop that job in a heartbeat to go to work with you."

He nodded. "She's practically an architect. Maybe someday, Ranahan Construction will design and build its own buildings instead of other peoples'."

"That's a nice thought."

Michael was silent for a moment, then he said, “Do you really think I’m old fashioned?”

She ruffled his hair that now has streaks of gray. “Maybe a little bit.”

“Maybe I am.” He stared off into the middle distance for a long time. Then, he said, “Ranahan and Daughter Construction Company. It has a nice ring to it, wouldn’t you say?”

Emily kissed him. “It does have a nice ring to it.”

The End

Made in the USA
Lexington, KY
06 March 2019